# VANGUARD STRIKE

# VANGUARD STRIKE

## JAROM STRONG

SECOND SKY

Published by Second Sky in 2025

An imprint of Storyfire Ltd.
Carmelite House
50 Victoria Embankment
London EC4Y 0DZ

www.secondskybooks.com

The authorised representative in the EEA is Hachette Ireland
8 Castlecourt Centre
Dublin 15 D15 XTP3
Ireland
(email: info@hbgi.ie)



ISBN: 978-1-83525-834-7
eBook ISBN: 978-1-83525-831-6

This book is a work of fiction. Names, characters, businesses, organizations,
places and events other than those clearly in the public domain are either the
product of the author's imagination or are used fictitiously. Any resemblance to
actual persons, living or dead, events or locales is entirely coincidental.

*To Marci,*
*Thanks for believing in me. Please don't get eaten by rippers.*

SIXTEEN YEARS AGO

It's amazing how bored one can be in the middle of a warzone.

I glanced up as I heard the familiar whistle of a Scourge rocket, tracing its flaring arc over our heads and down into the middle of a huddled mass of frightened Paragon grunts maybe thirty meters up range from us. Poor bastards. No armor or ordnance shields for them. The lucky ones died instantly. The rest of them started screaming, their cries mingling with the cacophony of the battlefield. If I hadn't seen a hundred scenes just like it, it might have been shocking to see. Instead, I found myself wondering idly what quiet corner of the galaxy they'd been dragged from, only to die here on the outskirts of... I frowned. Well, damn me if I couldn't even remember the name of the city we were invading. Brahmians had strange old earth names for their cities. *Gharseva*, I think. The capital of the Planetary Governance of Brahma.

Pretty place—or it looked like it had been before we got here. Rolling green hills now turned brown and red, charming countryside farm structures reduced to charred shells. A few weeks ago, sitting where I was now, you would probably have been listening to the sounds of farm animals braying, children laughing, and the occasional spacecraft taking off or landing from the nearby city. Today, though, all I could hear was the familiar lullaby of war: screams of pain, bullets and rockets whistling as they rushed to their targets, fightercraft screaming through the sky as they hurled ordnance down upon the enemy.

Nadus looked up from the small digital book he'd been reading. There was something amusing about the sight of the tiny device clutched between the bulky fingers of his armored Jericho CES-2 exosuit. "What was that, Lax?"

"How far out does SkyCom say we are?" I repeated.

Nadus shook his head. "No word yet from on high. But you can bet when it comes they'll want us in hot, so get ready to have your strings yanked."

The rest of the Vanguards grumbled their agreement and I nodded along with them. That was how it always was with SkyCom. A long, uninterested silence, and then suddenly they wanted you in there yesterday. How the hell had the Paragon managed to conquer the entire damn galaxy with a bunch of bumbling idiots for commanders?

I knew the answer, of course. And it had nothing to do with SkyCom. Nothing to do with the rich pricks in suits giving the orders. It was guys like us. Vanguards. Plucked from our homes as children, stuffed full of cybernetic and biological enhancements, wrapped in a suit of near indestructible armor, and then tossed out onto the battlefield.

*Puppets.* That was what the rest of the grunts called us. Far as they were concerned, we were mindless killing machines dangling by the Paragon's chemical strings. For a moment, I felt a surge of anger. You'd think I'd have learned to suppress that by now. After all, I'd been doing this for what... twelve years? Twelve years since Pa had dropped me off at the Vanguard recruiting station for a handful of credits. The thought still pissed me off. Enough so that it must have tripped my regulator. I heard a hissing sound and felt a sudden surge of calm as my exo shot a small dosage of frigicerin into my system. *Stay cool,* was the unspoken message, the proverbial string pulling me back into line. *It's not fighting time yet.*

"*Badger Green Seven,*" a female voice suddenly said over the comms. "*Prepare to move to designated co-ordinates. Expect both human and bioweapon resistance.*"

"Ah, *hell,*" I muttered, glancing down as an orange dot appeared on the minimap of my exo's wrist computer. Even through the recently administered frigicerin, I felt a chill run down my spine. *Bioweapon* was a laughably reductive term, one the Paragon used to make their monstrosities seem like the sort of weapon a respectable, civilized organization could deploy in good conscience.

Everybody else called them rippers.

"They already dropped them?" Nadus muttered, hefting his standard-issue Jackhammer rifle and checking the chamber. The gun was almost a meter and a half long with an industrial, box-like shape to it. Between the size of the rifle and the massive ammo drum attached to the bottom of it, it was far too heavy for anyone to wield without the assistance of the powered exosuits we wore. "Paragon is getting more and more trigger-happy with the rippers."

I rose to my feet, my exo giving a mechanical whir as I did so, and slung my own Jackhammer over my shoulder. "Same story as always. SkyCom makes the mess, we clean it up."

I heard a slight whimpering sound and turned to see Rafe staring at his minimap. I could hear his breathing—hot and heavy and scared. I fought back a chuckle. "You'll be alright, rookie. Just give a few seconds for the coolant to hit."

He looked up at me. Damn, but he reminded me of myself back when I'd first been pulled out of the factory. Looking almost as if he was wearing somebody else's body and it was a few sizes too big for him. "Just stay close to us," I said. "We'll make sure you come through this in one piece."

He nodded. Then his eyes suddenly went slightly glassy. That'd be the frigicerin kicking in. It took some getting used to. It was a violating feeling, knowing that the Paragon could just reach into your brain and switch your emotions on and off. Soothing you when your mind was screaming that you should be scared. Riling you up when all you wanted to do was find a rock to hide under. It took a while to stop fighting it. But you did stop... eventually. It was only a matter of time until you realized you belonged to the Vanguard. To the Paragon. If not in heart, then at least in mind and body.

Another rocket whistled overhead. This one hit closer, spraying us with chunks of debris—mostly dirt, with a few chunks of corpse thrown in.

With a thought, I triggered my neurointerface and commanded my visor to close. Two inches of hardened steel lowered over my face with a hiss, sealing me into my exo's helmet. A moment later, the darkness distorted into sight as my exo projected my surroundings directly to my brain. I looked around. The rest of the squad had visored up as well, their faces hidden behind blank, expressionless sheets of armor, identifiable only by the ID numbers printed on their chests, the info provided by my suit's HUD, and the occasional hand-painted images and slogans slathered across shoulder pauldrons. Travern had a crude image of an attractive woman on his, while Vint's said RIPPER BAIT in bold lettering.

I wondered idly what it must be like to be on the receiving end of a Vanguard assault. Faceless, merciless, nearly unkillable creatures of metal and flesh surging towards you. I felt a twinge of pity for the enemy. They hadn't asked for this. They probably just wanted to sit around and... I don't know, do whatever it was they did on this little green planet of theirs. And now, because they dared resist the Paragon's benevolent rule, we were going to kill them—that is, everyone the rippers didn't kill first.

"*Badger Green Seven*," the voice in the comms said. "*Go.*"

I took a deep breath. I knew what was coming. "See you on the other end," I said to Nadus. He nodded, bracing himself in the same way I was.

Rafe peered around the corner of the ruined structure we'd been taking shelter behind, then jerked back as a bullet slammed into his visor with a loud metallic thud. The round bounced harmlessly away, but it took a lot more experience than Rafe had to just shrug off a bullet to the face. "It's too hot," he gasped, swatting at his faceplate as if the bullet were a bug trying to sting him. "We can't. It's too—"

The words choked in his mouth, and he jolted up straight. I felt it too: a sudden rush of heat and fury in my veins as somebody sitting at a desk in a battlecruiser thousands of meters above us hit a button, sending a rush of ignicerin through our systems.

"*Badger Green Seven*," the voice in the comms said again. "*GO.*"

"Let's *GOOO!*" Rafe screamed, charging out into the open and rushing towards the enemy position. Nadus followed shortly behind him. I tried to resist. Tried to at least delay the urge to charge, to destroy, to kill. But I might as well have been a stone resisting the urge to roll down a hill.

Before I knew it, I was sprinting, my already powerful legs given godlike speed by my exo. Any pity I'd had for our enemies was gone now. Any resentment at the innocent blood we'd be forced to shed was twisted into hungry, almost giddy excitement. I surged past Rafe, past Nadus, towards the fight. Towards where the enemy was entrenched. Hiding like cowards behind their trenches and machine guns. But their paltry defenses wouldn't save them.

Not from *me*.

Bullets bounced uselessly off the hull of my exo and I laughed at them. An enemy rocket whistled directly at me. With a passing thought I triggered my exo's neurointerface to fire off an interceptor from my shoulder-mounted launcher, causing the rocket to explode harmlessly several meters in front of me.

I charged through the smoke and the debris and into the enemy position, leaping through the air to land in the middle of one of their trenches. Soldiers wearing ragged, filthy combat uniforms and wielding woefully outdated weaponry gawked at me from every side. They panicked and broke and ran, desperately trying to escape their own fortification as I lowered my Jackhammer and began spraying them with explosive rounds. They weren't people anymore—not so far as I was concerned. They were just targets. Targets with human-shaped bodies and faces and screams that burst into chunks of flesh and blood.

Something slammed into my side, causing me to stagger. Somebody was holding what looked like a shotgun, standing close to me and aiming down the barrel as he prepared to fire again. He was shouting something, but the words didn't register. Brave, meaningless words of defiance. He wanted to die a hero.

I don't know much about heroes—he was on his own there. But *dying*... that, I was an expert on.

I reached out one armored fist, wrapping my fingers around his skull. His shouts of anger quickly turned into cries of agony as I closed my fist with a meaty crunch. I discarded his remains like junk. More targets to kill. The rest of my squad had caught up now, and the rebel retreat had turned into a massacre. Rafe was laughing, his voice maniacal in the comms as he slammed the heavy boot of his exo into the face of a wounded enemy. Somebody was kneeling, hands held up in the air in what might have been a gesture of surrender, but Nadus simply raised his Jackhammer, and then they were gone. I felt no horror or disgust at the debauchery. Only jealousy that *I* wasn't the one inflicting it. I scrambled up and out of the trench, bellowing as I emptied my mag into the crew of a rocket system.

Movement behind. I turned to see the Paragon grunts following us, their eyes wide as they watched the carnage. I grinned. There was a part of me, morbid and bloodthirsty and swollen by the ignicerin, that wanted to know how many of them I could kill.

Suddenly, where there had been fire in my veins, there was ice. Sensation seared through my body like lightning. The fury, the bloodlust, the need to kill, vanished.

And for a short, terrifying, sickening moment, my mind was free.

The ground around me was littered with chunks of flesh. The surface of my exo's armor was coated in blood. The squad of Paragon grunts was pushing into the abandoned enemy position. One of them slipped in something scarlet and then doubled over and vomited. I felt like doing the same. Felt like turning the barrel of my Jackhammer on myself as I remembered what I'd done to that man with the shotgun. He hadn't been much more than a kid, really. What kind of monster *laughed* as he...

And then the frigicerin kicked in.

The disgust, the self-loathing, the hatred, all faded. I felt no relief in their absence. Just... nothing. Compared to everything that had come before, it felt pretty damn good.

"Position secure," Nadus said into the comms. His voice was flat. "The enemy has retreated."

"*Copy that,*" our commanding officer's voice said a moment later. "*Hold.*"

Our squad of armored Vanguard troopers came to a halt. Some Paragon grunts charged onwards, vanishing into the smoke and debris. We were within the city boundaries now, and in this sector at least, the fighting seemed all but over. Just clean-up now, and the grunts could handle that.

"Why are we stopping?" Rafe asked, his voice sluggish under the frigicerin's smothering calm.

"Because that's the order," I said.

SkyCom's voice crackled in our ears again. *"Badger Green Seven, assume defensive positions. Incoming bioweapons. Stand by for extermination protocol."*

Nadus swore, ejected an empty mag from his Jackhammer, and slammed a fresh one home. "Rippers inbound!"

*Fear.* I felt it lurking deep beneath the surface of my frigicerin-imposed calm. Rippers inbound. Claws and flesh and blood and death.

A few grunts who had lingered behind their comrades froze, their faces going pale as they heard Nadus's words.

I heard a sudden shout of alarm through the smoke. A barrage of gunshots echoed, muzzle flashes punching sharply through the gray haze. The gunfire faded from a cacophony into a few scattered bursts and then went dead.

Then it all went quiet.

I reloaded my Jackhammer.

We spread out slowly, raising our weapons and aiming them into the smoke. Rafe stepped up to the edge of the enemy position we'd captured, looking through a shattered doorway down the debris-filled street.

"I think I see them," he said, his voice heavy. As if he were trying to work up the energy to be afraid despite the frigicerin.

"Rafe," I said. "Get back. Now."

He stayed where he was. He wasn't used to the frigicerin yet. Wasn't aware of how it warped his thinking, his survival instinct. "I see shapes in the smoke. Moving towards us. They're—"

There was a burst of movement. Rafe staggered backward and collapsed, hands flailing at the *something* clinging to the breastplate of his exo. I got a good look at the creature that was attached to him. Roughly the size of your average human, it had pale, sickly-looking skin that seemed to be stretched too tightly over its lithe form. Its shape was nightmarish: a short, powerful body from which stemmed three sets of multi-jointed limbs and a long, scorpion-like tail. Long, curved claws made of jet-black biosteel extended from the end of each limb. Its eyeless head seemed too small for its body, save for its overextended, jagged-toothed maw.

Rafe didn't scream as the ripper's claws tore cleanly through his armor and into his abdomen. Too much frigicerin in his system. All he did was let out a ragged gasp as the creature burrowed into the hole it had made in his torso, pinning him down with its frontmost pair of claws while using the shorter middle claws to shovel innards into its maw.

"Hold fire," Nadus said. "Wait until—"

The handful of grunts that had stayed behind with us emptied their magazines in the ripper's general direction. Most of the bullets zipped past their target and into the smoke beyond. Some ricocheted off of Rafe's armor. A few struck the ripper. They tore through its flesh, leaving small, insignificant-looking holes.

The ripper turned its eyeless gaze towards us.

A grunt near me cursed under his breath and dropped his mag, fumbling as he tried to load a new one.

The ripper tensed, preparing to strike. Even as we watched, the bullet holes the grunts had dealt it were closing slowly, starting to heal. *Amateurs.* Regular small arms fire did about as much harm to a ripper as a handful of pebbles.

More shapes loomed in the smoke.

"Open fire," Nadus said.

More rippers came pouring into our little clearing. The grunts screamed in terror. Some of them turned and ran, discarding their empty weapons. Others frantically reloaded.

"SkyCom, we're too cold!" Nadus said into the comms, his voice urgent despite the frigicerin. A ripper charged towards him, but he dispatched it with a few rounds from his Jackhammer, splattering its wreckage across the already blood-soaked ground.

I squeezed the trigger of my own Jackhammer, feeling it jolt back against me as I fired. Three rippers died, the explosive rounds stopping them cold, but others replaced them, crawling over the ruined, twitching corpses of their companions. I felt my heart rate spike, terror gripping me before another dosage of frigicerin hit. That almost felt worse. Knowing that I *should* be afraid. That these creatures would rip me apart while I was unable to muster the fear needed to respond correctly. There were more of them now, seeming to materialize out of nowhere.

I felt waves of anger ripple across the frigicerin-imposed sense of calm. If SkyCom had held us back for a few more minutes, the rippers would have done our job for us, wiping out the enemy position like they were intended to do. And yet here we were, firing sluggishly into the hordes of biologically engineered killing machines, so stoned with frigicerin we could barely think straight.

I watched with idle curiosity as a ripper tore a mouthful of flesh from a screaming grunt and swallowed it. The ripper began to squirm and twitch. A moment later it split into two, its front half disconnecting from its rear half with a grotesque pop. Its front half dragged itself towards another victim, while its back half continued to shake until a pair of new limbs and an abhorrently childlike head stretched out from its bloody mass. *Mitosis.* That was how they reproduced. I aimed at the squirming mass of tissue and fired a few explosive rounds into it. Another few moments and it would have been a full-fledged ripper.


I glanced around. We were being overrun. Already it was down to just us Vanguards, and we were taking casualties at an alarming rate. Travern and Vint were dead, their corpses being used as chew toys. The words painted across Vint's shoulder pauldron were barely readable beneath a layer of scarlet viscera. Nadus was desperately firing into a mass of rippers attempting to flank us. A ripper leaped through the air, one claw flashing and shearing through the front of his visor. Nadus cried out in pain and swept up with the butt of his Jackhammer, the blow catching the ripper in the side and sending it spinning away.

We were all going to die. Through the haze of frigicerin the realization was sullen and ironic, rather than terrifying. We were going to die here in a city whose name I couldn't even remember, all because SkyCom had forgotten about us.

As if in response to my thoughts, a spike of sudden excitement shot through me. A fire running through my veins. I straightened as I felt ignicerin surge into my system, throwing me into a sudden blood rage. SkyCom had flipped their little switch.

The rippers kept coming. But now I felt no dread at the prospect. The thought of my own violent death changed immediately from a harrowing probability to a distant hypothetical. It was irrelevant anyways. Unimportant. All that mattered was *killing*.

I laughed and waded into the horde of rippers, firing as I went. I found myself wondering what exactly it was that I'd been so worried about as I reloaded my Jackhammer, slamming the new mag home and firing just in time to stop a ripper from leaping onto me. There was nothing to fear here.

Nothing except for me.

I don't know how long we fought for, or how many rippers we killed. I do know that after we broke through the rippers we ran into more Brahmian soldiers. They tried to surrender. We were too hopped up on ignicerin and bloodlust to care. When we were done with them we fought our way deeper into the ruined city.

Eventually the ignicerin wore off. We took a breather beneath the roof of an empty church. Half our squad was dead or too severely injured to carry on, which for a Vanguard meant they were missing at least one body part. Nadus had been fighting without a helmet after a ripper's claw destroyed his visor and half of his face in the first assault, but somehow he'd come through alive. He was hooked up to a MAMA device pumping healing chemicals into his body that interacted with his already enhanced Vanguard healing capabilities.

Our comms crackled to life. I grimaced as I prepared to hear the order to advance again. *"Badger Green Seven,"* our CO's voice said. *"Stand down and prepare for extraction. A ceasefire has been called."*

Nadus and I shared an incredulous look. "A ceasefire?"

*"That's right. They're surrendering. Congratulations, Badger Green Seven. It appears that you've won the war."*

———

Four standard earth weeks later, I stood at parade rest as I watched the Last War come to an end.

The anthem of the Paragon blared over the crowd of Brahmian civilians and the ranks of victorious Paragon soldiers gathered in the central plaza of Gharseva. I snapped to attention with the rest of my unit as a flickering holographic image of a man in a crisp military uniform appeared above the plaza, looking fondly down upon us. Daren Thorne, prime speaker of the Paragon.

"Citizens of the Paragon, both new and old," he said. "Loyal soldiers—today, I send my voice from Earth across the stars to deliver the most important announcement in the history of our race: we are, for the first time and at long last, *united!*"

Cheers broke out. I noted with some amusement that most of the cheers were being blasted through the public speaker system—the crowd of Brahmians looked like cheering was the last thing on their minds. They were beaten well beyond the point of jeering, though. They watched the image of the speaker with weary, sullen, cowed hatred as he droned on about peace and prosperity and other nonsense. They looked ragged and desperate, and there was a conspicuous lack of fighting-aged people among them.

Except one of them. I noted a young woman with raven black hair standing at the front of the crowd. Her fists were clenched at her sides, and her eyes were filled with a burning, smoldering hate that she made no effort to hide. With a jolt of surprise I realized that she was not looking at the prime speaker as his patriotic speech droned on and on in the same exuberant circles. Rather, she was staring at a group of men and women clad in sharp suits. They were standing near where the high-ranking officers were gathered, and had their own security detail.

I triggered my neurointerface to open a direct channel to Nadus, who was standing next to me. "Who're the slicks? The civvies, up there with the brass?"

Nadus shifted slightly beside me. We were all wearing our visors down, so the crowds wouldn't be able to see him staring. "What, you don't recognize your own parents?"

I frowned. "What?"

"They're from Divinity. Here to see the new conquest."

*Oh.* Divinity Technologies was a technology corporation—no, more than that. They were *the* technology corporation. Their partnership with the Paragon was what had allowed the Earth-based government to conquer all of humanity. They produced the most important technology the Paragon had: the Vanguard soldiers, the rippers, and—most importantly—the ultracell batteries that made faster-than-light travel feasible. Now that Brahma was under the Paragon's thumb, Divinity would have access to their markets and resources.

The speaker wasn't done yet. "If we want to observe true peace, we must do more—we must throw aside our weapons of war. The long-suffering citizens of Brahma have, as many of their united fellow citizens across the fold, agreed to surrender their arms. Now it is our turn. And so, in honor of their sacrifices, it is my pleasure to announce that all Vanguard battalions who served on the Brahmian campaign are hereby released from duty with full honors. As of this day, noble soldiers of humanity, you are no longer bound to war. Go forth, and prosper in the harmony and peace you have earned."

The words hit me like an artillery round. I looked at Nadus, who looked at me. The entire Vanguard rank shifted as the implications of the news sank in. None of us had ever expected to be released from service—we *belonged* to the Paragon.

But not anymore, apparently.

"He's lying, right?" Nadus muttered into our direct channel.

"I..." I shook my head, staring up at the speaker as he finally concluded his speech. "I don't think so. What would be the point? The Paragon has plenty of soldiers. They can afford to lose a few battalions as a PR move."

"So we're... free?" he asked, his voice puzzled.

I nodded slowly. My mouth felt dry. Partially from exhaustion, partially from the sheer unexpectedness of the news. "I... I guess so."

"So what now?"

It was my turn to frown. Truth be told, I'd never really considered the possibility that I'd have a life beyond service to the Vanguard. A life where I was free to do what I wanted, go where I wanted. Where there was more to my daily existence than just killing and destroying. Where I'd be able to actually make something of myself. I'd been angry about the prospect of continuing to fight the Paragon's wars, but now I found myself facing something that suddenly seemed just as daunting: freedom.

"I don't know," I finally said. "But I know one thing. I'm done." I jerked my head at the ranks of armored soldiers around us. "Done with all this. Done doing dirty work for rich bastards on the other side of the galaxy. Done fighting for a cause I couldn't give less of a damn about." I gritted my teeth, my jaw rigid with determination. "And most of all, I'm done being a puppet."

"Freedom." I could hear the grin in Nadus's voice. "Sounds nice."

"Yeah." I found myself smiling with him. *Freedom.* "It does."

# ONE

## KARAK BLACKROCK PRISON SYSTEM



I'm a big guy.

I don't say it to boast. Just stating the facts. Hell, I'm big even for a Vanguard, and big is the only size us Vanguards come in. Six feet and eight inches of biologically enhanced muscle.

Still, though. Some things hurt no matter how big you are.

The steel pipe slammed into the side of my face. Lights burst in my head and my vision reeled, but I managed to stay on my feet. He was coming at me again, the pipe making a deadly arc towards my head, but I threw up an arm and blocked it, then shoved him backward. He staggered and fell, giving me a short reprieve before his buddies helped him back up.

"*Kill the puppet bastard!*" somebody screamed.

Hands. Hands on my back, on my arm. Venter. "*Hey!*" He leaned close, shouting up into my ear so that I could hear his voice over the clamoring of the other inmates. His breath reeked. Then again, everything in here did. "The hell you doing, Lax? You're making me look bad!"

I blinked away my dizziness. Blood dripped down the side

of my face and ran down my orange prison uniform. The words *Karak Blackrock Prison System* printed across my chest turned crimson as the blood spread through them. I grimaced. "You wanted a fight, right?"

The other guy was on his feet again now, holding his pipe and crouching in a defensive stance, trying to decide how to best get at me. He was nervous, his own orange suit dark with sweat, but he was becoming steadily more confident. He'd landed a blow against the fearsome Vanguard. He'd probably expected to be dead by now.

"Yes," Venter sneered. "A *fight*. Those usually have *two* participants. Keep letting him hit you and it becomes too obvious you're holding back. Even my grandma would know you stepped into that hit."

The other fighter glanced from side to side, a smile starting to grow on his lips as his bloodthirsty companions shouted encouragement.

"*You've got him, Jed!*"

"*Break the puppet!*"

Venter squeezed my shoulder. Not in a comforting "I've got your back" kind of way; rather, in a menacing, clutching "Don't screw this up" style.

"Just make it last a few more minutes. Milk it. The longer it goes, the better the wagers get. We need everyone to believe that brave Jed here is gonna be the one to finally take down the Vanguard."

"Fine," I groaned, stepping forward. "But I want double my normal fix."

"Just do your damn job!" He shoved me forward. From a guy as small as him to one as big as me the motion was more symbolic than practical, but I got the idea. Sighing, I stepped carefully towards Jed. He grinned at me, his confidence soaring now as I did my best to look exhausted. He raised his pipe again. Letting fighters use a weapon to even the playing field was the only way that Venter could get them to agree to go up against me these days. The weapon never changed the outcome of the fight, but it sure as hell made it more painful.

I stepped to the side, letting the pipe thud into my shoulder instead of my skull, and swiped at Jed with my right fist, making sure to give him plenty of time to duck beneath it. He darted around me, jerking the pipe back and slamming it into my side in a blow that would have shattered the ribs of any normal human. All it got out of me was a grunt.

I spun, putting my fists up to block a barrage of wild blows. The ring of inmates closed gradually around us, their shouts and cheers a wild, bloodthirsty cacophony.

Jed stepped out of the way of my sluggish jab and slammed the end of his pipe into my midsection. *That* one really hurt. I staggered away to the edge of the ring, gasping.

"I'm finishing this," I gasped.

"If you want your cans, you'll give me sixty more seconds," Venter hissed.

I snarled and stepped back into the ring. In fighting terms, sixty seconds is an eternity. Most brawls don't last more than a minute from beginning to end. Especially when I'm involved.

*One... two... three...*

Jed came at me hard, his attacks increasingly careless, overextended, and painful.

*Ten... eleven... twelve...*

The pipe came down again and again. I retreated and kept my guard up, trying to look more tired and defeated than I felt. There was nothing fake about the pain that lanced through me with each strike, though.

*Thirty-three... thirty-four... thirty-five...*

From the corner of my eye, I saw Venter arguing fiercely with another inmate. Probably trying to get a higher bet out of him.

*Forty-two... forty-three... forty-four...*

I made a pathetic attempt at grabbing Jed. He slipped beneath my clutching hands and slammed the pipe against my rear, cackling with laughter. Jubilant whoops of approval rose from the crowd.

*Fifty-seven... fifty-eight... fifty-nine...*

I glanced over at Venter. He nodded.

Jed raised the pipe, triumph gleaming in his eyes.

I punched him in the face.

It wasn't a particularly hard hit. Exhausted and hurting as I was, I wasn't interested in putting too much energy into it. But it was enough. My fist connected with his temple, and I felt something crack beneath my blow and then Jed was down, face first on the floor.

The cheers died suddenly.

"*Sixty*," I muttered.

The cold water hit me harder than Jed's pipe. I shuddered, then forced myself to relax as I felt the water washing away the blood and sweat. The showerhead was built far too low for me, so I had to bend over to let it run over my back and shoulders, leaning against the wall and staring downward at the water pooling pink and bloody around my feet. My blood and sweat would be filtered out and the reclaimed water would be flushed through the system again, to be drunk and then pissed and bled and sweated out back into the pipes. An endless loop.

Chatter filled the washroom as several inmates entered, grumbling among themselves about how much contraband they'd lost betting on the fight. I cursed softly and turned away from them.

"There he is," I heard one of them mutter. "Damn puppet."

I closed my eyes, sticking my head under the showerhead and letting the water run over my shaved scalp and battered face.

"Hey! Puppet!" one of them called. "You hearin' any voices in your head? What are they telling you to do today, huh?"

A new voice spoke up. "I hope you're not planning on doing anything stupid, young man."

I opened my eyes, looking up to see Venter standing next to a sink. Venter was old—old by prison standards, anyways—with gray stubble crowning his shaved head and wrinkles across his face that accentuated his malicious grin. As he spoke, several members of his fledgling entourage filed in behind him, younger and more muscular. They took up positions on either side of him.

One of the troublemakers looked from Venter to me and back again. "You're crazy to trust that puppet, old man. He's gonna go psycho and kill you someday. Rip your throat out and eat it."

"Not while *I'm* holding the strings," Venter said, his grin widening. "Now, if you'll excuse us..."

"I ain't even pissed yet," the young man complained.

"Not my problem," Venter snapped, his good humor suddenly gone. "Get out. Now."

The troublemakers grumbled and fled, shooting dark looks at Venter over their shoulder. When they were gone, the old man gave a sigh and took a few steps towards me, leaning against the shower entrance.

"You know," he said, "they're starting to call me the puppet master."

I grunted. "You really think you control me?"

"Actually, I do." Venter gave me a nasty grin that showcased a mouthful of mismatched, dirty-looking artificial teeth. "Not the way *they* think, of course. Nobody in this tin can has the tech to reach into those implants of yours. And besides, even if they could, I assume you had yours deactivated when you left the Vanguard corps. Wouldn't want anybody to be able to just reach in there and push your buttons."

Right on both points. But I didn't like sharing more than I had to—not with greedy, ambitious bastards like Venter, at least. For guys like them, information was ammunition. The more they knew, the more firepower they had.

He continued. "No, I've no illusions about that. But *this*, on the other hand..."

He held a hand out to one of his cronies. The man stepped forward and slapped something metallic and cylindrical into his extended palm.

My arm twitched.

"With *this* stuff," Venter continued, "I figure I have more sway on you than the Paragon ever did."

I forced myself to look away from the can and fought the urge to rub at the port on my shoulder. How long had it been since my last hit? Two days? Three?

*Deep breaths...* I closed my eyes. *Don't look desperate. Don't look weak. You're in control.*

"That all you got?" I asked, keeping my voice level.

"You're lucky I even got this much," he said, tossing it up in the air and catching it. "Hard to come by out there and even harder in here."

I glared at him. "You promised me two cans."

"And you're getting one." He said the words calmly, like he was explaining something obvious to a young child. "Because *I* control the supply. And so you'll take what I, in my infinite generosity, choose to give you, while you, in your infinite wisdom, will continue to do as you're *damn. Well. Told.*" He spat out each of the last three words, his formerly calm voice laced with venom and vitriol.

My eyes narrowed and my fists tightened. Venter's body-guards tensed, giving each other nervous glances. They were big, and they outnumbered me, but nobody in their right mind goes willingly into a fight against a Vanguard, battered and exhausted or not. They'd seen what I could do, time and time again.

"Yeah?" I took a menacing step towards Venter. "How you figure?"

Venter stepped closer, his eyes swimming with malicious delight. He had balls, I had to give him that much. "Because if you *don't,*" he hissed, "I'll cut you off entirely. And I'll sit back and watch your mind tear itself to pieces, like the worn-out, broken piece of machinery it is. Reliving every little bit of pent-up trauma that led you here, unable to escape or do a damn thing about it."

My arm twitched. I tried to think of something to say. Some sort of retort to show that I wasn't afraid of him or his threats. But nothing came. Instead, I found myself just standing there, staring blankly past him, helpless as the memories—the *nightmares*—came washing over me.

Ruined, discarded bodies like trash all around me.

I opened my mouth, tried to speak.

A long, dark corridor. *Green dots, flashing red...*

Venter grinned.

Her face, haggard but smiling. *It's alright, Lax...*

I blinked away Kessa's face and reached out for the can, my hand shaking slightly. Venter jerked it just out of my reach. "Nuh-uh. Not so fast. I have something I need you to do."

I blinked, staring at the can. Kessa's face swam ghost-like before my eyes, that bit of yellow paint still on her cheek.

"You're getting a new cellmate," Venter said. "A Scorcher, from York 13. Ratted out some of his buddies. His gang wants to get at him, and we're charging them a fee for access. So when they show up, you let them have him and make sure they don't get disturbed, you understand?"

The paint on Kessa's face vanished, her skin now pale and eyes wide with fear. I forced my eyes shut, trying to chase away the image. "Fine," I croaked. "Just give it to me."

Venter gave a low chuckle. "You see?" He leaned forward until he was breathing in my ear. "I *own* you. Don't you forget it."

I reached for the can. He dropped it, letting it clatter on the shower floor. I fell to my knees, grabbing for it. Venter gave it a kick, sending it spinning away across the shower, and I crawled after it, water splashing. I heard him chuckle and say something to his gang as he left, but the words sounded far away. All of my attention was focused on that can—and on Kessa. I could still see her, her eyes soft and tired. Not afraid anymore. Smiling. Smiling, through it all. *Why was she smiling? WHY?*

I grabbed the can and fumbled the cap off of the narrow end of it, then brought it up to my shoulder port and plugged it into the narrow metal opening. I hammered the release button on the side of the can. There was a soft hissing sound as the chemicals surged out, through the port, and into my nervous system.

*"We had a good run, Lax,"* she says, and closes her eyes, her smile still there, milliseconds stretching into eons, and there's red tarnishing the warm blues and yellows—

And then, finally, blessedly, the frigicerin hit.

I gasped, my body giving a slight shudder as relief flooded through it. Everything disappeared. Kessa—gone. The battlefields—as if I'd never been there. The years of war, my few short years of freedom, and my imprisonment—no more than a vague concept in my mind. My rage at Venter, the lingering aches and pains of the fight against Jed, my shame and humiliation—all of it vanished. Gone. Replaced by absolutely nothing.

I don't know how long I sat there, stretched out on the shower floor with my back propped up against the wall. By the time I finally came back to myself, the showers had turned off and a few other inmates were standing at the sinks, washing their hands and shooting nervous glances in my direction.

I groaned, pushing myself more upright against the wall,

and pulled the can out of my arm, letting it fall with a hollow clink to the floor and roll away.

*Eight years.* My head drooped, and I found myself looking down. *Eight years in this hellhole.* The same amount of time I'd had as a free man. Eight years of blissful freedom, no longer tied to the Paragon, no longer being forced to fight in its wars. Eight years to make my own life, on my own terms, with the people I wanted. Eight years of thinking I was the luckiest man in the universe.

And then I'd gone and lost it all.

I stared down at the puddle I was sitting in, some of it water, and examined the all-too-familiar face staring back up at me. Broad and ugly, bruised and bleeding. A twisted nose that had been broken far too many times. Brown eyes, deader than the depths of space, staring back into my own.

Yep, there he is, ladies and gentlemen. The Luckiest Man in the Universe.

# TWO



The metallic voice jerked me out of a tumultuous half-dream and into the harsh white light of my prison cell. I groaned, holding up a hand to block out the light. I lay there for a few minutes, waiting for the door to open while I tried to gather the quickly scattering remnants of my dream. It hadn't been about Kessa this time, thankfully. This one had been my home—my old home, where I'd grown up, before my dad had pawned me off to the Vanguard corps for a few credits. I'd been dreaming about my mother. I remembered her smile, and the exhaustion around her eyes, and that was about it.

I wondered, idly, if she ever thought about me. If she ever looked up at the stars and wondered what had happened to her sandy-haired little boy.

I hoped not. The answers sure as hell wouldn't give her any comfort.

The door to my cell slid open and I looked up to see my new cellmate walk timidly through the door.

Venter had said he was a member of the Scorchers—a large

gang that had their fingers in a variety of criminal pies in the Karak system, known for their use of intimidation and brute force. With that in mind, I guess I'd been expecting someone more... *brute* looking.

The kid before me looked about as far from a brute as one could get. Lanky, with sharp features, pale skin, and vivid blue eyes. Maybe in his late teens or early twenties—I couldn't tell. His hair looked like it had been black before it had been buzzed down to stubble as part of his prison processing. He clutched a small prison-issue duffel bag to his chest like it was a lifesaver keeping him afloat in a storm-whipped sea. A tattoo of what seemed to be four blank playing cards was etched across the back of his right hand.

The tattoo that caught my eye, though, was the one across his neck. A flaming skull, jaws open wide in a devious cackle, inked in glowing red. The unmistakable mark of a Scorcher. I'd seen tattoos like that before—they used bioluminescent ink. Hard to hide, but maybe that was the idea. Once a Scorcher, always a Scorcher.

He gave me an unreadable sideways glance, then took a deep breath and shoved his duffel bag onto his bunk, keeping his eyes fixed straight ahead, his shoulders rigid and his jaw tense.

I opened my mouth to say something. *Hey, relax. Don't worry about your giant, biologically enhanced killing machine of a cellmate—he's not that bad.* But why bother? What did it matter what this scrawny Scorcher kid thought about me? He was marked for death no matter what I did. I didn't know when the Scorchers would come for him, but come they would, and by the time they were done with him, the kid would wish he'd never been born. Thus, always to rats. It was the only way to make sure everyone knew that death was a preferable fate to betraying the gang.

I took another look at him. There was something familiar

about the kid. I was certain I'd never met him before, and yet... he reminded me of someone.

I finally spoke up. "What's your name, kid?"

He gave me a sidelong glance. "Does it matter?"

I gave it some thought.

"Guess not," I said.

The Rat, as I took to calling him in my head, tagged along with me for the rest of the day. Well—*tag* gives the impression that we were together, which was not the case. A better way to say it would be that he *stalked* me the rest of the day.

When I went to the run-down prison gym, he lurked at the edges of the room. When I went to the washroom to rinse off the sweat, I came back out to find him waiting furtively outside. When I went to eat the disgusting protein goop the prison doesn't even pretend to call *food* for lunch, he sat down at the far end of the table from me and stared in concern at his bowl.

"You get used to it," I said, shoveling a spoonful of "turkey-flavored" goop from my bowl into my mouth. I swallowed it as quickly as I could, trying not to let it linger on my tastebuds any more than strictly necessary. I wasn't sure what turkey was *supposed* to taste like, but if this came anywhere close to approximating it, I wanted nothing to do with it. I fought back a grimace and shoved my spoon back into the bowl.

The Rat, as usual, said nothing. But he did look at me. Then back to his bowl of goop.

"Yep." I ate another mouthful. "Just... takes a while for the taste of freedom to wash away. But once it does, well, this goes down just fine."

He glanced around the room. The mess hall was big, loud, and, true to the name, messy. Tables full of criminals of various calibers shoveled down their goop while talking or arguing loudly among themselves. My table was towards the edge of the room—a coveted position, where nobody could sneak up behind me.

I looked up to see Venter several tables down from me, laughing loudly with a gang of his cronies. As I watched, an inmate I didn't recognize approached the table. He whispered something to Venter, who turned, searching the room, until his eyes lit on the Rat. Venter's gaze flickered briefly to me, then back to the other inmate. He nodded.

The stranger glanced over at us, his eyes latching onto the Rat. The Rat stared back, his expression unreadable. The stranger flashed a smile full of jagged artificial teeth, then turned away. I caught the faint red glow of a Scorcher tattoo on his neck.

The Rat looked down at the table, his eyes flitting back and forth like he was thinking. Hard. His knuckles whitened around the spoon.

I pretended not to have noticed the subtle exchange, focusing on finishing my bowl of goop. "So," I said. "Scorcher. What'd you do for them? Distributer? Watcher? Trigger guy?"

He took a deep breath. Looked like he was trying to force himself to relax. "Lockbreaker."

"Ah." I nodded. "Technical work, huh?" I found myself wondering, again, why I bothered making conversation with a man who was, for all intents and purposes, already dead. Guess it just felt like the natural thing to do. "How'd you end up in here?"

"I talked," he said through a grimace and a mouthful of goop.

I gave a flat grunt. "I thought the enforcers were supposed to protect rats."

He didn't grace that with a reply. I wouldn't have, either. It was a dumb thing to say. There is a wide, gaping void between what Paragon enforcers are *supposed* to do and what they *actually* do, and everybody outside of a posh core-system planet knows it. Hell, even those people know it; they're the ones who profit from it.

"You?"

It took me a second to register that he'd spoken to me. I frowned. "Me?"

He shrugged. "How'd a Vanguard get here?"

"Oh." I stared into my bowl. That was the problem with digging around in a person's past—it implied an invitation to give you the same treatment. "I was a vulture. After I got out of the Vanguard, I mean. Salvaging dead spacecraft. Had a job go... *bad*." I grimaced. Damn me if that wasn't the biggest understatement I'd ever made.

I waited for him to press, to ask for more details, but he didn't even acknowledge he'd heard me. Just turned back to his bowl. I found myself breathing a sigh of relief. Just thinking about the *Panama* made my heart begin to pound.

*Green dots, flashing red...*

The Rat's voice pulled me back to the present moment. "I never wanted to be one of them."

I frowned. "Who?"

"The Scorchers."

I shrugged. "And I never wanted to be a Vanguard. But here we are. Guys like us don't get to choose who we are, and we don't get to change it, either."

I thought back to that day sixteen years ago on Brahma, listening in disbelief as the prime speaker announced that my unit would be released from duty. I'd thought things would change. And for a while, while I was with Kessa at least, things had. But now I was back. Back to being nothing more than a puppet. Back to fighting other people's stupid battles for them.

I shook my head. "Far as everyone in here is concerned, you're just a Scorcher and I'm just a puppet. Ain't nothing you can do to change that."

He shrugged. "Guess not. We've gotta try, though, right?"

A beeping sound jarred me from the conversation before I could respond. I frowned, looking down at the crude computer strapped to my wrist. Every inmate has one, and some of them even work. All they really do is allow the prison administrators to contact you. Supposedly, you can also contact them, but I've never heard of it working.

VISITOR REQUEST, the screen flashed.

"What is it?" the Rat asked, peering over at my wrist.

"I..." I cocked my head, feeling my frown deepen as I stared at the words. VISITOR REQUEST. "Someone wants to talk to me. From the outside, I mean."

The Rat raised an eyebrow. "That unusual?"

I shook myself. "It's the first time I've gotten that message in all the eight years I've been here."

He sat back, idly stirring his goop with his spoon. "Who'd you think it is?"

I finally lowered my wrist, staring into my empty bowl as I worked through the same question. Who knew I was in here? So far as I was aware, everybody I'd known on the outside thought I was dead. I shook my head slowly. "I've got no idea."

The Rat glanced around the room again, and I followed his eyes towards the other Scorcher. The man was sitting in the far corner, still watching us. "Well," the Rat said. "Should we... find out?"

"We?"

He turned back to me and shrugged.

I sighed. "Come on."

# THREE

I let out a heavy sigh as I surveyed the chaotic mess that was the Inmate Administrative Offices. This was the hub through which prisoners were meant to file complaints, review their records, make appeals, talk to attorneys or visitors, arrange work releases, and see to a hundred other miscellaneous details. Whoever had designed it either hadn't realized that the offices were nowhere near large enough to efficiently process the needs of all fifty thousand inmates in the system, or didn't care. And why should they? After all, they'd been paid, hadn't they?

As it was, the large annex in the center of the offices had turned into a winding mass of disorganized lines, full of inmates waiting with varying degrees of patience for whatever they were here for. The lines spilled out of the annex and into the hallways leading up to it. I'd already spent three hours working my way through that line just to be able to register my arrival with an automated assistant. The AI told me to stand by for a conference room to be available.

And so I waited. The Rat waited with me, furtive as ever. I couldn't help but feel bad for him. He had no illusions about what was going on here. He knew that the Scorchers were coming for him. He knew that they were most likely scared of me. And so, he figured that sticking close to me was the closest thing he had to a chance of survival.

The only thing he *didn't* know was that when they finally came, I wouldn't do a damn thing to help him.

It wasn't that I didn't want to help him. I had nothing against the kid. He was odd, sure, and weirdly quiet, but those weren't crimes. Hell, even if they were crimes, I wasn't one to judge. But Venter wanted him dead, presumably to court favors from the Scorchers, and I was done fighting the illusion that I had any power to defy Venter. I could feel old memories surfacing, and if I didn't get my hands on another can soon, I was going to have to face them.

I looked around for a distraction. An old screen was hanging from the ceiling above me—an attempt at providing at least some slight entertainment to those of us unfortunate enough to be waiting in line. I guess the prison officials had figured out that a bored prisoner is a dangerous prisoner. The screen's blurry image depicted a large, stately-looking building spewing smoke and flames. I frowned at it. It looked vaguely familiar for some reason.

A garbled, feminine voice accompanied the image. As the voice started speaking, the inmates around me turned their eyes upward with one motion, eyes glued to the screen in hopes of seeing a feminine figure.

*"Though the prime speaker declared the Last War to be officially over sixteen years ago,"* the reporter's distorted voice said, *"small pockets of terrorists continue to wage war against the Paragon and the dream of united humanity. The footage you're now seeing comes to us from Gharseva, Brahma, where a group of violent anti-humanity anarchists, who call themselves the Brahmian Independence League, have recently claimed responsibility for an explosion that damaged the Capitol building, claiming the*

*lives of dozens of innocent bystanders and hardworking Paragon officials."*

Ah. That was why I recognized the building. It was where we'd stood at parade rest watching the prime speaker's declaration that the Last War was officially over. The familiar sight stirred little in me, however, other than a vague gloominess. We'd all known that the end of the war would hardly mean the end of the violence—especially on Brahma. This Brahmian Independence League—or whatever it was they called themselves—had garnered an increasingly fierce and bloody reputation over the years since the official surrender.

The screen cut to an image of what appeared to be a row of body bags, followed by a huddled group of weeping children. Somber but patriotic music played in the background as the camera zoomed in on a suspiciously attractive-looking Paragon soldier kneeling next to the children and handing one of them a chocolate bar.

*"Loyal citizens of Gharseva can take comfort in knowing that Paragon enforcers are hard at work seeking the cowardly traitors responsible for this inhumanity. We here at Paragon Independent Information Studios send our condolences to the victims and their families."*

The footage cut again—this time to the newsroom. The inmates around me leaned forward, only to groan in disappointment as the reporter's features were hidden behind a warped portion of the screen. The reporting went on, covering other small acts of rebellion scattered across the Paragon.

I looked away and shook my head. *The Last War.* That was what the Paragon had called it. One last war to unite all of the colonies humanity had scattered across the stars, to bring us all under the same banner and usher in an age of peace and prosperity for all. Or, at least, that was what the Paragon propaganda departments had been saying for the last hundred years or so. According to the Paragon, it had ended on Brahma after we conquered Gharseva. But anyone who figured that humans were done killing each other just because the vast majority of us had been forced to live under the same flag were either full of Paragon propaganda or just plain stupid.

An inmate—tall and lanky, with skin so pale it hurt to look at—slid out of the room in front of me, slipping away down the hall without making eye contact and holding his hands awkwardly over his crotch. A metallic-sounding voice blared out through the speaker system above my head.

*"Inmate LV5933, given name Lackan VanDunn, please enter conference room 19C."*

The Rat glanced around, then pointed at the door the pale man had just left. "That's you."

"Thanks," I muttered, moving towards it.

"I'll just be..." He glanced around nervously. "Here."

"Sure." I stepped up to the conference room door, scanned my wrist computer against the doorknob, and stepped through before it sealed shut behind me.

It smelled like piss inside.

*"Inmate LV5933, given name Lackan VanDunn,"* said the voice. *"Please be seated."*

I sat, trying to ignore the stench and looking anywhere but the glistening puddle at the base of the seat. The wall in front of me started to glow. It was so covered in grime and the dried remains of various fluids that the words appearing on it were barely readable. *Inmate LV5933*, it said at the top, followed by a blurry picture that I guessed was supposed to be me and several lines of identifying information. In the center of the screen a blinking message said *Visitor Conference: Waiting for Guest.*

I scanned through the other information on the screen. At the top was a message that said *Recording*, followed by the current year—1906 *Anno Exodi.* Nineteen hundred years since humanity had broken the lightspeed barrier and begun the long process of settling the stars.

At the bottom was some basic information about me. *Given name: Lackan VanDunn. Year and Place of Birth: 1866, Gideon. Conviction: Salvaging without a permit. Total Sentence: twenty standard earth years. Sentence served: eight standard earth years, forty-three standard earth days.*

I let a long gust of air burst through my nostrils. Eight years of cold slop for meals. Eight years of fending off killers and thugs trying to prove just how badass they were. Eight years of smelling other peoples' piss. Eight years without Kessa...

"Lax? Is that you?"

I blinked and looked up at the screen, jarred from my memories. I had to squint to make out what exactly it was that I was looking at.

The blinking message was gone. Obscured behind a layer of dried green *something* was the blurry image of a man. Broad-faced and bald-headed. Sporting a short black beard and a gnarled, twisted scar across one side of his face.

*Wait a second...*

I found myself leaning forward in the chair. "*Nadus?* What the hell?"

Nadus Torsund's weathered face broke into a wide, familiar grin. "Well, if it ain't the one and only Lackan VanDunn."

I tried to speak, tried to find words to adequately express my shock. I found nothing but memories. Memories of that now weathered face, young and terrified as we were herded into the Vanguard training facility together. Laughing at the sergeant behind his back in the barracks. Fighting back tears as we reminisced together about the homes we'd left behind. Daunted but determined, and then increasingly cold and hollow as we fought from battleground to battleground, planet to planet.

Sixteen years since I'd seen that face. Last I'd heard he'd gone the mercenary route, making a living doing the only thing the Vanguard had taught us: killing. He'd tried to talk me into going along with him. But I'd already spilled more than enough blood for one lifetime by then.

"Nadus?" I finally managed to croak. "Is that you?"

His smile only broadened. "It's me, Lax."

I shook my head, still trying to force myself to believe it. "What... how..."

"Heard some rumors about a Vanguard—an especially ugly one, mind you—stuck in the tin can, right after you fell off the radar," Nadus said. "Figured it was worth looking into."

I sagged back in my chair, my brain barely able to process what was happening. "Why..."

He chuckled and turned his head towards somebody offscreen. "Hang on. Bentley, you're up."

The screen flickered. The *Recording* message at the top vanished. I glanced around. The red light on the security camera hanging in the corner had gone out as well.

"Alright," Nadus said, cracking his knuckles. "To business. I don't know how long we've got so I'll make it quick. I've got a job lined up for you."

I frowned. "A job? You mean, in here?"

He barked out a harsh laugh. "Hell no! I don't care about what's going on inside that tin can. No, *out here.*"

"But..." I blinked stupidly.

He grinned. "That's right, Lax. We're gonna bust you out of there. You ready to taste some sweet, sweet freedom again?"

*Freedom.* After eight years in the tin can, I wasn't even sure what that meant anymore. But if it involved not being Venter's punching bag or sitting through meetings in another man's piss, it seemed pretty damn appealing.

"You ready to work again?" Nadus went on. "Armor on your back and a gun in your hands?"

Damn, but that sounded good. For the first time in eight years, I felt something like *hope.* A smile crept cautiously across my face.

"Hell yeah," I said. "You got a plan for getting me out?"

Nadus nodded. "Yep. We're gonna kill you."

I raised an eyebrow.

"Ever heard of *The Count of Monte Cristo*?" Nadus asked.

"No."

"Me neither. Our contact in the prison kept talking about it, though, like it meant something." Nadus shrugged. "Anyways, most of the corpses in there just get cremated and jettisoned. If you're willing to pay, though, the morgue workers will pull your body aside for pickup, so you can get towed back to wherever you came from for a proper burial." He shook his head as if the idea was ridiculous. "And, if you're willing to pay *extra* money, they'll even overlook a few vital signs."

My eyes widened. "So, what, I just need to play dead?

"They've got a system in there—the guys who run this op, I mean. I dunno what it is. All I know is that tomorrow during your lunch someone is gonna slip you something. You gotta drink it, then head to... uh... what was it again?" He craned his head to the side and listened as somebody I couldn't see said something, then turned back. "Sanitation Room 42C. Right next to the cafeteria, supposedly. Someone's supposed to meet you there."

I nodded, practically giddy with excitement. "If it meant I could get out of *here*, I'd trust a damn ripper."

"Damn right." He grinned. "We're gonna get you out. Give you a chance to stretch your legs. I'm telling you, you are *just* the man we need for this job."

"Yeah." Damn, but it felt good to let myself smile. "Yeah, that will be nice. What *is* the job?"

"Salvage," Nadus said.

A chill ran down my spine.

*Green dots, flashing red...*

"Got ourselves the real mother-lode," Nadus was saying, but his voice was harder to focus on with each passing word. "And I mean, *really real*. Bigger than anything you've ever done. Bigger than anything any vulture has *ever* done, I figure."

I was trying to talk, trying to get words out. But they didn't come. Kessa was smiling. Why was she smiling? "I..."

"I'm not talking a few ultracells," Nadus continued. "I'm talking real money. *Quitting* money. Make it out alive, and you'll never have to work a day again in your life."

*We had a good run...*

"That's the catch, though," Nadus said. "High risk, high reward. From what we can tell, there's a decent chance we'll have a lot of rippers on our hands. But that's why I want you along, Lax. From what I hear, nobody knows the salvage game like you." He frowned. "Hey, you alright?"

My breathing was getting heavy and fast. My heart was thumping in tight, painful contractions. I squeezed my eyes shut for a long moment, trying to get ahold of myself. I could see her. Could see the rippers swarming her and I wasn't doing anything and—

*A can. I need... a can...*

"LAX!" Nadus's voice jarred me out of my stupor. "I think the screen froze up for a second. Lax, can you hear me?"

"Yeah," I said softly.

"Alright. Well, the Bear will be in your cafeteria tomorrow at lunch. Just do what he says, and—"

"No thanks," I found myself saying.

Nadus frowned. "Sorry, what?"

"I..." I shook my head. "I'm sorry. I just... I can't." I forced a weak grin. "I appreciate you thinking about me, and I'm sure it must have been a hell of a lot of trouble getting ahold of me in here like this, but... I ain't your guy."

Nadus stared intently at me through the screen. "Damn, Lax. If I didn't know you better, I'd say you were scared."

I found myself looking down. "Maybe you don't know me as well as you think, Nadus."

"Huh." He rubbed his chin. "You'd really rather keep on rotting away in there?"

I hesitated. Don't get me wrong: there was nothing fun about the tin can. But thinking about doing another salvage run filled my head full of memories I'd spent the last eight years trying to forget. About the family I'd lost. And if I was being honest with myself, I wasn't sure I could handle going through anything like that again.

"Fine," Nadus said after a moment. He gave a long sigh. "Look. I heard about what happened to you. You've been through hell. And I'm sorry about that. But I'm offering you a second chance here. A chance to make things right. And you know those don't come around often."

"Some things can't be made right, Nadus." I said weakly. "No matter how badly I wish they could."He gave a sad smile. "Good luck in there, Lax. I'll see you on the other side."

He vanished.


*Green dots, flashing red...*

I gritted my teeth and turned on the faucet. Cold water hit me like Jed's pipe. I tried to focus on my breathing. On the sensation of the wet tile against the palm of my hand. On the icy water running down my body, washing away the lingering scent of urine from my meeting just half an hour ago. On anything other than the memories.

*If I didn't know you better, I'd say you were scared.*

Damn right I was scared. I was terrified. After everything I'd seen—everything I'd been through—you'd have to be crazy not to be. I groaned, letting my head thud against the wall and watching the water pool beneath my feet.

"Bad news?"

I turned my head, regarding the Rat with bleak, unfocused eyes. "What?"

He shrugged. He was standing near the edge of the large, open shower area. Weird. Normally he just waited outside. Harder to get cornered there. There was something in his eyes as he looked at me... worry, almost. Not for himself, though—for me. "You got a visitor. Don't seem too happy about it. Bad news?"

I sighed and turned away. "The hell do you care so much all of a sudden?"

He went blessedly quiet. I squeezed my eyes shut. Kessa was there. I saw her. Oh, *hell*, I could see her, and I wanted to vomit.

I could hear mumbling behind me, the sound of the doors opening and other inmates coming into the washroom, but I ignored them, too busy trying to tread the violent seas of my vivid memories. Just to keep my head above the water. Because there sure as hell was nothing good beneath it.

"There he is," somebody was saying. "Just like Venter said."

"Hello, Rat," somebody else growled.

I heard a cry of alarm, followed by a short scuffle. Somebody grunted in pain, then there was a soft thud and a splashing of water.

I opened my eyes.

Six inmates had come into the washroom, all of them bearing vivid red Scorcher tattoos on their necks. Two of them were grappling with the Rat, pinning him against the wall, while another one was getting back to his feet from where he had been knocked over into the shower area. One other Scorcher waited by the door while the other two stood by with shivs in hand.

The one who had been knocked down climbed back to his feet and glared around, his gaze settling on me. He seemed to be the leader, with a glowing skull tattooed over his face in addition to the one on his neck.

"What are you staring at, puppet?" he growled.

I glanced from him to the Rat. He had stopped struggling and was looking around wildly now for any chance at escape. He found none. Finally, his stare settled on me: a desperate, wide-eyed plea for help.

"Nothing," I muttered, and turned back to the wall.

*Breathe. Just... breathe.* Stepping in now wouldn't do me any good. And the Rat... well, they'd get him eventually anyways. No escaping fate. Not in here. Like I'd told him earlier, you can't change who you are.

The man scoffed. "Guess the old man was right. Puppet really is on a string. Now... where were we?"

My knuckles were white against the wall. I was dimly aware of the hissing sound of my breath pushing ragged through the gaps between my clenched teeth, hot and angry. *I own you. Don't you forget it.* Venter's face swam through my vision, blurred and distorted, his mouth twisted in a demonic grin.

The sound of flesh hitting flesh mingled with the Rat's grunts. The lead Scorcher gave a harsh chuckle. "Oh, you're regretting it all now, ain't ya? Seemed like a good idea to talk at the time, didn't it?" Another thud and another grunt. "You thought you could get away. Just stop being one of us. But once a Scorcher, always a Scorcher. It's all starting to come back to you, ain't it?"

*Don't look back.* I forced my eyes shut and lowered my head, trying vainly to block out the Rat's grunts of pain and broken protests. *Don't you dare look back.*

"The mistakes," the Scorcher continued. *Thud.* "The regrets." *Thud.* "The things you wish you would've done." *Thud.* "And the ones you wish you hadn't."

The Scorchers gave a laugh, and I heard the sound of the Rat's limp body splashing to the floor, followed by a desperate whimper. He tried to say something, only to be cut off by what sounded like a swift kick to the ribs.

"You're wishing you could take it all back now, ain't ya?"

The lead Scorcher gave a hungry sounding growl. "Well, friend, sorry to say, but you can't. Ain't no way of changing what you are—a rat. Hold his mouth open, boys."

I couldn't restrain myself any longer. I opened my eyes and glanced over my shoulder. One of the Scorchers was kneeling on him, pinning him to the floor, while the other grabbed him roughly by the mouth and pried his jaws open. The Rat's eyes widened even further as the lead Scorcher took a jagged-looking shiv from one of his companions and held it up.

"Tongues that wag," he said, a grin tugging at the corners of his lips, "get cut out. This next part works out better with a sharper blade, but I guess we're just gonna have to make do with what we've got, ain't we?"

The Rat's eyes flitted back to mine. He kicked and fought and gave a muffled scream of defiance as the shiv crept closer, and I suddenly realized who he reminded me of.

Rawlins. He reminded me of Rawlins, from my old salvage crew. Bright-eyed and naïve and in desperate need of help I couldn't give him.

My body moved of its own accord. One moment I was standing there in the shower like an idiot. The next I was striding towards the Scorcher boss.

He glanced at me, his brows furrowing. "What the—"

I swung my fist, and time seemed to slow.

I don't really consider myself a violent person. Which might seem a bit delusional, given my past, but the honest truth is that I don't enjoy hurting people. Usually.

But damn me to hell if the way his nose folded and snapped beneath my fist wasn't the best feeling I'd had in a long, *long* time.

The force of the blow lifted him off the ground and sent him flying backward. His body slammed into the sink and tumbled to the floor. The Scorcher that had been pinning the Rat to the floor blinked, his eyes wide with shock. He didn't even attempt to dodge as I drove my knee up into his forehead, slamming his skull back against the wall with a wet crack. The shock in his eyes turned to glassy nothingness as he sagged sideways, leaving a smear of blood on the wall behind him.

The other Scorcher—the one who had been trying to pry the Rat's mouth open—gave a sudden shout of pain as the kid bit down hard on his fingers. I started to intervene, then hesitated as the kid crawled on top of the bigger man and began pummeling him with blows, biting down on his hand all the while. Instead, I turned and faced the remaining three Scorchers.

"Anyone else?"

I took a step forward. They shuffled backward.

"Get out of here," I growled.

They stood still for a moment. Then the one with the shiv turned and bolted. Within seconds, the others had fled as well.

I turned back to the Rat. The Scorcher was barely conscious now, his protesting mumbles only just audible over the mixed sounds of the kid's fists raining down repeatedly over his battered face.

"Alright, kid," I said. "You got him."

He paused, then landed one more blow on the bridge of the Scorcher's nose before climbing shakily to his feet.

"Nice work," I said.

The Rat spat a mouthful of blood onto the still-groaning Scorcher, then wiped at his lips.

"Rid," he said.

I glanced over at him, raising an eyebrow.

"What's that?" I asked.

"Rid," he gasped, then gave a short laugh—the laugh of a man who's lucky to be alive and knows it. "My name is Rid."

I nodded, then turned and surveyed the washroom. The leader's body twitched once where it was lying beneath the sink, blood beginning to pool beneath his head. I didn't bother checking if he had a pulse or not. The guy I'd kneed in the face didn't look like he'd be getting up any time soon, either. I stood there in silence for a moment, letting the adrenaline slowly fade away.

I felt *great*.

"V...Vent..."

I frowned down at the sound. The Scorcher the Rat had been beating was trying to put words together, his pulped lips oozing with blood. "Venter... *lied*..."

And that was all it took to break the spell. Any elation I'd felt—the sheer, unbridled joy of the fight—vanished, replaced by a sinking weight in my gut. Venter.

"You think..."—the Scorcher groaned—"this is the end of this..."

This deal with the Scorchers had been important to Venter. And I'd just bludgeoned it to death. The Scorchers would think he'd screwed them, and the only way he'd be able to placate them would be to make an example of me. He'd have to put me down. Hard.

"Ah, *hell*," I muttered under my breath.

# FOUR

That was the last we saw of the Scorchers that day. Didn't hear anything from Venter, either. But I knew it was coming. More likely sooner than later. And when it did come—well, *mercy* was as foreign a concept to the old bastard as brushing his artificial teeth. His entire little prison kingdom was based on his unquestioned authority, and his most feared bruiser had just broken rank. If he wanted to maintain any of his power, he was going to have to make an example out of me.

Not just me. Us.

I glanced over at Rid from my place lying on my oversized cot. He was standing next to the door, gazing through the small peephole out into the corridor.

*Us.* The word felt wrong in my mind somehow. For eight years it had been me against the world. I had no illusions that Rid and I were anything like *friends*, but after my little demonstration in the washroom, we were stuck together. For better or worse.

"Relax," I said, turning back to stare at the bottom of the bunk above me. "Once those doors seal at night, nobody's getting through them."

Rid grimaced. "Even the wardens?"

I scoffed. "If the wardens want us dead, then there's nothing we can do about it anyways. And the guys who want you dead, they don't have those kinds of strings to pull."

"You sure?"

"Get some sleep, Rid."

He sighed and complied, climbing up into his bunk. A few minutes later, there was a clicking sound as the lights automatically shut off. Bedtime.

Sleep didn't find me, though, and I didn't go looking for it. I just lay there, staring up into the darkness and trying to work through what I was going to do.

I could hold Venter off for a while. I doubted he'd be able to talk his cronies into mounting a full-on assault on me, which meant he'd have to resort to catching me off guard. Which was the problem. Eventually, I'd slip up. Venter wasn't going anywhere, and neither was I. One day I'd let my guard down at the wrong time and that would be it.

Another thought struck me, somehow more daunting than the prospect of being stabbed in the back, and I felt myself grow cold. If Venter was really smart, he wouldn't do any of that. Wouldn't do a thing. Just... sit back and wait for me to come to him. Because his cans were my only source of sanity in this hell-hole and he *knew* it. He *knew* that eventually I'd come crawling back, desperate for blessed relief, no matter what I had to do to get it. Hell, he might even take me back under his wing if I...

*No.*

Disgust overcame me suddenly. What the hell was I thinking? I'd spent too long following that bastard's orders. And now that I had a chance to try to break free, I was already trying to figure out how I could get back under his thumb? Resolve surged through my mind. No matter what happened, I was done working for Venter.

My knuckles tightened. If I struck first, I could cut the head off the snake. Keep him from being a threat. I didn't know where his cell was, but I knew most of his routine. With just a bit of stealth I could hit him where he least expected it and turn him into nothing more than a stain on the prison floor. If I played my cards right, I might even be able to find his can supplier.

But then, of course... I closed my eyes, letting a long, exasperated breath filter through my nose. Then, of course, I'd just have to deal with the next overly eager self-made criminal mastermind that decided to fill the power vacuum. And on and on. There was no escaping it. As long as I was in here, it would just be one headache after another.

I let myself think about Nadus. About his mysterious offer. A way out and a good paying job. *Freedom.* The more I thought about it, the more appealing it became. Why the hell had I turned him down?

*Green dots, flashing red...*

I felt my breathing start to get heavy, the familiar fear beginning to worm its way into my nervous system, chewing me apart. I tried to relax, to calm myself, only to find my fingers scratching at my shoulder port, feeling the cold, metallic edges, and wishing desperately that I had a can. *Just a small hit.* That was all I needed. Just a small hit to make it all go away...

———

"What'll it be today, Rid? Brown goop or gray goop?"

Rid ignored me, too focused on swiveling his head back and forth to keep an eye on the inmates surrounding us. Based on the lines beneath his eyes, I hazarded a guess that he hadn't gotten much sleep last night.

I sighed and turned back to the line. Rid was nervous. I was too. But I tried to force a hint of playful levity into my voice. "Ooh—maybe *green* goop today?"

The guy behind Rid growled. "Hurry the hell up. I'm hungry."

Rid said nothing.

"You know what I could really use a hit of right now?" I continued, not letting myself be discouraged. "Mars Pop." I actually started to salivate at the thought. "A hit of good, cold, sugary Mars Pop. Damn, that sounds nice."

The guy behind Rid scoffed now. "What are you, six?"

I sighed and stuck my bowl under the gray goop dispenser, burying my dreams of red, sugary carbonation beneath the flood of discolored slop. When it was full, I turned and headed towards my usual table, scanning the room as I did so. Venter was noticeably absent. Concerning.

"Why did you do it?" Rid asked softly.

I glanced at him and frowned. "Huh?"

"Yesterday. You didn't have to get involved."

I stared down at my bowl. What was I supposed to say? *You reminded me of an old friend?* "Does it matter?"

Rid shrugged. "We're stuck together now," he said through a mouthful of goop. He twisted two of his fingers together and held them up. "Like this. Scorchers'll have you marked. Whatever happens now, it happens to both of us."

I raised a spoonful of goop only to find myself fighting the urge to gag at the thought of forcing down another mouthful. I stared down at it. What was it I had said to Rid yesterday? *You've just gotta let the taste of freedom wash away.*

I'd had a chance at freedom. I'd turned it down. And now, if I survived the day, it would be ten more years of this. Ten more years of goop. Ten more years of uniforms that smelled like piss.

"We need a plan," Rid said. He'd been quiet when I'd first met him, but it seemed that once he started talking he didn't stop easy. "Not, like, an *escape* plan—that'd be too complicated for now—but just something to keep us safe. Keep the Scorchers off of us." He glanced down at the tattoo of playing cards on the back of his hand. "What do we have to work with? There's gotta be something..."

I opened my mouth but something thudded onto the table next to me before I could speak. Dammit, I'd let my guard down. Any second I'd feel a shiv in my back. I jumped, raising a fist and turning, expecting to see Venter's gang surrounding me.

Instead, I saw a scruffy-looking man wearing a white uniform that marked him as an inmate volunteer. He'd set down a tall, opaque bottle on the table next to me.

"We weren't sure how much dosage was right," he whispered. "So we made it extra strong. Drink it here, fast as you can, then get to the washroom around the corner through that door"—he jerked his head towards the far side of the cafeteria—"and sit tight. You'll have to hurry. You'll start fading out not long after you've drunk it."

I blinked at him. "Wait, I thought—"

"No time. Follow the plan and you'll wake up a free man. If you're not in position in..."—he glanced up at a dingy old digital clock on the wall—"fifteen minutes, the whole deal is off."

I tried to say something else, but he just pushed the bottle towards me and turned back to pushing his cart full of sanitation equipment. Then he was gone.

I stared at the bottle.

"What was that about?" Rid asked suspiciously.

I ignored him. I'd figured Nadus would have canceled whatever little plan he'd made. Apparently not. Or, at least, these guys hadn't gotten the memo that the deal was off. Which meant that there was no way for me to know what would happen to me after I drank this bottle.

Rid was craning his head to get a better look at the bottle. "What is it? Booze?"

It wasn't worth the risk. And even if it was, I couldn't leave Rid behind. Not now. Whatever torture the Scorchers had been planning on him would be increased tenfold due to my interference once they caught him. Plus, even if I *did* bring Rid along with me, there was no guarantee that they'd take him. If I'd understood Nadus's plan correctly, this bottle contained some sort of sedative. We might both just end up dead in the bathroom. So, again—it just wasn't worth the risk.

Was it?

I looked around me, taking in the sight of a hundred jumpsuit-clad inmates forcing down their protein goop. Took in the smell of sweat and piss and long-dead dreams. Then looked back to the bottle.

"Damn you, Nadus," I muttered, then—quickly, before I could talk myself out of it—I grabbed the bottle, unscrewed the top, and lifted it to my lips, chugging its contents.

It tasted sour. I drank two thirds of the bottle, then handed it to Rid and wiped my mouth.

"Drink this," I gasped. "All of it. And fast."

He frowned suspiciously at the bottle. "Why? What is it?"

I shoved it into his hands. "Our plan. Just *do it.*"

His eyes widened. He lifted the bottle and started drinking. He coughed as soon as it touched his lips and almost pushed the bottle away, but when his eyes met mine he kept drinking until it was empty.

"Good." I rose to my feet, feeling slightly unsteady. "Now follow me."

I turned towards the exit the janitor had indicated. *Sanitation Room 42D.* Or had it been C? No matter—I'd see what was closest. I just had to make it there. The time for mulling things over was long gone. Now it was time for action. Before whatever I'd just put into my body started its work.

For the first time since I'd talked to Nadus, I felt just a spark of hope. A taste of freedom. Might be that I was getting both Rid and myself killed by doing this. But somehow it still felt better than just sitting around waiting for Venter's thugs to come after us.

I glanced up at the clock. Five minutes had passed since the janitor had plopped the bottle on my table. Which meant I had ten minutes left to get to that washroom.

I'd get there with time to spare.

Somebody loomed in front of me. I halted as several other inmates suddenly rose from their tables, forming a semicircle and blocking my path. The one in the center—a big guy I recognized as one of Venter's bodyguards—sneered at me, revealing a long, jagged shiv in each of his hands. The others all drew makeshift weapons of their own.

Behind me, Rid hissed a curse.

"Lax, my boy," said a tired, familiar voice. "I must say, I'm disappointed in you."

I inched my head sideways, not letting the guy with the shivs out of my sight, until I could see Venter standing off to the side, arms folded. "Your job was *so* easy. All you had to do was keep your head down and do as you were told, and everything I had was yours."

I blinked. I could feel myself growing dizzy. The seconds were growing longer—or were they growing shorter?

"Evidently, however," Venter continued, his voice waxing loud and showy, "this was too much for your feeble puppet mind to bear. And now I must make an example of you. I wish it hadn't come to this..."

He went on. I stopped paying attention. I could feel my legs growing weak. Whatever was in that bottle was potent. And I was running out of time. Fast. If I passed out before I could reach that sanitation room, I'd never wake up.

The big guy took another step forward. His eyes were gleaming with excitement. His knuckles were white around the grips of his twin shivs. I knew his type. He'd been waiting for this. A chance to prove just how badass he was. As soon as Venter gave the word, he'd step forward and cut me into ribbons.

I never gave him that chance.

Before Venter could finish his speech, I darted forward, closing the gap between me and the big guy. Mind you, he was only big by a regular human's standards, a fact that became immediately obvious as I stepped in close. I swung my right in a short, brutal hook that collided with his temple like an explosive round from a Jackhammer rifle. There was an audible *crack* as something broke and the big guy went down.

Then all hell broke loose.

They charged me all at once and from every angle. I knew with a certainty that comes with years of fighting that if I stayed where I was I'd be dead within seconds. So instead I charged forward, bellowing as I shoulder-checked two of my attackers and sent them flying through the air to collide with other inmates who weren't part of the confrontation. The neat little semicircle broke as they all scrambled to reposition.

A sharp pain bit into my back. I snarled and whirled. It was one of the Scorchers I'd faced down yesterday—one of the ones I *hadn't* left as a broken wreck, anyways. He was wearing a triumphant grin like he thought he'd just achieved something.

Some people never learn. I backhanded him, slamming his head into the corner of a nearby table with a jarring thud. His eyes went glassy. I whirled, dodged an incoming blow, kicked the legs out from under my assailant, and slammed my foot down onto his head. He twitched and went limp.

I retreated and scanned the room, blinking through the steadily growing fatigue. What had started as a targeted attack had spiraled out of control into a chaotic brawl. An alarm started blaring overhead, warning the inmates to return to order or risk consequences. Venter was shouting, face red with anger as he pointed at me. I counted three of his goons that were still on their feet and hadn't been distracted by the chaos around us.

I could take them. Probably. But my head was getting light and my vision blurry. I didn't have time for this. Any second now I might keel over. And from the predatory light in my opponents' eyes, I could tell they knew. The probably thought it was the shiv that was still sticking out of my back. They'd never have guessed that I'd voluntarily downed a bottle full of an unknown sedative just moments ago.

As had Rid. Whom, I realized with a start, I couldn't see anywhere. Had he run off in the chaos? Had he already passed out?

No time to find out. Three shiv-wielding inmates charged me in a co-ordinated attack. I staggered backward, narrowly avoiding their cuts, only to feel my foot catch on something. I grunted as I fell onto my back.

They were on me, barking their bloodthirsty joy like wild dogs. I could barely track where they were. I caught one with a solid kick to the chest that broke a few ribs and sent him flying backward. Another one stabbed his shiv into my shoulder. I cried out in pain, grabbed his head, and slammed it into the concrete floor as hard as I could. I swept out with a leg and knocked down the third, then rolled onto my hands and knees, grabbed the shiv that was still protruding from my back, and slammed it into his chest.

I tried to climb to my feet only to feel myself grow faint and sag. I groaned, rolling as a shape loomed over me.

"Got you, you big bastard," Venter hissed, holding up a blade. My vision flickered as he knelt above me, grinning demonically. "My face is the last thing you're going to—"

Warm liquid sprayed into my face. Venter's eyes rolled back and he fell sideways, head thudding against the floor. Rid pulled a bloody shiv from his neck.

"*Come on,*" he hissed, grabbing my hand.

He pulled me to my feet. Well—I climbed to my feet and he pulled. He wasn't nearly strong enough to budge my weight, but the effort was appreciated nonetheless. I staggered groggily towards the exit. I knew that I was trying to get somewhere, but could remember only vaguely where... or why. *Escape*, I thought. *Something... to do... with escape...*

I pushed through the doorway and into the hall beyond. The hallway was crowded with fleeing inmates. I could hear metallic thudding as mechanical wardens stomped their way down the hall towards the scene of the chaos. *The washroom.* That was where we needed to go.

I stumbled through the door marked SANITATION ROOM 42C. It was empty. I managed to make it to the far wall before I fell against it, sagging to the floor.

Blood pooled around me. Some mine, some Venter's. I could barely think straight, but I found myself chuckling. Seemed like I was spending a lot of time in bathrooms these days.

Rid swayed on his feet, staring down at me with heavy eyes. "Why... what are we..."

"Sit down." I waved vaguely at the floor.

"No way." He shook his head, his slurred words barely intelligible. "People piss down there."

"You're gonna..."

He sagged to his knees, then toppled over, his head landing on my leg. I gave another coarse, incoherent laugh. I didn't even know what was funny. I was dying on the floor of a washroom in a prison station with some random kid I'd met a few days ago by my side. And I couldn't even remember why.

Someone was standing over me. Wearing white. Saying something and pointing at Rid. I just nodded. I was tired. So very tired.

I wondered if this was how she had felt, before the end. Watching the world shrink slowly around you. It didn't look like much. Not from here, anyways. Maybe when I was gone, to wherever it was we all went, she would be there.

The figure in white drew closer, and I passed out.

# FIVE

## DEEP SPACE, NEAR THE BRAHMA SYSTEM

EIGHT YEARS AGO

She didn't look like much.

Not from here, anyways. Just a dark rectangle blotting out the dim light of a few stars behind it, growing steadily larger as we approached. But I knew, as soon as I saw it, that it was what I'd been looking for.

The Big One.

"That's it?"

I glanced over my shoulder. Rawlins was short and baby-faced, his eyes bright with excitement. There were five of us waiting together on the bridge right now, waiting to get a glimpse of our target, but nobody was more eager than him. He leaned forward as he spoke, craning his head to get a better look through the bridge window of the *Orpheus*.

Ah, to be a rookie again.

Behind us, Liung laughed. "What were you expecting, a big damn welcome sign?" He held out his hands with fingers forming a rectangle as if mimicking his imaginary sign. "*Atten-*

*tion vultures: riches beyond imagining inside. Please wipe your feet on your way in."*

The rest of the crew chuckled. Rawlins scowled, sagging back into his seat. "No, I just figured it would be more than a..." He gestured vaguely out the window. "Whatever *that* is."

I chuckled and put a heavy, hopefully reassuring hand on his shoulder. "Oh, it will be. We just need to get closer. You'll see." I turned away, ignoring his continued grumbles. "Sev, what does the scan show?"

Sevani shook herself, looking sharply up from a handheld quantum communicator and pushing it into her pocket. "Sorry, what?"

"The scan."

"Oh. Right. One sec."

Black and I shared worried glances. That wasn't like her. Typically she was on top of those details long before I was. Today she seemed distracted, her jaw tight with stress and her eyes glassy and distant.

"Clean ship," she said finally. "No sign of rippers. Easy money."

*Rippers.* I grimaced, forcing away a barrage of memories. Rafe, gasping as he was torn apart by flashing claws. Nadus, missing half of his face. But that was behind me. Eight years behind me, to be precise. I wasn't a Vanguard puppet anymore, charging recklessly into battle as ignicerin flooded my body, obeying orders nobody bothered to explain to me. I was a vulture now. Fighting battles I chose to fight, with the people I wanted to fight alongside.

I turned to Black. "Start getting everyone ready. I'll go tell Kess."

Black turned his big, serious eyes towards me and nodded. "Sure thing, boss."

I nodded in return and descended the hatch into the crew quarters. Rawlins was green and cocky, Liung was easily distracted, and Sevani's head seemed to be somewhere else today, but Black I could depend on. I made a mental note to chat with Sev after the run and see what was going on with her. Didn't want to have to worry about her freezing up on me on some future job.

Then again... if this job went right, we might never have to work another salvage operation again.

The thought gave me pause. If Trent had been right, and the *Panama* really *was* stocked full of ultracells, that would be game over. Enough money to go wherever we wanted. *Do* whatever we wanted. No more living off of processed protein bars, no more struggling to make enough cash to keep the *Orpheus* running. Hell, we'd never have to work another day of our lives if we didn't want to.

It was an alluring thought. And yet, as I ran my hand along the *Orpheus*'s battered bulkheads, I had to admit that the notion of leaving this all behind was bittersweet. In the eight years I'd been running salvage, this ship had become my home, the crew my family. Parting ways felt... wrong, somehow.

After the Vanguard had cut me loose I'd wandered from station to station, planet to planet, doing odd jobs here and there to pay my way. Not a whole lot of folks were eager about the prospect of hiring a puppet. Not for anything other than fighting, that is. Eventually, though, I'd run across a crew of vultures looking for somebody who knew their way around rippers. Turned out there were a lot of derelict ships scattered across the stars with plenty of goods left for the taking—so long as you were willing to run the risks involved, which often included rippers still hibernating on board, waiting for their next meal.

Turned out I was a pretty good hand at the salvage business. I worked a few jobs with a few different crews. Made some connections. Built myself a reputation. It wasn't until I met Kessa, though, that I had the idea to put together my own crew.

I thumbed the scanner next to the door of my room and it

slid open. The scanner was *supposed* to be a security measure that only let me or Kessa in, but it had a hard time differentiating between thumbs. Liung kept on saying he was going to take a look at it.

I ducked under the low doorway. This spacecraft had certainly *not* been built for a man of my size, but after almost eight years aboard it, I'd learned to get around just fine. Inside my cabin, I glanced around for Kessa, stepping forward and—

"Hey, watch it!"

I grunted as my foot thudded into something heavy and cylindrical. I doubled over to grab it before it could fall. Despite my quick reaction, several large drops of deep-blue paint spilled out of the can and splattered over the hard composite surface of the floor. I winced down at my handiwork.

Kessa gave an exaggerated sigh. "Guess I'm always gonna be cleaning up after you, huh?"

I looked up at her, a retort on my lips, but it sputtered and died before I could vocalize it, and I was left just standing there, gawking like some sort of idiot.

After the life that I've lived—all the things I've seen—there's not a lot that can stop me in my tracks. I've seen cities burn and crumble, watched spacecraft fall from the sky. I've seen the most incredible things humans have built in the two thousand years we've had since leaving Earth—majestic cities, breathtaking monuments. I've watched a foldgate activate for the first time, tearing a hole through the fabric of space to the other side of the galaxy. Eventually it all just starts to blur together, somehow, and you lose that sense of awe.

So damn it all if I can't figure out why the sight of *her* never ceases to amaze me.

There was nothing particularly extraordinary about her, really. Nothing that would set her aside from most other women you might meet in a crowded space-station cantina or a planetside marketplace. Slightly taller than your average woman, though she was still a full foot shorter than me. Short red hair that fell around her face to frame her sharp green eyes and freckled nose. A smirk that was slightly skewed to one side. Beautiful, surely, but in a quiet sort of way.

She was wearing her painting clothes—a baggy shift that covered her from the shoulders down and was splattered with a dozen different colors—and was holding a broad-headed paintbrush in one hand and some sort of aerosol can in the other. A few tiny flecks of yellow paint had fallen onto her cheek, but somehow it only added to her... *her-ness*, if that makes any sense. She made it look like they belonged there, a part of her.

"Lax!"

I shook myself. "What?"

She gave an amused smile. "You have something to say, or did you just come in here to look?"

I *wanted* something to say. Wished I could have come up with something grand and romantic, like she deserved. But finding the words—much less saying them—felt like trying to shove a bullet into a magazine that it just wasn't built for. It just... didn't fit, no matter how hard I tried to force it.

"No," I said finally. "Just that we're almost there."

"Ah." She gave me that knowing smirk of hers and turned back to her work, running the brush along the ceiling in a short circle. "How's it looking?"

"Fine." I shrugged, forcing my eyes away from her, and crossed the room, sitting down on the side of our bed. "Scans show a clean ship. Should have it all to ourselves."

"Good. Guess that means I need to finish up here." She lowered her brush, then sprayed something from the can over the paint. Our previously barren ceiling was now filled with a deep, darkly blue night sky, punctuated by the light of several warm, yellow stars painted in broad brushstrokes.

"Huh," I said. "That's the same pattern you put on your exo. New style?"

Kessa smiled. "Don't suppose you've ever heard of Van Gogh, have you?"

I shook my head.

"He was an old earth painter." She paused in her work to shake the can. From what I could tell, the contents of the can were applying a finish over the paint that sealed it in place and prevented it from dripping down. "One of the most famous. This is my attempt at imitating his style."

I nodded. "Well, I can't compare it to the original, but it's pretty."

She finished spraying and set the can down, then suddenly turned towards me, pulling herself onto the bed. She kissed me, gently at first, hands wrapped around the sides of my head, and then harder as I kissed her back, wrapping her slender body in my oversized arms, pulling her tight against me. Her hands wandered down the base of my skull, combing through my hair and brushing against the metallic surface of the cybernetic port installed in the back of my neck. She didn't flinch or hesitate, fingers continuing on down my back despite the cold steel reminder of what I was.

After what seemed like an eternity, she pulled back, our lips breaking apart, and pressed her forehead against mine, our breath mingling together. And all at once, that *something* I'd wanted to say clicked into place. Nothing fancy. Nothing grand or poetic. But true, every word, and I figured that that was what mattered most with this type of thing.

"You're the best thing that's ever happened to me," I found myself whispering.

She gave a short, breathless laugh. "Well, that's not hard. I *am* pretty great."

I chuckled, then kissed her again, pulling her close and feeling the warmth of her body pressed against mine, the gentle rhythm of her ribcage moving up and down, the quickening beat of her heart as we sagged together backward onto the bed. And I knew, suddenly, that even if this job didn't pan out—even if the rest of my life was going to be consigned to living in a spaceship, scraping by from job to job, eating protein bars and struggling to keep the lights on——that as long as it was with her, I'd be the luckiest man in the entire damn universe.

Then the door to the room slid open, and the moment ended. I broke apart from the kiss and turned to see Rawlins standing in the open doorway, his face bright red as he stared at us. "Uh—I mean—*dammit.*"

Kess gave a wry chuckle, kissed me on the cheek, and rolled off of me, giving me a chance to sit up. "Liung tell you to use the thumb scanner?" she asked.

"Yeah," Rawlins said, staring down at the floor. "He said it would just sound the ringer."

"Gonna throw him to the rippers," I muttered under my breath. I imagined Liung and Sevani sharing a laugh at our expense up on the bridge. I *definitely* needed to get that thumb scanner fixed.

"What did you say?" Rawlins asked.

"Nothing. What's up?"

"Black said to get you," Rawlins said, still not looking up from the floor. "We're closing in."

"Alright. I'm coming. Gimme a minute."

"Okay. I... uh... sorry." He turned and darted away.

I sighed and fell back into the bed. "Ugh. Damn kid."

"Cut him some slack." Kessa shrugged out of the painting gown and let it slide to the floor. Much to my disappointment, she was wearing her regular clothes beneath it. "He's just excited. You're a legend in the salvage business—he practically *worships* you. Besides, you were green once too."

"I was never *that* green," I grumbled. I stared up at the ceiling for a moment. "Maybe he's not ready for a run yet."

"Everybody's got to make their first run eventually." Kess

knelt and gathered her painting equipment. "May as well be now."

"First run," I muttered. I sat up abruptly, staring at her. "This could be our *last* run, Kess."

She raised an eyebrow. "Oh?"

"I'm serious. If this job is as good as Trent says, we'll never have to work again. We can go wherever we want to. Sell our shares of the *Orpheus* to Sevani. Or, hell, buy her out and turn it into a house ship. Go from system to system, see the sights."

She gave me a knowing look over her shoulder as she shoved her supplies into a box and slid it into place on a shelf. "You really think you could leave the salvage life behind?"

Once again, I felt just a pang of sadness at the prospect of moving on. I pushed it away, though. "This is no way to live a life. Jetting from one job to the next, barely scraping together enough credits to keep the *Orpheus* running. You deserve better, Kess. A real life. Breathing real air, under the heat of a real sun. I just wish I..." I grimaced, the flow of words choking to a halt. "That's all I want for us."

She smiled, then rose, kissed me on the cheek, and turned towards the door. "You're cute when you wax poetic. Come on, let's go see what Black wanted." She waltzed out of the room. My eyes followed her until she was out of sight.

"*Luckiest man in the universe,*" I whispered to myself.

# SIX

"You know, I think you might be the luckiest man in the universe."

My eyes opened slowly. Everything was blurry. I was in a white room. Something was attached to my shoulder port—a long, black tube. I followed it until it ended at a small rectangular device with a glowing screen. As I watched, the screen flashed green, and the words PATIENT STABLE appeared.

A Mobile Accelerated Medical Administrator—or, as we'd called them back in the Vanguard, MAMA. They were designed specifically for use on Vanguards, plugging into our ports, reading our vitals, and pumping us full of whatever chemicals the computer decided we needed to get back into fighting shape as soon as possible. At a glance, I saw that the chemicals MAMA had given me included serrepine, darezac, and frigicerin—the same chemical in the cans Venter had given me. No wonder I felt so calm.

Something moved in the corner of my vision. I turned my head to see a large man rising from a chair in the corner of my room. As he moved closer, my eyes focused and I could make out his features: broad, scarred, and missing an eye. Recognition flooded my brain as the last of my missing memories settled into place.

"Welcome to the *Jonah*," Nadus said with a grin. "You ready to get to work?"

———

"You've been out for nearly a full day," Nadus said, not slowing his brisk pace as we walked down the ship's corridor together. I hurried after him, zipping up the light gray jacket he'd given me. After wearing nothing but prison jumpsuits for eight years, the jacket, T-shirt and black trousers felt like the height of fashion. "Whatever it was they drugged you with put you out real good."

I frowned, trying to process everything he'd said. My head was aching—probably the lingering effect of the sedative. I was half convinced that I was still in the prison station and this was all a dream. "Slow down. First off: where are we?"

"We're on the *Jonah*," Nadus said. He jerked his head towards a painting of the Last Supper projected onto a wall as we passed it. "It's a missionary vessel for the Sacred Order of the Stars. Runs a constant loop through the sector, providing transport free of charge to poor, misguided sinners such as yourself in the hopes of offering them redemption.

I raised an eyebrow. "Sinners such as myself? You're one to talk. I seem to recall a night in the red district of Shinda station—"

Nadus shook his head. "Different time, friend. Different time, different place, different me. I'm a *pilgrim*, now. Got myself baptized and redeemed and all that." He paused as a gray-haired man dressed in a black robe embroidered with tiny gold stars walked past. Nadus nodded his head reverently. "Father Eladrius."

"Brother Nadus!" The man paused, turning and giving a priestly smile. "So good to see you again—I had no idea you were aboard. And I see you've brought another friend! Where are you bound this time?"

"Getting off at Albeni 7," Nadus said. "Got myself a mining job there. And I brought a few friends." He clapped a strong hand on my back. "I've got to warn you, though—this one here's as black-hearted a sinner as ever set foot upon this blessed heap of metal. It's a wonder the ship didn't turn to ashes the moment he set foot aboard."

Eladrius gave a polite laugh. "Well, nobody is so lost that they cannot be found." He offered a hand towards me. "I'm Father Eladrius. Should you need anything, please ask—I'm at your constant disposal."

"Thanks," I muttered, taking his hand. I guess after eight years in the tin can my social skills were a bit rusty. Eladrius smiled again, nodded to Nadus, and continued down the corridor.

"Got yourself reformed, huh?" I asked, watching the priest walk away. He paused before he went around the corner, giving me what seemed like a measuring look.

"Yes sir," Nadus said with a grin as he resumed walking. "Reformed from top to bottom."

"Huh." I followed. "Not so reformed as to give up the life of a criminal, though."

"*Shh.*" He put a finger up to his lips and looked around. "Don't say that so loud."

I raised another eyebrow. "*And* you lied to your priest about it? For shame, Nadus."

His face flushed slightly. "I tried going straight, you know. Tried leaving this life behind." He took a deep breath. "After they let us go, I lived off my pension for as long as I could while I looked for other work. But—well, I don't need to tell you how it is. Ain't nobody looking to hire the leftovers of an old Vanguard trooper like me. Even the loyalists look at us like we're some sort of monsters."

I nodded solemnly. I knew it all too well. I'd wandered down the same road after I'd been dismissed. Our pensions were paltry, barely enough to get us through a year. Not to mention the fact that spending the majority of your life moving from one bloody warzone to another hardly gets a fellow adjusted for a civilian lifestyle. The only place I'd been able to find work was under the table and in the stars, sweeping rippers from abandoned ships and looting them for goods to sell on the black market.

We walked in silence for a few minutes. I studied the architecture of the hallway as we went. It was impressive. The walls were dark blue, punctuated by artificial wood beams, white doors, and projections of various religious iconography. I could tell the wood was artificial because I could see several small scratches in various places where greedy pilgrims had tried to carve a sliver of the precious material as a keepsake. They'd all been disappointed, their knives only leaving shallow white cuts in the hardened composite.

A projection caught my eye. It was a painting of a man, wreathed in light, preaching to a group of enraptured listeners. With one hand the man held a book, extending it down towards his followers, while the other one was extending above his head towards the starlit sky above him. There was a line of text at the bottom of the image: *Let us take to the stars, a place pure of sin.* I bit back a chuckle at that. Now *that* was optimism in its highest form. If my experience had taught me anything, it was that humans tend to take our sins with us wherever we go.

The painting seemed to be putting a religious twist on humanity's mass departure from Earth, usually known as the

Exodus. In reality, of course, the Exodus had been a centuries-long period of history in which colony ships fled mankind's dying, massively overpopulated homeworld, and embarked on long nullspace voyages to distant systems with planets that were either habitable or close enough to be terraformed.

As we continued walking down the hall, I realized that the paintings formed a sort of brief, mythologized history of mankind. The next projection showed a small ship racing into the darkness from Earth towards a distant planet, connected to Earth by a long, thin thread of light. Probably symbolic of quantum communication—the technological breakthrough that had made pan-galactic communication possible.

"The projections are nice, huh?" Nadus said as he noticed me studying them.

"Yeah," I said, looking closer at the next one. It looked a bit like a Venn diagram, showing several different star systems arrayed in a ring of rings, with a large ring in the center overlapping and connecting them all.

"The foldgates," Nadus said. I nodded. Made sense. The foldgates were massive, man-made wormholes between systems. The foldgate network connected every inhabited system, allowing for trade and travel. Created in a time when humanity had *actually* been united, rather than just conquered.

I didn't pay as much attention to the next few images. I knew the next part all too well. A golden age of trade and prosperity... followed by centuries of conflict that had eventually turned into the Paragon's Last War. The Paragon claimed that under their benevolent guidance, humanity would reach greater heights of peace and prosperity than ever before.

Maybe somebody in the galaxy was having that experience. I hoped so. But it sure as hell ran contrary to everything I'd seen.

Nadus paused next to an entry to one of the ship's private suites and moved his thumb over a scanner next to the door. He paused before he pressed it down, the little glowing dot next to the scanner blinking red as it waited for him to confirm his identity.

"Before we go in," he said slowly, "I gotta ask you something."

I frowned. "Sure."

He looked up, meeting my gaze with his one good eye. "What made you change your mind?"

I hesitated. I didn't know the answer to that myself, other than the fact that I sure as hell couldn't handle staying in prison any longer. Some dark part of my brain was whispering that this had all been some big mistake, and that I was better off back in the tin can with Venter and his cans.

I shook my head. "Hell, Nadus. I don't know."

He sighed, not moving his thumb any closer to the pad. "Look. This job ain't gonna be like any you've worked before—I guarantee it. Once we go in there, you're locked in. No turning back. Don't get me wrong—I *want* you in on this. I know you. I trust you. There's nobody I'd rather have on my side for what we're up against. But if you want out, you've gotta say so now."

I hesitated, staring at the little red light on the scanning pad. *Walk away.* I knew that I should. I wouldn't be walking away to much, but at least I'd be out of prison. I had a few stashes tucked away in various banks and other, more shady establishments. I could survive. And it would be better than going back into... this, wouldn't it?

And yet...

"You said something when we were talking through the prison comms system," I said finally. "Something about second chances. And how they don't come around all that often." I gave a frustrated sigh. "I should be dead, Nadus. Torn to bloody chunks, or blasted into oblivion, or shanked in my sleep. But, somehow, I'm not. So now I've got to figure out what to do with myself. And then, somehow, you show up out of nowhere with this. So I'm working with what I've got."

I looked up and met his gaze, forcing the fear and uncertainty quelling in my gut to still. "So, yeah. Whatever bullcrap scheme you have drawn up, I'm in."

He grinned. "Good."

He pressed his thumb down. The red dot flashed green, and the door slid soundlessly open.

The room on the other side of the door was larger than I'd expected it to be, closer to what I imagined a luxury suite aboard some high-class cruiser might look like than a church-run charity project. Most folks might not have considered it much, but it was a veritable palace compared to my cell. It was bright and open, with a small kitchen and adjacent dining area towards the front, elevated by a few steps from a large sitting area towards the back. The room was longer than it was wide, with two closed doors on either side.

There were two other people in the room. The first was a dark-skinned man sitting at the table in the kitchen and typing away at a computer. He was wearing a bright red shirt with yellow flowers printed on it. As we entered, he looked up and gave a friendly wave.

"This is Miles Bentley," Nadus said, gesturing towards the man. "Our resident techie."

"VanDunn," Bentley said. "Heard a lot about you."

I gave Bentley a nod, but I was too distracted by the second person in the room to pay him much mind. It was a scrawny, familiar-looking figure sitting on a chair with his arms tied to his sides, wearing a prison jumpsuit. A glowing tattoo of a skull burned on the side of his neck. He was slumped over in a state of deep unconsciousness.

"And *this* guy," Nadus said, "we were hoping you could introduce us to."

Hell. Somehow, with all that had happened, I'd completely forgotten about Rid. I wasn't sure how long it had been since we'd passed out in that washroom, but he was still out cold. The only indication that he was alive was a barely discernable movement in his chest.

"Our inside guys made us pay triple for him," Nadus said, "since he was an unexpected addition. But they said he was with you, so we did it."

"Against my advice," Bentley muttered, not looking away from his computer screen. "*And* our boss' wishes. We don't need a Scorcher around here."

I hesitated. I didn't know anything about these people Nadus had fallen in with. On top of that, it had been years since I'd seen Nadus himself. They might not take kindly to being conned into freeing some random Scorcher kid. But—honesty was probably the safest route for now. "He's just a kid I took under my wing. He's harmless. The extra fee can come out of my cut from this job of yours."

Nadus rubbed his jaw, regarding Rid. "You always did have a soft spot for kids. Fine. Long as he doesn't know anything, we should be good to just let him go at the next stop. Catch and release. Assuming he ever wakes up."

I nodded, looking down at Rid. He seemed resourceful enough. He'd do just fine on his own.

"You guys are vultures, right? Salvagers?" Rid said, suddenly perking up.

Nadus started. "The hell?" His eyes narrowed. "How long have you been awake?"

Rid's eyes darted between the two of us. "Long enough to pick up what's going on. I think. You're one of Lax's old friends."

Nadus and I shared a glance. "Yeah. So what?"

"So I want in." Rid's eyes grew eager. "You've got a big job planned. It's the only thing that makes sense. You guys broke Lax out because he used to be a vulture and you need him. I'm a lockbreaker. I can be useful." His eyes flitted over to me. "Let me on your crew. You won't regret it."

Nadus folded his arms. "If you were awake, you heard that Lax here just offered to take a cut from his own earnings to let you off a free man. Why not just take that deal?"

It was a good question. I turned to Rid.

His eyes drooped. He shifted so that the glowing Scorcher tattoo was more visible from beneath his jumpsuit. "Because no matter where I went, *that's* all people would see me for. All I would be." He looked up at me. "This is a chance for me to become something else. I gotta play the cards life dealt me, and right now this is seeming like the best one."

I felt a slight tug of guilt. That was what I told him I had done. Only way for me to get out of being a Vanguard was to become a vulture. Now he thought the same thing would work for him.

"We are gonna need a lockbreaker," I said. "Unless you already have one."

Nadus shook his head. "We ain't got nobody yet. Except us in this room. And the boss. She's got final say. And like Bentley said, she didn't even wanna bring him on board. I had to talk her into it."

I frowned. "She sounds like a piece of work."

"No," said a voice from behind me. "But I am the one *offering* work, so I get to choose who does it."

I turned to see the speaker. One of the doors leading into the sitting room had opened, and through it walked the most beautiful woman I'd ever seen.

Now, look. I know that sounds like an exaggeration. And it probably was. But after having spent the last eight years of my life crammed into a floating tin can full of nothing but angry men, she looked like an angel fresh down from heaven. Long hair blacker than the depths of space and eyes bluer than oceans of Earth—or at least bluer than the pictures I'd seen. She was dressed in a sharp but utilitarian jacket and trousers.

I jolted to attention as I realized people were talking to me. "Sorry, what?"

Nadus sighed. "Yeah, he's the one. Lax, this is my—*our*—boss."

I extended my hand. "I'm Lax. Thanks for busting me out of prison and whatnot."

"Hmm." She turned and walked towards the kitchen area, ignoring my outstretched hand. "Nadus says you're the authority on salvage operations, especially when rippers are involved. That you had over a hundred successful runs."

"That's right," I said cautiously. A hundred successful runs. And look how it ended. *Green dots, flashing red...*

She pressed a button and a portion of the kitchen wall opened, revealing a small fridge. She bent over and reached inside of it. "But it just takes one bad one, doesn't it?"

The familiar spike of dread was trying to work its way from my gut up to my brain, but I was able to keep it down for now. Maybe it was the novelty of finally being out of prison, or maybe the frigicerin from the MAMA was still wearing off, but so far, managing the flashbacks and the old panic was proving easier than I'd anticipated.

"That's right," I said

She straightened and descended the steps back down into the main area, a six-pack of what appeared to be cans of beer dangling from her fingers. She pried one loose, popped the tab, and took a sip before stopping in front of me and giving me a long, hard look in the eyes. I stared back.

She handed me the remaining beers. "The name's Artemis. Welcome to the crew."

I took one of the cans and handed the other three to Nadus. Nadus took one for himself, then tossed one over my head to Bentley. The techie gave a yelp as he missed grabbing the can out of the air and it bounced off the table next to his computer.

Nadus ignored him, glancing down to Rid and then back to the woman. "So, uh..."

Artemis sighed and sat down. "Yes. The issue at hand. Tell us about yourself, Mr....?"

"Rid," Rid said.

"Rid." Artemis nodded. "You claim to know what's going on here. I can assure you that you do not. We're running a very delicate, high-stakes operation and don't have room for passengers. So even if I decided to trust you, how can I know that you're what you claim to be?"

"Well," said Rid, "For one thing..."

He lifted his hands, and the cords that had been binding him to the chair fell away.

Artemis raised an eyebrow, then turned to Nadus. "Secure, huh?"

"He was unconscious," Nadus muttered, sounding slightly embarrassed.

"When I was with the Scorchers I pulled heists for them," Rid said. "High-risk infiltrations. I've never done anything like this, but I'm used to working under high-stress conditions. Anything I don't know I can learn."

Artemis folded her arms, studying him. "Nadus?"

Nadus turned to me. "He's your guy. What do you think?"

I hesitated. Poor kid had no idea what he was getting himself into. But at the end of the day it was his mistake to make. "I ain't known him long, but he's got a good head on his shoulders and he's fast on his feet in a pinch. With a little training he'll do just fine."

"Very well, then," Artemis said. She turned away. "Bentley, you look about the same size. See if you can find him something to wear that doesn't shout *escaped convict* quite so loudly."

Rid's face broke into a relieved grin. Bentley grumbled but obliged, standing and walking into one of the rooms off to the side. "Sharing my wardrobe wasn't part of the job description."

"Hope you like floral," Nadus said. "Oh. And another thing."

Rid looked expectantly towards him. His eyes widened as a knife suddenly appeared in the Vanguard's hand and moved with blinding speed to Rid's throat. The polished blade gleamed sullenly with the crimson light from Rid's Scorcher tattoo.

"Screw us over," Nadus growled, "and you'll wish you'd never left that prison of yours. You understand?"

Rid nodded almost imperceptibly, being careful not to move his neck.

"Good." Nadus removed the knife, grinning, and held out a hand. "Welcome to the crew."

Bentley found Rid a change of clothes that roughly fit him—in size, if not in style; I had to restrain a laugh at the sight of Rid's gaunt features and grim, burning Scorcher skull peering out from beneath a brightly colored beach-style shirt with garish patterns—and before too long our strange little crew of five was gathered again in the suite's central common area. Artemis and Nadus discussed something quietly outside of my earshot as we waited. I found I needed to exert considerable effort to keep myself from staring at Artemis.

"Very well, then," Artemis said when Rid and Bentley were both seated. "Let's proceed to business. What's the biggest vessel you ever raided in your time as a vulture, Mr. VanDunn?"

"The ships I salvaged were smaller ones. Salvagers of all kinds have been busy scouring the stars looking for leftovers since the war ended. Paragon-contracted salvagers already got to most of the big ships, so small ones are all that's left. Homer class cargo ships are the biggest I ever worked. About six hundred meters from end to end. Had a few good runs on those." *And one really bad one.*

Artemis nodded. "What are the challenges that come with raiding a bigger ship?"

I shrugged. "Well, first off, you need more of everything. More crewmembers, more equipment, more cargospace, more coordination. Plus, bigger ships are likely to have more rippers. Higher risk, higher reward."

She nodded thoughtfully.

I glanced from her to Nadus and back again. "How big are we talking here? Thousand meters?"

Nadus chuckled. Artemis pulled a handcomputer from her pocket and pressed a button on its touchscreen, activating a holoprojector that had been placed on the table in the center of the room. The machine blinked to life, throwing up a computer screen with several files on it.

I frowned, hazarding another guess. "Fifteen hundred?" It couldn't have been bigger than that. According to all of my sources, the Homer class cargo ship I'd raided on my fateful final run had been the last one left. And Paragon research vessels tended to be a lot smaller, anyways.

Artemis smiled as she navigated through the files until she came to one labeled OVERVIEW_01 and clicked on it. An image sprang to life above the projector—a spaceship, long and blunt. It took me a minute to recognize the familiar sight. Not a Homer class cargo ship. Not a humble Paragon researcher. The sight before us was a Titan class battlecruiser. Three thousand meters of destructive power. The Paragon's most favored and feared weapon.

"You've gotta be kidding me," I said.

"This," Artemis said, pointing the remote towards the hovering image, "is the UCS *Revelation*. Well—not this image specifically. Nobody I'm aware of has schematics of the actual ship. But the ship is based off a Titan class battlecruiser, a vessel I am sure you and Nadus are intimately acquainted with."

Intimate was a stronger word than I'd have used, but I was definitely familiar. Our unit had traveled on plenty of these ships throughout the course of the war. "And *that*," I said, raising my half-empty bottle of beer and pointing it at the spectral battlecruiser, "is the ship you want to hit?"

Artemis nodded.

I studied her for a moment, leaning forward. My first instinct was to laugh. Battlecruisers were the backbone of the Paragon navy. The ship that had conquered all of humanity. So far as I knew, there were no recorded instances of a battlecruiser being captured, destroyed, abandoned, or otherwise lost to the Paragon. But there was no hint of mirth in Artemis's cold blue eyes. Nothing to indicate that she thought this task impossible.

I settled back. I didn't like it, but she had my interest. "Then I'm assuming there's more to hear. You seem smart enough to know that vultures only raid dead ships. And so far as I know, there ain't no such thing as a dead battlecruiser."

Artemis's severe face folded into a tight, cold grin. "The horizons of your knowledge, Lackan VanDunn, are far, *far* more limited than you believe them to be."

She took a deep breath, as if she were about to plunge into deep water. "The *Revelation* was built shortly after the Battle of Draden. Like all of its Titan class counterparts, it was designed to be the backbone of a planetary siege, providing Vanguard, artillery, and ripper support from orbit." She spoke the words with what seemed like an almost practiced coldness, ascribing none of the venom that people usually did to hateful, destructive words like *ripper* and *Vanguard*. "After serving with distinction in several different campaigns, it was recalled to the Vulcan shipyards for a short while, despite having not received any notable damage. After a year-long stay there it was assigned to a new planet: Brahma."

I locked eyes with Nadus. *Brahma*. The final showdown of the Paragon's Last War. I remembered lush green fields turned brown and bloody, majestic stone cities reduced to rubble. That final show of pomp and ceremony in the planet's capitol, where they'd announced that our unit would be released from duty. The place Nadus had lost his eye. The place we'd won our freedom, while everybody else had lost theirs.

Something didn't add up, though. I remembered the battlecruiser that had carried us to Brahma. It had been called the *Unity*. And while they certainly didn't tell us Vanguard puppets everything, we'd sure as hell have known if there had been another battlecruiser orbiting the planet.

Artemis resolved my confusion before I could voice it. "As I'm sure you're about to mention, however, the *Revelation* never reached Brahma. Nobody knows what happened to it. The last communications received from the bridge indicated that it had exited the Brahmian foldgate and was preparing to breach null-space for the final leg of the journey towards Brahma. But that was the last that was ever heard from the ship."

That got a frown out of me. An entire *Titan* class battlecruiser just vanishing? That seemed far-fetched. I would have heard at least *something* about it. I kept on listening, though.

"The Paragon covered it up as best they could," Artemis pressed on. "Fabricated all sorts of stories to explain away its disappearance. Internally, though, they had no idea what had happened. The generally accepted theory was that there had been some sort of massive malfunction that destroyed the ship. Regardless: the *Revelation* vanished. In the years that have passed since then, nobody has been able to uncover what became of it."

I glanced over at Rid, then Nadus and Bentley. Rid was focused on the hologram, studying the schematics while his eyes grew wider by the moment. Bentley was watching the presentation and tapping an impatient finger repeatedly against his arm.

Nadus winked his good eye at me, the message clear: *I told you this was a big one.*

I waited for Artemis to continue. When she didn't, I raised an eyebrow. "So. I'm guessing from the dramatic pause and everything, you're insinuating that you know where it is?"

"No." Artemis gave me a serious look. "But I know something just as good. I know where it's *going* to be."

"Roughly," Bentley said.

Artemis shot him a withering glare. He raised his hands defensively. "What? It's true!"

"Would *you* like to tell the story?" Artemis said sourly.

"Sure. I've heard it so many times by now it feels like an old bedtime story." Bentley cleared his throat. "So, let's see. After the *Revelation* disappeared, the Brahmians are all like, what the hell? So their navy goes to snoop around. Obviously they don't find the *Revelation*, but what they *do* find is a Paragon escape shuttle. So they capture it and interrogate the crew. And according to *them*, as soon as the *Revelation* got into the Brahma system, everything went haywire. I mean, *really* crazy. All the security systems shut down. Gravity generators turned off. Doors all opened and everything. Then suddenly rippers started attacking everyone." He held up his fingers like claws and made a scratching motion. "You know. Blood and guts and all that. Some message kept going over the intercom saying something about penitence. Our guys were smart, though, and didn't want to wait around to get out. Even though the escape pods were all shut down they managed to launch one anyways and escape—just to get picked up by the Brahmians a few weeks later. Poor bastards."

"And the *Revelation* breached into nullspace right after they ejected," I clarified.

"Exactly," Artemis said, taking the reins of the conversation back from Bentley. "The captured crew didn't know what had happened or where the *Revelation* went. But they didn't need to. The shuttle had a black box in it that received the *Revelation*'s route as it breached."

I nodded along. *Breaching* was the common term for when a spacecraft entered into the dimension known as nullspace, taking a shortcut through spacetime to travel at many times the speed of light. A ship in nullspace—like the *Jonah* was now— can't interact with the rest of the world. But it also can't change route. Once you're locked in, you're locked in until you get to wherever you're going. Which meant that if the Brahmians had found the *Revelation*'s pathing co-ordinates, they'd know for certain where it had gone to.

I said nothing, though, as it was obvious that there was more to the story. Artemis continued.

"As you know, though, the Paragon wasn't put off by the *Revelation*'s disappearance for long. When the *Unity* arrived to finish the job, the Brahmian ship carrying the black box was hit by a ripper strike. All communications lost. Crew presumed dead."

"So you don't 'roughly' know where the *Revelation* is," I said, feeling my heart drop slightly. I'd actually been on the verge of being excited about this job. Nadus had been right— nobody had *ever* pulled off a job like this. "You have no idea where it is. And even if we do find that black box to get its location, it'll probably be long gone by now, whether from simply drifting or from being taken over by whoever sabotaged it in the first place."

"Let me finish," Artemis said. "I wouldn't have invested so heavily in this operation if I wasn't reasonably certain we could at least find the *Revelation*. I have *one* piece of information from the black box that was transmitted by the Brahmians. Not the *Revelation*'s destination, but rather, the duration of its programmed nullspace journey: twenty years."

I fell silent as I absorbed the information. Twenty years. Hell of a long journey—enough to put the *Revelation* just about anywhere. More importantly, though, it meant that the battle-cruiser was *still in nullspace*, and we had time to get to wherever it would emerge from its long trip.

If we could figure out the destination.

"And you know where the black box is?" I asked.

She nodded. "I've no reason to believe that it's *not* still on the same Brahmian ship it was stored on. An interceptor called the *Guardian*."

"So before we can find the *Revelation*," Rid said, eyes thoughtful, "we have to go to the *Guardian*."

"And deal with the rippers on board," Nadus said grimly.

I felt a shudder at the thought of going onto another ripper-infested ship but managed to shove it away. I looked at Artemis. "Alright. Next question, then. How do you fit into all of this?"

She raised an eyebrow. "What do you mean?"

"I mean that people don't just stumble across this kind of intel." I gestured at the hovering image of the *Revelation*. "Back when I was a vulture we paid good money to get tips like this. Tracking down lost ships' whereabouts. It takes lots of work, lots of connections, and lots of luck to find. So when somebody like you shows up with information like this, that tells me that you have a personal connection to this job."

A ghost of a smile haunted the corner of Artemis's mouth for just a moment. "There's just one thing you need to know about me, Mr. VanDunn. I'm the woman with the money. This job won't be like your other endeavors as a vulture. We won't simply be wandering around looking for batteries. I'm paying for all of you to get me on the ship, help me do what I need to do, and then get out again. Any loot that you find along the way you can split among yourselves as a bonus."

I glanced at Nadus. He shrugged. "Her money's good. I just do what she tells me to."

I thought about it.

An entire Titan class battlecruiser, all to ourselves. The

amount of ultracells needed to power that would be *astronom-ical*. I ran some loose numbers in my head. The ten ultracells we'd tried to salvage from the *Panama* had been enough to retire on. The amount of ultracells we'd be able to harvest from the *Revelation* would make that look like nothing. All of that, plus whatever Artemis was paying us up front. Nadus was right—this really was quitting money.

I felt my lips start to curl into a smile. Maybe this wouldn't be so bad after all.

SEVEN

I've always figured it's the simple things that make life worth living.

A hot shower. A cold beer. Clean clothes. Decent food. *Especially* decent food. You have all of those things and maybe a few more besides, and you're looking at a pretty good life. That said—it's amazing how easy it is to take those simple things for granted until you lose them.

The food on the *Jonah* was basic. Lightly seasoned greens, fried potatoes, and a modestly sized piece of synthetic beef. Simple. But after eight years of nothing but protein goop—well, you get the picture.

I gave a sigh and pushed back my platter. I'd have eaten more if I had it, but I didn't. Plus, my mom had always told me that enough was as good as a feast. I smiled for a minute, thinking about her and our farm. What a little idiot I'd been, not realizing how nice I'd had it.

I glanced around the room. Most of the passengers aboard the *Jonah* ate in a communal mess hall, but not us big shots. We had food brought right to our own suite, to eat at the tiny dinner table stuffed to the side. Nadus and I each took up a full long side of the table, leaving Artemis and Rid at the ends. Rid had almost choked several times on his beef—kid had probably never had anything like meat before. Bentley was crammed in one corner, his expression annoyed as he shoveled food into his mouth from the awkward angle. A lovely little family dinner.

"So," Artemis said, sawing at a piece of her beef with a disdainful expression. "You know the situation. Now that you've finished *inhaling* your food, give me your take on it."

I glanced over my shoulder towards where the projector sat, the image of the *Revelation* long since gone. Artemis was careful like that. Didn't want to risk a passerby seeing it when they delivered our food. I got the sense from her that she was a true professional. Cold, calculating, efficient, and, I didn't doubt, ruthless when necessary.

"I ain't gonna lie," I said. "It's a tall order. Might be impossible. If those crewmembers were right—and right now there's no point in assuming they weren't—the rippers would have taken out the entire crew. That would give them enough substance to at least quadruple their numbers. Maybe more. As soon as they ran out of crewmembers to eat, they'd cluster around the generators and start hibernating. Which is tough, because that's where most of the ultracells will be located."

"The ultracells are a bonus," Artemis said. "Not a priority. Objective number one will be reaching the bridge. Is that possible?"

I grabbed the projector and put it in the middle of the table, then turned it on. Artemis put down her fork long enough to navigate to the ship blueprints. I spent a few minutes studying them, trying to work out the answer to her question.

"Maybe," I admitted. "But it'll be tough. That right there is the bridge..." I caught a hint of a rolled eye as I pointed at the bridge on the holographic image: a large room, several layers deep into the ship. "Which you clearly already know. But what you might not know is that the slightest vibration in the ship could wake up hibernating rippers. Which means that we'd have to go a long way being very, very quiet. The bottom line is that sitting here, who knows how many thousands of lightyears away, there's just no way of knowing what we're gonna find when we get in there. We don't know how many rippers there will be. We don't know what the condition of the ship is gonna be. We don't know whether the artificial gravity has gone out, or whether any of the ship's emergency systems can be salvaged."

Artemis nodded slowly, setting down her fork next to her half-finished meal. "Alright. What do we do, then?"

I eyed the last of her potatoes. "We plan for everything we can, assume everything is going to go to hell, and improvise when it does. Are you gonna finish those?"

"There's a couple things you need for any salvage job," I said. We'd finished dinner and now it was back to business. I held out a finger over the projector and waved it lazily through the air. A sharp blue line trailed behind my fingertip, hovering in place. I erased it with a swipe of my palm and then began scribbling notes.

"First: a ship." I jotted it down. My handwriting was far from pretty, but it would do the job. "Something small enough to get into the *Revelation*'s landing bay, but big enough to carry in all of our supplies and carry out all of our loot. Ideally, with stealth capabilities as well as a good scanning system. And, of course, somebody to pilot it."

Artemis nodded. "I can get us a ship when we reach Albeni 7. A pilot will be harder."

I gave it some thought and for a brief moment let myself wonder if Sevani was still out there somewhere. She'd been on the *Orpheus* when everything went to hell, after all. The fact that she hadn't picked me up when I'd been drifting in space must mean that the ship had been damaged in the explosion. Or she'd been long gone by then. I pushed the thought aside. "As soon as we're off this ship I can reach out to some of my old contacts. See if any of them are still flying. After that..."

I turned back to the words hovering above the projector and started jotting down more notes. "We'll need a hacker. Somebody who can access the ship's communications, security, life support, and weapons systems. This will be extra important for us, because the data we steal from the database is going to be our biggest payout. But it will also let us monitor the ship's security cameras, close and open doors, and turn the artificial gravity on or off."

"That's why Bentley is here," Artemis said, nodding her head towards him. "He used to be a Paragon technician, so he knows his way around their computer systems."

Bentley raised a hesitant hand. I fell silent, but he still didn't talk until Artemis sighed and said, "Yes, Bentley?"

He grimaced. "I won't actually have to go onto the ship, will I?"

Artemis and I shared a glance. Having him on board would be ideal, but Artemis's eyes seemed to hold a warning.

"We'll..." I hesitated. "We'll see. Moving on." I grabbed the words I had written and tried to move them up, only to curse as I apparently used the wrong maneuver and instead left five ugly lines scrawled across my notes. "Dammit."

Bentley made a motion with his hands. "No, you have to..."

I mimicked his motion only to leave another mark. "*Dammit.*"

Artemis sighed, rose, and grabbed my notes with pinched fingers, sliding them upward so I had more room to write. I muttered my thanks, tried to remember where I'd been, and started a new section below the two prior ones.

"We've got our lockpick," I said, jerking my head towards where Rid was staring off into space. It was all I could do to hope that he was as good as he said he was. "That'll get us through the more technical lockwork."

Rid nodded. "I'll need to learn about these specific mechanisms. And get some equipment."

"All in good time," I said. "Once we've got our shopping list taken care of, we'll be training as a group for many, many hours. Next step is firepower."

Nadus perked up at this point. I mimicked Artemis's pinching motion, moved all of the text I'd written off to the side, and wrote FIREPOWER in large lettering. "We know for a fact that we'll be facing rippers. More than likely, it will be a massive amount of them. So we need to put the bulk of our resources here. We're gonna need fighters—people who know how to use an exosuit, shoot a gun, and can keep their head under pressure." I hesitated. "And they're gonna have to know that there is a very, very good chance that they won't walk away from the job alive."

"That's been taken care of," Artemis said. "I have professionals waiting for us on Brahma."

"How much do you know about them?" I asked. "Experience-wise, I mean. Or anything else you're willing to tell me."

She grimaced slightly. I'd already learned that she saw information like money—she never liked giving any away when she didn't have to. "Experienced, but not necessarily against rippers. They'll need training. I'll tell you more when it becomes necessary."

Now it was *my* turn to roll my eyes. "Fine. The more the merrier. But we need to know how many we can fit on our ship first. And we'll need to know how much gear to wrangle." I scribbled a few notes down. "Speaking of which. We'll need exos, the heavier the better. Jerichos for Nadus and me. And batteries to keep them powered, along with repair kits. We'll need guns. Lots of guns. Ideally, Jackhammer assault rifles, along with a few heavy machine guns or laser turrets. We'll want ammo—high grade, explosive. Explosive ordnance. Shoulder-mounted grenade launchers to break up swarms, and incendiary grenades to block off chokepoints."

I stepped back and studied the list we'd made. "Quite a grocery list." I turned and peered at Artemis. "You can afford all this?"

She nodded. "My funds will hold. And we should be able to find all the gear we need on Brahma." She turned away from the table and walked down the stairs towards her room. "It's a thirty-hour trip from here to Albeni 7. Enjoy your beds while you can—they'll be the nicest we'll have for a while."

"Sounds like a plan," Bentley yawned as he left, inserting a pair of earbuds as he retreated to one of the rooms.

I watched Artemis cross the room and vanish behind the door to her room. Near silence fell behind her. Rid's head was resting on the table and he was snoring gently. Nadus was staring at the list and rubbing his jaw. I pulled my gaze away from Artemis's door and to the floating words above the projector.

First to Albeni 7 to get a ship. Then to Brahma to meet up with Artemis's contacts, get supplies, and train. After that we'd have to go find the *Guardian* and get the black box to see if this operation would even be possible, which would be enough of a pain on its own. Only then would we be able to actually go after the *Revelation.*

"Hell of a job," I mused.

Nadus just nodded.

We sat in silence for a few minutes, nursing our beers while I mulled over all that had happened. It was hard not to feel whiplashed—one day I was in prison with years to serve ahead of me, the next I was on a spaceship plotting the biggest illegal salvage job of all time. But that was the way my life had always been. One day I was living happily on a farm, the next I was getting shipped off to a Vanguard training facility. One day I was a Vanguard, the next I was out of a job. One day I was on top of the world, with my own ship and crew and the love of my life by my side, and the next...

"You good?"

I stirred. Nadus was watching me, his eyes lined with worry. I realized I had been scratching at my shoulder port and jerked my hand back. "Yeah. I'm fine."

He watched me for a few long moments, studying me through eyes far more serious and thoughtful than I remembered them ever being. Damn, but the years had changed him. The loudmouthed, hot-headed soldier I'd known and fought beside seemed long gone. The new Nadus was weathered, experienced, somber.

"So how did you get pulled into all this?" I asked.

He shrugged. "She was hiring. Looking for muscle. I was between jobs. Sorta just happened. She paid well and I did what I was told without asking too many questions." He eyed me. "That's kinda her thing, if you hadn't noticed. She likes asking the questions, not answering them."

"She hired me 'cause I know salvage," I said. "If I'm gonna plan this job, I need all the info I can get."

"You get used to it." Nadus pushed his computer away and settled back into his chair. "To not knowing. To the secrets. She'll make sure you know what you need to, but never more than that. If you're gonna work for her, you're gonna have to accept that you'll always feel slightly in over your head. Her secrets have secrets, and her agendas have agendas. Like I said before: all you need to know is that her money is good, and she'll take care of you."

I frowned. "It doesn't... *bother* you? Not knowing why we're doing what we're doing?" I hesitated. "Feeling like..."

"*No.*" Nadus shook his head sharply. "It's not like it used to be. Artemis might have her own way of doing things, but she doesn't see us as puppets." His good eye grew distant. "Funny, though. Never thought I'd be going back to Brahma, of all places."

"Yeah." I shrugged. "Guess it'll be nice to see it when it's not in the middle of a war."

He nodded slowly, still staring into empty space. Probably remembering the last days of the war. The final, brutal pushes through the dense city blocks. "You ever think back and wonder... if we could have done more?"

I raised an eyebrow. "Seems like we did a hell of a lot."

"No." He shook his head. "I mean—more to fight back. To keep the Paragon from turning us into their attack dogs."

I shrugged. "I gave up on wondering about that a long time ago. Past is past, Nadus. No going back and changing anything. No matter how badly we might wish to."

"Yeah." He shook himself back into the present moment. "Yeah, you're right. Well—I'm gonna get some sleep. We've got maybe thirty or so hours before we hit Albeni 7. You ever been there before?"

"Yeah," I said, throwing my mind back. "Long time ago. Actually, it's where I found my old pilot."

"Seems like a good sign," he said. "Get some sleep. Enjoy your new freedom." He got to his feet and gave my shoulder a squeeze. "Glad to have you with us."

I nodded. Nadus went into his own room. I wondered briefly if I should bother waking up Rid but I decided against it. I took one of the unoccupied rooms. The bed wasn't quite long enough, but it came a lot closer than my prison cot had. Plus, it was soft and entirely devoid of yellow stains.

Like I said. It's the simple things that make life worth living.

# EIGHT

"Good morning, sunshine."

I groaned, sitting up. "Nadus? What time—"

It wasn't Nadus.

It was Venter. The old man was standing at the door to my cell, pulling it quietly shut behind him. He raised an eyebrow at me, holding one finger up to his lips with a mischievous grin.

I frowned. "Venter? What... Where..."

"*Shh.*" The old man hissed, spittle flying from his lips. He grinned. "We need to have a *chat*, you and I. My old friend."

Something was wrong. *This* was wrong. My head was foggy, my thoughts cloudy, but I *knew* that something here was broken. I tried to move, to climb out of bed, but my limbs seemed to be stuck fast to my sides.

Venter moved towards me. "We never had a chance to finish our conversation, remember?"

"What..." I grunted, trying to extricate myself from whatever invisible bonds held me down. "What conversation?"

Venter reached my bedside and knelt down next to me, lowering himself until we were eye to eye. "Why, don't you remember?"

I blinked. Something was wrong with his eyes. They were... *empty*. Where his eyeballs should have been, there was nothing at all. Not flesh. Just two vast, empty voids, calling to me.

"You don't *remember*?" he hissed again. "Here. Let me help you."

With a sudden flash of speed, he swung up and into my cot, straddling me. His old, wrinkled hands gripped my head with a brutal strength, his mismatched artificial teeth shining in a lurid grin.

"You were only ever good for breaking things," he said, his words growing sweet and honeylike. "And so they sent you away."

He leaned over suddenly, his sandpaper lips clenching tight around mine, despite my grunts of protest, and exhaled into me as if he were forcing the memories down my throat. And I did remember. Violently and against my will I saw my father's face, cold and emotionless, as he shoved me towards the Paragon recruiting officers. I saw the sudden smile on his lips as the officer handed him a handful of credit chips.

Venter let go, pulling back. I gasped, feeling the memories soak through me like poison.

"They liked you in the Vanguard program," he said, the words lyrical and soothing. "But it took you a *long* time to like them."

He pulled my face up to his and I remembered. Remembered half-forgotten blurred visions of doctors in white coats stained red. Of screams that might have been my own as a thousand different needles were plunged into various parts of my body. Of waking up in the night to find bits of metal attached to me that hadn't been there before.

Venter pulled back again with a hiss, like air escaping a tire. "But when they finally turned you loose, you *knew* that killing was all you were good for. All you'd *ever* be good for."

His smile grew wider, until his whole face seemed stretched out by it. His teeth were coated in blood. "And, oh, Lax, you were *so* good at it."

His teeth grated against my bleeding tongue, and I remembered. I remembered blood. Years and years of blood. I remembered the thrill of power that came from charging into a battlefield, feeling invincible beneath the Jericho's armored shell, raining fire and death upon my enemies. The fear and anguish in my victim's faces before I crushed them beneath a steel-clad boot.

Venter's mouth broke free from mine with a tearing sound, and I felt blood trickle down my jaw. He pressed his forehead tight against mine, forcing me to stare directly into the nothingness of his eyes.

"And then you got out," he whispered. "And you met... *her*."

My breathing stopped. I remembered her.

"And for some reason," Venter said, his voice growing softer with each word, "she *trusted* you."

I saw her. Smiling over her shoulder at me as she painted. Or grinning over the cover of a book.

"She trusted *you*. She decided that you were more than a brute killing machine." Venter's smile turned sad. "That somewhere, deep down, behind all of the layers of blood and violence, was a man capable of goodness."

I still saw her. Saw the *Orpheus*. Saw our dreams and plans, the life I'd wanted so badly to give to her. To *us*.

Venter drew back suddenly. The sad smile vanished, replaced by a mouthful of long, jagged fangs. Ripper teeth.

"And *you*," he shrieked, his voice dripping with venom and rage, "LET. HER. *DIE!*"

He plunged down towards me.

·  ·  ·

I jolted upright. My chest heaved in and out, wracked by my ragged breaths, and my skin tingled with cold sweat.

Silence.

A dim light turned on above my head, most likely motion controlled. I blinked, taking in my surroundings. I wasn't in my cell. Venter wasn't here. I was on the *Jonah*, alone in my room.

My mouth tasted like iron. I wagged my tongue and groaned as pain lanced through it. Must have bitten down hard on it during the nightmare. I pushed myself out of bed and staggered to the trash can in the corner, spitting a wad of blood into it. It glistened in the dim light, red and viscous, like the blood on Kessa's armor after the—

Oh, *hell*. I staggered backward, until I collided with the bed and collapsed onto the floor.

*I own you*, Venter's voice whispered in my head.

A can. I needed a can. I rose, staggering into my shirt and jacket, then opened the door to the main room of our suite and poked my head out. Rid was exactly where I'd left him, snoring with his head on the table. Other than that, it was quiet and empty. I walked out into the corridor beyond, closing the door behind me.

A can. Where to find a can? The medbay! I started striding in what I thought was the right direction. The hallways were wide and well lit, but still seemed dark and oppressive somehow. Like I was back on the *Panama*, watching as the rippers closed in...

I swallowed a mouthful of blood, my heart pounding so loud I could hear it. Several other passengers gave me frightened looks as I strode past them, my breathing ragged and my steps uneven. They didn't matter. This ship didn't matter. I didn't matter. *She* was the only thing that mattered. The sounds of my footsteps echoing on the walls sounded like her voice in my ears, and the faces passing by looked like her face to my eyes, and the stars on the paintings adorning the walls looked like *her* stars.

*You let her die.* And Black. And Rawlins, and Liung, and all of them. *Green dots, flashing red...*

A sign on the wall pointed to the medbay. I quickened my pace. I wasn't sure how it worked; most likely I would need to break in. I might need to subdue whoever was on duty. But that didn't matter. All that mattered was *her*, and getting her out of my damn head before she tore me apart like a ripper's claws.

"Lax, isn't it?"

The voice was calm and soothing. I turned to see the speaker. It was an old man, dressed in the simple robes of a priest of the Order of the Stars. He looked familiar. I frowned.

He chuckled, taking a step closer to me. "It's Eladrius. You can call me Eli, however. Our mutual friend Nadus introduced us briefly earlier." He held out a hand.

"Oh..." I shook myself and took his hand cautiously, hoping I didn't look as much like a raving madman as I felt. "Yeah. Lax."

"Lax," he repeated, looking me up and down. "Well, Lax, you don't look too good. Is something bothering you?"

Maybe it was his priestly aura, or maybe it was the sobering realization that if I didn't pull myself together I would botch the whole job before it even started, but there was something in his voice that cut through the urgency I was feeling, splashing me with cold reality. I shook myself, feeling some of the panic fade away into the background.

"No," I said. "I'm fine, I just..." I stammered, then shrugged. "Just couldn't sleep. Needed to stretch my legs."

Eladrius studied me for a long moment, then gave me that nod that said *we both know you're lying, but it would be rude to point it out.* "I understand completely. Well, if you're thirsty, I just so happened to be on my way to the dining hall for a drink. Care to join me?"

I raised an eyebrow. "Guess I figured this was a dry ship."

The old man smiled. "The Order has no issue with the responsible consumption of alcoholic beverages. Many members choose to abstain from it of their own choice, but there's no overarching rule against it."

I hesitated. I *should* be getting back to the room. If Artemis found me missing, she might get suspicious. But on the other hand, I had to admit that a drink did sound nice. No alternative to a can. But under the circumstances, it seemed like it might be the best I could get.

"Sure," I said.

"Excellent." He reached up to give my shoulder a fond squeeze, then set off down the hallway. I had to keep myself from recoiling. After so long in the tin can, the notion of a friendly touch was still alien to me. I hardly remembered what it felt like to be surrounded by civilized people. Much less, people who treated me like an actual human, rather than... well, a Vanguard. I managed to shrug off my discomfort and follow him.

The dining hall of the *Jonah* was bathed in dim white light and accented with dark blue highlights against the artificial wood walls and furniture. A large window on the ceiling offered a view into the vast nothingness of nullspace enveloping us. The bar was mostly empty. I followed Eli's lead, sitting down at one of the tables and glancing around.

I stared up through that window for a few moments. It had been a long time since I'd actually looked out into space... not that this was really space, of course. Or maybe just not *our* space. Nullspace is an alternate dimension—a little pocket of reality, cut off from the rest of the universe, that ships use to travel faster than the speed of light. It was strange to think about. So far as the rest of the galaxy was concerned, right now, the *Jonah* and everybody on it simply... didn't exist. Gone, until we popped back into reality at our destination.

"If you're worried about nullspace," Eladrius said in a conspiratorial whisper, "don't be. Despite the rumors you might have heard, nullbreachers are perfectly safe."

I found myself chuckling. "I wasn't worried about that. I was wondering how the hell—sorry—how does your church afford all this?"

Eli chuckled, tapping a few buttons on the table's built-in computer to order our drinks. "Honestly? I have no idea. I just keep my head down and do what I'm told."

"Smart man." I frowned. "I... just realized I don't have any money on me."

Eli waved a hand in dismissal. "On me. I enjoy this." He smiled. "Getting to know new people, hearing their stories. It's well worth the price of a drink."

"You haven't seen me drink yet."

"Hah! Well, if you can outdrink your friend Nadus, I'll eat my—" He stuttered, seeming to catch himself. "My robes. I'll eat my robes. He's a good man, your friend Nadus."

I nodded cautiously. "He is. How did you meet him?"

"Oh, just a chance meeting. Like this one. He was seeking passage on our ship, and I made his acquaintance."

I raised an eyebrow. "Nadus never seemed the... *spiritual* type."

"I doubt anybody does, in the Vanguard."

"Hmm." I glanced as a man with a disfigured face and several prosthetic limbs approached our table and set down two bottles of beer. Based off the cold glare the kid gave me, I guessed he'd lost his good looks and his legs in a Vanguard assault.

Eladrius unscrewed his bottle and took a swig. "So, a mining job, eh? Was that what Nadus said?"

"Yeah." I kept my tone casual, taking a pull from my own bottle.

"Albeni 7 is no tame place," he said. "Not that that's a

problem for the likes of you, though. They say the criminals run it more than the station administrators do."

I gave a noncommittal grunt in response. Even in prison I'd heard about the underworld on Albeni 7. They ran the black market in this part of space. Supposedly even had lines running in and out of the prison.

"Done much mining before?" Eli asked.

"Nope." I figured that lies were best swallowed with a glassful of truth.

"Nervous?"

I grimaced. "You could say that."

Eli gave a broad shrug. "If you want to talk, feel free. I find it often helps to... clear the mind. Steady the nerves."

I stared at my bottle for a long moment, shaking it slightly in my hand to watch the golden liquid within swirl around—a dark whirlpool. I couldn't talk. I found that I wanted to, though. Wanted desperately to let some of the darkness in my heart ooze out, like squeezing pus from an infected wound. Finally, I spoke. "Have you ever heard the term *dead-in-transit?*"

Eli perked up, his eyes growing suddenly sharp and interested. "No."

"That's what happens when a ship gets disabled while it's en route. Could be the engine is blown, or the crew jumps ship or dies. But the thing is, the ship keeps on going. Just... gliding along through the emptiness of space." I took a deep breath. The words had felt unnatural in my mouth at first, but now they flowed almost against my will. "That's what my life feels like sometimes. It feels like I was created, given a purpose, and blasted off into the void, and now—no matter how much I want to, or how hard I might try, I'm stuck on that course."

"Hmm." Eli took another sip, his expression thoughtful. Like he was trying to work out a puzzle. "Well, here's the good news. *You're* not a ship. You're a human. Despite everything the Vanguard might have done to you, you're still a human being, capable of making your own choices and forging your own destiny. If you don't like the way you're headed, it's up to you to change the course."

I smiled at that. "That's the thing. I tried that. I thought I *had* changed my course. And then, suddenly, I was right back where I started."

He leaned forward, studying me through furrowed brows. "This isn't about mining anymore, is it?"

Dammit. I'd said too much. I sighed and took another swig. "Doesn't matter what it's about."

Eli shrugged. "Well, the more specific you are, the more I can help."

"I don't need help," I growled, feeling suddenly irritated. I gulped down the rest of the bottle. "I just need a drink."

"Well, then let me get you another one."

I wanted to. I wanted to stay and drink myself to oblivion. I'd figured talking would help, but somehow, I only felt more confused. But I knew it wasn't smart. The more I drank, the more likely I was to let something slip. I shook my head and rose. "I shouldn't. I need to get back. But thanks."

"Any time. Here—why don't you take this with you?" He slid what looked like a small computer chip across the table towards me. I picked it up and inspected it. *Eladrius*, it said in tiny letters on one end. A routing chip. Inserting this into a communication relay would link me through the expansive galactic relay network to Eladrius's personal device. It wasn't strictly necessary to use a chip to connect with somebody, but it did make it a whole lot easier. Eladrius closed my hand around it. "In case you ever want to continue this conversation. For now, though..." He hesitated, seeming to search for words. "Just remember, my son: you choose who you are. Nobody else. You."

I gave a weak smile and pocketed the chip as I turned away. "I wish I believed you, sir."

# NINE

Albeni 7 was long and cylindrical, relying upon good old fashioned centripetal force to simulate gravity rather than a more costly and modern artificial gravity generator. According to the station's official log, it was home to nearly a million people. By most people's best guess, though, the actual number of human beings crammed into the vessel was closer to double that.

The loading terminal was massive—certainly far bigger than any open space the prison could boast. Somehow, though, it still seemed just as crowded. The station administrators had seemingly given up on imposing any sort of order on the whirlpool mass of humanity fighting their way to or from the ships. My ears were full of the sounds of shouting and cursing intermingled with a constant stream of unintelligible announcements made through a worn-out public address system. My nose was bombarded by a dozen different smells, none of them particularly pleasant.

Ah, station life.

At a nod from Artemis, Nadus led us through the crowd, his

intimidating presence clearing a path through the press. I got a good look at our fellow travelers as we pushed through them. Most were adult men, faces blank as they marched begrudgingly to or from the shuttles that would carry them to the nearby mining stations. There were a few families clustered together, faces pale and gaunt with hunger. I found my eyes drawn to a group of three children bound together by a length of cord tied around their waists, seemingly alone as they fought the crowd to make their way to the *Jonah*. The oldest one was clutching at a datapad like it was a life preserver, while the youngest was crying and trying desperately to pull the others back the way they'd come. I felt my jaw stiffen. More than likely their guardians couldn't afford to take care of them here any longer, had sent them off to stay with... well, who knew? Hopefully someone kind. Someone that could give them some sort of life. Maybe even somewhere planetside. Not likely, but still. I figured anything had to be better than growing up here.

I'd grown up thinking I had a rough life, but at least I'd had fresh air and real sunshine every day—which was a hell of a lot more than any of these poor bastards could say. Most citystations were overpopulated far beyond their safe limits, making food, water, and vitamin D dangerously scarce. When you took those factors and combined them with the high amount of disease, poverty, and crime, you had yourself a nice little piece of hell just as bad as any prison. The station managers didn't care, so long as their cans were bringing in more money than they cost.

"Poor bastards," muttered Nadus, looking away from the line of hopeful passengers. "Bet good money most of 'em have never even set foot on a planet."

"That's the miracle of humanity," Artemis said, keeping her eyes straight ahead. "Adaptation. Where other creatures would be confined to the boundaries of their own habitats, we bring ours everywhere we go."

"Doubt *they'd* see it that way," I muttered, forcing myself to look away from a pale, malnourished woman holding a crying infant.

I glanced over at Rid. He had an odd look in his eye as he studied the waiting throng. Jaw set and eyes distant. I figured he'd probably grown up on a station like this. It struck me again how little I really knew about him.

I let myself fall slightly behind the others, drifting into step with Rid.

"How you holding up?" I asked Rid, keeping my voice soft.

He shrugged. "We're out of prison, right?"

I nodded. "True that. I reckon that's as good a start as any."

He shrugged again.

I cleared my throat awkwardly. "I don't recall if you ever told me, did you grow up on a station?"

He nodded. "York 13. Whole life."

That made sense. York 13 was the Scorcher gang's base of operations. They practically owned the station. If Rid really had ratted out some of his fellow gangsters to enforcers, he was lucky to have made it off York 13 alive. His earlier remarks about not wanting to be a Scorcher suddenly made much more sense. On York 13 it was either work with the Scorchers or be crushed beneath their heavy boot heels. It also explained—at least in part—his determination to join Artemis's fledgling crew. He'd been part of a gang his whole life. Going off on his own in a strange new place probably seemed a daunting challenge in comparison to sticking with us.

"Right," I said. "Listen. I get that you're excited to see the universe and all that. And that you want to stick with a crew. It makes sense. But I'm telling you, you have *no idea* what you're getting yourself into."

He frowned up at me. "I heard the same rundown you did."

"Yeah, but..."

*Green dots, flashing red.* Gleaming claws in the darkness. *Why was she smiling?*

I shook myself, fumbling for words. I wasn't sure why I was saying any of this, but I felt compelled to. Rid was staring at me, brows furrowed in confusion, the collar of Bentley's garish shirt folded outward to conceal his Scorcher tattoo, but all I could see was Rawlins. Young, and eager, and on the verge of making the worst decision of his life. "But you've never dealt with rippers before. I have. Albeni 7's a good station to lie low. So just... think about it."

His face curled into a frown. "Why don't you want me on the crew? Do you not trust me?"

"Would I be sending you off if I didn't trust you?" I shook my head. "Kid, this is a hell of a job. Especially for a team of rookies. Our odds aren't great. I'm just giving you a chance to get out before it's too late."

He studied me, eyes sharp with a suspicion I hadn't seen in him before. He jerked his head towards our companions. "You trust them?"

I hesitated.

Nadus? Yes. There was some small part of my brain saying not to be too hasty, that it had been years since I'd last seen him. And yet—I did trust him. We'd been through hell and back together. We'd gotten each other out of a dozen hairy situations. Fought side by side across more battlefields than I could count.

Yes. I trusted Nadus. Artemis, on the other hand... I studied the profile of her face as she turned to say something to Nadus. Her sharp, cold blue eyes and the serious set to her jaw. Her full lips and the slender form of her—

*Crap.* I shook myself out of my trance. She was beautiful, but that wasn't what made me hesitate to trust her. She was determined. She had a goal in her mind and nothing else mattered except achieving it. Folk admire people like that. The go-getters, the ambitious leaders who drive our civilization forward. I suppose there's a need for them. But the same thing that makes them effective makes them dangerous. When a person wants a thing bad enough, there's no knowing just how far they'll go to get it. Or who they'll be willing to sacrifice.

"Mostly," I said finally.

Rid nodded, then held up his hand, pointing at the tattoo on the back of it. The four blank playing cards. "My dad always used to tell me that you can't change the cards life deals you. Just how you play them. For better or worse, this is what life dealt me. So it's what I'm playing. We've been pretty lucky so far."

"I don't think you want to trust my luck for too long," I said.

The others had paused outside of a loading zone for the station shuttle—a transport that ran a loop around the entire Albeni 7 station. The three of them waited for us, Artemis and Bentley looking tiny next to Nadus's hulking form just as Rid must have looked next to mine.

"Let's split up for now," Artemis said. "Nadus, get us some lodgings arranged while I start looking for a ship. Lax, you come with me."

"Fair enough." Nadus looked between me and Rid, then pointed one beefy finger at my companion. "You're with me. I ain't taking my eye off you yet."

Rid gave me a slightly nervous glance. I gave him what I hoped was a reassuring smile. "Go along—he'll keep you safe. Just don't let him get hungry or he might eat you."

Nadus chuckled at that, turning and heading off towards a shuttle that was currently taking passengers. Bentley followed after him. Rid, for some reason, didn't seem to find my joke amusing. He lingered for a moment before he scurried off after Nadus, his face sour.

"He seems very... *attached* to you," Artemis said, a hint of amusement in her voice as she walked away.

I followed. "Well, I did save his neck in prison."

"Why?"

I frowned. "What do you mean, *why?*"

"What did you get out of it?" Artemis spared me a scrutinizing backward glance.

"I didn't get anything out of it. We were cellmates, and he's..." I searched for words. "He used to be in a gang. Had a lot of enemies waiting for him in prison. They tried to jump him. He's not a big guy. But I am. So I stepped in."

"Ah." She smirked knowingly. "I see. You're just a sucker."

I shrugged. "Yeah. I guess so."

"At least you're honest about it. I don't know whether that makes you more or less of one."

From the way she watched me, I figured she was goading me. Seeing how I would react, how far she could push me. Trying to figure out how I thought. I kept my face blank and my voice even as I replied. "Anyone's guess. Don't really care too much either way. I trust easy. A lot easier than I forgive broken trust."

Artemis came to a halt at an empty platform and turned to face me, cocking her head to one side and smiling wryly. "Why, Mr. VanDunn. Are you threatening me?"

"No." I came to a halt and looked down at her. "You feel threatened?"

"I don't know yet."

"Well, let me know when you make up your mind." I looked around us. "You know where we're going?"

"Roughly," she said, not breaking stride. We mounted a moving catwalk and headed in the direction of a sign that read *Terminal 17.* "They say there's one person to talk to on Albeni 7 if you want something. Somebody who can guide us to a suitable ship—and keep us off the Paragon's books."

"We'll need to be *on* the books," I said. "Can't get through the foldgates without Paragon-issued vessel identification."

"I know that," Artemis sneered. "But I've no intention of

marching down to the nearest Paragon administrative office with two escaped convicts, a mercenary, and a blackhat hacker and telling them *yes, this is my ship, we're going to go rob your long-lost treasures in it.*"

I sighed. "Obviously, we'll get something forged. For now, let's focus on what we're looking for. Emphasis should be on speed and stealth capabilities. Ideally with some decent cargo space too." I thought back to my old ship, the *Orpheus*, with futile, wistful longing. "Maybe they've got a Blackbird. That's what my old crew used to run. You get one of those outfitted right, there's not a scanner built that can pick you up. I had a pilot that could fly our ship through the eye of a needle."

"You mean the one who abandoned you after your crew got wiped out?"

I felt my face harden. I hadn't talked about my old crew with anyone—not even Nadus, yet. I wasn't keeping it a secret, but it wasn't exactly the kind of thing that I brought up in a casual conversation.

"It's not that simple," I said.

"Sure it is," Artemis said. "I did some research and I know what happened on the *Panama*. You let your entire crew get wiped out. Well—other than Sevani."

I stopped, coming to a standstill in the middle of the moving catwalk. Confused commuters passed around me like water flowing past a rock in the middle of a river, muttering their irritation. I ignored them. I didn't even really hear them.

*Green dots, flashing red...*

Artemis had stalled as well, studying me with that cold, calculating look of hers. We were still playing her little game. She was prodding me, like I was some sort of caged animal. Seeing how far she could push me before I went feral. Before I broke.

I *wanted* to break. I wanted, suddenly and with a fury I had not felt since my days in the Vanguard, to grab her and snap her in half. She looked tiny and fragile, standing there, looking up at me with that half-smirk on her face. I could practically feel the way her bones would crack beneath my hands, brittle and frail as I twisted them. The way her eyes would bulge as I squeezed my hand around her throat.

I forced myself to take a deep breath.

"I don't know you very well yet," I said softly. "And so I'm going to give you the benefit of the doubt and let that slide. But unless you want your spine tied into a knot, leave my old crew out of this."

She raised an eyebrow. "Well, I've made up my mind. I *definitely* feel threatened."

I opened my mouth to retort, but my words caught in my throat as I noticed something odd. The man in the dark red leather jacket that had been walking behind us had stalled and was now standing awkwardly on the edge of the catwalk, looking intently down at a handheld computer. The moment I set eyes on him, he suddenly shut his computer and kept on walking, disappearing into the crowd.

Weird. He certainly looked like he'd been following us. I turned my attention back to Artemis.

"We don't have time for this," I growled.

Artemis was still watching me, taking in every little twitch of my face.

"Agreed," she said, turning heel and continuing down the catwalk.

"Does anybody else know about the job?" I asked Artemis. I followed behind her, looking over her shoulder for the man in the leather jacket. He was nowhere to be seen.

"No." She shook her head emphatically. "Why?"

I didn't reply. My anger at Artemis and her prodding into my past was quickly transitioning into anger at myself. *Idiot.* She was testing me. Finding out what cards she could play against me. And I'd handed her a damn ace. She knew my emotional weak link, now.

I realized with a jolt of dread who she reminded me of. Venter. The way he had always hoarded every bit of information he could. Using it to control everybody around him. Dammit, had I just traded one control-freak of a boss for another?

I shook myself. There'd be time to worry about that later. For now—a ship.


Space ports on cylindrical stations are... complicated, to put it mildly. The gravity for the main portion of the station comes from the centripetal force of the rotating cylinder. That makes docking ships onto it difficult. To solve this problem, docking stations are built onto an attached arm that remains stationary rather than rotating with the rest of the structure. A complicated system of rail shuttles interconnect the station's primary cylinder to the outer docking rings, accelerating and decelerating depending on where they're going.

This particular docking bay appeared to have built-in artificial gravity generators—more expensive and modern than centripetal gravity but easier to control. A digital sign overhead as we'd come into the bay had warned that gravity was currently running at a comfortable sixty percent of the standard, making heavy cargo easier to move and putting a nice little jaunt into my heavy step. I was still caught up thinking about my old crew. If I recalled correctly, this port was where Kessa and I had found Sevani. Kess and I had worked a salvage job together on a different crew and decided to pool our resources to start our own team. All we'd needed was a ship... and a pilot. We'd found Sevani here, and the three of us had pitched in our resources to buy and outfit the *Orpheus*.

"That's a sleek-looking ship," Artemis said, pointing out

through a window at a large, luxurious-looking craft flying in to dock. "Maybe she's for sale."

I shook my head. "Sticks out too much. We want something that blends in." I looked ahead and spotted another ship in the process of docking. A Blackbird—same make as my old ship. I pointed. "Now something like *that* is what we want. Hell, that even looks like... wait..."

It had the same sullen red stripe painted down the side as the *Orpheus*. Same extended cargo bay.

"I think that's my ship," I muttered.

I pressed forward, anticipation forming a knot in my gut as Artemis scrambled to keep up. *Stupid,* I found myself thinking. *It's not your ship. The odds are...*

Not that bad, actually. The more I thought about it, the more plausible it became. I'd met Sevani here. Who was to say she wouldn't return here as her base of operations? Hell, she had probably found a job working for this smuggler queen. A capable pilot with a good reputation, a ship, and a sudden lack of work after...

Thinking about the *Panama* made my step suddenly falter. What if Sevani *was* here? What the hell was I going to say to her? *Hey, it's me, your old boss, back from the dead. Wanna drop whatever you're doing and come help me work the most dangerous job I've ever done?*

"Where are we going, exactly?" Artemis asked behind me, sounding annoyed.

"I just need to see something," I muttered, pushing through the crowd towards where I thought I had seen the *Orpheus* dock. Most likely it was nothing. Probably just a ship that looked similar. Or Sev had sold it. I couldn't blame her if she'd decided she was done doing salvage work for good.

Screw it. Only one way to find out. I took a deep breath as I rounded a corner—and there she was.

Sevani was standing with her back to me, giving orders to

several dock workers unloading large crates from the *Orpheus*. She had the same short, wiry frame. Same short shock of wild, defiant hair. Same faded crimson pilot's jacket, though it was rolled at the sleeves to reveal an arm full of tattoos I didn't recognize.

I came to a halt just a few meters away. It took me a few tries to muster up the courage to speak. When I finally did, my voice came out closer to an incredulous whisper. "Sevani?"

She turned. "Yeah?"

"I—" But the words choked in my mouth. It wasn't Sevani.

And yet it was. This Sevani was younger than the one I'd known, the weathering in her face mysteriously vanished. She looked to be near twenty or so. Her eyes were the wrong color, gray instead of green, and her cheekbones too low. But she wore the same cocky, self-assured expression that Sevani had always had. She raised one eyebrow as she looked me up and down.

"Well, damn me if you're not the most oversized chunk of fleshware I ever saw," she said, putting her hands on her hips. "What do you want?"

I found myself taking an uncertain step backward. "Sorry, I thought... I'm looking for Maren Sevani."

I registered a flicker of movement to my side and glanced over to see one of the not-Sevani's companions moving to flank me, hand placed firmly on the butt of a pistol. She had a large, athletic frame. Her dark skin was lined with vividly white geometric tattoos along her arms, and she carried a short sword in a sheath strapped to her waist. One of the Roamers, then. Odd to see a Roamer apart from their people.

"Who's asking?" the dark-skinned woman asked in a thick accent.

"Old friend," I said, my frown deepening. I registered that I was being threatened, but somehow still couldn't quite move my attention from the not-Sevani figure. I studied her again, trying to convince myself that I wasn't in a dream. "I'm sorry—who *are* you?"

The not-Sevani gave a wide, malicious grin. "You first, big man. You're the stranger here. It's only polite."

I opened my mouth to reply, only to be cut off by a disturbance behind me. I turned my head to see a cluster of people moving towards us, centered around one woman: Maren Sevani.

Sevani—the *real* Sevani, *my* Sevani—was surrounded by a variety of followers, ranging from well-dressed assistants sporting datapads to tough-looking bodyguards flashing pistols and shock batons. Maren Sevani herself was almost unrecognizable. The snarky, rebel-without-a-cause pilot had crystalized into a smartly dressed leader, her cocky swagger replaced by a purposeful stride.

"Tell Vatheson that twenty-five percent is our final offer," she was saying to one of her assistants. "If he doesn't like that, he can find somebody else to move his goods. He won't be able to." The assistant nodded crisply and typed something into her datapad. Sevani turned towards us. "Rose, I was wondering what—"

She locked eyes with me and froze.

"Hi, Sev," I said. "Long time no see."

Maren's mouth dropped slightly open. "Lax?"

I forced a grin onto my face, hoping my nerves didn't show. "In the flesh."

She took a step closer, staring at me like she was trying to convince herself I was real. "I... I'd heard rumors that you made it out, but I never believed them. I thought you were dead."

"Not yet. Sorry to disappoint." I glanced around at her men, who were watching me warily, and then towards the *Orpheus*. "Looks like the *Orpheus* is still running strong. I—"

She stepped quickly forward. I found myself tensing, as instincts developed over a lifetime of violence screamed at me to protect myself. But I didn't. I just stood there, like a big dumb tree, as Sevani strode towards me, reached out, and wrapped her arms as far around me as she could in a tight hug.

After what felt like forever, she pulled away, seeming to remember where she was. She straightened her suit jacket, took a deep breath, and then gave a slight smile, glancing between me and Artemis. "How about a drink?"

TEN

The cantina was run-down, lit by a neon sign that read *Tyrell's Bar* and a few flickering overhead lightbulbs. I smirked at the wave of discomfort passing over Artemis's face as we eased into a well-used, poorly cleaned booth. Might have been a sight less classy than our suite aboard the *Jonah* had been, but it felt like home to me. Hell—sitting here, in a run-down back-space mining station bar with Sevani, it was almost enough to feel like old times. Like nothing had changed.

Except that a lot had changed.

Sevani had changed. When I looked her in the eyes, I saw the same woman I'd known eight years ago. But beyond that, she was unrecognizable. She dressed more like a business-woman than an outlaw, carried herself with the calm profes-sionalism of an administrator rather than the plucky attitude of a pilot. And she certainly hadn't been flanked by bodyguards and assistants back when we'd worked together. Her flock had dispersed, leaving Sevani, Artemis, and me alone at a booth.

It was a strange feeling, seeing how far she'd come. Some-how, I'd expected that the world would wait for me, freezing in place while I moved through life behind bars. Now, I was faced with the disquieting notion that the exact opposite had happened. *I'd* frozen in place and the universe had spun on without me, not caring how far it left me behind.

"You seem to have done well for yourself," I said. "You finally go legit?"

Sevani smirked. "Hell no. Well, only a little bit. Officially, I run Odyssey Logistics, a galaxy-wide shipping enterprise. Unofficially, I'm Albeni 7's currently reigning smuggler queen." She leaned back and heaved her legs up onto the table with a happy sigh, stretching her arms out to gesture grandly at the run-down bar around us. "To my kingdom. Damn, but it feels good to be able to loosen up a bit. Gotta act 'respectable' these days."

I smiled. "You? Respectable?"

"I know!" She waved at a waitress, who brought over a bottle of dark liquid. Sev took the bottle and poured it into three cups. "It's outrageous."

I took my glass and swirled it, staring into the alcohol's turbulent depths as I tried to figure out how to say what was on my mind. Sevani spoke up before I could. Her voice was quiet and taut, like a string she was worried would break if she put any more pressure on it. "So. How'd you make it out?"

I spared a sidelong glance at Artemis, who was watching me intently. I really wished she wasn't here. All I wanted to do right now was catch up with an old friend. I knew that Artemis was absorbing and analyzing every word I said, tucking it away for use against me later. Learning how she could manipulate me. She didn't look like she was going anywhere, though.

I sighed. "I got lucky. Let's leave it at that."

Sevani nodded slowly, her face grim. "I... I know what the answer is, but do you know if by some miracle any of the others..."

She trailed off.

"No," I said.

Sevani put her feet down and leaned forward, face all serious. "You say that, but that's what I thought about you. Did you *see* it? How can you be—"

"I saw enough," I snapped.

Sev's face flushed with guilt. I grimaced. I hadn't come here to chastise her. There was nothing she could have done. I sighed. "They're gone, Sev. All of them. Trust me."

She nodded slowly, looking down at her drink. "Yeah. Figured. Well, then." She raised her glass. "To the ones we left behind."

"Yeah." I raised my own glass, clinked it against hers, and downed it.

Somebody approached the table. I set my glass down and looked over to see Sevani's young doppelganger approaching us. Sevani wiped her mouth and set her empty glass down, gesturing briefly with her head. "You've already met my daughter, Rose. Rose, this is Lax VanDunn, a very old friend of mine."

Rose's eyes lit up at the mention of my name. "Lax? I've heard *so* much about you. I thought you—"

"Cool it," Sev said with a fond smile. "Take a seat, hotshot."

Rose sat down. I frowned at her, then back at Sev. Rose looked to be at least twenty years old, and Sev had never said anything about any daughter back in the day.

Sev read my mind. "I kept my lives separate back then," she said, a hint of tension in her voice. "Not because I didn't trust any of you. I just..."

"Didn't wanna risk getting them caught up in any of it," I said.

She grimaced. "Yeah."

I nodded slowly. That made sense. With the types of characters we ran with back in the day, having loved ones was a liability. Sevani wouldn't have wanted to take any chance that her family could be used as leverage against her or the crew. Still, though. It stung a bit, realizing that there was such a large part of her life I'd never known anything about.

Rose's companion—the one with the knife and pistol who had threatened me in the docking bay—filed in behind, slinking into a seat and studying me curiously for a moment before turning her attention elsewhere. Her hand never moved more than a few inches from her pistol, though. Rose's bodyguard, maybe?

"She's grown into quite the pilot," Sev continued. "Flies the *Orpheus* these days. Transports my most lucrative goods." She gave her daughter a sidelong look. "One of these days, she might even become as good as me."

Rose scoffed. "You wish. I could fly circles around you. In my sleep. With my hands tied behind—"

Sevani smiled and wrapped one arm around her daughter. "Yeah, yeah, I know. Keep dreaming, kiddo. Anyways." She raised an eyebrow at me. "Lax VanDunn, the legendary salvage runner, suddenly materializes from the dead, with a mysterious companion whose class *considerably* outmatches his own by his side. I'm guessing this isn't just a social call."

"No." I glanced at Artemis. "We need a ship, and a pilot."

I noticed Rose perk up, her eyes focusing in on me. Sevani's pleasant smile disappeared, replaced by a look of professional concentration. "Why?"

I hesitated. I could trust Sevani, couldn't I? From the sounds of things, she was out of the salvage game now. Still—we were in a public place, and even if I could trust her, who knew what her guards might go around repeating.

"Salvage job," I said finally. "Big one."

Sevani's face grew even more serious. Her eyes searched mine. "Back at it already, are you?"

I shrugged. "Can't teach an old dog new tricks."

She laughed without humor. "I'm living proof that's not true."

I smiled ruefully. "Well, maybe some old dogs are just more stubborn than others."

Sevani glanced from me to Artemis. "And you have the funds to pay for a ship?"

Artemis nodded. "I'm sure we can come to a satisfactory deal."

Sevani studied her. "And you are?"

"Artemis." Artemis gave a joyless smile.

Sevani waited for a moment, presumably to let Artemis elaborate. When that didn't happen, she cleared her throat and continued. "Well, I'll be honest with you. I'm not particularly interested in the salvage game these days." Her eyes locked mine. "And, frankly, I'm a little surprised you are."

"Then that should tell you just what kind of job it is," I said. I leaned forward, lowering my voice to a whisper. "Sev, we're not just talking another salvage run for a few ultracells here. This is a game changer. Bigger than anything we ever did, by one hell of a long shot."

Sev sighed. "That's what you said about the *Panama*, Lax."

My words choked in my throat. I had nothing to fire back at that.

"I'll do it," Rose said before I could reply.

All eyes turned to her. Her friend in the back perked up, teeth bared in a concerned grimace. We must have looked skeptical, because Rose's brows furrowed and she gave an angry huff. "What? I can do it! Salvage running doesn't even sound that hard. All I have to do is dock the ship. I'd practically be a parking valet." She turned to me, her eyes bright and earnest. "I've researched salvage. I know what it takes. I just need—"

"Absolutely not," Sevani said firmly. She turned back to me, her expression cold and professional. "It's simply not happening. I can help you find a ship and I know plenty of pilots that I'm sure would be interested, but I will *not* be getting involved."

I nodded slowly. I didn't blame her, of course. Not in the slightest. There was even a slight part of me that was relieved she had the good sense to stay away from a job this risky. But both of us knew that I had one card left to play: the *Orpheus* itself. Kessa, Sevani and I had each owned a third share in it. By virtue of my relationship with Kess, her portion fell to me. There was no binding contract enforcing it, no standing law to guarantee it, but we both knew that I would be well within my rights to demand use of the *Orpheus*.

I opened my mouth to say as much, only to pause as I met Sev's eyes. She knew what I was about to say, of course, and there was no anger or resentment in her expression. Just a quiet, desperate plea. *Don't. Please.*

There was a long moment of silence.

"'Preciate it," I finally said.

What I thought was a relieved smile broke across Sevani's face. "No hard feelings?"

"Nah." I grinned. "I get it. You're all settled down here. Besides, you left me behind for the enforcers last time anyways. Figure it'd be bad luck to get you involved."

Sevani made a face. "You're a dick, you know that?"

I rose. "Really, though, Sev. I'm glad you're doing well. Thanks for chatting."

Her smile turned sad. "I missed you. And everyone."

"Yeah." I felt my smile slipping and forced myself to keep it up. "Yeah. Me too."

Artemis went out first, her face as expressionless as ever. No way for me to gauge her reaction to the whole incident. Before we left, though, Sev pulled me aside, just out of Artemis's earshot.

"Please let me know if you need anything at all," she said earnestly, holding me by the arm. "Anything other than... well, you know." She grew hesitant. "And about the *Orpheus*. I'm more than happy to pay out your shares. With interest. It should be enough to set you up quite nicely." She glanced towards Artemis, who had turned and was watching us. "Nicely enough that you don't have to work for snakes like *her*.

I could always use some more muscle around here if you're interested."

I looked towards Artemis myself. I wanted to take her up on it. Just take a nice, quick payout and lie low for a while. But like it or not, I'd signed on for this job. I'd given my word to Nadus. Plus, I didn't know what Rid would do if I left him in the lurch like that.

"Thanks," I said softly. "But..."

"...but no," Sev finished for me. "You're a real stubborn bastard, you know that?"

I grinned wanly. "Guess so. And about the *Orpheus*. Don't worry about it. I'm just glad it's still in the family, so to speak." I stepped away, speaking over my shoulder. "I'll come back, assuming everything goes well. We'll catch up."

"I'd like that," Sev said.

I caught up with Artemis. She said something as we started walking away, but the words didn't stick. I was too busy thinking. Feeling. Remembering.

# ELEVEN

## THE PANAMA



Somehow, no matter how many times I do it, I can never quite get used to the eeriness of boarding a dead ship. Maybe it's the darkness—the shadows, thick and oppressive, clinging to the sharp corners and long hallways. Maybe it's the silence—the quiet so loud that you can hear every sound your body makes, every mechanical click of your exo's inner workings. Or maybe it's simply the mind's natural reaction to being someplace it knows it shouldn't be.

It had been two years since anybody had heard from the *Panama*. Trent, the man I'd gotten the tip from, said that a surveyor ship inspecting nearby asteroids for minerals had documented what seemed to be a derelict ship drifting aimlessly past, but hadn't bothered to investigate. They'd sold the tip to Trent, who had done some researching to validate and then had sold the information to me.

And now I was here, staring down the lifeless halls of a ghost ship, listening to my breath cycling through the life-support systems of my Jericho CES-3 exosuit, that eerie feeling slowly settling into my gut.

"What's the hold-up?" Rawlins's voice rasped in my ear through the comms system. "Scans showed a clean ship, didn't they?"

"*Squeaky,*" Sevani's voice affirmed. She was still on the *Orpheus,* while the rest of us had suited up and were currently in the process of boarding the *Panama.* "*If there're any rippers on there, they're long dead. I'm not getting any signals at all.*"

I nodded. Rippers were designed to emit a faint electromagnetic pulse so that Paragon clean-up crews could find them without fear of being ambushed. The detection technology wasn't easy to get, but Sev had always had a gift for finding things she wasn't supposed to. If she'd had any brains at all, she'd have ditched our sorry crew a long time ago to take up smuggling. She hadn't, though, because our crew was a family. And, as she had said when I'd raised that very subject with her, *you don't leave family behind.*

And yet, here I'd been talking to Kess about our retirement plans. I felt a flush of irrational guilt but pushed it away, pulling my thoughts back to the task at hand. If Sev said the scans detected a clean ship, that meant we could put our minds at ease where rippers were concerned. Still, though...

"Crews don't just disappear without a reason," Kessa said. "If it wasn't rippers, then it was something else. Either way, no point in being stupid."

As per usual, Kess had managed to not only guess what I was thinking but articulate it far better than I ever would have. Something had happened here. The last message that had been received from the *Panama*'s crew indicated that they were investigating an SOS broadcast. After that... nothing. The systems that the shipping company used to track their cargo vessels had stopped working. The ship had never arrived at its destination and investigations along its estimated trajectories had yielded no results.

*"Probably pirates,"* Sev said. *"Common enough tactic. Send out an SOS to lure in the target, then hit them fast and hard and take out their comms."*

Sev had a point. Pirates did seem like the most likely explanation for what had happened here. I could already feel my elation at the thought of the riches awaiting within slipping away.

"Well," Liung said, his voice hopeful, "maybe they left us a little something. Out of the goodness of their hearts. It ain't polite to eat the last cookie, after all."

"And if there's *one* thing pirates are known for," Black said, "it's their manners."

I grimaced. "Well, we're here, so we might as well have a look around. Liung, take Gomez, Jackson, Vargus and Pollock and go to the cargo bay. Kess, Black, Rawlins and I will head along the core of the ship towards the bridge and see what we can find. And make sure that everybody keeps their heads on a swivel."

"Or else the rippaz'll getcha," Liung said in an exaggerated accent, reaching out and grabbing Rawlins by his armored arm. The rookie jolted with startlement, then cursed and shook Liung's gauntlet off of him. I bit back a smile. Oh, to be young and full of the desperate need to prove myself again.

"You know how the rippers like to eat?" Liung said. His face was concealed behind the visor of his helmet, but I knew his mischievous grin well enough to picture it. "They like to start down low." He patted his stomach. "Where it's nice and soft and warm. Then work their way up from there."

"Knock it off, Liung," Kess said. "Kid's scared enough as it is."

"I ain't scared," Rawlins insisted, his voice cracking slightly.

Liung laughed and then gave me a nod as he led his group

towards the cargo bay, using the built-in thrusters of their exos to propel them in the zero gravity.

"There's no rippers on the ship, though, are there?" muttered Rawlins, staring into the darkness Liung's team had vanished into.

"No," I said. "The *Orpheus*'s scanners would have picked them up."

"Right. And..." He hesitated. "That ain't true, is it? About the guts, and all that..."

The image of Rafe, flat on his back as a ripper burrowed into his lower abdomen, tearing through armor and flesh alike, rippled against my will through my brain.

"No," I lied.

He nodded and let his hand move away from the grip of his SVAG submachine gun holstered on his exo's hip. We all had them. It wasn't much of a weapon, but it was light and unobtrusive, and we wouldn't need it anyways, so it was a good emergency option.

I glanced down at my wrist computer, pressing a button to activate my minimap. A fuzzy, blue holographic image flickered to life, detailing the blueprints of the *Panama* I'd gotten from Trent. Eight green dots were clustered at one of the *Panama*'s docking ports where Sevani had unloaded us. As I watched, the group began to split into two as Liung's group separated.

The eerie feeling in my gut didn't go away.

"Alright," I said with a grimace. "Let's get this done."


There are a few rules I like to follow when running a salvage op. Nothing too fancy, just some simple common sense to minimize risk. For example: don't split up more than necessary. If something goes wrong, you don't want to be alone. Others include keeping a low profile when you can (no point in drawing attention from anything that might be on the ship) and keeping the general comms channel clear for important information.

Rawlins seemed determined to break all of those rules.

"How often do you run into rippers on these things?" he asked over the comms.

I winced as I watched him bump into a wall up ahead of us. He still wasn't used to moving around free from gravity. "Often enough, kid. Watch where you're going."

"Sev said the ship is clean," he said.

Sev's voice crackled over the comms in response. "*Plenty of ways to die out here without getting rippers involved.*"

Kess reached out and touched my arm. "Take it easy on him," she said over a direct channel to me. "He's just a kid."

"Doesn't make him death-proof," I muttered back.

I glanced down at the map projected from my wrist computer. The dots representing Kessa and I were clustered together in the middle of one of ship's long corridors, while Black's dot was trailing shortly behind us and Rawlins's was pushing increasingly far ahead. Liung's team had just reached the cargo bay.

"Aw, *man*," Liung said, his voice leaden with disappointment.

My heart sank. "The cargo bay wiped out?"

"I was really looking forward to running salvage and living in poverty the rest of my life," Liung said. "But, alas, my friends, I fear that will not be our fate."

I frowned. "Wait, what?"

A flashing message on my wrist computer indicated that he had sent an image. I glanced down at it and felt my eyes widen.

The image showed a several large crates, each of them marked with the words CAUTION in large red lettering. A few moments later, Liung sent another image showing the interior of one of the crates. It was lined with carefully packaged cylinders, each one roughly a meter long and a third as wide, with a white shell and the words *Divinity Technologies* printed across the side in crisp blue.

I felt a grin spread across my lips, looking up from the image at Kess. She smiled back.

"Now *that's* quitting money," she said.

"Sev."

I spoke the word gently into a private channel, not stopping my work. There was a long delay before she responded.

"*Yeah*," she replied.

"What's going on? Something's wrong. I can tell." I carefully pulled the ultracell I was currently focused on from where it was installed in one of the *Panama's* back-up power generators. Ultracells are mostly safe, but they do hold an unbelievable amount of energy. An impossible amount, actually—there was a reason that nobody had been able to figure out how Divinity made them, much less imitate them. Mishandling them had led to catastrophic results for several vulture crews.

"*Don't push me, Lax,*" Sevani said, her voice brittle. I knew her well enough to pick out the threads of the different emotions woven into her tone. Anger was the strongest. Hidden beneath that, though, was just a hint of fear. Panic. Maybe even guilt.

I didn't press her. Sevani was as stubborn as they came—if she didn't want to talk, not a damn thing this side of Earth would make her. I sighed. "Fine. But when we're done here, I'm buying drinks and we're having a chat."

Liung's voice sounded over the general channel before she could reply. "*Uh, Lax?*"

"Yeah." I handed another ultracell to Black. He caught it and carefully slid it into place in the cargo pod he had been pulling behind him. I had to restrain a grin at the sight. This was one hell of a haul.

Liung cleared his throat. "*We just got back from dropping off the first load, if you know what I mean—*"

"Ugh," Kessa groaned.

"*Get your mind out of the gutter, Kess,*" Liung said, his tone playfully indignant. "*Very unladylike of you. Anyways, I noticed something in the docking bay. It looks like an escape shuttle.*"

"Meaning an escape shuttle ready to launch?" I gave it some thought. "That could fetch us a few—"

"No." Liung cut me off. "*Not that. A used escape shuttle, one they picked up. It looks like a Paragon craft.*"

Kessa and I shared a look. She shrugged, the shoulder pauldrons of her exo rising and falling, the starry night sky painted across them glinting briefly in my floodlights. "Guess that's the source of the SOS they responded to," Kessa said.

Sevani's voice crackled to life on the public channel, her tone urgent. "*Hey, not to rush you guys, but it looks like we've got a Paragon patrol on its way.*"

*Dammit.*

"There's no way that's a coincidence," Black said. "Trent must have tipped them off."

"How far out?" I growled.

"*On current trajectory we've got forty-seven minutes before they're on top of us.*"

I gave it some thought. The Paragon did not look kindly upon vultures, and I somehow doubted they'd accept the old *rippers ate my permit* routine if we were still here when they arrived. Plus, I was increasingly certain that something was wrong on this ship. I mean, more wrong than normal for a ghost ship. The fact that the ultracells were still here meant that it hadn't been pirates who had hit the ship. But if it was rippers, we'd almost certainly have run across them by now. Rippers aren't known for their subtlety, and despite my efforts, we hadn't exactly been keeping a low profile.

My gut told me we should pack up and leave. We already

had a decent haul loaded onto the *Orpheus*. And yet, with just a few more minutes of fast work, we could more than double that amount. *Quitting money.* A little cottage next to a lake on some nice, quiet planet, with just Kess and me.

I glanced at my wrist computer and was greeted by the sight of my minimap. An assortment of green dots scattered across the ship blinked back at me. We were spread out and exposed. But we were so damn *close.*

"*One more load,*" Liung suggested. "*Quitting money, right?*"

I grinned. "Damn right."

TWELVE

"Catch," Artemis said.

Her voice jarred me from the memories I'd been stewing in just in time to spot a small object hurtling through the air towards me. I snatched it.

"Quantum communicator," Artemis said, holding up an identical device. "Directly linked to mine. Instant, untraceable communication."

"I know how it works." I looked down at it, then back up. "Why do I have it?"

"You're getting dinner," Nadus said.

After our meeting with Sevani, Artemis and I had made our way to the room Nadus had picked out for us. It was small and cramped compared to our lodgings on the *Jonah*, but it did the job. Rid was currently stretched out on a sofa, snoring, and Bentley's voice was drifting from the washroom over the sound of running water as he sang—very loudly and very poorly—in a language I didn't recognize.

"Right." I shook myself and rose to my feet. I'd had a hard time focusing since leaving Sev's bar.

The sound of running water cut off abruptly, and Bentley's singing twisted into a disappointed groan.

"Somebody's not used to water restrictions," Nadus said with an amused grin.

I pocketed the communicator and headed out the door. The corridor outside was long, claustrophobic, and littered with trash. I thought again about how many people across the galaxy had never known anything *but* this life. An old, faded sign on the wall caught my eye—a set of quarantine instructions from the neurovirus outbreak almost a decade back.

It was about a fifteen-minute walk through twisting corridors and flickering overhead lights to the commissary. I passed a few people along the way. The first was an older woman with two children. She gave me a frightened look and hurried past. The second was a scantily clad lady standing seductively next to an ajar door. She wasn't quite able to keep the fear or desperation out of her voice as she tried to lure me towards her. The third was a group of station hooligans wearing hoods and gang tattoos across their foreheads. One of them tried to stare me down but I ignored him, brushing past. I listened to their footsteps and banter fade behind me. Another set of footsteps replaced them.

I glanced casually over my shoulder—just in time to catch a glimpse of somebody slipping around a corner, out of my sight. The footsteps stopped. I kept on going and heard them resume again after a moment of silence.

Dammit.

I turned at an intersection. Not the one I was supposed to, but I figured that the chances were decent whoever was behind me was just going to the commissary same as I was. No such luck. The footsteps followed me around the corner.

Dammit.

I thought about the guy I'd seen earlier in the day at the loading bay. He'd sure seemed as if he was following me. But he'd gone off after I spotted him. Maybe he'd just been trying to throw me off. If he'd managed to follow me back here, though, that meant he most likely knew where our room was.

Dammit.

I took another turn to put me back on the path towards the commissary. After all, food was food, hunted or not, and I was starving. Plus, it was best if whoever was following me didn't know I was onto them. Easier to turn things around. There's a fine line between the hunter and the hunted, and the truth is that you're never quite as far over one side of it as you think you are.

I quickened my pace. After a few moments the footsteps behind me quickened as well. I waited until I passed another group of people—this one a group of drunken men wearing miners' gear, likely coming home from work—and used their noise to mask my disappearance as I slipped into a dark corridor.

I waited there with my back against the wall, listening to the footsteps draw closer. As they neared, they slowed, the soft padding sounds of soles striking the cold concrete floor growing further and further apart, until they came to a stop.

I felt my fist clench. Whoever was following me, they were almost certainly armed. I wasn't in the tin can anymore, fighting gangsters with dirty shivs and eating utensils. Didn't matter how strong I was if I had a bullet lodged in my skull. The only way to make this go my way was if they moved near enough for me to safely close the distance.

*Come on. Just a little closer.*

My pursuer took a few cautious steps forward. I tried to estimate where they were. Probably just a few meters away from the corner. I heard more footsteps coming from the other direction, down the hall, and cursed under my breath. If somebody else came down that way and saw a big guy like me waiting around the corner, they'd assume I was a mugger or worse.

*Come on. Hurry. Let's get this over with.*

I heard three more slow steps. A dark shape moved into the corner of my vision, and I pounced, darting out from behind my corner, wrapping my pursuer in a bear hug with one hand clamped over their mouth, and pulled them into the dark hall-way. The person was small but strong, resisting with a series of futile kicks.

I pivoted and shoved them up against the wall, keeping one hand clamped over their mouth while I drew back my fist, only to see—

"Sevani?" I growled.

Not Sevani. I furrowed my brow. "Rose. What the hell?"

Her eyes flitted to the side. I moved my hand and stepped back as another group of miners came down the main corridor. One of them glanced at me. I gave an awkward smile and nodded my head. He looked away, his eyes uncaring as he continued down the corridor with his companions. I could have been murdering children down here and he wouldn't have cared.

Their footsteps faded down the corridor and I turned back to Rose. "What the hell are you doing, following me like that? Could have gotten yourself killed."

She gritted her teeth, and I saw an anger flash through her eyes that reminded me of her mom. "Why does everyone assume I'm so fragile?"

I raised an eyebrow, looking her up and down. "Well, you don't exactly look like a fighter."

She scoffed. "Whatever. I'm here for the pilot job."

I studied her for a minute. "Your mom know you're here?"

"No," she said angrily. "And she doesn't need to. I'm a grown-ass woman—I can go where I want."

I shrugged. "I ain't gonna argue with that."

"Good." She stepped away from the wall, straightening the fabric of her pilot's jumpsuit with her palm. "Anyways. You need a pilot. I want a job. You need a ship. I have a ship."

"The *Orpheus?*"

"Yeah."

"I was under the distinct impression it belonged to your mother."

Rose glared at me. "Are we doing this or not?"

"Not." I turned and continued down the hallway.

It only took a few moments for her to chase after me. "Why not? What, are you afraid of her?"

I raised an eyebrow at her without slowing down. "Of Maren Sevani? Hell yeah, I'm afraid. You would be too if you knew half the stuff she's done. How much do you even know about your mom's past? About me?"

She shrugged. "I know you guys used to run salvage together. That's how she got her reputation. I've heard about pretty much everyone on your crew. And I know about you and Kessa."

I didn't slow down. "And you know what happened to them?"

She didn't answer.

"I'll take that as a yes," I growled. Up ahead of us I could see where the corridor widened into what looked almost like a city street, with windows looking in on various commercial establishments. I noticed a large line of people standing towards the end, waiting in front of several electronic kiosks marked CREDIT. The commissary was just beyond.

"I *know* it's dangerous," Rose said, still following behind me. "That doesn't bother me. That's why I want to work for you. I'm never gonna get out of here if I don't take some risks."

"There's risks," I said, pushing through the doorway into the commissary, "and then there's *risks*. This is the latter. Trust me —you should stay away from this."

She paused inside the doorway. "Wow. I assumed you were going someplace more…"

"…Exciting?" I paused in front of a kiosk, tapped a button to activate it, and began scrolling through a list of the items available. Most of it consisted of fabricated meal packages, various beverages, and a smattering of random household items—all of it far more expensive than it should have been. I picked out some basic meal kits, intending to call it good there, and then paused when I saw an image of bright red liquid in a bottle. Mars Pop. On a whim, I added it to my list and hit order, scanning the payment chip Artemis had given me.

"Seriously, though," Rose said as she tailed me over to the receiving line, where I waited with a few other people next to a door for the machinery to put together my order and deliver it. "I'm a damn good pilot," she continued. "Even my mom thinks so, and she's the best there is. And I have a mechanic ready to go. We could leave right away."

I raised an eyebrow. "You've really thought this through."

She crossed her arms and gave me something that was halfway between a smirk and a scowl. "So what's the hold-up? You *know* I'd be an asset to the team."

"The hold-up," I said impatiently, "is that you're not listening to a word I'm saying." I gave her a hard look. "This isn't like any of the jobs I did with your mom. It's not like anything that *anyone* has done before." I glanced around at the other customers and lowered my voice. "And it's not just because of rippers. Look, I get it: you want to make your own reputation, get out from under your mom's shadow. But this ain't the place to start."

An automated voice called out my order number and I took my bag from the machine, searching briefly through it to make sure that it had everything I'd paid for. Five meal packages, check. One bottle of Mars Pop, check. I pulled it out of the bag and started making my way towards the exit.

Rose saw the bottle of bright red liquid and giggled. "Mars Pop? What are you, six?"

"My mom used to buy this for me when we went to the city center," I said, twisting off the top and feeling a rush of nostalgia as I heard the hissing sound of carbonation escaping the bottle. I held it up to my nose, savoring the overly sweet smell. "Haven't had one of these in decades." I put the edge of the bottle on my lip, pulled my head back, and got just the smallest taste of my childhood before I locked eyes with him.

He was standing at the commissary entrance, one hand on the open door, the other hidden beneath his jacket. It took me only a split second to recognize him. It was the same guy that had been watching me earlier in the day in the space port.

Dammit.

There was a glint of metal as the man moved the hand under his jacket.

*Dammit.*

THIRTEEN

"You're not exactly the guy my mom made you sound like," Rose was saying. "I wonder if—*hey!*"

The man's hand came up from under his jacket. I shoved Rose out of the way with one hand, sending her flying into a nearby shelf, while I flung the bottle of Mars Pop into the face of the stalker. He grunted as the plastic bottle bounced off of the bridge of his nose and splashed bright red liquid all over his jacket. It wasn't enough to seriously hurt anyone, but it was at least enough of a distraction that the pistol coming out of his coat wavered.

I lunged forward. He brought the gun up—too slow. I slapped it out of line with my body, slamming the back of his hand with brutal force into the corner of the doorway. He gasped at the pain and the gun clattered to the floor. I drew back my other fist and shot it towards his face but he ducked beneath it. There was another flash of steel and I felt a sharp pain across my side as he darted under my extended arm and behind me.

I pivoted, fists clenched, to see him standing in a fighting pose with a bloodied knife in one hand. The other hand—the one that had been holding the gun—was mangled and broken.

I touched a hand to my side. It came back up wet with blood. One for one so far.

"Who the hell are you?" I growled.

He grimaced and pressed a button on the back of his knife. There was a soft whirring sound as the edge of the blade suddenly began to blur with vibration.

"Fair enough," I said.

He darted forward, feinted to the right, and then made a sudden upward cut. I stepped backward, avoiding the blade by mere inches. He slashed downward too quickly for me to get in a retaliatory strike and forced me back again. I stumbled as I backed up into one of the kiosks and he lunged forward, driving the tip of his knife towards my gut.

I grabbed his wrist. The knife's tip stopped no more than an inch away from my belly. I could feel the blade's vibrations working through his hand and into mine.

He growled, pushing forward in vain. He was athletic, but nowhere close to my size.

"What do you want?" I growled, not loosening my grip. "Who are you working for?"

"Screw yourself," he growled, and threw all of his weight forward onto the handle of his knife.

The sudden assault caught me off guard. I felt the tip of the rapidly vibrating blade kiss my midsection, tearing up my shirt and skin. I jerked his hand to the side, holding his arm stretched out to his side, and then slammed my free hand palm first into his elbow. There was a *cracking* sound as his arm bent in a way arms are decidedly *not* meant to bend.

He screamed.

"Last chance," I growled.

"Let him go!"

I glanced over his shoulder. Two more men were standing

near the entrance to the commissary. Both were holding pistols. One was aimed at me, while the other was pointing at Rose, who was crouching on the floor, hand frozen in the process of reaching for the first hitman's discarded weapon.

*Dammit.* I could make a break for it, use the first attacker's body as a shield. Make it out the side door. But there could be more of them. And I wouldn't make it more than a few steps before they sprayed Rose's brains across the floor.

"I'll kill her," said the man pointing a gun at Rose's head. He was wearing a black coat. "You better believe me."

"We just want to talk," said the other one calmly. That guy was wearing a stupid-looking old-timey hat pushed back on his head. Probably thought it made him look classy. "Let him go, and we won't have to hurt you."

"Too badly," his companion muttered, eyes settling on their friend's mangled hand and broken arm.

I gritted my teeth, then finally let go. The injured hitman staggered away, moaning.

The man in the black coat sucked air through his teeth. "Bad news," he said, and moved the barrel of his gun from Rose to me. "I lied. Better luck next time."

There was a sharp metallic flash. The black-clad man's eyes bulged as the end of a long, straight blade punched suddenly through his chest. His companion gawked at the wound, then spun to avenge it only to find himself staring down the barrel of a pistol.

The gunshot echoed down the corridors outside the commissary. The thug's head jerked backward and he slumped to the ground.

The man in the black coat gasped as the knife tip disappeared. His gun clattered to the floor and he dropped to his knees, coughing wetly. My eyes moved upward, to the figure standing behind the two would-be assassins. Rose's friend, from the docking bay, holding her pistol in one hand and her long knife in the other, blade glistening with blood.

"You tried to ditch me," she said accusingly to Rose, eyes not leaving the man in the black coat.

"I had it under control," muttered Rose. She gestured towards the discarded gun. "I was about to... you know..."

The first hitman was standing with his back against the wall, eyes wide as he surveyed the devastation. He looked down at his two mangled arms, mouth hanging open in shock.

"Thanks," I said to our apparent rescuer, then turned to the wounded hitman. "Let's try this again. Who sent you?"

"I—we don't know," he said, eyes wide with terror. "We never know."

The man in the black coat wheezed uselessly, fumbling for his fallen gun. Rose's friend stooped casually and stabbed him through the base of the skull.

The surviving assassin swore viciously. "I'm telling the truth. I don't know. But—they're going after your friends."

I frowned. "Explain."

"The other Vanguard," he said, eyes flitting from his fallen friends to me. "And the lady. And the two skinny guys. They're gonna kill 'em all. That's the job."

Ah, *hell.*

"Thanks," I muttered, then shot my fist out without warning. It slammed into his forehead and smashed the back of his skull against the wall behind him. His eyes went glassy and he sagged to the floor, but I was already sprinting long before he got there.

"Where are you going?" Rose followed me. Her companion jerked her blade free from the corpse and wiped it off on the black coat before following us.

"Back to my room," I said, digging in my pocket for my own communicator as I left the commissary. I stooped to grab one of the fallen pistols, then glanced around, scanning for other threats. The coast seemed to be clear. "He was an assassin. There will be more."

I held the quantum communicator up to my lips and activated it, striding back down the corridor towards our room all the while. "Artemis. Nadus. Rid. Anyone, you copy?"

Rose's footsteps slapped loudly against the floor behind me. "We're coming with you."

I activated the communicator again. "Guys? Anyone there? We have a problem."

Nothing.

I broke from a fast walk into a sprint, my mind racing as I went. Somebody knew. Artemis had insisted that the intel was secure, that we were the only people who even knew that the *Revelation* was still out there. Obviously she was wrong—wrong, or lying. Somebody knew what we were up to, or at least something about us. Either they were trying to get the *Revelation*'s co-ordinates from Artemis, or they were a rival crew of vultures just trying to thin out the competition. Maybe both. Or neither.

I slowed as I reached the corner our room was adjacent to. Rose came to a panting halt next to me, leaning on her knees. Her friend fell in behind her. All things considered I was impressed they'd managed to keep up with me. I ignored them for now, leaning to get a look around the corner.

There were seven men standing outside of our room. One of them was kneeling next to the door, fiddling with some sort of device that he had placed flat against the surface of the door. The others were standing furtively behind him with drawn handguns. They were dressed in casual streetwear.

I drew back behind the corner, gritting my teeth. With a sudden attack I'd be able to take at least a few of them out before they got me. If nothing else, it would alert Nadus and Artemis. Why weren't they answering?

"I'm not picking anything up," I heard a voice say.

"Alright, then," somebody else said, his voice grim. "Let's move."

I turned to Rose. "You still want a job?"

Rose's frightened eyes hardened suddenly into a wicked grin. "Hell yeah."

"Rose," her friend hissed. "We should talk about this before we—"

"It's too late now, Shell," Rose retorted.

"Get out of here, both of you. Go prep the *Orpheus*," I said.

She nodded and began backing away. "What are you going to do?"

"Something stupid," I muttered. "We'll be down there as soon as we can."

"You better." She turned and ran down the hallway, vanishing from view. Her friend—Shell, apparently—gave me a dark look before following.

I took a deep breath. As soon as I engaged the assassins, I'd be subjecting myself to an overwhelming amount of return fire. My only chance was to catch them off guard, thin the herd, and then hope that Nadus could get them from the other side.

*Showtime.* I quickly inspected the stolen handgun, making sure a round was chambered and safety off, then leaned out from the corner and took aim.

I took a few seconds to line up my shot. Those seconds were just enough time for one of the guys by the door to notice me and shout something to his buddies. That way, when the man kneeling next to the door looked my way, the last thing he saw in this life was the flash of my muzzle.

He slumped to the floor, blood leaking from the hole in his head as the rest of his gang turned and opened fire on me. I drew back behind my corner, gritting my teeth as a hailstorm of bullets blasted tiny chunks of concrete off the walls. Under ordinary circumstances these smaller caliber weapons wouldn't have had too much of a bark, but here, surrounded by concrete, the cacophony of gunshots and ricocheting bullets was deafening.

I backed up until I found another intersection and took shelter behind it, aiming my gun down the hallway towards the corner I'd been at earlier.

I saw a flash of movement as one of the gunmen poked their head out of cover. I squeezed off a shot. I missed my mark, but I heard a yelp of dismay come from around the corner as the bullet ricochet off of the wall and—I hoped—into somebody's flesh. Chances were against it, but hey, a man can dream.

Something small and tube-shaped flew around the corner, bounced off of the wall, and slid to a halt in the middle of the hallway. I swore and drew back around my corner, ducking my head and protecting my ears with my arms as I waited for the concussion to sound. When it did, it was significantly softer than I'd expected. I glanced around the corner to see a ball of thick red smoke expanding outward from the canister. I couldn't see a thing through it.

A smoke screen. I hesitated. There was no knowing what they were doing back there. I thought through what I would have done in their shoes. Probably split into two groups: one to keep pushing me down this hallway, and another to go around the other way and get behind me. That was the problem with fighting in spaceships—you're either going one way or the other. Made it too easy to get trapped.

Well, I wanted none of that. The smokescreen meant I couldn't see them, but it also meant that they couldn't see me. With the numbers on their side, they'd assume I was taking up the defensive. Which meant it was time to do the opposite.

I left the cover of my corner and sprinted down the hall towards the smoke, drawing my stolen knife. The world turned crimson as I plunged into the cloud. A split second later a shape loomed in front of me. I hit the button on the knife and felt a slight tremor run down my wrist as the blade turned into a deadly blur. I lashed out and heard a scream as the blade sliced cleanly through somebody's wrist. I let my momentum carry me forward, slamming my shoulder into the unfortunate would-be assassin and sending him flying backward.

He collided with one of his companions and they both fell to the ground. A gunshot sounded and a muzzle flash illuminated the sheet of crimson hanging around me. A shout of pain followed it. I found a grim smile tugging at the corners of my mouth. Fighting solo had its advantages: unlike them, I didn't have to worry about who I was killing.

I raised my pistol and fired three shots in quick succession at where I'd seen the muzzle flare, then quickly ducked and rolled to the other side of the hallway. I was rewarded with a yelp, followed by several more gunshots and a whining ricochet sound as bullets bounced off of the wall I'd been next to just moments before. I fired a few more shots, trying to guess where my attackers were, based upon the muzzle flashes, and then had a moment of panic as the trigger suddenly became stiff to my finger.

Out of bullets. I thumbed the magazine release and reached down for the spare clip, deactivating my knife and setting it aside to do so. As I grabbed the clip a shape loomed through the smoke in front of me, arm extended and pointed just to my right. I reacted on instinct, charging forward and slamming my shoulder into his gut. I drove him backward, across the hall, and slammed him into the wall on the other side.

Except it wasn't the wall. There was a splintering sound as the door unfortunate enough to be in our path was torn from its hinges. For a second, I lost track of up and down as my opponent and I both tumbled head over heels. By the time I regained my bearings he was already climbing to his feet. He kicked out and I grunted as the hard toe of his boot smashed into my brow, driving me backward. The world spun for a short, violent moment.

"Got him," he gasped. I heard the telltale buzzing sound of another one of those vibroblades activating. By the time my vision stabilized the blade was plunging down towards my chest.

I lashed out with one hand, knocking the blade out of line with my body. Sparks flew as it slammed into the concrete floor and went skittering away. I heard myself bellowing, adrenaline surging through my body as I reached up, grabbed my would-be killer by the throat, and threw him to the side. He grunted as he hit the concrete wall. I seized him by the back of the neck, jerked him back, and then drove his skull forward with all of my strength into the jaggedly sharp corner of the doorway.

That did the job.

Somebody else loomed in the doorway, stepping through the smoke. I reached around for some sort of weapon and found nothing. I looked up to see one of the assassins standing above me, holding a pistol at the ready. His eyes flickered briefly to the gory sight of his companion's body and his eyes lit with rage.

There was a deafening concussion, echoing with a volume that made the other gunshots sound like firecrackers. The assassin's head practically inverted itself as a bullet smashed through it. What was left of the man swayed and then fell over backward. A few seconds later a huge form loomed through the smoke as Nadus materialized like a vengeful demon, holding a Mjolnir T21 handcannon that made the other guns look like kids' toys.

Relief washed over his face as he saw me. "You good?"

"Yeah." I sat up, groaning. "We get 'em all?"

"I count six dead out here."

I jerked my head towards the guy I'd plastered to the corner. "He makes seven. We're good."

Nadus nodded, glancing around the corridor. "Sweet. Let's get the hell out of here."

"Yeah. Be right there." I sagged backward slightly, trying to catch my breath. Holy hell, that had been a fight. I glanced around the room. For the first time, I realized that it was occupied. A man, a woman, and two kids were sitting on a sofa in the middle of the living room, their shocked expressions lit softly by the light from an old television hanging on the wall.

I groaned and pushed myself to my feet, giving them a brief nod. "Those corners are a safety hazard," I said. "You oughta cover them up or something."

The woman vomited.

## FOURTEEN

In the hallway outside the smoke had started to clear out. Doors all along the corridor were cracking open, eyes filled with fear and curiosity peeking out to see what was going on. Nadus was kneeling over one of the fallen assassins. I realized with a start that the man's chest was still moving.

"Who the hell are you?" Nadus growled.

The man only wheezed.

Nadus took his Mjolnir and pressed the barrel against the bottom of the man's chin. "I doubt dying is ever pleasant, but I can make it a lot easier for you. Or a lot harder. Your choice. Tell me who sent you."

The man groaned. "I don't know. We never know. We were just filling an order."

"Local muscle," I mused. "Probably got contracted anonymously."

"Why?" Nadus growled.

"I don't—" The man coughed up blood. "I don't know. All we got was your descriptions."

"Then I guess you're of no more use to us," Nadus growled, his finger tensing on the trigger. The man's eyes widened.

"No—wait," he wheezed. "There was a name. Let me go. I'll tell you."

"I'm listening," Nadus said.

"Our clients use codenames," the man said, eye not leaving the barrel of Nadus's gun. "This one went by 'Penitent'."

Nadus and I shared a quick glance.

I shrugged. "Means nothing to me."

Nadus glared at the terrified thug for a long moment, then swore and stood up, glaring into an open doorway and the pair of frightened eyes peering out through it. It closed immediately.

"We need to get going," I said. "This place will be crawling with enforcers soon."

"Yeah." Nadus turned down the hall, leaving the thug bleeding on the ground. I followed behind.

Artemis emerged from our room, holding a sleek-looking black pistol that she lowered when she saw us. She raised an eyebrow as she looked me up and down. Between the cuts on my side and chest, the kick to the face I'd received, and the blood of the men I'd killed coating my clothes, I probably looked like hell.

"You look like hell," Artemis very considerately confirmed.

I grimaced down at the corpses littering the floor. "We need to go. Now."

"Go where?" Artemis hoisted a duffel bag over her shoulder, scrambling to keep up with me as I stalked down the corridor. "We don't have a ship!"

"Yeah, we do," I said. "Sevani's daughter. She's prepping her ship now."

Rid came out behind her, straining under the weight of a duffel bag of his own. Nadus grabbed the bag from him and tossed it over his own shoulder, making it look like a pillow, and then gave Rid a shove that propelled him down the hallway towards us. Bentley came out last, his eyes wild with fear and his shirt only partially buttoned.

I skidded to a halt at the end of a corridor and slammed the interface to call the elevator that would take us up—or down—or wherever it was—towards the shuttle stop. From there it would be just a short trip to the docking bay.

A few moments later, the doors grated open to reveal an elderly couple inside. They gave my blood-streaked face a frightened glance and scurried past us. I cursed under my breath and looked around for something to wipe my face with, only to find Rid holding out a clean rag.

I frowned and took it. "Where'd this come from?"

He shrugged and followed Nadus into the elevator.

I shook my head and followed, wiping the rag across my face and soaking up the flow of blood as best I could. Artemis punched a button on the elevator control panel and the machine lurched as it began moving.

I pulled the rag away. It was soaked red.

"What's going on, Artemis?"

Artemis turned, glaring at me. "What do you mean?"

"I mean that you're *obviously* not telling us something." I reached down to remove my shirt and winced as the movement agitated the multiple wounds on my chest. I settled for tearing the shirt down from the neck, and then started inspecting my injuries. "Whoever those bastards were, they knew something. Who else knows about the *Revelation*?"

Artemis gritted her teeth. "Nobody. I swear it."

"Then why are we being hunted?"

"Somebody must have talked." Artemis turned her gaze towards Rid.

Rid's eyes hardened. Nadus, to my surprise, shook his head. "Nah. It ain't him."

Artemis raised an eyebrow. "You two must have really bonded in the last couple of hours."

Nadus gave a slight grimace. "Nothing like that. Still wouldn't say I trust him. But he hasn't left my sight since I untied him on the *Jonah* yesterday. I'd know if he had contacted anyone."

"It's none of us," I said grimly, holding up the computer I'd taken from the first assassin. "They had descriptions and kill orders for every one of us." I glared at Artemis. "You're *absolutely certain* none of the other 'interested parties' are onto us?"

"Yes," Artemis snapped.

Silence fell. Nadus rifled through his duffel bag until he found one of his spare shirts, which he handed to me. I did my best to put it on, trying not to burst into swearing as pain lanced through me. I glanced at the screen showing our transport's progress towards the docking bay. *Faster*, I silently urged it. For all we knew there was a full squad of assassins waiting for us there.

"Sevani," Artemis said.

"*No.*" The word left my mouth sharper and louder than I'd intended it to. "There's no way."

"She's the *only* possibility," Artemis insisted. "The only one who has even the start of a notion of what we're doing. Maybe she decided she wants the job for herself. All she would need is to get the co-ordinates from us."

"We don't even have the co-ordinates yet," Bentley said in confusion.

"*She* wouldn't know that," Nadus said grimly.

I forced myself to consider it. Artemis had a point. And yet —there was too much that still didn't add up.

"The guy that attacked me in the commissary," I said after a moment. "He was following us before we met with Sevani."

"We were on her turf," Artemis shot back. "He might just be part of her security detail."

True enough. "But I was *with* Rose when he attacked me. They took her hostage. There's no chance in hell she would put her daughter in harm's way."

"Rose being involved is probably just a coincidence."

Artemis shrugged. "She probably went after you on her own and just got tangled up in it. Those hitmen probably had no idea who she was."

Also true. I felt a knot growing in my stomach. Would Sevani really turn on me like that? After everything we'd been through together?

"So what do we do?" Nadus looked from me to Artemis. "It's her daughter we're flying with, ain't it?"

Artemis nodded thoughtfully. "Yes, but that may be an unexpected opportunity. The only reason Rose would be in the middle of the crossfire would be if she was there unbeknownst to her mother. We can therefore assume that Rose and Sevani have no knowledge of each other's intentions. If we can escape the station with Rose on her ship—"

"The *Orpheus*," I muttered.

"—then we'll have an unexpected advantage: a hostage." Artemis smiled coldly. "Sevani won't dare to attack us again so long as we have her daughter with us."

I shook my head, trying to stay calm. "No, no, no. This is all wrong. I know Sevani. She wouldn't do this."

Artemis gritted her teeth in frustration. "You *knew* Sevani. Eight years ago. And even then, you didn't even know she had a family until today. Face it: she's a criminal. And we just walked into her territory, announced that we had something valuable, and then tried to walk out. Of *course* she's going to try to take it from us. That's what criminals do."

"No. That's not what *she* would do." I felt like I was trying to convince myself more than anyone else. "We were a crew. A *family*. She wouldn't turn on me like that."

Artemis sighed. "There's no such thing as *family*. Only individuals with mutual goals. When you worked together, your priorities aligned. As soon as you split..." She shrugged. "That's just how the world works. You can't trust anyone further than their own well-being." She fell silent for a moment, seeming contemplative. "I don't know much about your final job, but let me make some guesses. Was Sevani in the ship the whole time?"

I nodded. "That's how we always run it." I grimaced. "*Ran* it."

She folded her arms. "Had you already loaded your loot onto the ship when everything went to hell?"

"A decent chunk." I frowned. "But not all of it. What are you getting at?"

She smiled. "And, from what you mentioned earlier, *she* was the one who said the scanners showed a clean ship. And she was the one who reported a Paragon patrol that just so happened to be in the area. Then, once you do happen to run into her again, she's apparently somehow accumulated the funds to start her own criminal enterprise." She raised an eyebrow. "Even you have to admit. Adding all of that together..."

Silence fell again.

I didn't believe it.

I still didn't believe it when the elevator finally groaned to a halt. I wrestled with the idea as we boarded the shuttle to take us to the docking bay. I fought against the possibility that it could be even remotely, partially true as we left the shuttle and started working our way through the crowds to where the *Orpheus* was docked. But by the time I could see the sign marking the docking bay a gnawing, sickening uncertainty had settled in my gut.

Had Savani betrayed me? Betrayed *us*?

Rose emerged from the gaping maw of the *Orpheus*'s cargo bay and looked me up and down, raising an eyebrow. I couldn't help but notice again how much she looked like her mother.

"You look even worse than the last time I saw you," Rose said.

My mind was too cloudy to respond with anything other

than a grunt as I pushed past her and into the cargo bay. It was cavernous and empty inside other than a few crates that looked to be full of basic supplies. Shell was inside, hastily making a few last-minute preparations. She watched me warily as I walked past.

"We need to hurry," Artemis said, breezing after me into the cargo bay. "How soon can we take off?"

"As soon as you're all packed," Rose responded.

I turned. "Did you tell anyone we're leaving?"

Rose shook her head, brushing past me and towards a computer at the far end of the cargo bay. "No, other than the launch authorities. I've been scrambling to get cleared for take-off."

"Not even your mother?" Artemis asked, shooting me a sideways glance.

Rose scoffed. "I don't need her permission."

"Good." Artemis waved at Rid and Bentley, urging them to move faster as they scrambled aboard. "Let's get the hell out of here."

"So, where to next?"

Rose's voice was quizzical as she glanced between me and Artemis. Artemis's eyes were fixed on me, and mine, in turn, were staring out of the rear window of the *Orpheus*'s bridge and watching as Albeni 7 grew smaller and smaller, until it was little more than a blinking light on the edge of the giant red gas planet.

"Brahma," Artemis said. "We'll be going planetside."

"On it." Rose spun in her chair and began working the navigational computer, determining the most direct route there.

"NavCom is saying it's a three-day trip," Rose said. "With thirty-nine hours in nullspace and two foldgate connections." She turned and gave me a disapproving look. "You're bleeding all over my bridge, Lax. There's a medbay down the—" She caught herself, flushing slightly. "Sorry. Forgot you know this ship better than I do."

I shrugged. "I used to. I can find the way." I moved towards the hatch down to the second deck, only to pause as I heard a familiar beeping sound. An incoming transmission, picked up on the *Orpheus*'s communications panel.

Rose glanced over at it. Her face hardened. "Crap. It's my mom." She hesitated before moving her hand towards the *reject* button.

"Wait." Artemis stepped closer and held up a hand. "Let's talk to her." She gave me a knowing look. "She deserves to know who you're with, at least. We won't be able to talk to her after we activate the nullbreacher."

"Fine. Your funeral." Rose shrugged and hit the *accept* button. Artemis leaned close to my ear.

"Don't give up anything you don't have to," she whispered.

A blurry image of Sevani's face flashed onto the screen. "Rose? Rose, what the hell are you doing?"

"Your daughter is safe," Artemis said calmly, stepping into frame. "She decided to come with us. Of her own volition."

Sevani narrowed her eyes. "Artemis. Is Lax there?"

I sighed and moved over to the camera. Artemis and Rose both moved aside to make room for me. "Yeah, I'm here."

Sevani's voice turned from concerned to livid. "Lax, you bastard, I told you not to—" She cut off abruptly. "What happened to you?"

Every instinct I had was screaming at me to just confront Sevani with the suspicions Artemis had seeded in my mind. *Did you put out a hit on me?* Surely, knowing the truth couldn't hurt worse than living in this damn uncertainty. I opened my mouth to say it, but a glance at Artemis stopped me. She shook her head slightly.

"Got into a scrap," I said finally. "That's why we had to get out of Albeni 7 so quickly. I'm sorry, Sev. I wouldn't have let her come if I had any other option."

"A scrap?" Sevani leaned in closer to the camera. "With who?"

"I dunno," I said. At least that I could be honest about. "Hired thugs. Local, I'm guessing." I hesitated. "You got any ideas?"

"No." She shook her head. "But I'll do some digging. Just..." She sighed. "Rose, are you still there?"

I stepped aside, letting Rose inch closer. "Yeah."

"Rose, just be *careful*, alright?" Sevani's voice softened. "This isn't a game. You're not going to be able to throw around my name to get what you want. And don't you *dare* set foot on any ripper-infested ship, you hear me?"

Rose rolled her eyes. "I know, Mom. Relax, Shell is with us."

Shell. She was a killer, that one. There had been no remorse in her eyes as she'd dispatched the hitmen in the commissary. Just cold, brutal efficiency. I made a mental note to do what I could to stay on her good side.

"Good," Sevani continued. "And Lax?"

I stepped back up to the camera.

Sevani's voice grew as hard as ever I'd heard it. "Just so that we're clear. If anything happens to her, it will not matter how long we've known each other, or how far away you are, or how well armed you are. There is no *amount* of distance that will be able to keep me from you. I will find you, and I will make you wish you'd never gotten off the *Panama. Do you understand?*"

I nodded. "You have my word, Sev. I'll get her back to you."

"I don't want your word. I want my daughter back." Sevani sighed. "Just keep me updated."

"Will do." I hesitated. "I'm sorry, Sev."

"Yeah." Her face turned hard again. "Me too."

Her face vanished, replaced by the words

TRANSMISSION ENDED.

# FIFTEEN

I'd thought that being on my old ship would give me some sort of comfort. It didn't. Instead, as I made my way down the corridor towards the ship's medical bay, I found myself scrutinizing every familiar sight with a sense of paranoid suspicion.

The ship had changed in the eight years since I'd last set foot on it, of course, but the things that made it *home*—the details big and small, like the dent in the doorway at the end of the second deck, or the space near the middle of the corridor where the grav generators were glitched and you felt like if you just lifted your feet, you would just hover—were all still there. And yet, it didn't feel like I was home. It felt... *wrong*. Uncanny. Dreamlike.

*Sevani betrayed us.*

I could feel the thought worming its way through my brain like an all-consuming disease, infecting everything it touched and withering it. Every memory I had on this ship or with my old crew was suspect. The shadows in the familiar corridor seemed suddenly to be deep and impenetrable, hiding vile treacheries within their boundless voids.

*The ones we left behind...*

The faces of my crewmates flashed before my eyes. Black, with his big, serious eyes. Liung, never to be caught without a smirk and a quip. Rawlins, eager and naïve. Did Sev have it in her? To condemn her friends to the rippers? I found my fists clenching involuntarily.

*Stop it.* I shook myself. I needed a can, desperately. The door into the medbay was marked with a red cross symbol. I pushed it open, went through, and then winced as I peeled Nadus's spare shirt off. It was stained an ugly brown in several places with my blood. I made a mental note to go shopping for clothes at Brahma. At this rate I was going to bleed my way through Nadus's wardrobe within the week.

The medbay was similar-looking to the one I'd awoken in on the *Jonah,* if a bit more run-down. A small rectangle of a room with a bed in the middle and several medical devices along the wall. My eyes found one in particular—a rectangular box about the size of a briefcase with the words MOBILE ACCELER-ATED MEDICAL ADMINISTRATOR printed in boxed letters across it, shoved into the corner of the room.

I took it off the wall. There was a small screen and several buttons on the other side of it. I pressed the biggest button. There was a slight hiss as the end of a tube stuck out of the box.

HOOK UP PATIENT, the screen read.

I grabbed the end of the tube and pulled it out, extending it until it was long enough to plug into the port built into my shoulder. As I did I glanced down at the warning label on the box. *For use on Enhanced Vanguard Personnel Only,* it declared in bold, authoritative lettering. I'd always thought it was odd they felt the need to include that. Only Vanguards had the right ports anyways.

I plugged the tube into my shoulder port. The screen flashed green. READING.

I sat down on the bed and sighed, looking at myself in the mirror. I really did look like hell. My forehead was a mottled mess of bruised flesh where I'd been kicked. There was a long cut along my ribs that was black with dried blood. The skin along my midsection was torn to shreds where the tip of the vibroknife had almost killed me. In addition to that, my scars from the prison brawl just a few days ago were still angry and red.

I sighed. I might heal faster than most folk, but at the rate I was getting hurt that wasn't gonna do me much good.

The screen flashed again. I glanced over. PATIENT STABLE, the screen said. It began spitting out various little factoids about my medical health. There was a slight bubbling sound as it injected some sort of compound into my system through the tube. Probably just something to make sure I didn't get infected. I let out a sigh as I felt the frigicerin starting to work, soothing away my worries, blunting the sharp edges of my anxiety.

The door into the medbay swung open. I glanced up to see Artemis slip into the room, making sure the door closed behind her.

I grunted a greeting.

She stood there silently for a moment, and for the first time since I'd met her, I detected just a trace of uncertainty in the awkwardness of her pose as she looked from my bare, bloodied torso and around the small room. I glanced at the MAMA. The screen had a flashing heart symbol in the corner, meaning it wasn't safe for me to disconnect yet.

Artemis fixed her eyes on my torso, running down my body. "That's a lot of scars."

I looked down. "Yeah."

She cocked her head as she studied the MAMA and the tubes running into my body, her eyes glinting with morbid fascination. "You know, despite years of trying now, nobody can quite figure out how Divinity managed to pull it off."

I frowned. "Pull what off?"

"You. The Vanguards. And the rippers." Her eyes widened slightly as she watched one of my wounds healing faster than should have been possible, the flesh knitting itself together just fast enough to notice with the naked eye. "Countless captured rippers and Vanguards have been experimented on by various groups. Dissected and studied. Nobody can figure out how you heal so fast."

"Yeah, I'm a real miracle." I raised an eyebrow. "You come in here just to gawk?"

"No. I..." She hesitated, a few lines of uncertainty creasing across her usually stoic face. "I came to apologize."

I raised an eyebrow. "What for?"

She took a deep breath. "I pride myself on being able to see a situation clearly, my judgment unclouded by sentimentalities. I sometimes get too caught up in that, and forget to account for the emotional impact of my words and actions. I still don't trust Sevani. But I should have factored in the importance of your relationship with her before I aired my concerns. I didn't mean to disturb you."

I studied her. She seemed sincere. As sincere as I'd ever seen her, at least, standing there with her head held high and her gaze fixed unmoving on mine. Any awkwardness that had been there a moment before was gone, but she no longer seemed so cold and unapproachable. She just *was*.

I moved over, clearing some room on the bed, and she sat down next to me.

"That's alright," I said. "For all I know you're right. I guess I'd just never thought about Sevani like that. But, I have to admit..." I took a deep breath. I didn't like it, but if Artemis could show some sort of compromise, then I could too. "It does make a... terrible sort of sense. There's nobody in a better position to take advantage of us than Sevani."

She nodded. "It hurts, but it's true. I've been betrayed too many times not to question things like that."

I hesitated. "Did you mean what you said earlier?"

She gave me a quizzical look. "Which part?"

"About... people, in general. You said there's no such thing as family. Just people using each other."

Her face turned serious. "Yes."

"I call bullcrap." I shook my head. "I get that you have this whole ice-cold killer persona going on, but that just ain't true. Humans are a mess, but if we've got one redeeming quality, it's that we stick together."

She looked down at the floor, a sad smile twisting the corner of her mouth. "I wish I agreed with you. But the sad reality is that we only stick together so far as it's valuable to us. We stick together because it increases our chances of survival. That's all we want at the end of the day, like any other animal: to survive just one more day. To persist. To keep on existing. And we'll do *anything* to achieve that goal. No matter who we have to leave behind to do it."

I nodded slowly. The truth was that it made sense to me, in a gut-wrenchingly familiar sort of way. That was the way I had seen the world before I'd met Kessa. Before I'd met the people who made me think there might be more to life than just... *surviving*. But maybe Artemis was right. Maybe *I'd* been right.

Artemis turned and opened the door to leave. I held up a hand to stop her. "Wait," I said, wincing as the motion sent a lance of pain through my side. "Do you still think Sevani..."

She nodded crisply. "Until we know for certain who is pursuing us, I have no better alternative than to believe Sevani wants us dead. And so we will continue to act as if that is the case. Our conversation with her earlier left me unconvinced in either direction." She cocked her head. "Unless you have an argument to persuade me otherwise."

I thought about it and then shook my head. "I guess I don't."

Her eyes turned slightly curious. "What do *you* think?"

I didn't know what to think. I knew how I felt—angry, confused, lost. But it didn't seem like emotions like that would mean much to someone like Artemis, even after our little heart-to-heart. I shrugged. "I think we have a job to do."

Artemis gave a tight-lipped smile. "That's what I like to hear. It's a two-day trip from here to Brahma via the foldgate. Rest up, then come find me. We need to plan our next move."

She vanished around the corner. I let myself sag backward onto the bed. The machine had stopped pumping and the heart symbol had stopped flashing. I squeezed the end of the tube and disconnected it from my shoulder port with a hissing sound, then cleaned off the end of it with a disinfectant wipe and shoved it back into the MAMA. I could still feel the frig-icerin working in my system. I resisted the urge to try to coax more out of the device. I wasn't sure how much there was on the ship, and I didn't want to waste it. Most likely there wasn't much. What reason would Rose have for keeping around a bunch of compounds that only Vanguards could use?

After a few minutes of just lying there I sighed and sat up. I took a few minutes to inspect my wounds in the small, dirty mirror on the wall opposite the equipment and made sure that they were healing up right. The cuts on my chest were already just angry red scabs. The bullet hole and the cut along my side both looked like they could still break open again, so I wrapped some bandages around them. If nothing else, it would remind me not to move around too much. When I was satisfied, I picked up Nadus's shirt, decided against putting it back on, and tossed it into a disposal chute before pushing my way out of the medbay.

Nadus, Bentley, and Rid were walking down the corridor, peering into rooms. As Nadus saw me he raised an eyebrow and tossed me a fresh shirt. "Feeling better?"

"Yeah." I jerked my head into the medbay, shrugging into

the garment. "They've got a MAMA in there. And I've walked away from a lot worse."

"I'll say." An old smile flitted like a ghost across Nadus's face. "I remember when you took that round through the back at Reven. I thought you were a goner."

"Oh yeah. Went right through my guts." I chuckled. "Now, *that* sucked."

Nadus shook his head, slapping me on the shoulder as he passed me and poked his head into another room. Rid had already crossed the hall and was pushing open another door.

"I swear," Nadus said, "you must be the luckiest man in the universe."

I fought back a grimace. Nobody ever seemed to get tired of telling me that. "At least I never got my face torn off."

His face went grim, and he nodded slowly. I knew that we were both fighting back the same memories. Fallen rebels carpeting the ground. Screaming in the air as rippers poured over the walls and into our ranks.

Nadus shook his head grimly, glancing at Rid and jerking his head towards me. "If you think that he was a barbarian in that hallway back on Albeni 7, you should have seen him back in the day. Pumped full of ignicerin, strapped into a Jericho..." He gave me an odd look—an almost *scared* look. "Heck of a thing to see. I don't think rippers get scared, but if they did, this here is the guy they'd be afraid of."

I forced a chuckle. "That was a long time ago."

"I know." Nadus walked down the hall, opening another door. "I'm glad to see you can still kick some ass when the occasion calls for it. Quite the piece of art you made back there."

"I guess so," I said. "Here, I'll show you around."

I walked Rid and Nadus through the *Orpheus*'s three decks. The lower deck was primarily dedicated to cargo. As it sat now, it was a long, empty space. In a similar fashion to the docking bay of Albeni 7, the gravity generators for the cargo space were turned down to a lower setting than the rest of the ship to make moving supplies and goods easier.

"Back when I ran the ship, we had this area split into two," I said, pointing down the cargo space. "One half for storing our salvaged goods, and one part as an armory. That was where we'd suit up before we boarded a ship." I pointed towards the airlock at the far end of the cargo bay. "We modified the ship to make the airlock bigger so that we could board depressurized ships with more personnel at one time."

I led them back up to the middle deck. The majority of it was dedicated to living quarters—bunkrooms, a mess hall, the medbay, and a washroom. I saw Rose climbing down from the command deck, Shell coming down right behind her.

"You giving them the tour?" Rose asked.

"Figured I may as well," I said, looking back to Rose. "Gotta say, I'm surprised at how little has changed."

Rose gave a mischievous grin. "Oh, you ain't seen *nothing* yet. Follow me."

She walked ahead, Rid falling in next to her as she proudly rattled off facts about the ship. I let the rest of the group walk ahead. Shell lingered as well, studying me.

"You're a Roamer?" I said.

She looked at me sharply. I shrugged back. "Recognize the accent and tattoos. And I never knew anyone but a Roamer to carry a weapon like that."

Her scowl lightened. Slightly, at least. "You're dragging us into a bad situation."

"How much has Rose told you?"

"Not much. I don't think she knows much." Her eyes settled on the form of Rose walking next to Rid up ahead. "She just jumped at the chance to prove she can do what her mother used to do."

I nodded. "You're not wrong. On any of that. It is a bad situation. And if we had any other choice I'd have told Rose to stay well away from it. But you're both in it, now." I studied Shell as she walked beside me. "What are you, her bodyguard? Sevani pay you to keep her safe?"

"I'm her mechanic," Shell said flatly.

"Awful handy at fighting for a mechanic."

"Tell me about this job."

Well, so much for that line of conversation. I hesitated, trying to figure out how much to say. If Artemis was right about Sevani, Shell might be reporting everything she saw back to her.

"Salvage," I said finally. "Long-lost Paragon ship. Lots of rippers. Those are the broad strokes. We'll fill you guys in on the other details later."

At the mention of rippers, her face hardened. I bit back a grimace of my own. Not a soul in Paragon space had what could be called a *good* impression of rippers, but you could always tell when somebody had personal experience. I wondered if her homeship had been hit. But she didn't seem to be in a mood for talking, let alone digging into the darkest moments of her past, so I let her be.

I let my thoughts wander, and soon they were looping back to the matter of Sevani—and whether she'd just tried to have me killed. I was torn. Artemis seemed certain. But Sev had seemed genuinely surprised when I had told her about the attack. Or maybe she was just a better actor than I gave her credit for. After all, she'd been able to hide her family from us.

Rose came to a halt in front of a familiar door.

"Wait," I said. "That's my old..."

She just smiled and pushed the door open. I stood rooted where I was, breath stuck in my throat. Going in there seemed... wrong, somehow. It wouldn't be *our* room anymore. Not after all these years.

"After you," Rose said.

I forced myself to breathe, ducked my head under the too-small doorway and felt my eyes go wide as I stepped inside.

The bunkroom that Kessa and I had shared was exactly the same as we'd left it. An oversized bed stuffed awkwardly into the far corner of the small room, leaving just enough space for a bookshelf to be crammed between it and the opposite wall. A small desk and a drawer in the corner closest to the door, where Kessa had done her painting. And painted across the ceiling above the bed—a starry night, painted in broad, warm strokes of yellow and gold against a backdrop of swirling dark blue.

"When my mom gave me the ship, she said this was the only room I wasn't allowed to mess with," Rose said, rubbing at the back of her neck.

I looked back to the room, nodding slowly. I noticed now that there were several knick-knacks on top of Kessa's desk. A set of dice that had belonged to Liung. A puzzle cube that had belonged to Black. A dozen or so small objects that Sevani must have collected from their rooms.

"I think she kinda felt guilty," Rose said quietly.

I froze. "Guilty? Why?"

Rose shrugged. "Because she was the only survivor. That the rest of the crew died while she got to walk away with the ship and the batteries you guys salvaged." She hesitated. "I think she knows it wasn't her fault, but all the same, I don't think she ever forgave herself for what happened—for leaving you behind. I think this was kinda her shrine to you guys."

There was a soft thud as Rid fell backward onto my bed and spread his limbs out in every direction, grinning. "This room taken?" he asked.

I grabbed him by the shirt, and easily lifted him out of the bed, shoving him outside. "Very funny. Find your own damn room."

I turned to Rose, who was fighting an amused grin at Rid's antics. "Thank you," I said, jerking my head towards the room. "For this."

"You got it." Rose turned away, walking out of the room and beckoning for Rid and Nadus to follow.

Their footsteps retreated down the corridor. I shut the door and fell back onto the bed, just staring around me and... absorbing. Thinking. Reflecting.

I felt suddenly sick as I thought about what Sevani must have gone through after the *Panama*—going through all of our rooms, clearing out our junk, trying to contact any loved ones or family—not that most of us had many of those. I suddenly felt almost lucky that I'd gone straight to prison. I'd been forced to move on. I tried to imagine the wide, empty, bleak future Sevani must have faced. At least she'd had her family to fall back on.

Sevani hadn't betrayed me. I felt a sudden surge of resolution as my mind wrapped itself around the thought. The situation looked bad for her. And talking to Artemis, seeing the world from her cold, calculating perspective, had almost been enough to make me forget who we'd been. Kessa, and Sev, and me, and the rest of them. We'd been a family, and this had been our home. Maybe it was naïve of me. Maybe it was a mistake, and it was going to get me killed. But I decided then and there that I still trusted Sevani.

I looked up, staring into Kessa's starry night, and wondered about the old guy that had originally painted it. I wondered if he'd had any idea that thousands of years after he died, people would still be inspired by his work. And I thought about Kessa, standing there with paint on her face, looking down at me with that knowing smile.

*Home.* It felt good.

I fell gradually asleep beneath a swirl of warm yellow stars.

# SIXTEEN

## THE PANAMA



"Why stars?" I asked Kessa over a private channel.

"What?" She grunted in confusion as she took the ultracell from my hands, the painted night sky on her shoulder pauldrons shifting in the dim light as she moved. She turned and passed the cell to Black, who secured it in the cargo pod.

"Why stars?" I gave as close to a shrug as I could through my Jericho. "I mean, sure, they're pretty, but come on, we live on a spaceship. You can see the stars whenever you want."

"*Now?*" she said incredulously. "We're kinda in the middle of something."

"Sure." I carefully extracted another ultracell from its port in the auxiliary power station I was currently disassembling. The timer in my heads-up display indicated that we still had roughly twenty minutes before the arrival of the Paragon patrol Sevani had spotted. The incoming patrol was certainly a concern, but overall I had started feeling much more relaxed about the job. If there *had* somehow been rippers on the ship, they surely would have attacked us by now. "We can talk while we work."

"Fair enough." I could picture the contemplative tuck of the lower lip she always assumed when she was thinking something through. "A few reasons. First off is that this is based on Van Gogh's most famous work. But second is that back on Earth, before the Exodus, before people even knew what stars *were*— when they looked up at the stars, they saw beauty." She gestured vaguely towards a window we had passed that looked out into space. "Bright, burning points of beauty in the otherwise dark sky. I think that might be why Van Gogh liked this painting. His life was kinda miserable. But somehow, he found beauty."

She looked back at me and smiled through her visor as I handed her another ultracell. "I guess I chose this painting because I like that reminder to look for beauty in the darkness. To find the good things in the ugliness of life."

I opened my mouth to reply only to be cut off by Black's voice on the public comms. "We're cutting it awfully close."

"We'll be fine," I growled. So long as we were back on the *Orpheus* in fifteen minutes or so from now, we should be able to breach safely. Once we were in nullspace we'd be out of the Paragon's reach. And if all of that failed, I trusted Sevani's piloting abilities to evade the incoming fire. "Focus on the prize. We get out of here with all this, we'll never have to work another day in our lives."

"Wait." Kess's voice sounded alarmed. "Where's Rawlins?"

I paused. I'd been so engrossed in my work that I'd completely drowned out the kid's near constant chatter. Or had he even been talking?

"Damn kid," I muttered under my breath as I glanced down at my wrist computer, bringing up the map. Four dots showed Liung and his team still hard at work in the cargo bay. Three others showed Kess, Black and me in one of the ship's main corridors. And one solitary green dot indicated where Rawlins had wandered off to, farther down the main corridor and around a corner.

"Rawlins!" I snapped, pulling another ultracell free from the fixture I had been dislodging them from and handing it to Kess. "Get the hell back here. We don't have time for sightseeing."

"One sec," he replied. "There's something back here."

I frowned, looking up at Kess. Through the sheen of her transparent visor her face was creased with worry. "What do you mean?" she asked.

His voice was low and intrigued. "I don't know. It looks like —wait—"

Rawlins's voice didn't cut off so much as it transformed, twisting suddenly from words to an unintelligible shout. A burst of fear and adrenaline so visceral that it turned my blood cold and washed my mouth with the bitter taste of iron.

And then there was silence.

"*Rawlins!*" Kess yelled. "Rawlins! Do you copy?"

There was no response. I glanced down at the map. Rawlins's solitary green dot flashed red.

## SEVENTEEN

The *Orpheus*'s mess hall was much the same as I remembered it. Big enough to fit everybody in while still somehow feeling crowded. Stains of various colors marked the walls and floor here and there. It would have been easy to think of them as a sign of sloppiness, but I preferred to think of them as war wounds. Or medals of honor, worn proudly on a scarred veteran's chest. This mess hall had *earned* those stains.

I let out a comfortable sigh as I finished warming a bowl of oatmeal and sat down at one of the only slightly large enough tables. Dammit, why'd they thrown out my old chair? It was the only one I really fit in. Guess it *had* taken up a lot of space, though.

"Morning." Bentley yawned, walking into the mess hall. He was dressed in an off-white bathrobe decorated with bright green palm trees, a pair of fuzzy-looking, bright pink slippers, and from what I could tell, nothing else.

"Looks like you've made yourself comfortable," I said cautiously.

"Comfort," he said, walking to the fridge and pulling it

open, "is one of life's few great gifts, which should be exploited whenever possible."

Strange as Bentley was, I found myself in complete agreement with him. I shoveled a spoonful of oatmeal into my mouth. Damn, but it was good. Probably synthetic rather than naturally grown, but still—sprinkle some equally synthetic brown sugar on top, and you had a breakfast fit for a king. Probably. I had no idea what kings actually ate for breakfast. But I doubted it could be much better than this.

Bentley sat down across from me, tearing the wrapper off a chocolate-flavored protein bar. I studied him over my oatmeal as he dug into his breakfast.

"So, what's your story?" I asked eventually.

"Well," he said. "Once upon a time, a man and a woman had the unfortunate notion that they should bring a child into this world, and as a result of that notion, *I* entered existence, and have been stuck in that state ever since."

I raised an eyebrow.

He sighed. "I was a Paragon computer technician. Stationed at a shipyard in the Jackson system, doing security audits. I got a bit too... *comfortable* for my own good. Left my job under some unpleasant circumstances, just about managed to stay out of jail, and went off the grid. Been working as a freelance hacker ever since. Artemis reached out to me and offered me a job, and here I am."

"So you specialize in hacking Paragon computer systems?"

"I mean, I'll hack whatever." He shrugged. "But there's a lot of money in being able to hack Paragon systems in particular. And I'm uniquely qualified to do it."

"Security protocols haven't changed since you left, huh?"

"Oh, they have. But I have some inside sources that keep me updated."

"Nice." I found myself thinking back to Liung, the techie of my old crew. He'd have *loved* having an inside Paragon source.

Then I remembered the sounds he'd made when the rippers had gotten their claws into him. My food suddenly tasted bland, and I found my hand creeping towards my shoulder port.

"I always wanted to ask." Bentley waved his protein bar towards my shoulder port. "Those implants. Do they itch?"

I pulled my hand back. "Sometimes."

"Huh." He stretched, and I heard a cracking sound as his back rearranged itself. "I always wondered what it was like down there on the ground. I worked on the Vanguard oversight program for a little bit. Security. Making sure you poor bastards were safe from people hacking your receivers and frying your brains. I've gotta be honest, though, biotech has always scared me a little bit."

"Yeah?" It was hard to keep the disinterest out of my voice. Scared of biotech? Get in line. Nobody in their right mind *wanted* to have dozens of bits of machinery inserted into their body. Some of us just hadn't had a choice.

"Yeah." He rubbed the back of his neck, where my neck port was. "I remember falling down a research rabbit hole during the project. Divinity literally created a new *gland* for you guys. And to top it off, made it so they could control it remotely." He shuddered. "Freaky stuff."

I stared at him, a frown forming on my face more out of puzzlement than offense. "You're kind of a dick, huh?"

He gave a vaguely apologetic shrug. "Heard it once or twice before. Sorry. Far as I can tell, I'm built a little differently too. Genetics, not tech, though. The part of my brain that's supposed to care what people think never seems to have developed. I think that was what made me a good security auditor."

"Can't have been that good if the Paragon fired you."

He raised a finger. "I got *so* good at finding loopholes in their security systems that I couldn't help but utilize them to make a little extra profit. Paragon pay is piss-poor. No wonder there's such a problem with corruption. Their own fault, really. But it does mean a small bribe can go a long ways, so, you know. That's good, I guess." He leaned forward, voice lowered in a conspiratorial whisper. "We called bribes *charitable donations* in the security department, if you can believe it."

I could. I found it hard to care much, though. I looked up as Artemis walked into the room. She was wearing her usual outfit —a jacket and trousers that was the perfect blend of nondescript practicality and professionalism. She studied the mess room with a look of distaste, then gave a resigned sigh and moved to the fridge.

"Let me guess," I said. "You're wishing we'd gotten something fancier."

"Let's just say I'd rather we hadn't been forced to settle for the first bucket of bolts that came our way," she said, annoyance lining her voice.

Despite the fact that I hadn't seen the *Orpheus* in years, I found myself indignant at the comment. "The *Orpheus* is a bit on the old side," I admitted, "but she's perfect for what we need. Fast enough to outrun most Paragon ships and with enough stealth to slip through most of their blockades. Trust me, she'll do the job."

"We'll see," muttered Artemis, shutting the fridge. "We have *got* to get some fresh food once we hit Brahma."

"Speaking of Brahma," I said as she started mixing a bowl of oatmeal, "what's the plan when we get there?"

"We'll touch down outside of Gharseva," she said. "It's the oldest city on the planet. When the first colony ship arrived, almost a thousand years ago, that was where they set up base. Then we meet up with my contacts."

"Don't suppose you're gonna tell us who they are," I said.

"All in good time."

My knuckles tightened around my spoon in frustration. "Not sure how I'm supposed to plan a job like this when I don't know half the details," I said. "We'll be at Brahma in a few days. What's the point in delaying it until then?"

"You know all the details you need to know," Artemis said, her voice growing colder. "Your job is to get us onto that ship and off again. My contacts on Brahma will provide us with supplies and more personnel. You don't need to know who they are, and apparently we've already had at least one security breach in this operation, so I'm not feeling inclined to share more than is strictly necessary."

"We're in nullspace," I said. "Even if somebody aboard *wanted* to leak some intel, they couldn't. Not until we resurface."

Artemis sighed and set her spoon down. "Bentley, will you give us some privacy?"

Bentley gave an annoyed sigh and rose. "Fine. But you're doing my dishes."

When he was gone, Artemis raised her hands and started massaging her temples. "Do we have a problem, Mr. VanDunn?"

I grimaced, trying to decide how honest I should be. I hadn't expected her to confront me. I'd figured she would just brush me aside.

"Did Nadus ever tell you about what it's like being an active Vanguard?" A sneer of disgust curled my lip. "A puppet?"

She watched me closely. "No."

I took a deep breath as I opened the door to a piece of my brain I generally kept sealed tight, and tapped the back of my neck with one finger. "There's a device installed there, just at the base of the neck. Called a regulator. Command used it to keep track of us, monitor our vitals, all that. But it also let them control us. They could control our emotions. Rile us up when they needed us to attack, cool us down when the fight was over, with drugs called ignicerin and frigicerin."

I felt my hand drifting on its own up towards my shoulder

port, and I forced it down flat against the table to control it. "I remember spending entire weeks without sleep, some campaigns. Not knowing where we were going or why we were doing it. Just... a list of cities to burn, enemy positions to over-run. The minute you started to wear down, or to stop to think about what you were doing—all the innocent people you were killing—they'd just... press a button, and you'd get another hit of ignicerin, and pretty soon you were blasting away again. When the fight was over, same thing: pump up the frigicerin and cool us down.

"Eventually, when the war 'ended', I was lucky enough to be in one of the battalions Paragon disbanded as a show of peace. The first thing I did was get my regulator deactivated. And I made a promise to myself, then"—I looked up, meeting her eyes—"that I was never gonna be anyone's puppet, ever again."

I felt guilty saying those words, as Venter's grinning face swam through my vision. I'd broken that promise already, of course. Maybe this really was all I was destined to be. But what was it Eladrius had told me? *If you don't like the way you're headed, it's up to you to change the course.*

"So, yeah," I continued. "We do have a problem. Because I know your type. You're a puppet master. And I don't want to find myself dangling from your strings."

Artemis nodded slowly, drumming her fingers on the table in a thoughtful rhythm. Finally, she sighed. "Well, I suppose I can't blame you for that."

"Yeah." I muttered the word, my cold anger spent and replaced by a sense of sullen embarrassment.

Artemis studied me as if seeing me for the first time. "You are not at all what I expected."

I frowned. *That* didn't bode well. "What do you mean?"

"I mean that..." She hesitated, seeming to search for words. "I suppose I expected a second Nadus. Simple, straightforward, efficient, reliable. All the things a Vanguard is supposed to be. And you are those things. But there's more to you." She looked at me, and I once again got the distinct impression that she was cutting me apart with her eyes, dissecting me and trying to figure out what was going on behind my skull. "Nadus is hard-shelled. His pain is hidden, smothered beneath layer after layer of his psychology. But your pain..."—she reached forward and tapped a finger against my chest—"it's all out here. A gaping tear in your soul. For all your strength, you're... *delicate*."

I felt my throat tighten. The point of her finger felt like a scalpel. She kept on talking, though. Something in the lilt of her voice made me think she was talking more to herself than to me. "You didn't just lose your crew, your friends, your lover."

My heartbeat grew fast. I felt my breathing growing short and shallow, hissing through my clenching teeth. Kessa's face— smiling, trusting, happy—swam through my mind's eye.

"You lost *yourself*," Artemis said, her eyes lighting up in a sort of triumphant satisfaction. She prodded me with her finger again, poking me to emphasize each sentence. "You *died* on that ship. What's her name, Kessa, was—"

I snatched her wrist with a speed that shocked even me. Artemis's eyes widened slightly.

"We're done here," I growled, then let her go and stood up.

Artemis watched me go, her expression unreadable as ever. I shut the door behind me and stood in place for a moment, breathing heavily. I shut my eyes. Kess was still there, smiling. Why was she smiling? *WHY WAS SHE SMILING?*

"You alright?"

I looked up to see Rose walking down the corridor, with Shell trailing right behind her as always. Rose raised an eyebrow at me.

I forced a grin. "Yep. Just... thinking."

"Don't think too hard. You looked like you were about to

give yourself an aneurysm." She sidled past me, into the mess hall. Shell followed.

I found my hand inching up towards my shoulder port. A can. I could *really* use a can right now. Kessa's face was still there, and I knew what would happen next if I didn't escape.

I let my feet lead until I found myself in the medbay. The MAMA was right where I'd left it, sitting innocently on the counter. I picked it up, hefting it in my hands, considering. If I just hooked it up to my shoulder port it probably wouldn't register that I needed frigicerin. I glanced over my shoulder to make sure the door was shut, then pried open the compartment on the back of the device and inspected the inside. There were several small vials hooked up to the delivery device, each containing a different chemical. I studied them until I figured out which one was the frigicerin, then pried it loose.

I just needed a hit. Something to take the edge off.

EIGHTEEN

I woke up to a crackling sound as the intercom next to my bed came to life. *"Lax? You awake?"*

I frowned, leaned over, and pressed the *talk* button. "Yeah."

*"We're a few minutes from dropping out of nullspace,"* Rose's voice said. *"You said to let you know."*

"Thanks." I slid out of my bed and pulled on my clothes, then made my way towards the bridge.

I pulled myself up the hatch with a groan. Rid, Rose, and Shell were there too—Rose and Shell busy working the navigation while Rid stood behind them and watched.

"What're you doing up?" I asked him, settling into a seat.

His eyes flitted back and forth across the large window. I followed his gaze. Outside it was dark. Utterly, completely dark. But that's how it always is in nullspace. No flashing lights, no stars zipping past. Just... sheer nothingness. I had forgotten how eerie it could be.

"I want to see it," Rid said. "The foldgate."

"Well, you're about to," Rose said. She cleared her throat. "Ladies and gentlemen, the Karak Sector Foldgate."

The ship jolted slightly as it tore itself out of nullspace. The darkness vanished like a curtain being pulled abruptly away, and suddenly I could see the gate. Nestled among the stars, looking small and insignificant from this distance.

"Been a long time since I've seen one of those," I muttered.

"Let's get a closer look," Rose said. She manipulated the *Orpheus*'s controls, and the ship jolted as it thrusted forward.

The foldgate loomed before us, a massive ring of silver, blinking with various lights. Compared to it, the ships passing through looked almost tiny—massive Homer class cargo haulers looking like toys. Hell, I'd have bet that you could fit a dozen battlecruisers through that gate at once.

More remarkable than the gate itself, though, was what I could see looking through it—or, rather, what I couldn't. The foldgate was locked in orbit around a massive gas planet. Looking through the gate, however, I saw only darkness where the gas giant's vivid yellow surface should have been. As I focused, I could see distant stars through it. A slight chill ran down my spine, like it did every time I traveled through a foldgate. We were looking through to another solar system, thousands of lightyears away.

I glanced over at Rid. He had taken a step forward and was staring at the foldgate like it was something out of a dream.

"You ever seen one of those?" I asked him, settling down into a chair.

He shook his head. "Only in pictures."

"Not even when they took you to the tin can?"

He shrugged. "No windows."

"We're cleared for entrance," Rose said, looking up from her computer. "I'll line us up in the queue. Should be through in about twenty minutes."

I nodded, suddenly feeling nervous. "Keep an eye out for any..." I hesitated. "Suspicious activity."

Rose turned to me with a frown. "Like what?"

"Any ships that are getting too close to us." I sat down next to the scanner station and pulled up a holographic display mapping the ships around us. "Whoever sent those assassins on Albeni 7 might know what ship we're in, and this would be the perfect place for an ambush."

Rose nodded, turning back to the cockpit. "Got it."

I searched through the ships nearby. Most of them were cargo ships, mingled in with a few passenger vessels. Nothing that looked like a threat. Still—safe was a hell of a lot better than sorry. So I watched them like a hawk as the minutes ticked past and we drew closer to the foldgate.

"I see it!" Rid gasped.

I looked up sharply. "See what?"

He pointed. I followed his finger and realized that he wasn't talking about a ship. He was pointing through the foldgate. I could see a small blue and white orb through the gate, surrounded by blinking dots.

"What, the planet?" I said, equal parts relieved and annoyed.

"Yeah," Rid said. "Is that Brahma?"

Rose spoke up. "No. That up ahead is the Alpha Centauri system."

Rid frowned. "I thought we were going to the Brahma system?"

"We are." Rose never took her eyes off of the screen in front of her. "But it's more complicated than that. Each foldgate connects directly to just one other foldgate. Some of the foldgates are just built in gate systems, with a bunch of gates all close to each other to make it easier to get around."

"Alpha Centauri..." Rid's eyes widened even further, which I hadn't thought possible. "*We're going through the Alpha Centauri system?*"

Rose grinned. "That's right, pilgrim. Less than five measly lightyears from the birthplace of our species."

Rid's expression took on a sort of solemn reverence at the thought. I chuckled.

"You ever been to Earth, Lax?" Rose asked.

"Nope." I shook my head. "Centauri's the closest I've been." That could be said for most of humanity, I figured. At least, whatever chunk of humanity had ever been off whatever station or planet they'd been born on, which amounted to a tiny minority. The Alpha Centauri system was the densest gate system in the galaxy. Chances were that if you wanted to get somewhere, you'd have to go through Alpha Centauri to get there.

"And we're actually gonna go *down* to Brahma? When we get there, I mean?" Rid spoke the words with a sort of cautious optimism. Like a kid who had spotted some candy but wasn't sure it was meant for them.

"Yeah," I grunted. "That's right, I forgot. You've never been planetside, have you?"

He shook his head, turning back to fix his gaze on the foldgate. I found myself watching him with a dumb little smile on my face. I'd seen that side of him more and more the past few days. It was a hell of a thing, freedom. I turned my attention back to the holograph. Everything still looked good.

Finally, it was our turn. I felt my hair stand on end as we approached the foldgate. Up close it looked even bigger—an impossibly large arc wrapping all around us. I craned my head to get a better look at the inner surface of the gate. It was lined with thousands of emitters emitting... something. I'm not a scientist. I don't know how it all works. But looking up there at the inside of the gate I could see where the light seemed... bent. As if the fabric of reality was being stretched and warped.

"Here we go, folks," Rose said. "Get ready to say goodbye to the Albeni sector."

She nudged the ship forward, and we passed through the gate. There was no flash of light, no rush of sound. The only sensation I felt was a slight moment of—I don't know how to describe it. Vertigo? No—more than that. It felt like, for just a moment, I was in two places at once, and I wasn't sure which one of them was real and which was a dream.

Rid swayed on his feet, blinking and looking queasy. Rose was grinning like a kid on an amusement park ride. Shell sat stone-faced, only a glint of amusement in her eye as she watched Rid struggle.

But then the moment was over, and we were in the Alpha Centauri system.

Space is big and empty enough that you generally don't have to worry about coming across other travelers. Kids love stories about harrowing encounters with deep-space pirates and the like, but the truth is that unless you're very close to a planet or station, you're not likely to run into anything at all.

The Alpha Centauri system, however, took that generalization and smashed it into a billion tiny pieces. Here, the usual deadness of space was alive, thrumming with activity and energy. Ships of all shapes and sizes drifted together in carefully controlled lanes from one foldgate to another, carrying cargo and passengers across the galaxy. Paragon gunships patrolled the lanes, enforcing order. Glancing at Rose's screen I saw a flood of information coursing across it, relaying data about nearby ship trajectories, public messages being broadcasted from the traffic control stations, and various other miscellanea.

Rid leaned forward, standing on his toes to get as close to the window as possible as he pointed through it. "What's that over there?"

It took only a few seconds to see what he was talking about. Two massive ships were passing near us, surrounded by an escort of dozens of smaller vessels. The first ship was smaller than the second, coated black and silver. If not for the light sources of the thousands of other ships it would have been completely invisible. I squinted to make out the logo on its side.

A circle containing two hands on opposite sides, with index fingers outstretched and just about to touch each other. Apparently it was a reference to some old earth painting. That was what Kessa had told me, at least.

"*Divinity Technologies,*" I muttered.

"Why are there so many Paragon ships with them?" Rid asked. "Are they being boarded or something?"

"It's an escort," I said idly. I glanced over at Rid. He still seemed confused, so I continued. "Divinity is the company that produces rippers and Vanguards. Most importantly, though, they're also the only ones in the galaxy who know how to make ultracells which means they have a monopoly on superluminal travel. And they have a deal with the Paragon."

"One reason why the Paragon is so powerful," Artemis's voice said. I glanced over my shoulder to see her climbing up the hatch. She'd been acting differently around me since our last conversation. Avoiding me, I thought.

Rid spoke again. "Why doesn't the Paragon just... attack them and take them over? Seems like that's what they do to everyone else."

"I'm sure the Paragon would love that," I said, "but they say the Divinity factories are all hidden in deep space."

"Then what are the stations they have all over?" Rose asked. "Every system I've ever been to, you can find a few big, mysterious Divinity tech stations nobody is allowed near."

"Research," Artemis said as she sat down. "The first thing that happened after each system was conquered during the war was a series of quickly deployed Divinity satellites, followed by several larger stations. Nobody's quite sure what they do. But they're not factories. Not that it matters—the Paragon would never move against Divinity. If anything, they work for Divinity more than Divinity works for them."

I frowned. "The hell is that supposed to mean?"

"It means that the Paragon is really closer to a bundle of

corporations masquerading as a government than it is an actual nation," Artemis said idly, pulling out her handcomputer and checking it. "Once you strip aside the patriotic, fascistic façade from Paragon propaganda, you'll see that almost all of their military operations and laws are driven by protecting corporate interests. *Especially* when it comes to Divinity."

I nodded slowly as I remembered the sight of the group of Divinity representatives on Brahma during the unification ceremony. Their fancy suits and their utter disregard for the destruction around them. I guess a few million lives lost or ruined was a small price to pay to control all of humanity.

The Divinity ship drifted past, and the second large ship loomed above us. This one was bigger. Far, far bigger. Still tiny in comparison to the foldgates, but a damn sight larger than any spaceship had any right to be. The shape was familiar: long and rectangular, with jagged edges making it look almost knife-like from this angle.

"Battlecruiser," I said.

The room fell silent as we watched the battlecruiser loom larger, and then smaller as it moved in the opposite direction to us. There was something unsettling about looking at it. Talking about boarding the *Revelation* from the safety of our room on the *Jonah*, studying the schematics, had been one thing. Actually seeing the scale of it, though, was another entirely.

Rose finally broke the silence with a low whistle. "That's a lot of spaceship."

I'd convinced Artemis to give Rose and Shell the full rundown of our endeavors earlier, so we were all thinking the same thing.

I glanced over at Artemis. She was studying the battlecruiser intently, her expression grimly determined.

"Yeah. It is," she finally said. "Rose, how long until we touch down on Brahma?"

Rose glanced at her computer. "Roughly six hours. Still gotta make it through the Brahma system foldgate."

Artemis gave a nod, turned, and descended the hatch. I lingered for a few moments before I followed, staring at the blinking lights that marked the battlecruiser as it passed through a foldgate and to some distant solar system.

"A *lot* of ship," I muttered to myself again, then turned away.

# NINETEEN

*"Touching down in just a few minutes. Find something to hold on to."*

The intercom on the ceiling of my room clicked off and Rose's voice silenced. The *Orpheus* rattled with turbulence as it tore through the skies of Brahma—a strange sensation after the long stillness of nullspace travel. I double-checked to make sure that all of my belongings were secured.

*Planetside.* It was impossible not to be excited. I'd breathed nothing but recycled air for well over eight years. To soak in real sunshine, breathe real air, feel real wind in my hair... well, I still didn't have much hair, thanks to prison sanitation standards, but, still. You get the idea.

Somebody knocked on the door. "Open," I said.

Artemis entered, shutting the door behind her. "Got a minute?"

"Sure."

The *Orpheus* jumped slightly as it cut through a particularly robust gust of wind. Artemis steadied herself with a hand on the wall.

"When we touch down," she said, "you'll come with me."

"To where?"

"To meet our contacts."

I raised an eyebrow. "Don't suppose I get to know who they are yet?"

Her mouth drew into a line. "I suppose there's no point in delaying it any further. You won't like it."

"I don't have to like it," I said. "I just want to *know* it."

"Our partner on this job," she said, "is the Brahmian Independence League."

That stirred a memory. The news footage I'd seen in prison, of a bombing. The news studio had claimed it was the work of the Brahmian Independence League, but I'd learned a long time ago to take anything reported over public news channels with a hefty dose of skepticism. Still, the news that we'd be working with a known group of rebels—or terrorists, depending on who you asked—got me to raise an eyebrow.

"You see why discretion is of the utmost importance," Artemis said. "They're under quite a bit of pressure at the moment, so if they suspect that working with us could compromise them, they'll be... *unhappy*."

My eyebrow inched even higher as I recalled the footage of body bags in the streets. "As in, 'deal's off' unhappy, or 'dump their bodies in an incinerator' unhappy? They don't exactly have a reputation for pacifism."

"I have a good relationship with them," Artemis said. "So long as we—and by we, I mean *you*, just to be clear—don't do anything abundantly stupid, we should walk in and out thoroughly un-incinerated."

I couldn't help but think back to the war. The havoc we'd unleashed on their peaceful cities. Beautiful rolling green hills turned into muddy scarlet killing fields. Meticulously crafted stone buildings blasted to rubble. Streets slick with blood as rippers gorged themselves on fleeing civilians. Hell, if I was in the rebel's shoes I wouldn't be in any kind of mood for pacifism, either. I did wonder, however, what the rebels wanted with the *Revelation.*

"What's their stake in this?" I asked.

"That's their concern," Artemis said.

I gave her a pointed look. "You one of them?"

"No. I'm an independent contractor." She stared back at me, face as unreadable as ever. "Would it be a problem if I was?"

"Not necessarily. But I spent a good chunk of my life fighting other people's wars. If I'm getting dragged back into that, I'd at least like to know."

"You're not getting dragged into anything," Artemis said. "We do this one job, you get paid, and you're free to sulk off to whatever quiet corner of space you want."

I thought about it for a moment, then gave a brisk nod. "Alright."

She cocked her head slightly. "I imagined you'd be more... *disgruntled* by working alongside your former enemies."

I shrugged. "I'm a Vanguard. Just about everyone is my former enemy. You get used to it. Real question is, are they gonna be willing to work with me?"

Artemis gave a shrug of her own. "They'll have to. I could have found a different, less morally offensive salvage specialist, but Nadus insists that you're the only one who can make this job work. They'll understand that, even if they don't like it. They've learned to be... *flexible* the past few years."

"Alright, then. Thanks for telling me." I looked around at my room. "Guess that means I better get packed."

She looked around, and then up at the ceiling, as if noticing Kessa's old décor for the first time. "This place is... *quaint.*"

"Yeah." I reached under my bed, feeling around beneath it for my old backpack. After a few moments of groping, I felt my hands close around it and drew it out. It was a simple daypack, but it had some basic emergency medical supplies, some food, a small box of liquid ammo. "Not what you expected?"

"Not quite. I expected something a bit more... utilitarian."

I turned to the wall next to my bed and ran my hand over it until I found a slight indentation. I held my thumb over the catch. A moment later there was a slight clicking sound and a small section of the wall swung open, revealing a compact but hidden safe.

"Oh, there's plenty of utility," I said.

The contents of the safe didn't look like much, but it was all valuable in one way or another. A few credit chips, legal tender just about everywhere you could go, even if you didn't have a secure connection to a banking system. A pocket watch with an engraving of a spacecraft on it—an old hand-me-down from Kessa's grandpa, if I recalled correctly. A few photographs of Kessa and me, along with a charcoal drawing she'd made of the two of us.

I left all of that alone, though, and felt a grin spreading across my face as my fingers closed around the object of my search. I withdrew it.

Artemis raised an eyebrow. "What is *that* monstrosity?"

"Slugthrower. Blackstar Technology's *Peacebreaker* LPP-36," I said, feeling a rush of embarrassingly boyish excitement as I hefted the familiar weight of my old handcannon for her to see. It didn't look like any regular pistol. It was bigger, for one thing, with an oversized grip that made it fit perfectly in my oversized hands and a girth that made other handguns look like squirt guns. The magazine was attached to the bottom of the barrel rather than the grip, making it look unwieldy and front-heavy.

Artemis raised an eyebrow. "It doesn't look like a particularly... *elegant* weapon."

"I'm not an elegant person." I pressed the magazine release and slid the clip out, hefting it in my hands. A small green light blinked back up at me, indicating it was full. I slid it back in, and it connected home with a satisfying metallic ring. "Shoots hardened liquid metal rounds." I fingered a dial near the trigger. "This dial lets you modify the density. Softer for more stopping power, harder for more penetration."

"You know we're planning on working *with* the rebels, right? Not shooting them?"

"Well, sure." I found Peacebreaker's holster and clipped it to my belt, then shoved the weapon home and pulled my jacket over it. "But, hey. Plans change."


The cargo bay doors groaned open. I stepped out, and for the first time in over eight years, felt fresh air in my lungs and real sunshine on my face.

Damn, but it felt good.

I took in a deep breath and let it out with a contented sigh. Rose had put the *Orpheus* down in a large starport. There were a few other ships around us, all of them smaller craft capable of both atmospheric flight and interstellar travel, like the *Orpheus*. Most of them were in the process of either loading or unloading cargo. The air was heavy with the sound of whirring mechanisms, igniting engines, and shouting voices. Rose had already started exchanging words with a port technician, who spoke in a thick accent I'd never heard before.

Beyond the confines of the starport, I could see the peaks of several jagged mountains, covered by a thick blanket of lush green foliage. Much more... *alive* looking than the last time I'd been here. I searched my brain, trying to remember what details I could about Brahma's history from our pre-invasion briefings. I knew that it had been one of the last planets to be colonized during the Exodus, long before the birth of the Paragon. Before quantum communication allowed mankind to speak across the endless void, and before the foldgates had shrunk the galaxy from unfathomably huge to just inconveniently massive.

I tried to imagine what it must have been like—dropping out of nullspace into orbit around Brahma, knowing that the rest of humanity was utterly out of your reach. That it was up to you and your fellow passengers to reinvent society in whatever manner you deemed fit. I wondered if Brahma had been fully habitable when the colony ship arrived, or if they had been forced to terraform it.

Artemis came down the ramp, pausing beside me as she sucked fresh air—well, *starport* fresh air—deep into her lungs.

"Feels good, doesn't it?" I said, more quietly.

"Yes," she said, closing her eyes. A smile—an actual, happy smile, not her usual cynical smirk—flitted across her face for an almost imperceptibly short moment.

Then it was gone. Her eyes snapped open.

"I'm wearing this dress to blend in," she said, all business. "And to make the right impression to our contacts. I'd have tried to find something for you but frankly you'll stick out even more if you dress like a native. Just stick close to me, and if anyone presses us, I'm a Brahmian national who has been living off planet returning to visit friends, and you are my bodyguard. Understood?"

"Yep." I glanced down at my own outfit—a light jacket that covered my weapon, a faded shirt, and worn trousers, all taken from my old wardrobe. Even if she had been able to find more native-style clothing, she'd never have anything that fit me anyways.

Rid came down the ramp. He paused just before he stepped off the boarding ramp, one foot dangling over the concrete of the starport landing bay. As if he worried that the planet might open a gaping maw and swallow him up if he stepped onto it with too much confidence. Finally, he took a deep breath and plunged forward, almost wincing as he stepped onto the ground.

I gave him a grin. "Welcome to Brahma, kid."

Rid took a few more cautious steps forward, looking around and then up with a look of undeniable terror. I followed his gaze up into the wide, open sky, and chuckled. "Pretty damn big, huh?"

He gulped.

"Stay here with everyone else," I said. "You'll get your chance to explore soon enough, if you want it. Help Rose and Shell get the ship restocked. Make yourself useful. We'll be back soon."

He nodded, seemingly grateful for an excuse to shuttle back into the ship.

I turned back to Artemis. "Shall we?"


Gharseva was unlike any other city I'd ever been to before. Where most cities, at least on Paragon-ruled worlds, focused on rugged, unremarkable utility, each building here was an intricately crafted work of art, built from light brown stones, layered with vine-covered balconies and decorated with ornately engraved designs. Some seemed to be shops, others restaurants. Vendors patrolled the streets, offering various wares. Not so much as a bullet hole in a wall remained to hint at the horrors that had torn through this city not so many years ago.

I scanned the crowds as I trudged along. We hadn't been attacked at the foldgate, but I wasn't convinced we were out of the woods yet. Whoever had wanted us dead wasn't likely to give up after one failed attempt. I inspected every vendor, every traveler, every shopper that came close to our group, tracking their eyes and watching their hands. Both of us got stared at, though for very obviously different reasons. I made a mental note to keep my guard up. Vanguards were despised most places, but here—on a planet that had been so brutalized by the Paragon—I was willing to guess that it went far beyond that. So far as they were concerned, I wasn't a person. I was a monster, every bit as bad as the rippers, who was responsible for every bad thing that had happened to their home since the invasion. Truth be told, I didn't blame them for feeling that way. I probably would too if our places were swapped.

"The city's not looking too bad," I said to Artemis. "Beautiful, actually."

She gave a scoff. "We'll see. This is where the money is—the façade of normality the Paragon slapped over the wounds they left behind."

I nodded. Made sense. The reconstruction efforts had started as soon as the city was deemed reasonably safe. What was the point of conquering a booming, verdant planet if you couldn't benefit from taxing its economy, after all?

"Where exactly are we meeting these contacts?" I asked quietly.

"In a safe place," Artemis said. "There are eyes—and ears—everywhere up here."

At her words, I noticed a cluster of enforcers clad in black tactical armor standing on a street corner. They had stopped an agitated young man and were searching through his backpack.

"Rebel activity has been on the rise," Artemis muttered to me as we passed the scene by. "Riots. Bombings. Sabotage. Enforcers are more vigilant than ever."

I nodded, recalling the footage I'd seen in prison. For the most part the Paragon let the locals handle law enforcement. The fact that there were so many enforcers on duty meant the Paragon was worried. They wanted to make a show of strength. Remind the Brahmians who was in charge. If things got to open combat, as they had on a few other worlds, then they'd deploy Vanguards.

If that didn't work, there were always the rippers. So far as I knew, no rippers had been deployed since—well, since the last time I was here.

"Recognize any of this?" Artemis asked me.

I shook my head. "These buildings were mostly rubble last time I was here."

We rounded a corner. "How about this?" Artemis asked again.

I looked around. We were in a large, open plaza. It was paved with pale white stone tiles. A large, modern-looking building made of massive glass windows and steel beams glinting in the sun stood imperiously at the far end, marked by a large sign that read *Offices of the Governor*. A large fountain gushed in the center. There was a statue in the center of it, featuring two men and two women standing together in a circle and clutching hands, their stony faces staring outward at the plaza. A ring of glowing words around the base of the fountain read *To those who gave their lives, that we might live forever Unified.*

Yes. I did remember this place. I remembered standing right over... *there.* With Nadus by my side, clad in gleaming Jericho armor, standing among the unbeatable ranks of the Vanguard as the Paragon declared its final victory. I remembered seeing the battered, defeated Brahmians and the bored Divinity representatives. I remembered listening to the prime speaker as he released my battalion from duty. It all felt like a different life.

"Yes," I said softly. "I do."


With each step deeper into the city more memories arose like ghosts from forgotten graves, haunting me. The farther away from the wealthy city center we got, the more scars of the war we found. The well-dressed foot traffic was replaced by increasingly worn and dejected-looking locals. Where before vendors had laid claim to the street corners, offering their wares, now beggars sat in huddled blankets, holding out empty bowls. A group of sullen-looking youths sitting on the steps of a crumbling building watched us hungrily but made no motion to follow. I kept an eye on our rear just in case.

Near the starport, the buildings had all been pristine. Here, they were lucky to be standing. Several buildings that must once have been beautiful residences were now piles of rubble, seemingly untouched since the invasion. A slight chill ran down my spine as I noticed several deep grooves in the walls of an abandoned structure that seemed to have been a bank. Ripper claw marks.

Eventually Artemis led the way into an abandoned old church. We walked silently through a room full of barely conscious drug addicts and into a musty cellar, where—with the help of a flashlight—we found a hidden door with a keypad. Artemis input a sequence and the door clicked open.

"Watch your head," she said as she walked through the doorway and into a spiral staircase.

I did—for a long time. The stairs wound their way down through the earth for several minutes' worth of cramped walking before ending in a long, narrow tunnel.

"How old is this place?" I muttered as I followed Artemis downward.

"Old," she said. "It's part of a network of tunnels that spans the entire city. They say smugglers built them, well before Brahma re-established contact with Earth. But they've been used for a dozen different purposes over the years. During the war people took refuge from the rippers down here... until the rippers found their way in, at least."

I instinctively put a hand on Peacebreaker. "Any still down here?"

"I doubt it. Not this section, at least. Rebels use it frequently." She turned a corner that led into a larger open area.

I scoffed as I followed her. "Doesn't mean that—"

Somebody moved beside me. I saw a glint of steel as a rifle barrel was lifted towards my head. Moving instinctively, I grabbed the barrel of the gun and jerked it away from me. There was a grunt as somebody fell to the floor. I whipped the rifle around, aiming it down at my ambusher and pinning him to the ground with one foot.

"*Hold it!*"

I looked up. A dozen people dressed in light tactical gear surrounded us, holding up weapons—most of which were pointed at me.

Artemis raised her hands slowly. "Good to see you too, Tekka."

One of the men lowered his weapon and stepped forward, pulling down a mask that had been concealing his face. He looked to be about my age, with tall features, grizzled salt-and-pepper hair, and piercing green eyes.

"Artemis," he said, voice wary rather than welcoming. "I'm hoping there's a good reason you've got a damn puppet with you."

"Have you ever known me to do anything without a good reason?"

"You always say your reasons are your own, or some mysterious crap like that."

That did sound like her. I didn't move, keeping the barrel of my stolen gun aimed at the face of the young man sprawled on the floor beneath me. He stared up at me with wide, shocked eyes.

"He's my salvage specialist," Artemis said, sounding irritated. "He's as experienced a vulture as you can find. We need him."

"We're used to working without things we need," Tekka said. "Question is if we can *trust* him."

"Don't insult me, Tekka." Artemis sighed and turned towards me. "Lax. Put the gun down."

I hesitated, locking eyes with my hostage. His terror had crystalized into cold, steady hate as he looked up at me.

"Pretty please?" Artemis asked.

I gritted my teeth—last time I'd let go of a hostage when somebody had a gun pointed at me I'd nearly been killed—but I finally stepped back and dropped the rifle into the disarmed rebel's lap. He scrambled away from me, swatting aside an outreaching hand from one of his buddies and climbing to his feet himself.

The other guns didn't lower.

Artemis gave an exasperated sigh. "Oh, come now. He put his down. Play fair."

Tekka gave a reluctant nod, and one by one, his troopers lowered their weapons.

"Well, then," Artemis said, injecting a false cheeriness into her voice. "With all that unpleasantness behind us: Tekka, meet Lax. He's a vulture and he works for me. Lax, meet Tekka. He's a captain of the Brahmian Independence Forces and he and his men have bravely volunteered to board the *Revelation* with us."

I folded my arms, staring at Tekka. He grimaced back at me, then turned to Artemis. "They're not gonna like this."

"They're grown-ups," Artemis said calmly. "They can handle it."

"*I* don't like this," Tekka said.

"You're the one who's always saying that the current strategy isn't working," Artemis replied. "That new, unorthodox methods are needed. This is what *unorthodox* looks like."

Tekka glanced back at me one more time, his face twisted sourly, then nodded. "Fine. We're blindfolding him, though. Non-negotiable."

"Negotiate with *him*," Artemis said.

All eyes turned to me.

I sighed. Any kind of dignity I'd ever possessed had rotted away in prison a long time ago. "You got a scarf or something?"

. . .

Somebody tore the makeshift blindfold away. I blinked as light flooded my eyes. How far had we traveled? After letting them blindfold me we'd walked for some time before getting in some kind of vehicle. Then we'd disembarked and climbed into an elevator before arriving here... wherever here was. They'd let Artemis in alone for a few minutes before allowing me to proceed. The whole journey had been filled with a tense, awkward silence. The few times one of the rebels had started to say something, Tekka had shut them up fast.

I took a few moments to orient myself, squinting around. To be honest, I'm not entirely sure what I'd expected. Something dark and utilitarian, perhaps, full of desperate-looking people and cobbled-together weaponry. What I saw before me now, however, was about as far from that as it was possible to get. I was standing in a large, ornate, sunlit room. The walls were made of dark wood paneling, supported by vine-covered pillars. A large window was built into the wall opposite me, looking out over the city of Gharseva and allowing sunlight to pour in. A long, oval-shaped table sat in the middle of the room, covered with various breads, jams, fruits, and vegetables.

There were three people sitting at the table. The first two were clearly Brahmians. They were a man and a woman, both looking to be at least in their sixties, dressed in fine but simple clothes. They were sitting on the opposite side of the table from me. The last one was Artemis, sitting with her back to me. She was eating. And smiling.

And *laughing*.

The mirth on her face was so alien that it took me a moment to recognize her. I glanced around me, checking if I was the focus of some sort of practical joke. Tekka and the kid I'd taken hostage in the tunnel were the only rebels left in the room with us, both of them standing a meter or so behind me.

Artemis waved me forward, laughter fading away. "Sit down, Lax. This is Restell Khendar and his wife, Nalis. Restell and Nalis, this is Lackan VanDunn, the man I've hired to lead the job."

Restell studied me disapprovingly. "You always did have a penchant for strays, Artemis."

Artemis shrugged. "I suppose so. Or maybe I just care more about getting the job done than how it gets done."

I looked from Artemis to the Khendars, frowning. "So you guys... know each other?"

Artemis gave a smile—an actual smile, brimming with warmth, rather than her usual thin-lipped smirk—at the Khendars. "Oh yes. The Khendars are great... *benefactors* of the cause of Brahmian Independence. They've agreed to help us."

I ignored the fact that Artemis hadn't actually answered the question. Instead I found myself focused on the couple sitting across the table from me. *Benefactors.* Judging by Artemis's penchant for guarded language, that probably meant these two were in charge of the Brahmian rebels, or at least very high up in the chain of command. If anyone else had told me that these two kindly looking gentlefolk were responsible for an organization that was actively waging a bloody guerrilla campaign, I'd have laughed at them. But Artemis wasn't one to joke, and the looks the couple were giving me now were anything *but* kind.

I felt a chill creep along my spine. These people were dangerous.

Tekka took a cautious step forward. "Maybe we shouldn't speak so openly with"—he glanced at me—"*that* in our midst."

Artemis waved a dismissive hand. "He has no loyalty to the Paragon. He's an independent contractor, like me." She gave me a meaningful look. "And if he's going to help us, he should know everything he needs to."

"Yes," Nalis said. "Except that you work independently in order to protect those you care about. Whereas I suspect that this... *individual* works independently because there is nobody he cares about."

Something about the way she pronounced the word *individual* seemed to suggest that she had a different word in mind she was far too polite to say. I opened my mouth to speak, but Artemis spoke up first. Which was probably a good thing, seeing as my manners were stretched about as thin as could be by then.

"I trust him," she said firmly. "That should be everything you need to know about him."

Restell and Nalis shared a glance. Restell shrugged and waved me closer. I slowly lowered myself into a seat next to Artemis.

"You too, Tekka," Restell said. "We've much to discuss."

Tekka sat down at the head of the table to my left, carefully not making eye contact with me.

Artemis leaned next to me. "You wanted to know all the details? Well, here you go."

I just nodded. Obviously, there was a lot going on here I didn't know about—these people were clearly more than just *connections*. But even more obviously, nobody here except *maybe* Artemis was very happy about my presence. So I kept my mouth shut and listened as Nalis began speaking.

"Based upon your prior messages," she said, "the situation has become more complex."

Artemis nodded. "We've had some positive developments— and some complications. I now have a ship, crew, more intel, and a salvage expert." She nodded towards me. "The complication is that somebody seems to be onto us. We were attacked by hired assassins on Albeni 7."

Restell gave a heavy sigh, shaking his head. "Already this plan spirals out of our control."

Nalis placed a hand on his arm. "You're *certain* that they were after you specifically?"

"They had each of us identified by photograph," I said. "It was a co-ordinated attack. Paid for by somebody called the Penitent."

The Khendars shared a questioning glance. Restell shrugged. "I've never heard of any *Penitent*."

"Regardless," Artemis said, "The plan stays the same. We have the ship. We have the personnel. Now we simply need the equipment, the training, and the intel."

Restell gave me a sourly skeptical look. "You're the salvage expert, are you?"

I stuttered, searching for words. My mouth tasted dry and my skin crawled with discomfort. I'd spent most of my life trying to stay as far away from powerful people as possible. When Artemis had said we'd be working with rebels I'd assumed that meant covert meetings with people like Tekka. Not... whatever *this* was. I was used to working with people who said what they meant. Here, it seemed like every word had a dozen layers of hidden meaning I was too slow to catch on to.

"Ran over a hundred successful salvage ops," I finally managed. "Most of which involved rippers." I resisted a sudden impulse to add *sir*.

Tekka grunted. "We don't need a damn puppet to tell us how to deal with rippers. We've been cleaning them up ever since your kind left sixteen years ago. We've got plenty of experience on our own."

Well, at least one person here said what was on their mind.

"Not in these kinds of numbers you don't," Artemis said. "Nobody does. This job won't be like anything attempted before. But if there's someone who can pull it off, it's Lax."

I found myself straightening slightly with the words of confidence. Even if she was just acting, Artemis said the words with so much authority that I couldn't help believe them. Artemis was just full of surprises today.

The Khendars, however, didn't seem convinced. Restell

sighed and looked away. Nalis, however, studied me intently, eyes cold. "So, then, Mr. VanDunn," she said. "In your *expert* opinion, how should this job be done?"

I glanced over at Artemis, but she simply nodded at me. I straightened, trying to act as professional as she'd made me sound. "Well, like Artemis mentioned," I said, "first step is getting our gear and getting trained. We'll need exos, ordnance, guns, and ammunition. After that I'll need some time training everyone."

"How much time?" Restell asked.

"Much as we've got." I glanced at Artemis. "Which I'm thinking ain't much."

"The data currently available suggests that the *Revelation*'s journey will end in approximately six standard earth weeks," she said. "So that'll have to be enough."

"Once we're feeling confident we'll need to go get that black box," I said. "And then we just need to pray like hell that the *Revelation* is dropping somewhere we can reach in time. If it just shot straight out into deep space, away from any foldgates" —I shrugged—"then we're screwed no matter what we do. It's been going for sixteen years."

"Maybe that would be for the best," Restell muttered.

"It won't be out of reach," Artemis said. "I'm certain of it."

Nalis gave her a searching look. Almost the same way a parent studies a child caught in a lie. "Certain because of research, or because of..."

"I've independently corroborated it," Artemis said stiffly.

"And you're sure you want to go to the *Guardian*?" Nalis pressed.

Artemis fought back what seemed to be a grimace, but nodded. "It's essential. All the data we need to find the *Revelation* is there. Once we have the box, we'll be ready to go. And even if we get the box and find out that the *Revelation* is a lost cause, recovering all of the equipment and data aboard the

*Guardian* will be invaluable. And potentially lucrative," she added to me.

Nalis studied Artemis carefully—skeptically, almost. I frowned as I found myself recognizing the look. The same look Nadus gave me whenever I tried to convince him that I was alright. That I *wasn't* constantly pushing away memories of Kessa's last smile. That I wasn't perpetually yearning for a can to dull the pain of old wounds still bleeding.

Clearly, Artemis knew the Khendars in a deep, personal way. More than professional associates. Nadus's words flitted through my mind. *Her secrets have secrets.*

"For the sake of argument," Nalis said, "let's assume that you do successfully locate the *Revelation*. And that you manage to find what you're looking for without being killed. What comes next?"

Artemis glanced at me. I raised an eyebrow. I was curious about that myself. Clearly I wasn't the only one who *didn't* know what intel Artemis was hoping to find on that ship.

"Then," Artemis said, looking back to the Khendars, "we take whatever we find. And we use it."

Restell held Artemis's gaze for a long moment before nodding slowly and settling back in his seat. "I still think this is an exercise in futility. But it's your choice. And on the slim chance that it does prove fruitful I'm willing to hold to our previous agreement. We'll connect you with local arms dealers, provide the data you need to find the black box, and provide a squad of volunteers to fill out your ranks." He turned to Tekka. "You understand the risks that will be undertaken, Tekka. Do you still wish to do this?"

Tekka eyed me, then nodded. "We'll need to have at least one loyal Brahmian on this mission."

I noticed Artemis frown slightly at those words. She nodded, though. "Very well. Then let us proceed."

. . .

I couldn't help but breathe a sigh of relief as we left the Khendars' estate behind us. Rebel soldiers escorted us through the tunnels back to the same abandoned church we'd entered through, leaving us to make our own way back to the starport. My head was spinning with so many questions that it took me a few minutes to decide where to start.

"How do you know the Khendars?" I asked.

She walked on in silence until I figured she either hadn't heard me or was just ignoring the question. When she did reply, it was in a quiet voice. "Old family friends," she said.

I nodded slowly. Made sense, seeing how familiar they'd been. "So you're from Brahma?"

"My parents were both immigrants," she said. "They relocated here after their homeworld fell to the Paragon."

"Ah. Are they—"

"Any of your concern?" she interrupted. "No."

That shut me up. After a few moments of sullen silence, Artemis sighed. "I'm sorry. I don't like talking about... any of this, really. All you need to know is that my parents knew the Khendars. My father is dead and my mother is not a part of my life."

I nodded, letting it go. If there was one thing I understood, it was not wanting to talk about a painful past. "What about the Khendars? Who *are* they, exactly?"

"They own the largest mining corporation in the Brahma system," Artemis said, seeming relieved not to be talking about herself. "They're loyal Brahmians, but when the invasion was imminent, they were shrewd enough to see the writing on the wall. They aligned themselves with the new powers, getting into the Paragon's good graces so that they could keep their mining empire. Then, after the invasion, they and a few other like-minded patriots used their resources to secretly fund what would eventually become the Brahmian Independence League." Her face turned slightly sour. "Not that it's done much good. A decade and a half of guerilla warfare and all they have to show for it is an increasingly long body count. They're smart enough to know when something isn't working."

"Thus, *your* plan," I said. "Whatever it is."

She gave a crisp nod.

I hesitated. "I don't need to know the whole plan. Whatever you do after this job is your own business. But I've *got* to at least ask. What's on the *Revelation* that you want so badly? After everything I've heard, it seems obvious that it has something to do with fighting the Paragon. Khendars wouldn't be interested if it wasn't."

Artemis glanced at me. "Would it bother you if it did?"

I glanced at her. "Why would it bother me?"

She shrugged. "You spent most of your life fighting for the Paragon. And now I'm paying you to help bring it down. Maybe."

I gave a short, humorless laugh. "What, you think I *wanted* to be a Vanguard? That I volunteered to go fight the Paragon's wars?"

She frowned. "I guess I don't know."

"My parents sold me into it," I said. "When I was ten. Paragon had a program going on my homeplanet, buying young boys to turn into Vanguards. Guess my folks needed the money, 'cause one day they dropped me off at a recruiting station, turned around, and never looked back." I shook my head. "The Paragon has taken just about every good thing I've ever had. My childhood, crappy as it was. My body. My sanity. And even after I got out of the Vanguard, it wasn't enough." I took a deep breath. "They took my crew. My family. And after that, they took my freedom." I looked up at her. "You think I'd turn down a chance to take something back?"

She fell silent for several minutes. Finally, she spoke. "Before the *Revelation* departed for the Brahma system, it spent several months in the shipyards being modified. Whatever they did to it was top secret, but internal communications indicated that the Paragon saw it as a monumental advance for them. But afterwards—after it disappeared—rumors began to spread among the intelligence community. Rumors that Divinity was *not* happy with whatever the Paragon did to the *Revelation*. Dozens of Paragon scientists mysteriously vanished. The high-ranking officers involved were all suddenly demoted and replaced. The facilities that had been used to work on the *Revelation* were demolished."

I nodded, deep in thought. "So you think there's some kind of, what, super-weapon on there that you can use?"

"No." Despite the empty street, her voice lowered to a hush. "I think that the Paragon managed to crack Divinity's code. I think they were trying to get out from under their thumb." She gave me an earnest, excited look. "I think that they somehow managed to figure out how to build their own ultracells."

My step faltered.

Ultracells were what kept Divinity in power—and, therefore, the Paragon. Only Divinity could make them. That meant that anyone who wanted to travel faster than the speed of light was a slave to their products. Divinity controlled the ultracells, and therefore controlled the Paragon, who in turn controlled everything. If the Paragon had figured out how to make their *own* ultracells, though, that meant that they wouldn't have to rely on Divinity anymore. They'd be completely unstoppable.

But if *somebody else* happened to figure it out...

"You're sure?" I asked.

"No." She shook her head. "But multiple other sources support the idea. Another report said that the Paragon wanted to turn the Brahma system into a *New Eden*. They planned to conquer it and use it to produce something that they'd ship all over the Paragon."

"Alright, then," I said. "Why Brahma? Why not use any one of the dozens of systems they already controlled?"

She shrugged. "Maybe for the symbolism, with Brahma being the last to fall. Or maybe *because* Brahma was the last to fall. There's a reason it took so long. Brahma is the most remote inhabited system. Once conquered, it would have been the easiest for the Paragon to defend. Or maybe it was because they knew Divinity didn't have a presence here yet."

We walked in silence for a few minutes while I digested the information.

"I do have one request," I said. "The others deserve to know."

Artemis raised an eyebrow at me. "Don't forget who's paying who here."

"I'm not. But I'm also not forgetting what you're paying me *for*. If we want to build a crew that can hold together in the bowels of hell, we need to make sure they know that we've all got each other's backs."

She frowned at that, but I pressed on. "And they deserve to know what they're getting themselves into. This isn't *just* a salvage op. This is political. Especially now that the resistance is involved. Being a part of this puts every one of us at risk. Even if we succeed, we'll have to be looking over our shoulders for the rest of our lives." I stared at a patch in the street that clearly marked where a crater had been filled in. "If we pull this off, we'll be directly responsible for starting a new era of war, with no way of knowing the outcome. Billions of people could end up dead because of us."

"What about Sevani?"

I shook my head. "I don't think we have anything to worry about from Sevani. I don't have a better explanation for why we were attacked back on Albeni 7 but I trust Sev. Besides, even if she was trying to sabotage us, there's no way she'd risk putting the Paragon on our scent while we've got her daughter with us."

Artemis went silent. After several minutes, she gave a resigned sigh. "Fine. We'll tell them the basics. But they don't need to know everything, and knowing too much could put them in even more danger. The whole point of doing this as a group of independent contractors instead of just sending the Brahmians is that this way, if we're caught, it doesn't all get traced back to the same place. Your little crew will fare much better if the Paragon thinks they're just common vultures."

I nodded. "Fair enough."

The starport was in sight now. The city was gleaming with the evening sun. I took a moment to admire it all.

"I haven't seen a sunset in over eight years," I said softly.

Artemis paused beside me, looking up. She smiled. Then she straightened, and suddenly she was back to the cold, calculating Artemis I'd known before. "Don't get too used to it. You have a team to build."

## TWENTY

"Just to be clear," Bentley said, clenching his eyes shut as if he was trying to conserve energy for his rapidly overheating brain, "your partners are Brahmian terrorists—and we're working *with* them, but not technically *for* them."

"Consider it a joint venture," Artemis said, reposing calmly in her seat on the bridge of the *Orpheus*. The rest of the crew was gathered there too, each coming to terms with the information she'd just revealed in their own ways. "Their involvement makes no difference in the amount you'll be getting paid. All they're doing is contributing a team of soldiers to accompany us into the *Revelation* and connecting us with some of their suppliers."

"What're they getting out of it, then?" Rid asked suspiciously.

"Access to whatever data I find on the *Revelation*'s computers," Artemis said.

"Having them behind us gives us a lot of resources," I said. "And we're gonna need the extra personnel. But there is a layer of extra risk. We'll be doing our best to keep security high and to keep our two groups compartmentalized, but if everything goes to hell and it does get out that we worked with rebels... well, the Paragon treats vultures a lot kinder than traitors. And trust me, they don't treat vultures very well."

Rose raised an eyebrow. "Well *now* I'm sold."

Shell spoke up, surprising me. "What will you do with this data?"

"That's my business," Artemis said calmly. "But you have my word that it will bring no risk to any of you."

"Will it hurt the Paragon?" Shell asked pointedly.

Artemis hesitated, then moved her head in a slow, grim nod. "Yes. Yes, it will. Badly."

Shell gave a satisfied grunt and settled back into her seat, thumb tracing a circle around the butt of her long knife at her side.

Bentley groaned softly, massaging his temples. "This is *so* much more than I signed up for..."

Rose's eyes were blazing with excitement. "We could go down as *legends*."

"Best-case scenario is that nobody ever knows we were even there," I said. "That's the catch, though. Even if everything goes perfectly according to plan, we'll all be checking over our shoulders for the rest of our lives." I glanced at Artemis. "So if that's a deal-breaker for you..."

"Then you're free to go," Artemis finished, meeting my gaze. "I don't want anybody on this job that doesn't want to be here."

Artemis's words drove the rest of the group into a long, contemplative silence. Rid glanced questioningly towards me. Rose nodded thoughtfully, folding her arms. Nadus was watching Artemis carefully, brows furrowed slightly. Bentley scratched his head, eyes glassy.

Nadus spoke first. "Well, I'm still in. If anything, the fact that we get to rub some dirt in the Paragon's eye is a nice little bonus."

Rose leaned forward in her seat, eyes still bright. "You bet your ass we're still in."

I glanced at Shell."Everybody needs to decide for themselves."

Shell smirked at that but nodded. "If we're going after the Paragon, I'll be there all the way."

Rid gave a casual shrug. "Doesn't change anything for me. This is my crew."

All eyes turned to Bentley, who was still massaging his temples. Finally, he groaned and threw his hands up. "What the hell. We're still getting paid, right?"

"Assuming we don't die," I said, "that's right."

He grimaced. "Thanks for that."

Artemis stood up. "Glad to hear that everyone's still on board. The rebels have granted us use of one of their training facilities up in the mountains. We'll head there and link up with Tekka's squad. From there, preparations will begin in earnest. As soon as we're ready, we go for the black box." She withdrew a datastick from her pocket and tossed it to Rose, who plugged it into the navigation system. A few seconds later, a holographic map of the Brahma system appeared in the center of the bridge. A blinking red dot flickered to life on the edge of the map. Artemis pointed at it. "There. That's the projected location of the *Guardian*, a Brahmian Interceptor class vessel. It will almost certainly be infested with rippers. Think of this as a training run. Once we've cleared that and found the black box, we'll come back here, resupply, and then it's off to do the real thing. All clear?"

Nods all around.

"Good." Artemis nodded. "Get some rest. Over the next few weeks every second needs to count."

The room burst into life. The grave, expectant silence transformed into a cacophony of excited chatter as plans and hypotheticals crystalized into vivid reality.

Despite the air of excitement, however, I found myself feeling strangely grim. As the rest of the group filtered out I stayed put with my arms crossed, staring at the blinking red dot on the hologram that marked the *Guardian*'s location.

"You alright?"

I glanced up. Nadus had lingered behind, standing beside the ladder and watching me.

"Yeah." I forced a grin with more energy than I felt. "Just... thinking."

He studied me a moment longer, then nodded and left. I turned back to the map, staring at that blinking red dot.

It just blinked back at me.

# TWENTY-ONE

## THE PANAMA



EIGHT YEARS AGO

I stared down at the red dot that represented Rawlins on the minimap. It blinked back at me.

"*Uh, Rawlins's exo just went offline,*" said Sevani.

"I don't have eyes on him," Black said.

My mind raced through the possibilities, desperately trying to conjure up an alternative explanation to what I knew in my gut was the truth. He could have fallen and somehow damaged his comms. He could have stumbled across a corpse and startled in fright, accidentally turning off his relay system. It could be a simple exo malfunction. He could be playing some sort of demented, poorly thought through prank.

But I didn't believe any of it. I wanted to. Wanted to believe that there was some simple, mundane explanation. But Rawlins's final scream—that visceral, almost *tangible* burst of sheer terror—was still echoing in my ears.

"Abort," I said. "Grab what you have and *go*. Get back to the *Orpheus*."

"What about Rawlins?" asked Liung.

"*NOW*," I yelled.

Kessa and Black burst into motion. Black activated his thrusters and took off down the corridor the way we had come, towing the cargo pod behind him. Kessa and I followed. I hesitated for just a moment, looking down the hall in the direction Rawlins had gone. I saw nothing but shadows.

Maybe he was still alive. Maybe I could save him. Maybe—

"CONTACT!" Black screamed.

I whipped around to see Black firing his SVAG. Each round fired punched through the darkness ahead of us with sharp white light, painting a picture that lingered only for a fraction of a second before plunging back into darkness and then reappearing like some sort of macabre, low frame rate cartoon.

Within each of those paintings I could see a shape. Pale and spider-like. Eyeless, mouthless. Closer. Closer with each flash of light.

"*Ripper!*" Black bellowed. "*We've got—*"

The ripper's scorpion-like tail lurched forward. Black's words choked off into a wet gurgle as the long, glistening spear on the end of the ripper's tail punctured through the front of his helmet and out of the back.

Kessa let out a high-pitched scream of equal parts fear and fury, raising her SVAG and squeezing the trigger. The ripper launched itself towards her, claws flashing in the near darkness.

Instinct took over and I found myself launching forward, reaching out with one armored fist and grabbing the ripper's skull. I heard myself bellowing as I twisted and slammed the creature against the wall—once, twice, three times, the skull fracturing each time until it collapsed in on itself.

I took a deep breath, scanned our surroundings to make sure there were no more threats, and turned to Kess. "You alright?"

She nodded weakly, her eyes fixed on Black's corpse. He was still standing upright, his boots fixed to the floor by his exo's maglocks. The ripper's tail was still stuck through his head. I let go of the creature's twitching, ruined body, and it drifted aimlessly, still anchored to my friend as droplets of black blood oozed from the dozens of bullet holes in its torso and the ruined pulp of its skull.

I frowned as I studied it. There was something off about it. Something different. An untrained eye would never have noticed it, but I'd spent most of my life fighting rippers. Other than a few mild deviations, they all looked the same. This one, though... it was all wrong, even if it was in subtle ways. The claws shorter, more curved than they should have been. The torso and legs too long and lithe.

*The hell?*

"Oh, Black..."

I turned to see Kessa still staring at Black. She reached a trembling hand out towards him, then pulled it back.

Black had been the first to join our crew. Steadfast and reliable. In many ways it was thanks to him that the hare-brained scheme Kess, Sevani, and I had cooked up had turned into a reality. And now he was gone. A green dot, flashing red.

"Lax!" Liung's voice rasped in the comms. "What's going on up there?"

The words jarred me back to the present. "Rippers," I growled, activating my thrusters and grabbing the cord to pull the cargo pod with us. "Black is dead."

There was a moment of shocked silence.

*"That's impossible,"* Sevani snapped. *"The scans—"*

"Black is *dead!*" I yelled. "With a ripper's tail embedded in his skull. So it's pretty damn possible. Everybody needs to get off of this ship. *Now.*"

"Uhm... Lax?"

Kessa's voice was soft, confused. I turned to her. She stared back at me. I realized suddenly that there was a gash in her side, her exosuit compromised by the ripper's talons. The suit's emergency repair system had already started the self-sealing process, but I could see little red globules of blood floating around the breach. As I watched, one of them drifted downward and splashed itself across the surface of the starry night painted on her shoulder pads.

"I think it got me," she said weakly.

## TWENTY-TWO

I lay awake that night, staring up into Kessa's starry night sky painted across the ceiling and thinking about the *Revelation*.

Artemis was saying that based on her intel, the *Revelation* would drop out of nullspace fifty-four days from now. Where it would be and for how long, well, who knew? Maybe it would be twenty years of nullspace travel out of reach. Maybe I was secretly hoping that it would be. But my gut told me that wouldn't be the case. Whatever was going on—whatever malevolent forces had acted upon it to butcher its entire crew and escape into the void—wouldn't be satisfied with just vanishing. Surely somebody had plans for the *Revelation*.

I just had no idea who.

Did Artemis know more than she was letting on? I found it hard not to believe that she did. She claimed to have no idea who this "Penitent" was that had tried to kill us on Albeni 7. She claimed that nobody else knew what she knew about the *Revelation*.

Just a few weeks before we did this insane, laughable, possibly suicidal thing. Fifty-four days until I went charging back into the maws of death, even after it had chewed me up and spit me out last time.

Was I insane?

I gave it some serious thought as I lay there, fingers interlocked on my chest. They say that insanity is doing the same thing and expecting different results. Was that what I was doing here? Or was I secretly hoping that this time the rippers would finish what they couldn't last time?

I'd spent my entire life living on the fine line between life and death. Peril had become my one constant. By now it seemed like a comforting friend—one familiar aspect of my otherwise perpetually chaotic existence. It seemed somehow wrong that I'd survived for as long as I had. Other people would have gotten out of the game a long time ago—leaving it all behind for something safe and predictable. And here I was, getting sucked straight back into the life that had so nearly killed me before.

I could walk away. It would be easy enough. I could find a job somewhere here on Brahma and never worry about rippers or ultracells or rebels ever again. Easy.

But I wouldn't, and I knew it. I would ride this train until it careened off the edge of the cliff. Because Artemis had been right about me from the beginning. Deep down, I'm nothing but a sucker.

*Green dots, flashing red...*

I sat up and reached under my bed, feeling until my fingers wrapped around a small vial. The frigicerin I'd plundered from the MAMA. I inserted one end of it into my shoulder port and applied just a slight amount of pressure. I felt better within a few seconds, my worries suddenly no longer quite as urgent, the sharp edges of my fears blunted.

"Just a hit," I muttered, feeling sleep finally begin to take me.

—————

## FIFTY-TWO DAYS

In the two days since he'd ambushed me, blindfolded me, and begrudgingly escorted me to his leaders, Tekka did not seem to have grown any more comfortable with the prospect of working alongside a Vanguard. I found it hard to contain my amusement at his horrified reaction when he saw that there were *two* of us now.

"This the guy?" Nadus asked me as Tekka dismounted his hoverbike and approached us.

"The very one." I nodded to Tekka. "Nice bike."

The rebel was dressed in casual, if somewhat rugged, clothes now. From looking at him, I'd have guessed he was a farm technician rather than a combat-ready guerrilla. I could tell from his stance, though, that he was armed. The way he kept his right arm loose and slightly further back than looked natural made me think he had a pistol hidden in his waistband, just behind his hip. Glancing at his bike, I saw a scabbard with an assault rifle sitting inside it as well.

"Tekka," I said.

He grimaced and gave a nod of acknowledgment. "VanDunn."

"This is my associate, Nadus Torsund," I said, gesturing towards Nadus, who extended a hand. Tekka grimaced, but eventually gave it a brief, begrudging shake.

"Quite the place you've brought us to, Tekka," Nadus said.

I glanced around. The Khendars had given us a set of co-ordinates of what they claimed to be their most reliable arms dealer. The trip had taken us deep into the Brahmian mountains to what was either a derelict shipyard or a thriving scrapheap—it was hard to tell from outside the tall electric fence. All I knew for sure was that it certainly didn't seem like the type of place one went to find high-grade weaponry.

"There's more to it than meets the eye. Follow me." Tekka turned and walked towards the gate to the junkyard.

The gates started grinding open as he approached. "I called ahead to let them know that we were coming," Tekka said as he walked through.

Nadus and I followed. "Seems professional," I said.

As soon as the words left my mouth, a woman rounded a corner and waved at us. *Professional* seemed about the last word I'd have used to describe her. Wild hair that looked like she'd made a vague, unsuccessful attempt to tame into a ponytail, a gap-toothed smile, and an old Paragon technician's uniform with the words *Bullets are cheaper than lawyers* embroidered across the front, all combining to form a portrait of an individual with more than a few screws loose.

And we were here to buy weapons from her.

"Howdy there!" she half yelled, half drawled. "Why, Tekka, darling, it's been way too long! How's the operation going?"

Tekka glanced over his shoulder at us. "Can't talk about that right now, Mindy. I have some new customers with me who wanted to meet you."

Mindy looked us over, putting her hands on her hips. "Vanguards, huh?"

"That's right." Nadus extended his hand towards her. "We hear you've got the good stuff."

"Oh yeah." She looked us up and down, shaking Nadus's hand without hesitation. "You betcha. Good for everyone other than the poor bastards on the receiving end of it. Hear you lot are going after rippers. Hah! You'll need all the firepower you can get. Follow me."

She took us out of the office and into the junkyard. I glanced around, but there wasn't a weapon or piece of armor in sight. Instead, I found myself looking over heaping mounds of broken engine parts, decommissioned ground vehicles, and eerily empty hulls of ships. Mindy stopped in front of the lifeless corpse of a massive truck and pulled the gas tank open, revealing a keypad. She pressed a few buttons, and there was a grinding sound as a hidden door beneath the truck suddenly opened.

We followed her down into darkness. She fumbled around for a few moments, cursing, until she found a switch on the wall and threw it.

"*Let there be light!*" she shrieked.

A few seconds later, the prophesied light flickered into existence, illuminating a massive room cluttered with disorganized heaps of military equipment. I let out a low whistle as I stepped further into the room. Exosuits in various conditions leaned against walls. Firearms, grenades, and other weaponry lay in heaps. Crates and crates of various types of explosive ordnance were stacked in the center of the room.

"Hell of a collection," I said.

"Hah!" She chuckled as she pressed past me. "Most of this crap was just lying around after the war. I got the lion's share of it for free. Don't expect that to reflect your price, though. Over here—I got all the stuff you said you wanted sorted out."

Sure enough, there was one corner of the room wherein chaos did not reign absolute. Familiar-looking Jackhammer assault rifles, shoulder-mounted grenade launchers, crates of ammunition, and exosuit powercells were arrayed in neat lines. I stooped and hefted one of the Jackhammers. It was heavy, even for me, though that wasn't a surprise—Jackhammers were designed for use with exosuits. Without one they were too unwieldy to use.

"Looks like they're in good condition," I said, holding it up and inspecting it.

"They'll do the job." Mindy nodded, retrieving a cigarette from her pocket and lighting it. I figured that smoking in a room full of explosives probably wasn't the safest thing in the world, but from what I'd seen of Mindy so far, pissing her off was probably even less safe.

"Where'd you get all this?" Nadus asked, walking down a pathway between the stacks of killing machines.

"Here, there, yonder," Mindy said through her cigarette. "Some of it's salvaged. Some of it's stolen. But it's all in fightin' shape."

A tall shape covered in a canvas caught my eye. I put down the Jackhammer rifle I'd been inspecting, stepped up to the shape and tore the canvas off, then stood back with a long whistle.

A Jericho armored exosuit stood imperiously before me, its unpainted surface gray and menacing. It was at once hulking and lithe, heavy and dangerous. This was the Jericho CES-4, the newer version of the model I'd owned before the *Panama*. Looking at it made me feel small, vulnerable. I itched to climb inside of it. To shield my unprotected flesh in its armored embrace. This piece of machinery turned a Vanguard into a walking fortress, immune to all but the most devastating of armor-piercing rounds. Even ripper claws had a hard time piercing the Jericho's surface.

They still did, though. I felt my hand inching towards my shoulder port as the memories started worming their way through my brain again. *Green dots...*

Tekka and Mindy stayed back, quietly discussing something as Nadus and I began inspecting the gear.

"Admit it," Nadus said, stepping closer to me. "You miss being inside one of these."

I nodded slowly, rapping one knuckle against the Jericho's hardened steel shell. "I do. How long's it been since you were strapped in?"

Nadus shrugged, beginning to inspect the other exosuits. "A few years. I ain't been out of the merc game for all that long."

I hit a button on the Jericho's mounting frame, causing it to open with a mechanical whirring sound. I'd always thought that exosuits looked strange while they were opened up, like some kind of bizarre metal creature's dissected corpse. I felt a faint thrill of excitement as I studied the familiar sight. The best and worst years of my life had been spent inside one of these. The deeds I'd been most proud of and the ones I'd regretted most.

I glanced over my shoulder to make sure that Tekka and Mindy were out of earshot. "How do you feel about going up against the Paragon?" I asked softly.

Nadus thumped his fist against the back of the exosuit he was inspecting, then gave a satisfied nod and moved on to the next one. "Do you remember Nesting?"

I grimaced. Nesting was—or, had been, before we'd been there—a large city on the planet Redhawk. A particularly defiant city. "Of course I do."

"Me too. You remember that compound below the school?"

Screaming. The smell of death and rot. Blood pooled so deep it splashed when we walked through it. In the darkness and the chaos it had been impossible to tell cowering civilian from armed rebel, panicked human from frenzied ripper. Years ago, but I still felt my heart rate increase just thinking about it.

"How could I not?" I still had nightmares about Nesting. Nesting, and a dozen other once thriving cities.

"Me too. So to answer your question, pretty damn good." He leaned down to inspect a damaged part on an exo. "Eladrius is always telling me that real change—real penitence—only works when we try to fix the mistakes we made. I figure that this is the best shot we have at doing that."

"How'd you meet that guy, anyways?" I shook away the memories and turned back to inspecting the Jericho in front of me. "Eladrius, I mean. I would never have taken you for the type."

"Me neither. I didn't go looking for him—he found me. Met

on some middle-of-nowhere station while I was on a job for Artemis. Anyways, he seemed to take a real interest in me for some reason, and I needed somebody to talk to, so I just talked, and he just listened, and we became friends."

"Guy must have a thing for Vanguards." Satisfied with the condition of the Jericho, I hit a button to close it up and began inspecting the next one. "He gave me a routing chip on the *Jonah*. Said I could contact him with it if I ever wanted to talk."

"Yeah, that sounds like Eladrius." Nadus gave me a sideways look. "Have you talked to him?"

"No." I grimaced. "The hell would I talk to him about?"

Nadus glanced around, as if making sure that nobody else was in earshot. As if he was about to confess the most horrible secret in the galaxy. He leaned in close to me. "I know you're hurting, Lax."

My jaw stiffened. I said nothing, focusing on the mechanical suits in front of me.

"I see the way you reach for your shoulder port whenever somebody brings up Kessa, or the war. You're hurt bad, Lax. Real bad."

"Yeah." I looked up at the ceiling, down at the ground, anywhere but my old friend's eyes. "Well, that tends to happen when you've lived our kinds of lives."

"The hurt is unavoidable," Nadus said. "But it won't go away if you just keep running from it."

I gave an annoyed growl. "You deal with your pain in your way, Nadus. Let me deal with mine in mine."

"But you're *not* dealing with it, are you?" Nadus said, unfazed. "All you're doing is hiding it away. And that wound is just gonna keep on festering."

"Oh, well why didn't I think of that?" I snapped.

Nadus sighed. "Just *talk* to someone, alright? I don't care who. It can be Eladrius. It can be me. It can be a stranger on the street. Just find someone to share the burden with."

"We've got two Jerichos, like you asked," Mindy said, interrupting our conversation and walking up to us. She pointed towards a row of smaller suits of armor. "And then a handful of exos of various sizes for regular-sized folks. Plus some other Vanguard-only stuff that I'll throw in for cheap since I won't be able to sell it to hardly anyone else."

I glanced towards the pile she was indicating. Some MAMA supplies, neurointerface repair kits and diagnostic computers, and what seemed to be a box containing vials of ignicerin and frigicerin.

My shoulder port started to itch.

Mindy and Nadus started talking through the terms of the purchase. I distracted myself from the urge to immediately flood my system with frigicerin by glancing towards Tekka. He was standing off to the side, regarding the two empty Jerichos with dark, haunted eyes. He was just about the right age to have been a young man during the invasion. I wondered where he'd fought. How many of his buddies had been killed by men wearing exos like this one.

Tekka's glance shifted from the exos to me. Our eyes met. I saw a brief flash of burning anger before he turned away, walking off to inspect some more equipment.

I thought about what Nadus had told me. He was right, of course. And I'd have to be an idiot to deny it. Until I had faced that pain I would never be able to turn the page of that particular chapter of my life. I'd be stuck, not really living but not dead, either. My own personal purgatory.

My eyes wandered to a pile of scrapped armor off to the side. I recognized the model—a Brady LAFA-7. The same type of exo that Kessa had used. A chill ran down my spine as I noticed three long, jagged cuts running down the frontpiece of the armor. A ripper's claw mark.

Nadus shoved me. "Hey. That all sound good to you?"

"Yeah," I said absently, not taking my eyes away from the morbid pile of scrap.

"Great." I could hear the grin in Mindy's voice. "We've got a deal. I get a crap ton of cash, and you get some gear that'll maybe keep the rippers off of your backs. For a few minutes, anyways."

*Green dots, flashing red...*

"Yeah," I said again.

———

## FIFTY DAYS

"Just a few more," I said, wiping sweat from my brow. "After a quick break."

Shell nodded beside me, shoving her welding goggles up onto her forehead. Rid collapsed as soon as I said the words, sagging onto his back and panting. The Brahmian sun was out in full force today, turning the cargo bay of the *Orpheus* into an overheated oven. That plus the welding tools Shell and I were using to install the exo mounting frames made for a devastatingly uncomfortable combination, even with the ventilation systems working at full blast.

"Planets," Rid moaned, "are *stupid.*"

Shell set down her tools and lifted a canteen of water. She was wearing a vest that left her muscular arms bare. I studied her tattoos as she drank. A series of thin lines and jagged angles were laid out in what seemed to be a careful geometric pattern, with words of a script I couldn't read appearing occasionally.

"Your tattoos," I said as she lowered the canteen and handed it to me. "What do they mean?"

"They're records," she said. "From my home. Jobs I had. Accomplishments. Colleagues. Places I worked. Lots of Aboenians get them."

I nodded. She had mentioned before that the *Aboena* was the name of her homeship—a massive craft, bigger even than the Paragon battlecruisers, built for faster-than-light travel with the goal of spreading humanity across the stars, long before ultracells had been invented. After depositing their cargo to their destinations, some of the Exodus crews had decided to stick with their ships. Over a thousand years later, their descendants were the nomadic space-farers we called Roamers.

Rid sat up, studying Shell's arm. He pointed. "What's that one?"

I craned my head towards Shell's other arm to see what he was pointing at. Multiple lines coalesced to meet in a large hexagon etched in a thicker line than the others. An image of two crossed blades filled the center of the hex, and lines of unreadable text lined the outside.

Shell glanced down at it, her eyes growing distant. She ran her fingers over the tattoo. "I was a member of the... well, our ship's version of enforcers," she said. "Keeping peace between the cabals, enforcing our laws. One day something collided with the ship. Command sent me in with a squad to inspect for damage. By the time we got there it was too late."

"Rippers," I said.

Shell nodded. "They spread too fast. We killed as many as we could, tried to slow them down to give civilians time to escape, but they overran us. Command decided that the only solution to save the ship was to seal that section closed. With everyone in it."

Rid's eyes were wide. "How'd you escape?"

"I was outside the containment zone," she said in a clipped tone. "So that wasn't my problem." She reached up and tugged her goggles back down over her eyes. "Rid. I need that T-frame."

Rid groaned and climbed back to his feet, trudging off in

search of the part. I grabbed my own goggles but didn't put them on yet.

"If you don't mind my asking," I said, "why'd you leave? Never known a Roamer who left their homeship on purpose."

"I *do* mind." She lifted her tool. I lowered my own goggles as she resumed welding, then turned away and got back to assembling the next mounting frame. Rid came back and dropped off the supplies before being called away by Rose to help with something else.

We'd been working for another half-hour or so when Shell suddenly spoke up again. "You know, Rose worships you."

I scoffed. "She just thinks I'm a chance to get out from under Sev's thumb."

Shell shook her head. "She talked about you and your old crew all the time. Sevani used to tell her stories about you. From before your bad job. Says those stories were what got her through the hard times, after her dad died." Her face turned serious. "If you tell her that I spoke to you about any of this..."

I shook my head. "Trust me, I ain't telling anyone." Truth be told, I wasn't sure how I felt about it. I had nothing but loathing whenever I looked in a mirror even on the best of days. Whatever Sev had seen that was worth telling stories about was beyond me.

Shell nodded and turned back to her work, lowering her goggles. A thought struck me. "Wait. So you have experience with rippers, then."

She paused. "Yes."

"Then you know what we're up against here."

She looked over her shoulder at me. "None of us know what we're up against."

"No. But some of us know less than others." I stepped around the frame she was working on, facing her. "Right now, Nadus and I—and Tekka maybe—we're the only people on the crew with any experience when it comes to rippers. And whatever experience they've had will be far different from facing down rippers in a confined space."

She reluctantly raised her goggles again. "What's your point?"

"My point is I could use somebody I know isn't gonna panic on me. In there, with us."

She frowned. "I'm here to keep the *Orpheus* running and keep Rose safe."

I opened my mouth to press her only to pause. What the hell was I doing? Deep down inside I was still convinced that this whole job was suicide for everyone involved. Why was I trying to drag even more people into it?

"Why are *you* doing this?" Shell asked, leaning one shoulder against the mounting frame. "You know better. You know how dangerous this is. You know what *they're* like." She leaned closer to me, eyes burning with dark memories. "You know that the best way to deal with rippers is to never get near them in the first place. Only a fool would choose to walk right into their lair."

I looked for something to say. I came up empty-handed. That was the big question, after all. The one Sev had asked me back on Albeni 7. The one I'd been mulling over in my head every day since agreeing to this stupid job.

"Damned if I know," I finally said. "But I am. Like a fool. And this fool's job is to keep all the other fools alive. Which is why I need fools who have some experience under their belts. Real idiots. The kind who've been through hell and want to go back for more. So if you decide that that's you, just let me know." I stepped away back towards the frame I'd been working on. "No shame in saying no. Hell, it's probably the smarter thing to say. But just give it some thought. We could use you in there."

Shell watched me, shaking her head. "You're all crazy. All of you."

"I ain't disagreeing."

She gave a short, unbelieving laugh, then abruptly pulled her goggles down over her eyes and raised her welding gun. "You Vanguards. Crazy. Now get back to work before I test how good that healing of yours really is. No more talk."

"Artemis could probably be talked into paying extra," I said.

She waved the welding gun towards me. "*No more talk.*"

I grinned, then raised my hands in a gesture of surrender and turned away.

———

## FORTY-NINE DAYS

The truck came to a rumbling halt, then shut down. A few moments later, Tekka climbed out of the driver's seat, gave a defeated glance towards me, sighed, and thudded his fist on the side of the vehicle.

"He looks happy to be here," I said to Artemis.

She gave a snort of a laugh. "He'll get over himself."

Seven people climbed out of the back, while three more disembarked from the front of the truck. As they began trudging towards us I glanced upward. We'd put the *Orpheus* down and made camp in a valley just a short ways away from Mindy's scrapyard. Rocky mountains surrounded us, and a waterfall cascaded down the side of one of them to end in a small lake in the center of the valley. Pretty, as far as training grounds went. Supposedly the Khendars owned this whole valley. If any Paragon satellites spotted us down here they'd pass us off as surveyors, looking for a good place to open a mine. Or, that was what we were supposed to say if anyone showed up.

Tekka and his rag-tag team came to a halt a few meters away from us. They shuffled into a line, regarding me suspiciously. I recognized a few of them from the ambush in the tunnels. One of them was the kid I'd knocked to the ground. He was doing his best to stand extra tall and fixing me with a glare that he was probably hoping made him look dangerous. It didn't—unless you consider angry children dangerous.

Artemis smiled. It was her "I'm beautiful and intelligent, so you should trust me" smile. I'd been around her long enough now to recognize it. "Hello, Tekka. Quite a fine little army you've brought with you."

Tekka regarded her sullenly. "You won't find a more loyal group of patriots anywhere. Every last one of these men and women would march into hell for Brahma."

"They're going to," I said.

Artemis gave me a withering look. "This is Lackan VanDunn. Don't be alarmed by his... ah... *enhancements*. He has just as much reason to hate the Paragon as any of us do."

The kid I'd scuffled with in the tunnels scoffed. "Doubt it," he muttered to a young man standing next to him.

"But more importantly," Artemis continued, "he's been fighting rippers his whole life. He knows what he's talking about. His job is to teach all of us how to survive out there. So if you want to survive, you'll *listen to him*."

Tekka glanced at his group. "They know the deal. They'll listen. They don't have to like it, though."

The rest of the day was spent setting up camp and making introductions. Everyone got along, more or less. The rebels stuck to themselves for the most part, setting up tents, until at my suggestion, Artemis insisted on a group dinner around a campfire.

Despite their reluctance to engage with me, I did my best to learn our new companions' names. The kid I'd grappled with was named Jin. His buddy Rathen was never far from his side. Tekka's second in command was a gaunt, scrappy-looking woman named Tames whose prosthetic hand was never more than a few inches from the butt of her pistol. I did my best to interact with the other seven but never got much more than vague, distant politeness from them.

"Your hand," I asked Tames casually between spoonsful of the stew we were sharing. "Rippers?"

She gave me a sidelong glance. "Yeah."

I waved my spoon at Nadus. "Rippers took his eye too."

"Too little too late," Jin muttered from across the campfire. Tekka slapped the back of his head as he walked behind him, causing the kid to flinch and earning a chortle from Rathen. For her part, Tames just grunted and turned back to her stew.

By the time the fire had started to die down the rebels had already retreated to their little camp, while most of my crew had returned to the *Orpheus*, leaving me and Artemis sitting across the mound of fading embers from Tekka.

"Give 'em time," I said, holding my hands up close to the last vestiges of heat. I'd forgotten what it was like to be cold, somehow. Too much time spent in temperature-regulated space stations. "They'll start bonding as training starts."

Tekka grunted. "I wouldn't be so sure. It's not just you Vanguards that have their hackles up. Far as they're concerned, your whole crew's a bunch of opportunists, here to benefit from their misfortune. War profiteers."

"Then why'd they volunteer?" Artemis asked.

"They didn't," Tekka said. "*I* volunteered. They begrudgingly agreed to come with me. They're having a hard time seeing what raiding some long-lost Paragon ship with a bunch of vultures has to do with freeing Brahma from its oppressors. But I told them to trust me. That this mission could change everything. That it's a cause worth risking their lives for." His eyes glinted dangerously with orange firelight as he stared at Artemis. "I would sure hate to find out I've lied to them."

There was a long, tense silence as Artemis held his gaze.

Finally, Tekka forced a grin, slapped his legs, and rose to his feet. "Well, I'd better be getting to sleep. Long day tomorrow, I'd expect."

He wandered off towards his camp, humming as he went. Artemis leaned back in her chair with a frustrated groan, looking up at the stars. "I never thought I'd feel more at home with a bunch of criminals and Vanguards than with my own people," she muttered.

I shrugged. "It's like you said, back on Albeni. Miracle of humanity is that we can take our homes with us wherever we go. You adapted after the war, went out into the stars. I'd bet good money Tekka and his people have never left Brahma. Just the fact that you have is enough to make you an outsider in their eyes."

Artemis nodded slowly, eyes heavy with a sort of sadness I'd never seen in her. "He doesn't trust me. Thinks I'm leading his people to their deaths, all for my own gain."

My stomach constricted at those words. I thought of my old crew, laughing and joking as they followed me into the jaws of hell. Their screams echoed in my ears. *Green dots, flashing red...*

Artemis sighed and climbed to her feet. "Exos tomorrow?"

"Yeah," I said.

"Good." She walked back to the *Orpheus*. I watched her go, then looked up into the Brahmian night sky. The stars were vivid against the empty black. They looked cold and distant and alien. Nothing like the warm, swirling yellow orbs that Kessa had painted. Maybe that's the point of art, though. Pretty lies to make the universe seem a little less daunting.

Green dots, flashing red. A drop of blood smeared across a starry night sky.

My pulse started to race. I got up and walked into the *Orpheus*'s cargo bay, closing the ramp behind me. Among all of our supplies was a crate labeled WARNING: VANGUARD

USE ONLY. I hesitated, then opened it and withdrew a can of frigicerin and shut the box.

Just a hit. Something to take the edge off.

---

## FORTY-EIGHT DAYS

The Jericho closed around my body like a familiar blanket—that is, if blankets could be made of metal. It's not as uncomfortable as that makes it sound. There are layers to an exo—a good exo, at least. The inmost was a comfortable, temperature-regulating jumpsuit that would keep me cool—or warm—and protect my skin from chafing. Next came strategically placed pads to make the exo a bit softer on the inside. After that came the armor: three solid inches of hardened steel at the most vital areas, with thinner layers for less important parts.

I heard a mechanical whirring as the helmet closed over my head. The world went dark as the blast shield sealed shut over my face. Then the strangely violating sensation as a long, metal computer jack screwed itself into my neck port. As it tightened, I braced myself for—

*There* it was. A short electric jolt, tingling throughout my body. For a few seconds my vision went blurry; then the world was a mass of distorted images, sounds, and sensations. As quickly as it started, it was over.

Wearing a neurointerfaced exosuit is a difficult thing to explain. It felt as if the suit was part of my actual body. The limbs moved as I thought about it rather than waiting to react to the movements of my actual body, rendering my reflexes quicker. I saw and heard the world through the exo's sensors, projected through the neurointerface and directly into my brain. The two shoulder-mounted grenade launchers felt like I had gained two new limbs that I could move about and use just as easily as my actual flesh.

I let out a sigh. I'd missed this feeling.

Using the neurointerface, I commanded my visor to open. My vision swam for a moment, and then I was seeing through my own eyes again. I glanced around. The rest of the team—even those who weren't planning on going aboard the *Revelation*—were all wearing exos of their own. Artemis had finished putting on hers and was now carefully walking around. I strode over to her side, relishing the familiar mechanical movements of my Jericho, and helped her make her slow, unsteady way out of the cargo bay and into the Brahmian sunlight.

"That's it," I said, taking her by her gauntleted hand. "You're getting the hang of it. There's a sort of rhythm you need to hit with your movements. Before too long it'll feel as natural as breathing."

"It's actually remarkably intuitive," she said. "How much protection will these give us?"

I studied her exo. She was wearing a Granite Arms Ranger-34, a reliable all-purpose tactical suit. Standing next to my Jericho it looked almost petite. "Plenty. Small arms fire won't do anything more than tickle you. Even armor-piercing rounds will need to be a pretty good direct hit to do any real damage. Should hold up well against anything but the most high-powered energy weapons."

She turned to look at me through her open visor. "And against rippers?"

I grimaced, fighting a flood of memories, both from the war and from the *Panama*. Jerichos with gaping rends in the breast-plates, blood gushing from the wounds beneath. Black's helmet punctured clean through by a ripper's tailspike. Blood droplets pouring out of Kessa's side.

"And against rippers," I said finally, "it's better than nothing."

She nodded.

"Why are you going onto the ship with us?" I found myself asking.

"What do you mean?"

I shrugged. "You're the brains of the operation. Seems like it would be easier to send somebody else and hang back yourself."

"I need to be on location to make sure it all goes smoothly," she said. "And..." She hesitated. "Well, it doesn't feel right to send everybody else in to do my job for me if I'm not assuming some of the risk."

I raised an eyebrow. "Careful, Artemis. That almost sounded sentimental."

She gave a harsh laugh. "This place is a bad influence on me."

"Nothing quite like a reminder of where you came from to bring you back into old habits, huh?"

She nodded somberly, bouncing back and forth from foot to foot. "I'm getting the hang of this. Go help the others."

I turned away, monitoring everybody else's progress. Nadus was helping Tekka and his ten rebels into their exos. Rid, Bentley, and Rose were all staggering around. I found myself smiling as Rid and Rose collided with each other, falling to the ground in a heap of metal. They looked like a bunch of drunken robots. I stopped laughing when I remembered that in just a few weeks, I was going to be leading these untested rookies into the most dangerous salvage job I'd ever attempted.

Another figure staggered down the ramp onto the field outside of the *Orpheus*. Shell. I blinked in surprise. Based on the last conversation we'd had, I'd assumed she wouldn't be training with us. We'd outfitted her for an exo anyways for emergency purposes, but she'd seemed adamant that she wouldn't need it.

"Decided to join us after all, huh?" I asked.

She grimaced. "Did you mean what you said? About the extra pay?"

I nodded. "I haven't talked to her about it yet, but she'll go along. We need more experience in this crew. I figure that's worth some extra cash."

"I better not regret it."

"No guarantees of that, I'm afraid. I did tell you you'd be smarter to say no."

"Well, I guess I'm not that smart."

I grinned, putting a hand on her shoulder to steady her as she practiced her gait. "Neither am I. Seriously, though. I'm glad you'll be with us. I need at least a few people who aren't gonna lose their heads at the first sight of a ripper."

She nodded. I turned to the rest of the group.

"Alright," I said into a group comms channel as soon as everybody was securely inside of their exo. "Ladies and gentlemen, welcome to your exo. For simplicity's sake I wish we could have found the same model for everyone, but we work with what we have. Each of your exos will be a bit different, but the general idea is the same."

The group gathered in a semicircle around me. I pointed one gauntleted finger up into the sky. "Up there, your exo is your personal spaceship. The life-support systems will keep you breathing. The thrusters will keep you moving. Your comms system will keep you synced with the rest of the team. And the armor will protect you from bumping your head or from most small arms fire. But it will *not* save you from ripper claws. If a ripper gets close enough to you it will kill you, armor or no."

I glanced around, gauging reactions. They seemed focused. Good. "You're better off going in naked than wearing an exo you don't know how to handle," I said. "And right now, I'd say you're all better off naked. So first step is learning how to move." I pointed towards a tall tree a few hundred meters uphill from our campsite. "Let's start by having everyone sprint to that tree and back. *Now!*"

They broke out into a chaotic, unco-ordinated rush. Artemis, Tekka, and Nadus lingered behind.

"Good start, I think," Artemis said. "I—"

"You too, Artemis," I said. "Don't think I won't kick your ass just because you pay me."

She made a face and set off. Tekka glanced at me, chuckled, and started up the hill behind her.

Nadus stepped up next to me, watching the rag-tag group struggle up the hill. "Reminds me a bit of Mud Hill, from training," he said. "You remember that?"

"Oh yeah," I said. "Up and down, up and down…" I spat onto the ground. "Damn, I hated that hill."

"Made us tough, though," he said. "No denying that."

"Yeah." I watched as Bentley tripped over a stump and rolled down several meters of slope. He tried to get up only to collapse, then watched forlornly as his crewmates staggered on ahead of him. I frowned. "But more importantly, it taught us to rely on each other."

Artemis caught up to Bentley and proffered a hand, pulling him back to his feet.

"We'll get there," Nadus said.

———

## FORTY-TWO DAYS

"How many of you have ever seen a ripper up close?" Nadus asked, voice echoing slightly in the cargo bay of the *Orpheus*.

Our little army exchanged glances. Of the eleven rebels, five raised their hands: Tekka, his second in command Tames, and three other older-looking rebels. Of our little crew, only Shell's arm went up.

"Good," Nadus said. "We've got some experience. Consider this *Ripper 101*."

He turned to the mobile holoprojector in the center of the group and turned it on. An image of a ripper appeared in the air, its six grotesque limbs and tail splayed out like... oh, what was that old earth picture Kessa had shown me? The naked guy with his arms and legs spread- eagled. Not sure why it was considered such a masterpiece, but that had always been Kessa's department, not mine.

*This* was mine.

"Rippers are man-made violations of every law of nature God ever laid out," Nadus continued. "Evolution had no hand in their creation. They have no survival instincts. No emotion. All they know is hunger. They operate by a very simple rule: if there is a meal nearby, they find and eat it. If there isn't, they cluster together and hibernate until something wakes them up. They do not reproduce. Instead, when a ripper has consumed a certain amount of matter, it will *mitose*."

He hit a button on a remote in his hand and a three-dimensional video of a ripper appeared. Looked like live footage from some sort of testing chamber, showcasing the gruesome mitosing process. I had to force myself to watch it, pushing aside memories of the battlefields where I'd seen the awful spectacle firsthand.

"How the hell do they"—Rose waved a hand in a futile gesture—"*do it* so fast? I mean, I'm not a scientist, but that should be impossible, right?"

"Ask Divinity," Nadus said. "But trust me, impossible or not, it's real."

I glanced around the group. Tekka and Shell seemed to be the only ones unfazed by the bloody display, both of them watching with the grim acceptance veterans of ripper combat often adopted. Everybody else was staring in horror. They'd all breathed a sigh of relief when I told them we were taking a break from training with the exos. They didn't seem to be enjoying this any better, though.

"They travel and fight mostly in groups," Nadus continued. "But not *as* groups, if that makes sense. They have no concept of group unity, or of hunting as a pack, but they do communicate. I'll be damned if I know how, but whenever a ripper finds a meal, all the other rippers nearby know about it and they'll all rush to try to be the first ones there."

My shoulder started to itch.

"When they do get there, though," Nadus continued, "they don't work together or take turns. It's a mad scramble. They'll crawl over each other to be the first to get at a target. Far as I know, however, they'll never attack another living ripper. They will consume the remains of their fallen buddies, though, if there's nothing else around. If there's one good thing about rippers, it's that they're predictable and stupid. You can always rely on them to act in the same way. Every ripper looks the same, acts the same, and dies the same. Now, that doesn't mean they're easy to kill..."

He kept talking, showing more footage of rippers. I found myself looking away. *Every ripper looks the same and acts the same... except for the one time when it mattered. Was I remembering it wrong? Was the trauma of it all warping my memories of what I'd seen that day?*

*Green dots...*

Artemis was looking at me strangely. I nodded to Nadus to keep going and walked quickly away. When I was confident nobody could see me I scrambled through my pockets for the can I'd put there, raised it with shaking hands to my shoulder port, and carefully injected a short burst of frigicerin.

Calm flooded me. I wanted to keep going, to keep pushing until I could feel nothing at all, but I forced myself to stop. After a few seconds my breathing was level again. The memories were a vague construct with no emotional relevance. I took a deep breath, slid the can back into my pocket, and rejoined the others. Artemis raised an eyebrow at me. I ignored her.

Nadus had another video playing, this one of a ripper that was restrained to a wall by several heavy bolts that pinned its limbs, tail, and head in place. The point of the video seemed to be showcasing its rapid healing abilities. Watching the footage was easier now—morbidly interesting rather than deeply disturbing thanks to the frigicerin.

"So how the hell are we supposed to kill these things?" Jin demanded as the ripper survived one act of abuse after another. "I don't think they're gonna let us tie 'em to a wall."

"The answer," Nadus said, stooping and grabbing something, "is this." He grunted as he hefted his Jackhammer heavy assault rifle for all to see. "This right here is the ripper solver. It's a pretty simple weapon. No real bells or whistles. No fancy target acquisition, electromagnetic propulsion, or recoil stabilization systems. It does one thing and does it well: shooting a hell of a lot of bullets with a hell of a lot of stopping power, fast and without jamming."

He ejected the magazine and held it up. "A standard magazine holds fifty-two explosive-tipped rounds. Rippers can't heal what's not there anymore. If you pump enough of these rounds into them, it'll cause enough damage to stop them permanently. If you're firing like an idiot, though, you'll burn through that in a matter of seconds and then you'll be screwed. The time it'll take your dumb, panicking hands to reload will be more than enough for the rippers to swarm you. Which is why, now that you've all got a grip on the basics of handling an exo, the next two things we need to learn are weapons operation and how to work as a team." He turned to me.

I blinked. My thoughts felt sluggish with the frigicerin in my system. Nadus's eyes narrowed slightly. Everybody was looking at me.

"I..." I shook myself, forcing my thoughts into focus through the haze of the coolant. "Let's—"

An alarm sounded from the *Orpheus*'s intercom system. All eyes turned to Rose and Shell.

"What's that supposed to mean?" Jin asked. "We about to blow up?"

Shell shook her head as Rose frowned down at her hand-computer. "It's a proximity alert," the Roamer explained. "Rose set the system to warn us if—"

"*Crap*," Rose said, standing up. "There's a squadron of Paragon craft approaching our location."

There were about two seconds of shocked silence. Then a sudden rush of activity. Tekka immediately withdrew his own pocket computer. Rose and Shell climbed up the chute towards the command deck, while Rid and Bentley shared a confused glance then scurried after them. Artemis stood up and walked calmly to the open cargo ramp, peering out into the Brahmian afternoon.

"What do we do?" Jin hissed to Tames, voice pitched with panic. "Should we run to the truck?"

"Calm down and stay put." Tames raised a calming hand, glancing at Tekka. "We don't know that they're coming for us."

Nadus frowned at me, then walked over beside Artemis. I followed him, still feeling slightly disconnected from the situation by the frigicerin. I knew, logically, that Paragon ships flying in our direction was bad. Try as I might, though, I couldn't get myself to feel anything other than vaguely concerned about it.

"See anything?" I asked as I stood next to Nadus.

"Not yet."

There was a rumbling sound as the *Orpheus*'s engines started to power up. Artemis pressed the intercom button to talk to Rose. "Don't take off," she said. "Not until we're sure they're coming for us."

"We'd already be dead if they were focused on us," I said.

"One orbital barrage and this whole valley would be a smoldering wreck."

"Unless they want us alive," Nadus said grimly. "How many of them are there, Rose?"

*"Twelve,"* she said. *"Looks like four troop carriers and eight escorting fightercraft. They're going fast. Should be in visual range now."*

Sure enough, I saw a cluster of black dots on the horizon to our north, growing steadily bigger by the second. A tense silence fell as we waited to see what would happen. I glanced around, gauging everybody's reactions—partially out of curiosity and partially out of a need to know how scared I *should* be feeling right now. Nadus's eyes were narrowed. Jin and the other younger rebels were holding their breath, eyes wide. Tekka hadn't taken his eyes from his handcomputer. Tames had approached and was now standing next to me, watching as the flight approached.

The distant dots morphed with frightening speed into sharp black outlines—eight small, knife-like ones surrounding four larger, bulkier shapes. It was an eerily familiar sight—I'd seen flights like this pass over my head hundreds of times on this very planet. They'd been on my side back then, though, carrying reinforcements for us and ordnance for the enemy.

I waited for them to slow, to turn and descend towards us. I wasn't sure what I'd do if they did. I trusted Rose, but the *Orpheus* was built for space travel, not atmospheric pursuit. Our chances of escape would be slim no matter who was flying. But those chances would still be better than trying to fight off four full squads of Paragon troops.

I heard whispering. Nadus and Tames were each muttering their own quiet prayers under their breath.

The ships were above the valley now, but they showed no signs of slowing or descending. A moment later there was a deafening supersonic boom as they tore over our heads and away into the distance.

Sighs of relief flooded the cargo bay. Nadus and Tames stopped muttering. Rose's voice crackled over the intercom. *"All good. Not sure where they're going, but looks like we happened to just be on the way."*

"They're going to New Therida," Tekka said, his voice clipped. He glanced up at me, eyes hard. "It's a city to the south, if you don't recall from your earlier *visit*. And now it sounds like the rebel cell there has been compromised."

Tames turned sharply to him. "Are we..."

"No." Tekka shut his handcomputer and slipped it back into his pocket. "We're still secure. Sounds like the necessary precautions have been made so the damage will be contained."

Jin glanced from Tekka to Tames, eyes wide. "That's... good, right?"

Tekka's face was flinty. "Dozens of operatives will probably be caught. The lucky ones will die fighting. The unlucky ones will be captured and tortured. So no, it's not *good*." He glanced at Jin, then softened slightly as he saw the boy's wide eyes. "But it's better than the entire league being compromised."

There was a long silence as Rose, Shell, Bentley, and Rid filtered back into the cargo bay. I felt a surge of relief as the frigicerin started to wear off and I realized how close of a call that had been.

"I have friends there," Rathen said forlornly.

"That's the fight," Tekka said. He looked around, addressing his squad of rebels. "And if it's the cost of independence, it'll be worth it in the end. If. We. *Win*."

"What's any of this got to do with winning?" Jin muttered, shooting a dark look at me. "We should be *there*. Fighting back. *Killing* puppets, not working for them."

"You don't work for him," Artemis said, finally standing up. "You work for me. And Tekka wouldn't have led you here if he didn't believe that it would help your cause." She gave the rebel leader a pointed stare. "Isn't that right, Tekka?"

His lips drew into a thin line. He nodded sharply. "It's the same fight, Jin. Just a different kind of battlefield."

"Good. Since we're in agreement on that, then, I believe we should return to business." She turned to me. "What's next?"

"Shooting," I said, still slightly shaken. "Gear up. We'll be practicing live fire drills in the exos."

People shuffled to their exo mounts, muttering among themselves as they went. I watched them, mind reeling. What if those ships *had* been coming for us? I'd have been next to useless, my mind slowed by frigicerin all so I could hide from the memories for a few minutes. This wasn't sustainable. Eventually something would break me.

"Hey!" Nadus raised an eyebrow at me, already geared up in his Jericho. "You coming?"

"Yeah." I glanced towards the projector, where a holographic image of a ripper was still hovering. "Just... thinking."

# TWENTY-THREE



"This is going swimmingly," Artemis muttered to me over a direct channel.

The entire crew was geared up in their full outfits: exos, Jackhammers with empty mags, and the same amount of supplies strapped to their backs I estimated they'd be carrying on the *Revelation*. We weren't on the *Revelation*, of course. And it was a good thing, too, or we'd probably already be dead. Instead, we'd taken the *Orpheus* up into orbit around Brahma and turned off the gravity generator to run a few exercises. The groups were split into roughly the same two groups we'd divide into when we hit the *Revelation* for real: myself leading one crew with Artemis, Tekka, Nadus, Rid, Shell, Jin and Rathen, while Tames led the remaining seven rebels in the second team.

In theory it was a good breakdown. As for the practice... well, *swimmingly* was just about the last word I'd have applied.

We had started with simple tasks. Moving down the hallway without gravity, using their exos' thrusters to avoid bumping against walls and sending vibrations through the ship. That alone had been difficult enough. After doing that for a while we'd transitioned to having them maneuver down the halls in groups, practicing keeping a formation and covering all of the angles rippers might attack from.

After a few iterations of that I'd thrown in extra challenges. Moving from Point A to Point B while Bentley or Artemis hacked something. Making a covered tactical retreat down a narrow corridor. Making emergency field repairs on an exo. Maneuvering a cargo truck or a wounded companion around tight corners. We made use of every single square inch the *Orpheus* gave us.

The current scenario was breaching a locked entryway. That put Rid up front. He'd been hard at work practicing on some locks Mindy had found salvaged from old Paragon ships that would be roughly similar to what we'd find in the *Revelation*, but he was still slower than I'd have liked. And his response to pressure was to shut out his teammates so he could focus better. Which unfailingly sent Jin, whose competitive drive made him want to be at the forefront of everything, into a fit of rage.

And that was just one example of the friction between the two groups. The rebels regarded my little crew with suspicion at best and derision at worst. Rid, Rose, Shell, and Bentley, meanwhile, had banded together and frequently cut the rebels out of key decisions during the practice scenarios. It made sense, in an unfortunate way, and I gradually realized that it was probably my fault. I'd always explained the idea of the rebels joining as simply a way to get more guns on our side. Now I feared that my crew saw themselves as the real vultures, with important jobs, while the rebels were just the extra firepower, there to shoot rippers and stay out of the way.

They weren't entirely wrong, either. Bentley, Rid, Artemis, and Rose all had specific expertise that they brought to the table. I needed each of them for specific tasks, while the rebels were there for cover and backup. But they still needed to be able to work as a team.

I sighed and triggered the general comms channel. "Alright, let's take a breather. We'll run it back again in fifteen. Be ready."

There were grumbles as the group dispersed, awkwardly swimming their weightless ways through the corridors. I saw Jin approach Tekka and Tames to start complaining to them. Rid, meanwhile, gathered in a group with Bentley and Shell.

Artemis and Nadus approached me. "We might need a change of pace," Artemis muttered. "I think we're doing more harm than good here."

"Individually, everybody's doing fine," Nadus said. "There's improvements to be made, but everyone more or less knows what they're doing. As a group..."

"As a group they don't trust each other," Tekka finished, gliding next to us and using his thrusters to come to a halt. I grimaced. I'd been about to say the same thing.

Tames was right behind Tekka. "They don't trust each other because your little gang won't loop our people in."

Nadus bristled. "Or because your hotshot freedom fighters treat our people like a bunch of criminals."

"*Enough.*" I raised my hand, cutting them off before any more retorts could be made. "Nadus, go check in with Rid. Tames, get your people ready to go again."

"I don't take orders from *you*," Tames snarled.

"Do it," Tekka said. Tames glared at me and trudged off.

"Give them a few minutes," I said wearily. "We'll run it again."


We ran it again. And again. And again. Then, just for fun, we ran it a few more times.

Bit by bit, they got better. More efficient. Their formations became tighter, their communication clearer. They solved problems quicker. But by the time we called it a day and had Rose fly the *Orpheus* back to our valley training grounds, the two groups were as distrusting of each other as ever.

That night, Artemis, Tekka, and I sat by the fire long after everybody else had retired, discussing the issue and drinking cold Brahmian beers.

"If you're asking *why* they don't trust each other," Tekka mused, "it's obvious. Why should they? We have two teams here with two different goals: one for profit, and one for freedom. My crew doesn't trust yours not to screw them over at the first prospect of extra cash, and yours doesn't trust mine not to get them all killed in some zealous act of patriotism."

Artemis scowled. "When they're on that ship they'll either work together or die together. They know that. Shouldn't it be enough?"

"Logically, maybe," I said. "But they know that already. Trust isn't something you *know*. You earn it, bit by bit. It takes time."

"Time's one of *many* things we don't have," Tekka said. "We're already behind schedule. We should be going after the *Guardian* in three days, and we're nowhere near ready."

I was inclined to agree. The crew knew what they were doing, for the most part, but they were completely untested. When working under pressure they'd break, panic, screw up. And a mistake during a training exercise was one thing, but on a ship full of rippers...

*Green dots, flashing red...*

"We should consider delaying," I said. "Push our little expedition to the *Guardian* back—even if it's just by a few days. The extra training will make a difference."

A slight grimace had curled Artemis's lip at the mention of the *Guardian*. "Ready or not, we can't afford to wait any longer.

We'll have to hope that the training we've put in so far will suffice." She stood up. "We proceed with the original timetable. We'll fit in as much training as we can before we leave for the *Guardian*. After that, we'll consider if we need to readjust our expectations for the *Revelation*."


Tekka and I sat in silence for a few minutes. I swirled my half-empty bottle, staring into the fire and thinking sourly of the task ahead of us. Just as I was on the verge of tossing away the rest of my beer and calling it a night, Tekka spoke up. "You think this is going to work?"

I raised an eyebrow at him. "Is what going to work?"

Tekka shrugged. "This mission. Artemis seems so sure that it's got..."—he seemed to catch himself—"what we're looking for."

"The ultracell stuff? Divinity's plans?"

He raised an eyebrow. "Guess she really does trust you."

"Unless she's lying to me."

"Never can tell with her."

I chewed on that for a few moments before replying. "You know her? From before the war?"

He chuckled. "Not before the war. Before the war she was a rich brat. I was just a low-ranking officer. Never crossed paths. After the war, though, when I started climbing the ranks in the resistance forces, and after she'd started doing intelligence work, I ran a few ops with her. She always insisted on being her own agent, though. Never quite seemed to trust the Khendars."

I thought back to the conversation I'd had with Artemis our first day on Brahma. "I thought they were friends. Of her parents, or something."

"They were. They're also the reason her father is dead. Or, that's what she thinks, at least."

I paused in the process of raising my bottle, looking sharply at him. "What?"

"Yeah. There's a reason she's so obsessed with the *Revelation*. It was her dad's pet project before it was hers. He was obsessed with it. Was certain that it somehow held the key to beating the Paragon. He sabotaged just about every relationship he had trying to figure out what happened to it. His wife left him, his political allies distanced themselves from him. Especially the Khendars, who saw the writing on the wall and knew that the war would have to change once the Paragon had taken over. So her father died alone and friendless. And here she is, all these years later, pushing the same boulder up the same hill."

I glanced towards the dark shape that was the *Orpheus*. "No wonder she keeps insisting she's working independently. How'd he die?"

"She didn't even tell you *that*?"

I frowned. "No."

He shook his head unbelievingly. "He was on the *Guardian*."

It took a moment to sink in. When it did, my eyes widened. "The ship we're about to..."

"Yep."

My gut felt suddenly hollow. Funny thing was, I was hardly even thinking about Artemis. I was thinking about Kessa. And what it would be like going back to the *Panama*, the place she had died, after all these years. It explained the way she grimaced every time it was brought up. I'd assumed she was just... scared.

"So if there's some skepticism from *our* side on all this," Tekka said, "that's why."

"Why'd you volunteer, then?" I asked.

"I volunteered," Tekka said, "because if this doesn't work... then I don't know what will." His voice—usually full of grisly bravado—turned suddenly grim and haggard. "I've been in this fight my whole life. And I've been losing it my whole life. We can blow up a supply depot here, ambush a convoy there. Assassinate a few leaders. Bomb a government building. None of it makes a difference in the end. But if Artemis *is* right..." He shrugged. "Well, then, who knows? Maybe we will make a difference."

I thought about that for a bit before I spoke again. "Why are you telling me all this?"

He shrugged. "Because right now we're just two guys drinking beer around a campfire. It's dark enough that I can almost forget what... *who*... you are. And if I do that, I can almost find myself liking you. And if you *were* somebody I liked, I'd want you to know the truth about what's going on here."

I gave a short chuckle. "Well, that's mighty generous of you."

"Don't let it get to your head." His gaze turned dark and serious as he focused his firelit eyes on me. "And don't think for one minute that I'll ever truly forget what you are. No matter how much you might have changed, or how little a choice you had about the things you did to my home back in the war. I hate you, Lackan VanDunn, even if I like you, I'll always hate you."

I said nothing. What the hell are you supposed to say to something like that?

Tekka reached down and I felt myself tense. When his hand came up, though, it was just holding a rock. "Imagine somebody took this rock and used it to beat your momma's brains out. Then your best friend. Then everyone else you knew. You know it's not the rock's fault. But how could you *not hate it* all the same?"

"Damned if I know," I said.

He let out a long sigh, tossing the stone aside. "You know, it's funny, but I almost resent you more *because* you got out of the Vanguard. You finished your fight and moved on. I'm still fighting the same war."

"At least you're fighting *for* something," I said. "I don't think I've ever felt that way. I've always been just... a rock." I glanced at the stone he had been holding. "Just rolling around, bludgeoning whatever within bludgeoning distance."

"Hmm. Well, all I can say is that I'm glad that we're not bludgeoning each other this time around. You seem like you pack a hell of a punch." He stood up, stretching. "Who knows? Maybe we'll find the secret Vanguard recipe on the *Revelation* too. Imagine that. A whole army of you boys to unleash upon the Paragon."

I found the thought vaguely horrifying. I shook my head. "If it came down to that, I'm not even sure it'd be worth it."

He scoffed, shaking his head. "If you can say that, then you've never really hated. Or never really loved. Whichever side of that you decide you fall onto." He pointed up into the stars. "Because believe me when I tell you that there is nothing I would not do to hurt those bastards. I'd cut off my hand for a chance just to spit in their faces. So when you ask why I volunteered for this idiot's idea of a mission... that's why."

He rose to his feet. "Get your rest. In a few days you'll be leading this untested crew of ours into a ship swarming with rippers. And if Artemis is right about this crazy plan of hers..." He shook his head in slow, almost disgusted disbelief. "Well, then, the future of Brahma and a whole lot more might be resting on your oversized shoulders."

I couldn't help but crack a wry grin. "Life's a bastard of a thing, huh?"

"I'll say." He gave me one last disapproving shake of the head before trudging off towards his camp. "Going into battle on the same side as a Vanguard," he muttered as he disappeared into the night. "The things I do for freedom."

———

THIRTY-TWO DAYS

"Lax. My mom wants to talk to you."

My eyes snapped open and I sat up in my bed. Rose was peering through my ajar door. Crap. I hadn't meant to fall asleep. I was exhausted, though. We were only hours away from taking off to go find the *Guardian*, and I'd been pushing myself every waking minute to get the crew ready.

I rubbed one eye. "What does she want?"

"Said it's about what happened on Albeni."

"Be right there."

A few minutes later I dropped into the seat in front of the communications console. Sevani's face peered back at me through the screen.

"You look like hell," she said.

"I feel like hell."

"Going that well, huh?"

I hesitated. I didn't want to make it seem like I had no confidence in our chances—especially given that her daughter's safety might well depend on those chances. But I also knew she'd see right through me if I lied. "It's... not the strongest start to a job I've had," I said.

Sev scoffed. "You got our crew into shape."

"Yeah. But I had you and Kess to help. And a crew that had at least some experience working salvage. I'm starting from ground zero here."

"You'll work it out. You've got at least few solid people you can rely on there. I'd trust Shell with my life in a heartbeat."

I nodded. "She's something. Rose and I would both have died back on Albeni if not for her."

From the corner of my eye I saw Artemis ascending into the otherwise empty bridge. "I take it that's not what you called about, though," I said to Sevani, as Artemis took a seat off to the side.

"No. I'm calling because I dug up more information about this Penitent of yours."

I perked up. Artemis raised an eyebrow.

"Despite the mess you left in those hallways on Albeni 7," Sev said, "it turns out you let one get away. I managed to track him down."

I remembered the guy. Last man standing after Nadus and I had butchered the rest of his team. "We let him go," I said. "He didn't know anything."

"No," Sev said. "But his bank account did. I managed to trace the payment they received for taking the job. It's a secure account, of course, and I wasn't able to find out where it was located or any of its history. But I did put some feelers around Albeni 7."

"Didn't realize you were such a good detective," I said. "You should have gone into information brokering, not smuggling."

"I may branch out," she said. "But I haven't finished yet. I got a hit. A pilot accepted an under the table payment from the same bank account just a few days after you left the station. I managed to track him down. The payment was for passage for one person—to Gharseva, on Brahma."

Artemis grimaced.

"Ah, *hell*," I muttered. "Did he know anything else?"

"Not much. Just that the passenger was an old man with Roamer tattoos on his face, and seemed to be in a hurry."

I glanced at Artemis. She shook her head blankly. I turned back to Sev. "Well, thanks for the heads-up. Guess we're not out of hot water yet."

"You're not even *in* the hot water yet."

"Thanks for reminding me."

"What I'm here for." Her face turned serious. "I assume I don't have to remind you that no matter how important you think this job is, my daughter's safety comes first."

I nodded without reservation. "You have my word."

"Good. I'll let you know if I find anything else. For now, keep my daughter away from old men with Roamer tattoos. And get some sleep. Again, you look like hell."

She disconnected. I turned to Artemis.

"Old man with Roamer tattoos," she mused. "Doesn't stir my memory."

"If that was a week ago," I said, "then whoever this Penitent is, he's already here on Brahma." I frowned. "I don't suppose the Khendars could keep an eye out?"

"I can ask," Artemis said. "But it's a big city. And I imagine your friend Sevani was only able to trace that banking information because of the sway she has on the smugglers of Albeni 7, so that won't help us here."

I leaned back in my seat and groaned, massaging my temples. "So now we just... wait for him to try to kill us again."

"We've been careful," she said. "There's no reason to believe he knows where to find us."

"Other than the fact that he just happened to fly directly to the same city we did."

She pursed her lips. "True."

We sat in silence for a few minutes. I snuck a glance at her as she stared at the floor in deep thought. Since my conversation with Tekka two days before she'd somehow seemed more... *human* to me. I thought I could see past her carefully guarded exterior and glimpse—just barely—a more flawed, vulnerable person hiding inside. I thought again about the *Guardian*, and the fact that we would in essence be going to plunder her father's grave. I was about to say something about it when she suddenly sighed and rose.

"Well," she said, "we're not solving the problem sitting here sulking. I'm off to get some sleep. You should do the same." She crossed the bridge and began descending the hatch, giving me a wry, tight-lipped smile that reminded me somehow of Kessa. "You look like hell."

# TWENTY-FOUR

*"Twenty minutes till we drop out of nullspace."* Rose's voice echoed over the *Orpheus*'s intercom system.

"Final gear checks!" Nadus shouted. "You know the drill. Everyone checks a buddy."

They did know the drill. The staging zone we'd created in the *Orpheus*'s cargo bay bustled with activity as everybody double-checked that exos were sealed correctly, gear was secure, and comms and life-support systems were functional. They moved and spoke with a confidence they hadn't had a few weeks ago.

"All good!"

"Check!"

"Clear!"

"Good to go!"

I felt a satisfied smile tug at the corner of my mouth. We still had a long ways to go, but we'd made progress. This mission would consist of myself, Artemis, Tekka, Tames, Nadus, Rid,

Shell, Jin, and Rathen. Rose and Bentley would remain on the *Orpheus* to provide support along with the other six rebels.

I turned to choose a buddy for my own gear check and found myself face to face with Artemis. She nodded her assent and I started inspecting her exo.

"You sure you wanna go on board with us?" I asked quietly.

She frowned at me. "Why? You think I'm scared?"

"No." I tugged on her supply pack, making sure it was fastened tight. "But I wouldn't want to go back to the *Panama*."

There was a long silence. She studied me as I continued checking her gear.

"Tekka tell you?" she asked.

"Yeah." I hesitated. "Why didn't *you* tell me?"

"Because I liked having a clean slate." She glanced over at Tekka, who was in the middle of having his exo inspected by Tames. "The rebels think I'm delusional. That I'm doing this just to finish my father's work. To vindicate him, somehow. They only agreed to help because they're desperate." She turned back to me. "I didn't want any of you to have that distraction. I needed you to trust me. *Need* you to trust me."

"I do trust you," I said.

She raised an eyebrow. "You've pestered me with questions since the beginning. Wanted to know all the details."

"Trust's gotta go both ways," I said. "I'm just done being a puppet. Fighting other people's battles for them. But if you tell me that you really believe we'll find the *Revelation*, then I'll be there."

An amused smile flitted across her face. "At the end of the day, you really are just a sucker."

"Maybe." I gave her a mischievous grin as I plugged my handcomputer into her exo and ran a diagnostic. "Then again, I'm getting paid no matter what. So maybe *you're* the sucker."

"You'll get paid a hell of a lot more if we do find the *Revelation*, though," she said. "All that loot for the taking. You'll never have to fight any battle, for anyone, ever again if you don't want to."

"Yeah," I said, thoughtfully. Once that idea would have been enough motivation for me to jump into hell itself. But that had been with Kessa by my side. Thinking about what came after this job left me feeling... empty. Alone. "But if there's one thing I've learned as a vulture, it's not to count your money till you're back in port. Greed makes people stupid."

Satisfied that her gear was in order, I let her begin inspecting my exo. "To answer your earlier question," she said, "yes. I am certain I want to go. I know what we're looking for. And I have to face this. I've been dreading it for years. I'd never forgive myself if I took the coward's way out now."

She stood in front of me, hands moving across the surface of my Jericho to make sure everything was sealed correctly. Even in our exos, I still towered over her.

"There's cowardice," I said softly, "and there's knowing your limits. They're different. But I've got your back in there, no matter what happens."

She looked up at me, her cold, blue eyes searching mine. I realized suddenly how close our faces were. "Are you certain that *you'll* be alright in there?" she asked.

The question caught me off guard. I frowned. "Of course."

I expected a sarcastic response, but her face was serious. "The last time you did this you lost everything. Everybody. Are you certain you're ready to go back?"

My breath caught in my throat. All the fear and guilt and self-loathing started trickling back into my brain from wherever it had gone the past few days.

What the hell was I doing?

I didn't see Artemis standing in front of me anymore. I saw Kessa. Smiling, blood on the starry night painted across her shoulders. *Why was she smiling?* We were even in roughly the same place the *Panama* had been, the outskirts of the Brahma system. Granted, that was one hell of a big place, but still. The irony was disquieting.

I shook myself and forced what I hoped was a convincing grin. "Yeah. I'm ready. Like you said, gotta face it eventually, right?"

Artemis studied me a moment longer, then nodded. We finished the inspection in silence. When it was done I left her to go check on the rest of the crew.

Rose and Bentley were on the bridge to run remote tech support, and Tekka's people were staying behind as backup. The rest of us, though, would be going into the *Guardian* through the ship's main docking port.

The *Guardian* was an interceptor, designed for speed and firepower. It was about twice the size of the *Orpheus*. The plan was simple: go in through the docking port, hurry to the second deck where there was an excellent chokepoint, and let the rippers come to us. Once we'd killed them all, we'd move on to search the rest of the ship and find the data we were looking for. The rippers were a threat to take seriously, but I doubted they'd have enough numbers to overrun us provided we were careful and didn't let ourselves get surrounded.

"*Dropping,*" Rose's voice said.

I felt that familiar, twisting, two-places-at-once sensation as the *Orpheus* rematerialized into the real world.

"*And, there she blows,*" Rose said a moment later. "*Starting the scan and making our approach.*"

My heart started to beat faster. Rose's voice sounded so much like Sev's. Rid glanced over his shoulder at me, and for a moment I could believe he was Rawlins.

"*There they are,*" Rose said. "*Scan is detecting a cluster of ripper signatures next to the primary power generator. Just like you said.*"

I closed my eyes, trying to force myself to calm down. Dammit, but I wanted a can. I didn't dare go into this job with frigicerin in my system, though. I needed to be sharp. Focused.

"Moment of truth, eh?" Tekka said. I opened my eyes to see him standing next to me. "Let's see if all this training of ours worked."

I nodded. "Visors down!" I yelled. "Airlock positions. Just like we practiced."

My visor sealed around my face. My vision blurred, then sharpened as my exo's neurointerface kicked in. Nadus and I moved to the front of the airlock, Jackhammers held at the ready. Everybody else filed in behind us.

*"Give me just a moment,"* Bentley muttered over the comms. *"Using the codes the rebels gave us to initiate the docking protocols..."*

The *Orpheus* groaned slightly as it connected to the *Guardian*'s docking port.

I felt a bead of sweat form on my brow. *Green dots...*

*"And,"* Rose said, *"we are go. Good luck."*

*...Flashing red...*

The airlock doors opened.

Darkness loomed beyond.

My legs wouldn't move. My breath felt trapped in my lungs. My pounding heart echoed in my ears. I could tell Nadus was looking at me.

*Go, damn you.*

I took a deep breath and pushed forward. Within a few steps I was outside the reach of the *Orpheus*'s gravity generators and inside the dark, dead, empty, weightless space of the *Guardian*.

This first area was a loading bay. Stacks of supplies were strapped to the floor, keeping them from floating off. I triggered my thrusters and navigated around them, heading towards a doorway at the far end of the room. Nadus moved beside me, Jackhammer raised as he covered my blind spots.

I glanced down at my wrist computer. Eight green dots blinked back at me as the crew entered the *Guardian* in pairs. I hit a button to get an atmospheric reading. The *Guardian's* gravity generator was obviously out, but the rest of the life-support systems still seemed to be working.

"*Rippers are moving,*" Rose's voice said. "*Docking the ship must have woken them up.*"

*Focus.* I looked away from my minimap. *Remember the plan.* I entered the corridor at the far end of the loading bay and started down it, my floodlights shearing through the darkness. "Everyone stay close and keep your eyes open. Don't want any surprises. It'll take them a minute or two to start hunting. We need to be at the chokepoint by then or we'll get caught in the open. Rid, get up here."

Nadus shifted to the side, allowing Rid to glide next to me. I pointed down the hallway at a closed door. "You're up."

He forged ahead. I let him go past me, taking position at a four-way intersection with my Jackhammer aimed into the darkness. Nadus wordlessly slipped into his position covering the opposite hallway. The rest of the crew started filing past, stacking up behind Rid at the end of the corridor.

"*Rippers are really awake now,*" Rose said. "*They're scattering. I'm losing track of where they are. The signals aren't concentrated enough.*"

*Hurry,* I wordlessly begged Rid. I risked a quick glance at him. He was locked into his task, a plasma cutting tool hacking through a panel to let him access the innards of the lock that was keeping us from continuing down the hallway.

I turned back to my hallway. It was empty and dark. I could see a few bits of debris drifting aimlessly, though. A few spent shells. A badly torn, empty boot. A chill ran down my spine.

"I'm through," Rid said.

The crew pushed through the open door like water through a broken dam. Nadus and I abandoned our positions to take up the rear as the group rushed down the corridor. We went up a stairway and entered the second deck.

"*Looking good,*" Rose said. "*Rippers don't seem to know where you are. They're just sort of running around aimlessly.*"

"This way," Artemis said from the front of the group. She darted around a corner.

"Stay close," I hissed. "No spreading out. Rose, where are the—"

"*I see one!*" Rathen screamed.

"Hold your fire!" I shouted. "We're not in—"

Too late. Light flashed and gunshots echoed deafeningly down the narrow halls as Rathen fired his Jackhammer wildly down a branching corridor he was covering. I cursed and fired my thrusters, coming to a halt next to him with my own Jackhammer raised.

There was no ripper. Instead, what seemed to be a discarded white spacesuit spun in torn tatters from the momentum of Rathen's bullets tearing through it.

Rathen's voice trembled. "I thought—it looked like—"

"*Rippers are* all *headed your way,*" Rose said, voice urgent. "*And they're moving fast. Holy crap, they're moving fast.*"

I brought up my minimap. We were still maybe fifty meters away from the chokepoint. "*Go!*" I pushed off against the wall, launching myself past the others. "Nadus, take the rear. Get into position as fast as possible. Pair up and cover flanks. *Move!*"

I darted around corners, Jackhammer aimed in front of me, pausing only to check that the others were still behind. I passed a set of ripper claw marks engraved in the wall. My breathing sounded so loud I was sure everyone could hear it, and my heart felt as if it were trying to tear its way out of my chest. I ducked around an empty crate drifting in the middle of the corridor and there one was.

My brain froze.

I'd seen rippers hundreds of times before. Their grotesque,

insect-like legs and their faceless, tooth-filled maws. In the Vanguard I'd mowed down hordes of them. But when I saw that ripper, scuttling along the wall towards us, claws shining in my floodlights, I felt suddenly as if I was a rookie stepping onto a battlefield for the first time. My muscles were rigid, unresponsive. I couldn't breathe. Couldn't think. All this—all the training, all the experience, all the damn grief I'd been through over the years—and here I was, frozen in fear by just one of the damn creatures.

The ripper tensed, drew back, getting ready to launch itself towards me.

Then its head exploded.

I blinked, the sound of the gunshot still echoing. The ripper's body twitched as it spun towards me, blood fountaining from the wound and forming scarlet spirals in a macabre display. I looked around to see who had shot, only to realize that smoke was venting from the barrel of my own Jackhammer. I gawked. The entire exchange had lasted no more than two seconds, but the fear had made it feel like an eternity. Through it all my instincts had held firm, though. I'd even subconsciously triggered my thrusters so that the gunshot didn't send me flying backward.

I looked back down the hallway. Movement as more rippers scuttled into view, clinging to the walls with their biosteel claws. Reality crystalized around me. My brain kicked into action. No room for fear. No time for panic. This was what I was made for.

"*Contact front!*" I yelled.

More gunshots. "*Left flanks!*" Shell shouted.

We were in a bad spot. I used my neurointerface to fire a grenade down the hallway, then whipped around the corner. We were almost to the chokepoint. More rippers ahead, though, launching through the air towards me. I planted my feet, activated my magboots, and began firing in controlled bursts. One ripper down. Two rippers. Three. Soon the hall was empty again, save for a few mangled, spasming ripper corpses. Rid and Artemis flew past me, down the hallway towards our designated chokepoint. I turned off the magnetic locks on my boots and started after them.

"Almost there!" I glanced back over my shoulder. Despite the urgency of the situation I couldn't help but feel a surge of pride as I saw the crew moving down the corridor with tactical precision, taking turns covering flanks, tapping shoulders as they moved past each other, and shouting out targets as they appeared. Nadus was still at the very back, firing at rippers I couldn't see and letting the recoil of his Jackhammer propel him down the hallway.

I ducked through a doorway into a large, central open space. The ship's common area. One way in on each side. Rid and Artemis were already on the other side of the room, accessing the control panel to shut the far door. Once that was shut, the rippers would all be forced to funnel through the same entrance we'd used. We'd mow them down as they went through and then have free run of the ship.

"How's it going?" I said over a direct channel to Artemis.

"Almost got it," she said, her voice taut. "We just need to—"

Her voice cut off as a ripper suddenly loomed in the doorway, only a meter or so away from her. She scrambled backward, lifting her Jackhammer, but she squeezed the trigger too early and the bullets slammed into the doorway near Rid's head. Rid cursed and instinctively lifted his hands to cover his face, accidentally pushing himself away from the doorway.

The ripper lunged towards Artemis, claws slashing at her face. There was a flash of sparks. Artemis screamed. My blood turned cold. I aimed and squeezed the trigger of my Jackhammer. The barrage struck the ripper in the chest, slamming it against the corner of the entryway and sending it spinning away down the corridor.

"Rid!" I fired my thrusters and blasted towards Artemis. "Get that door closed!"

Rid twisted in mid-air. I landed next to Artemis and activated my magboots, facing down the hallway. More rippers were rushing towards us. I dispatched them, then quickly ejected my magazine and slammed a fresh one home, glancing down at Artemis as I did so. "Hey! You alright?"

She steadied herself against the wall. "Yeah! I think." She felt at her visor. Two long, shallow scratches were engraved in the front of it. Another few centimeters and her face would have been cut to ribbons.

More rippers were pouring down the hallway. Jin appeared next to me, Jackhammer roaring as he sprayed bullets down the corridor.

"Got it!" Rid yelled, who had finally stabilized himself next to the control panel. The doors shut with a mechanical whirring noise. I breathed a sigh of relief. "Good job. Now we just need to—"

"Help! Hey! Help us!"

I whirled. The whole crew had made it into the common room and were taking positions near the door. All except for three. In the far corridor—the one we'd entered the room through—I saw Tames and Rathen still lagging behind. Tames was facing away from us, firing wildly at a horde of rippers while she pulled an apparently unresponsive Rathen along with her. Nadus was even further behind, doing his best to cover their retreat. For every ripper he shot, though, more took its place.

"There's too many!" Tames was shouting. "I need—"

Her voice went suddenly quiet as her Jackhammer stopped firing. "Oh, *hell*," she hissed.

*Dammit.* I readied myself to leap down the corridor after them. Before I could, though, Shell was there, thrusters flaring with Tekka right behind her. Shell braced herself against the wall and fired a grenade into the swarm as Tekka grabbed Rathen and pushed him towards us.

"Flank!" I shouted. "Watch your flank!"

As I spoke, a ripper appeared in a doorway next to Tekka. He spun to face it. I raised my Jackhammer but I was too far away. The ripper's tailspike darted towards Tekka's chest. He grunted. The ripper lunged towards him. Nadus intercepted it, catching it in the chest with one armored boot and pinning it to the wall. It spasmed and flailed, claws flashing wildly. Something was stuck to its tail but it was moving too fast for me to make out what it was. Nadus fired a shot into its skull at point-blank range, then pivoted, grabbed Tekka, and blasted towards us. Tames and Shell came right behind him.

"Move!" I shouted at the rebels gathered by the door. "Let them through!"

They did. I caught Rathen. Nadus pulled a wriggling Tekka through. Tames and Shell were right behind them. The rest of the rebels closed the gap behind them, pouring covering fire down the hallway into the swarm of rippers.

Rathen suddenly started kicking. His rifle fired, sending a shot whizzing past my head into a wall. I jerked his gun away from him and pinned him down. "What's wrong with him?" I asked.

"Nothing." Tames was already at Tekka's side. "Just panicking. Tekka! How bad are you—"

There was a strange sound in the comms. It took me a few moments to work it out. When it did, I frowned. *Laughing.* Tekka was *laughing.*

"I'm alright," he wheezed. "I'm alright." He sat up, holding out empty hands. I realized all at once what had happened. The ripper's tailspike had struck his rifle. That was what I'd seen pinned on the end of its flailing tail after Nadus had kicked it.

Tames let out a long burst of air from her nostrils. "Tekka, you're the luckiest bastard I know."

I turned to back to Rathen. I was still pinning him to the floor. His arms were flailing. I tried to calm him down, but either he couldn't hear me or was too panicked to register the words. A few moments later Jin was floating over us, visor lifted. That seemed to do the trick. Rathen stilled.

I moved away from them towards the doorway. More rippers were still flooding down the corridor, but Nadus and Shell were firing at them, shooting in consecutive bursts to conserve ammo just like we'd trained.

Artemis flew next to me, sticking herself to the floor with her magboots. "Now what?" she asked breathlessly.

I glanced around. There were no other ways in, and the rippers that had been outside the far door had opted to take the long way around instead of trying to claw their way through it. Which meant that the plan had worked.

"Now," I said, "We just wait."

After just a few minutes, the flow of rippers had slowed to a trickle. Then they stopped coming.

*"I'm not picking up any more signatures,"* Rose said. *"Everyone alright in there?"*

"Yep." I glanced around. Rathen had more or less recovered. He was in a corner now, breathing heavily while Jin and Tames spoke quietly to him. Artemis and Tekka were both still evidently riding the high that comes after narrowly avoiding death. "We're all good here. Everyone did great."

We waited another fifteen minutes before I finally gave the order to move out and start searching the ship. In groups. Logically, any remaining rippers would have attacked us by now. But... well, that was what I'd thought on the *Panama* too.

I'd be damned if I was making that mistake again.


"There it is," Rid grunted.

The doors to the bridge opened. I went through first,

checking corners until I was satisfied that the room was empty. Artemis, Rid, and Tekka filed in behind me.

It was a much bigger bridge than what we had on the *Orpheus*. A few of the computer screens were flickering. Some of the chairs were soaked in long-dried blood. No bodies, though. The rippers never left bodies.

I glanced at Artemis. She had her visor down, but I could tell from her stance that she was nervous. Her hand was trembling slightly, and she moved her head slowly and deliberately, as if she was afraid she might see something she didn't want to if she looked around too quickly.

I switched to a private channel with her. "I can go ahead, if you want. Just make sure that..." I hesitated. *Just to make sure you don't stumble upon your father's mutilated remains.* Not that the rippers would have left anything behind.

"No." Her voice was quiet. "I can do it. I have to do it."

Tekka spoke up on the main channel. "All things considered, I think that went pretty damn well."

I nodded. No casualties. Our performance had been far from flawless but we'd pulled through. Other than Rathen, who was already back on the *Orpheus* with Jin, everyone had kept their cool. Even me. I was shocked at how relieved I felt that I'd made it through the ordeal without breaking. Once the action had started and I'd gotten through my initial burst of panic, I'd gone through the rest of the fight clear and focused.

"Here's my question," Rid asked. "Why didn't they use the escape pods?"

"They did," Tekka said, hitting a button on a keyboard. The attached computer screen only made a faint attempt at glowing before going dark. "A lucky few made it out. That's how we knew where to find the *Guardian*. But nobody had time to grab things like the *Revelation*'s black box on the way out."

Rid nodded, opening a cabinet and digging through it. "So, is this thing literally a black box?"

"No." Artemis activated her thrusters and flew to the back of the bridge. I followed. There was a blast door.

"Rid," I said. "Got a lock for you."

Rid started over. Before he could get there, though, Artemis raised a hand. She moved to a keypad near the door and pressed a few buttons. The door swung open.

Tekka and I shared a glance. He gave an "I told you so" sort of shrug.

Artemis took a deep breath, then went inside. I followed.

It seemed to be some sort of secure storage room. Shelves full of documents, data devices, weapons, and gear lined the narrow confines. I ignored all of that, though.

"Artemis," I said. "I'm..."

My voice trailed off.

A figure was stretched out in the center of the room. Looked like a middle-aged man. He was wearing a Brahmian naval uniform. I couldn't see his face. It was hidden behind an emergency life-support mask. I could see a bullet hole in the visor, though, and a pistol still gripped tightly in the man's right hand.

Artemis stood in silence for several minutes. I gave her space. Finally, she took a deep breath, moved forward, and gently pried something from the corpse's left hand.

"I have the black box," she said, her voice icy cold. "We can go now."

She turned and flew past me without another word. I lingered a few moments longer, unable to take my eyes from the corpse.

*We had a good run.*

My pulse started to pound.

*I'm sorry.*

I shook myself and turned away.

———

"You've really got a place you can stow a ship that size without the Paragon noticing?" I asked incredulously as I studied the *Guardian* through the *Orpheus*'s bridge window.

"The Khendars will come up with some reason to have it docked at one of their mining stations," Tekka said. "They can scrap it for parts or make it so it's not obvious it's an old Brahmian ship. Either way, the resistance will find a use for it."

"Well, then, I guess this little idiot's mission has paid off for you already," I said.

Tekka raised an eyebrow. "*And* for you. Don't think I didn't notice that ultracell Shell stole from the engine room. That's property of the Brahmian Planetary Governance, you know."

"Huh." I rubbed my chin. "Funny. 'Cause I seem to remember destroying that particular political organization."

Tekka's eyes went dark, and for a moment I thought I'd gone too far. Finally, though, he gave an unbelieving laugh and shook his head. "To the victor the spoils, I suppose," he said. "For now." He left me with that, leaving the bridge.

I glanced at Artemis. She was sitting at one of the *Orpheus*'s computers with the black box—which was, in fact, a bright orange, palm-sized datadrive—plugged in. She'd also taken several other datadrives from her father's collection. She hadn't spoken any more than strictly necessary since returning from the *Guardian*, and had gotten straight to work cracking the black box's mysteries. The rest of us, in the meantime, had gotten to work disposing of the ripper carcasses and getting the Brahmian ship ready to travel. Tames and a few of the rebels would fly it to a location designated by the Khendars, then meet us back at our camp on Brahma.

"Seriously?" Rose's voice echoed through the bridge. She, Bentley, Rid, and Shell were gathered near the pilot's station as Rid and Shell recapped their harrowing adventures. "His *Jackhammer* caught it?"

"Artemis nearly got cut too," Rid said. He drew two lines

across his face. "Just a bit closer and that ripper would've had her head off."

Bentley shook his head incredulously. "You guys are insane. No way am I ever setting foot on one of those ships. Not enough money in the world."

"That's fine," Rid said. "At least we'll know where to look if we need someone to type in an access code someone else gave you."

Rose burst into laughter. Even Shell cracked a smile. Bentley threw up his hands indignantly. "That was my job! Hell, I'd just have gotten in the way in there."

*Getting in the way* reminded me of the next task I'd been meaning to check off my list. I left them, going down the chute and heading towards the bunkrooms the rebels had been staying in. I searched until I found Rathen, sitting in a corner and staring down at the floor. Jin was nearby.

"You alright?" I asked.

Rathen looked up. His eyes were bloodshot. "Yeah," he said. "I... I'll pack my things. I'm just gonna get someone hurt if I do... *that*... again."

"Well, are you gonna do it again?" I asked.

He stared at me. "I'm... not *planning* on it..."

I studied him for a moment. "Rathen, I ain't your commanding officer. This isn't an army. You wanna go, you go. But I ain't kicking you out, if that's what you think. You made a mistake, which led to panic, which led to a sticky situation. We got through it." I glanced at Jin. "You've got buddies who're here for you. You've got training. Next time you'll do better."

"Lax!"

I turned my head to see Nadus standing in the doorway. He jerked his head down the hall. "She's got it."

I followed him back onto the bridge. Tekka had returned as well. We all huddled around the holoprojector as Artemis finished inputting instructions into the navigation computer. Her face was pale as she finished typing, her breath short.

"Done," she said. She met my eyes for just a moment before turning to the projector. We waited in hushed silence as the navigation system worked out the co-ordinates she'd inputted.

A starmap flickered to life in the center of the bridge. First it showed where we were, the edge of the Brahma system. It zoomed out. A long, thin line traced from where we were, through the bowels of space, across several different star systems, and then came to a blinking red point.

"And there it is," Artemis breathed. "Rose. How long would it take us to get there via foldgate?"

"Uh..." Rose scrambled to input some co-ordinates. She whistled. "Nineteen days. There's a foldgate nearby... well, not nearby. Several thousand lightyears. But near enough that we can beat the *Revelation* there."

I studied the starmap. What was so special about that location? It was deep space. No planets, stars, or registered stations. The only nearby object was a black hole. Why? What was the point of going to all the effort to take over the *Revelation* just to fly it to the middle of nowhere?

"So it's happening," Tekka said, voice unbelieving. "We're doing this."

I looked up at Artemis. She hadn't looked away from the blinking red dot. As I watched, a tear formed in the corner of her eye. She brushed it away immediately, looked around to make sure nobody had seen it, and locked gazes with me.

I gave a half-smile. "You were right all along."

Her face broke slowly out into a grin.

"We're doing this," she said.

# TWENTY-FIVE



It's the simple things that make life worth living, I've always figured.

Cold beer. A warm fire beneath the stars. The sound of friendly laughter hanging in the air. I settled against my log and found myself heaving a contented sigh. I hadn't felt this good since... well, not since I'd been with Kessa, that was for damn sure.

The entire crew—all eighteen of us—were gathered around our campfire. Tames and her people had dropped off the *Guardian* and made it back. Now it was just a matter of resupplying before we embarked.

I glanced across the fire towards Artemis. She was staring into the flames, holding a bottle of wine loosely in one hand. It struck me again, along with a pang of guilt, just how beautiful she was. I forced myself to look away.

"So let's say it does work out," Jin was saying, his voice only slightly slurred by the alcohol we'd all been drinking. He waved his bottle in the general direction of my crew. "We go in, we do the job, and you walk away with a crap ton of money. What are you doing next?"

"Honestly," Bentley said, taking a long pull from his bottle, "nothing. Gonna buy myself a nice place—planetside, doesn't much matter where as long as it's away from fighting and rippers and whatnot—fix myself up some clean records so nobody ever comes after me, and do absolutely nothing for the rest of my life."

Rose spoke up next. "Gonna keep doing this," she said. "Maybe get some upgrades for the *Orpheus*. Get the best gear money can buy. Then keep flying around, finding lost stuff and having adventures."

"Easy for you to say," Shell said with a smirk. "You won't be the one going into the ships."

"You *volunteered* to go in there!" Rose protested. "What would you do?"

Shell shrugged. "Keep traveling, I guess."

"You wouldn't want to go back to your homeship?" Rid asked.

"Don't think that's an option for me," Shell said grimly, meeting my eyes as she said it. She glanced sharply away from me towards Rid. "Why, would you?"

"Hell no." Rid shuddered. "Never going back there if I can help it."

"Where would you go, then?" Jin asked.

For some reason, Rid looked at Rose. "Dunno," he said. "I kinda like this life, though. Working with friends. A real crew. I wouldn't mind keeping at it a bit longer."

Rose smiled.

"What about you lot?" Bentley gestured towards Jin and his companions. "You could make some money too. What are you planning on doing? Surely there are places you're dying to see. You could visit Earth! Or go stay on a luxury station!"

Jin's smile faded slightly. He glanced around at the other

rebels. "I mean... we'll keep fighting. That's the point. This is our home. *My* home. I can't just leave to go wander around. Not until Brahma is free, at least."

"Ah." Bentley coughed. "Well, now I feel like a real bastard."

Laughter all around. Even Rathen was smiling, for the first time I was aware of since his panic attack.

"You know," Jin said, raising his bottle in a mock salute, "for a bunch of war-profiteering, criminal lowlifes, you guys aren't so bad."

"And we could never have hoped to meet a nicer bunch of terrorists," Rose said, returning the gesture with a grin.

I glanced over at Tekka. He raised one eyebrow at me. Somehow, our crew's little trust issue seemed to have resolved itself. Guess they'd just needed some pressure to bond beneath. Hell, even Tekka and I were somewhere close to friends now, regardless of what he claimed.

The conversation moved on, every person retelling their version of our harrowing adventures on the *Guardian*. I didn't feel the need to add anything. It felt good just to listen. I'd forgotten how it felt to be part of a group. To have a crew.

*Don't get cocky.* I tried to temper the triumph I felt with a hard dose of reality. We hadn't even left yet for our main task. And we still knew hardly anything about the *Revelation*. I felt myself start to tense as I thought about it.

Laughter caught my ear. I looked up to see Artemis across the fire, face lit in a wide smile as she laughed at some joke. Our eyes met and lingered before we both turned sharply away. It could have been the firelight, but I swore she was slightly flushed.

The tension faded. I found myself smiling without really knowing why. We had work to do yet, sure. For tonight, though... tonight I could afford to celebrate what we'd accomplished. I took another sip of beer.

. . .

By the time I left the fire I didn't feel much like sleeping. I went to the bridge instead, intent on catching up on some of the data Artemis had found among her father's files. There was a lot to it. I only found myself more confused as I searched through it all. Surely there had to be an answer. An explanation as to who had sabotaged the *Revelation* and how. Whatever it was, though, I was increasingly certain the answers weren't here.

"Tried that already," Artemis's voice said. I turned to see her head poking out of the hatch, staring at my screen. She grunted as she pulled herself up the rest of the way. "Got nothing helpful."

I glared at the screen, as if I could intimidate it into revealing its secrets to me. "I'll say. Just questions, dead ends, and endlessly looping paradoxes. I think I'm halfway crazy already."

She sat down next to me, studying the list of names. She still smelled faintly of the wine she'd been drinking. "That's the danger of it. You have expectations. Notions of what the answer is going to be. And so, you try to force all of the data we have to fit those notions, and when they don't you try again, over and over again, until none of it means anything anymore."

"And you don't? Have expectations, I mean. Guesses. Surely you have a few ideas about what might have happened, even if they're only half-baked."

She shrugged. "Theories come inevitably to mind, of course, but I try very hard to keep them malleable. The most important fact to keep at the forefronts of our minds is that we simply don't have the data necessary to properly formulate guesses, and doing so is an exercise in futility." She shrugged. "It's like you said, way back on the *Jonah*. All we can do is gather what info we can, get to the ship, and then improvise from there."

I rubbed at my bleary eyes. "Because that's worked so well for me in the past."

Artemis fell silent, watching me curiously.

I groaned. "Sorry. You're right. *I'm* right, I guess. That's all there is to it. I just... well, last time I underprepared, and it got everyone I loved killed. I'd like to avoid a repeat of that. Even if it does drive me crazy."

She gave an earnest look. "It'll be different this time. We're going in with our eyes wide open. Prepared."

I frowned. "You *just* said we have no idea what we're dealing with."

"Yes. But we *know* that we don't know." She flashed me a good-humored smile that made my heart skip a beat. "That's got to count for something."

I found myself smiling too. "Yeah. I guess so."

She leaned back in her seat, casting her eyes around the bridge of the *Orpheus*. The first few weeks the sight of her here had been incongruous, but now it felt right. Had she changed, or had my perception shifted?

"Is this what it was like? In your old life?" She waved a hand. "Obvious differences aside, of course."

"More or less." I took a few moments of my own to study the familiar sights. "Researching jobs, putting together a plan, finding the right personnel and equipment. Just felt more..."—I hesitated, searching for a word—"more personal back then."

She cocked her head to the side. "What do you mean?"

"Just that back then it felt like it all had purpose. Now it's just... what I do."

"It had purpose because you had a family."

I frowned at her. "I thought you didn't believe in family. Just people with similar agendas."

She shrugged. "I don't. Or maybe I do. Or did once. Or maybe I'm just drunk." She smiled, her eyes meeting mine, and

I was suddenly vividly aware of how close we were. "Or maybe all of this has just reminded me of what it felt like to care about people again."

I nodded slowly, not taking my eyes from hers. "Yeah."

She kissed me.

There was nothing sudden about the way she moved, no unexpected burst of speed or passion. And yet I found myself as shocked and frozen as if she had suddenly drawn a weapon. Less so, I imagine, as I had significantly more experience with that situation. She simply leaned forward, closed her eyes, and kissed me gently but lingeringly on the lips. I just sat there blinking.

She drew back slightly, her eyes opening and searching mine again. She must have been able to see the wires in my brain short-circuiting, the gears churning to try to make sense of any of this, because she gave an amused smile.

"That bad, huh? To be fair, I'm a little out of prac—"

My body finally caught up to my brain and I reached forward, wrapping her in my arms and pulling her close as I kissed her. She stiffened at first, maybe in surprise or perhaps in fear, but as the kiss endured, she relaxed, melting into me, the warmth of her body pressing tight against mine. I tasted the sweetness of the wine on her lips, felt her breathing, hot and desperate as her hands moved up my torso.

I pushed against her, and she sagged onto her back. There wasn't much room on the bench we'd been sitting on, but I did the best I could with what I had, my brain blind to everything else as I followed her down, kissing her with eight years of pent-up longing. Her hands moved up my back, touching, exploring, until they reached the nape of my neck and the hard metallic line of my port there, and she froze.

It was only for a moment, and a brief one at that. Tenseness where there had been tenderness, hesitation where there had been hunger, a quick, surprised draw of breath. She recovered quickly, her hand moving away and her body relaxing again. But it was enough.

Enough to break the spell. Enough to remind me that I was a monster, created to kill and destroy. Enough to make me think about the first person who had ever convinced me that I could be more than that.

In an eternally long moment between moments, I found that I wasn't here with Artemis anymore. I was with Kessa, kissing for what I didn't yet know would be the last time. A few brief moments of bliss before Rawlins burst in through that door. Before we climbed into our exos. Before we walked into that damned ship. Before the rippers had surged demonlike out of the darkness and taken away the only good thing that had ever happened to me in a storm of claws and blood. Before—

"Lax!"

I blinked and shook myself. Artemis was staring at me, her eyes worried and confused as they moved up and down my face. I felt myself breathing heavily, my chest heaving as a slight tremor worked its way up through the arm that was holding me above Artemis's slight frame.

"What's wrong?" she asked.

"I..."

*Green dots, flashing red...*

"Hey." Her hand rested on my cheek. "It's alright."

*We had a good run...*

"I..." I felt sweat beading on my brow. "I can't. I'm sorry."

She said something else, but I couldn't make sense of it as I stumbled off her and towards the hatch. I passed somebody in the corridor but brushed past them. Before I knew it, I was sitting on the floor of my room, clutching my head in my hands as I gasped for air.

A can. I needed a can. The walls were closing in around me,

the rippers leering eyeless at us through the darkness, and Kessa was looking at me, and if I didn't stop it soon, it would be too late. But there was nothing. No can to save me. No barrier between me and the relentless onslaught of remembering. Only her...

# TWENTY-SIX

## THE PANAMA



Time slowed as I watched the single globule of blood drift, spinning aimlessly until it collided with Kessa's shoulder pauldron, smearing itself dark and ugly against the night sky she had painted there. Red against the blues and yellows. Wrong. All wrong.

"I think it got me," Kessa said weakly.

"Come on," I growled, grabbing her by the arm and pulling her along with me. "We're getting out of here."

She groaned but activated her thrusters, following after me. I thought only briefly about taking Black's corpse with us before rejecting the idea. Under better circumstances I would have. But these weren't better circumstances. Every second now could push us to one side or the other of life and death.

"Liung. Status," I snapped.

"Hauling ass back to the *Orpheus*," he gasped. "No sign of rippers yet."

I felt a surge of relief. "Good. Sev?"

*"Ready to blast out of here. You guys gotta hurry, that patrol is only a few minutes out."*

As if I needed a reminder. At this rate we'd be lucky just to make it off of the *Panama* alive. I gritted my teeth, glancing down at the minimap on my computer. The flashing red dots representing the final resting places of Black and Rawlins were falling farther and farther behind us. Liung's team was almost to the docking bay the *Orpheus* was waiting at. "We can make it. Just hold tight—"

The green dot at the back of Liung's group flashed red.

"Aw *hell!*" Liung shouted. I heard a faint, muffled thunking sound over his voice as he fired his SVAG. "They're on us!"

My throat constricted. "How many?"

"Too many! I can't—"

His voice twisted into a scream.

"*LAX!*" Kess yelled.

I looked up, shining my floodlights down the corridor. Rippers. Dozens of them, crawling along the floor, the ceiling, the walls. Looking like pale, overgrown spiders in my flood-lights. The closest one tensed, its tail drawing back to strike. I raised my SVAG and held the trigger, clamping my magboots to the floor to keep the recoil from driving me backward. The ripper's body jolted as the barrage of bullets tore into it, tail spasming and slamming into a window nearby.

"Behind us!" Kessa shouted, opening fire. I wanted desper-ately to turn and help, but the rest of the rippers in front of me were surging forward. I fired the last few rounds in the SVAG, then used my neurointerface to unlock my magboots and trigger my thrusters at the same time, jolting me slightly to the right and out of the path of a set of flailing claws. I caught the ripper by the tail, locked my magboots, and jerked it like a whip, sending it hurtling into the oncoming monsters. It collided with one, bounced off, and slammed into another, causing the push to falter in a tangle of limbs and claws, the rippers tearing through each other in their eagerness to get at me.

I ejected the empty mag from my SVAG and slammed in a new one, glancing over my shoulder again. Kess had backed up a few paces, still firing her weapon. In my brief look I saw one ripper drifting aimlessly, limbs spasming uselessly—she must have landed a hit along its spinal column—while others moved silently forward.

Their silence was an unnerving contrast to the chaos playing out over the comms. Sevani was shouting, trying desperately to understand what was going on. Somebody was screaming—Liung, my heads-up display indicated. No words. No meaning. Just pain. Liung's own words flashed through my brain. *They like to start down low. Where it's nice and soft and warm. Then work their way up from there.*

I brushed the words aside, every iota of brainpower my body could muster focused on fighting off the swarm of demons that was now descending upon me. No room for terror, no time for grieving as the sounds of death filled my ears. A strange calmness filled me as I took a step forward and emptied my SVAG into the tangled mass of flesh from point-blank range. One of them managed to make it through alive, claws slashing wildly at me. I swung my now empty SVAG and slammed the barrel downward into the ripper's skull, knocking it to the floor. It was still alive. I raised my boot, ready to bring it down and crush the creature—

"Lax!" Kessa's voice was urgent. A glance showed me that she had backed up even further, just barely managing to stay out of the rippers' reach. "*I need you!*"

The sense of calmness shattered, replaced by a rush of terror unlike any I'd ever felt before. I whipped around, firing my thrusters and propelling me towards Kessa. She was stumbling backward as best she could, frantically reloading her SVAG as a ripper bore down on top of her.

The terror twisted into rage. I was dimly aware of my own scream mingling with the others—a guttural, animal roar of hate and fury as I threw myself between Kessa and the ripper. I slapped one claw aside with the SVAG and backhanded the creature across the face, sending it spinning away, then anchored myself to the floor.

Another ripper leaped towards me, using its tail to push itself off the wall it had been clinging to. I hurled the SVAG at it with enough force to temporarily stun it, then ducked past its wildly flailing claws, grabbing the ripper's torso in one hand and head in the other, and pulled.

Screams in the comms. My friends. My family. My *crew*. People who had relied on me to keep them safe. Dying slow, painful deaths, far outside of my reach.

I pulled.

A splash of red against a warm, starry night. Kessa's voice panting in the comms, lost amid the chaos, and yet somehow piercing through it all. Depending on me to save her. To get her out.

I pulled.

The ripper spasmed and went still as its flesh finally gave way to the Jericho's mechanical strength, the head tearing away from the body and pulling a few feet of metallic spinal cord with it. I flung the grisly wreckage down the corridor and snatched my SVAG from the air where it was floating.

Then paused.

The rippers had all frozen in place, clutching the floor and ceiling and walls and just staring at us—at me—with their eyeless gazes.

I waited, my breath catching in my throat. Slowly, I removed the spent mag from my SVAG and inserted a new one

"Lax?" Kess's voice hissed in my ear, sounding weak and faint. "What's happening?"

The rippers just sat there, so still they might as well have been dead. This wasn't right. Rippers *never* acted like this. Rippers were reckless—unstoppably aggressive. They had no concept of tactics, or timing, or fear. All they knew was hunger.

*So why were they waiting?*

"I don't know," I breathed. I turned back, looking in the other direction. Same story—rippers waiting silently everywhere I could see, more joining them with each passing moment.

My mind raced. A way out. There had to be a way out. The comms were still full of screams. I couldn't tell whose anymore. Another of the green dots from Liung's team had turned red. Sevani was shouting something over and over.

The rippers started moving. Slowly, but inevitably. Inching forward with movements so slow they were hardly noticeable.

Something loomed behind them. I blinked, certain my mind was playing tricks on me. A nightmarish shape was approaching. A ripper that was easily twice the size of the others. With... were those *wings?*

"What the hell is that?" Kessa groaned, staring at it.

"I don't know." I shook myself. *A way out. A way out.* There had to be one. I kept my gun trained on the rippers in front of me and swiveled my head to look behind us. Sure enough, more rippers were waiting there, mirroring the slow, dreadful approach of the ones ahead. Inch by terrible inch.

"Lax."

*A way out.* There had to be one. There was always one. I just needed to—

"Lax."

The nightmare ripper was getting closer, other rippers clearing the way for it. I got a better look at it now. Its wings were black and glinted in my floodlights. This couldn't be real. Rippers were all the same. This couldn't be—

Kessa's hand touched my arm. I looked down at her. Her face was pale and frail-looking, but she was smiling.

*Why was she smiling?*

"It's alright, Lax," she said. Her voice was soft and gentle, and yet it somehow cut through all the chaos in my comms like warm water through snow.

I shook my head. "No. No, it's not." My breath was ragged. I glanced towards the rippers, holding out my submachine gun like it was a holy symbol holding back the forces of hell, but they kept on creeping forward all the same. The nightmare ripper loomed larger with each careful step forward. I pivoted backward, waving my gun to ward back the horde behind us, then swung back. "It's not alright. I'm gonna get you out of here." I felt a lump forming in my throat, felt every emotion I'd ever felt—fear, love, anger, hope, hate, disappointment—clawing at each other, amplified a thousand times. "We're gonna get that life I promised you."

The screams had all gone silent. Where a cluster of green dots had been on my minimap were now four flashing points of red. Only two green dots were left.

"Maybe it's not the life we lived that matters," Kessa said, her voice fading quieter with each word. "Maybe it's just who we lived it with."

I looked at her. She was still smiling, even as a tear ran down the side of her face.

"We're not getting out of this, Lax," she said softly.

A ripper pounced. I fired a stream of bullets into its head, then grabbed its twitching form as it came close and hurled it aside. The other rippers recoiled slightly, making way for the nightmare to inch closer yet.

None of this made sense. I was dreaming. I had to be. None of this could be real.

I gritted my teeth. "No. I don't accept that."

"It's alright." She lowered the barrel of her SVAG from where it had been pointed at the rippers. A chill ran down my spine as I realized where she was aiming it instead.

"We had a good run, Lax," she whispered.

Another ripper lunged forward. I yelled, swinging my submachine gun and clubbing the ripper on the side of the head. It went spinning away. I turned back desperately to Kessa, reaching for her. "Kess. Please. Don't."

She closed her eyes.

"Wait." I spun just in time to fire a barrage of bullets at another ripper leaping at me from the other direction. "Kessa, don't—"

The nightmare was looming above us, wings outstretched. Its maw opened wide, glistening with jagged teeth. Watching. Waiting. For what? *What was it looking for?*

*Not real. This can't be real.*

"I'm sorry, Lax," Kess said.

She pulled the trigger.

Another green dot flashed red.

The nightmare lunged for me.

# TWENTY-SEVEN

I'm not sure how long I was there, sitting alone on the floor of my old room, beneath the stars that Kessa had never quite finished painting. Eventually, though, my breathing steadied and my vision cleared. I raised my hand to wipe a tear from my cheek.

My memories of what had happened after she pulled the trigger were rough and unstable. I remembered a moment of denial, of shock so overwhelming I couldn't even begin to process it. The nightmare ripper had lunged for me. I'm not sure how I evaded it. All I knew was there was a sense of rage stronger than any dosage of ignicerin I'd ever received in the Vanguard. I remembered hurling myself at the rippers, certain of nothing except that I wanted—*needed*—to kill as many of them as I possibly could. I'd killed them until I was almost out of ammo, and then I'd fired my last bullet into the cargo pod full of ultracells.

I remembered a flash of white light, and then... nothingness.

I'd woken up tied down to a medical bed on a Paragon patrol craft. The medtech working on me had been amazed I'd somehow survived it all.

*You must be the luckiest man in the universe*, he'd said.

I let my head fall back until it collided with the desk behind me. Something clattered and fell to the ground. I frowned, turning my head to see a glint of metal. It took me a moment to recognize it. Eladrius's routing chip.

*Talk to someone.* Nadus's voice echoed in my head. *I don't care who. Just find someone to share the burden with.*

I gritted my teeth, staring at the routing chip. It seemed futile and stupid. But I knew deep down that he was right. I *had* to overcome this. Until I did—until I stabilized myself—I was a liability to the mission and, more importantly, to my crew. I cursed and grabbed the routing chip.

The bridge was empty now. Brahma's sun had long since set. I felt a twisted knob of guilt form in my gut as I looked at the bench where Artemis had kissed me just a few hours ago. I wasn't even sure what about. Some of it because I'd hurt Artemis, who deserved better than whatever it was she thought she saw in me. Some of it out of a still-lingering loyalty to Kessa, who'd deserved a better fate than dying on my watch. But it didn't matter now. I sat down at the communication console and plugged the routing chip in.

*...Connecting...*

The screen flickered for a moment, lines of code running across it before the *connecting* message reappeared. I frowned. Maybe the system needed an update.

*...Connecting...*

I found myself growing nervous. What was I supposed to say?

*...Connecting...*

The message vanished. Eladrius's face appeared, surprisingly unshaven for a priest. He seemed to be planetside, somewhere dark. I could see stars behind him. He opened his mouth. "Lackan? Is that—"

I suddenly found myself reaching forward and jerking the

routing chip out of the terminal. The image vanished, replaced by an error message.

I sat there, staring at the screen for a few minutes. I wasn't sure why I'd done that. Somehow it just hadn't felt quite right. I found my hands navigating the computer almost of their own accord. Within seconds, the *Orpheus*'s communication relay was connecting to a different number.

There was almost no delay this time. Not more than a few seconds after I hit the *call* button the system connected and Sevani's tired but alert face jolted into view.

"Lax!" She rubbed at her eyes, her face lit only by the gentle glow of her computer. "What's going on?" She stared at me closer, her eyes narrowing. "You look bad. What happened? Is Rose—"

"Rose is fine," I said wearily.

She frowned. "What's going on, then?"

"Nothing much." I forced a grin onto my face, feeling stupid. "I just... figured..."

I fell silent. Sevani stared at me, her face gradually softening.

"Lax. Come on. What's up?"

"How do you move on from the best thing to ever happen to you?" I asked, my voice hoarse and broken.

Sevani let out a heavy sigh, sagging backward. Looked like she was in her bed. "Wow. Really coming out swinging, huh?"

I gave a weak chuckle. "Yeah. Sorry."

Sevani chewed thoughtfully on her lower lip. It was a look I knew well. The one she'd always had when she was trying to work out a more efficient flight path, or work out the best deal on ship parts, or any other number of puzzling problems. Finally, she spoke, her voice slow and reluctant. "You remember the neurovirus outbreak on Albeni 7?"

I searched my memories. "Yeah. I remember being glad we weren't there for it."

"Rose's dad caught it," Sev continued. Her voice was grim but matter of fact. "Before they'd come up with the cure. Ate through his brain in less than a week. He was smart, though, and managed to get Rose away as soon as he realized he'd been infected."

I stared at her, trying to process the new information. "How'd you keep from catching it?"

"Because I wasn't there." She gave a weak, forced smile. "Because I was with you guys. Getting ready to board the *Panama*."

A hollow feeling settled into my gut. "So... you found out you'd lost Rose's dad... and then you lost us."

"That's about the shape of it."

I watched her for a few moments, neither of us speaking. Sevani had always seemed unbreakable to me. An impenetrable fortress of self-confidence and defiance of the world and everything it had to throw at her. But now, curled into a ball on her bed, face illuminated only by the dim light of her computer screen, I could see the cracks in her armor. The frailty, the old, buried pains that lay just beneath the surface.

"What did you do?" I finally asked.

"I went and found my daughter. Then I sold off what I could from the *Panama* job, lived on that for a while, and when it was safe, went back to Albeni 7 to take advantage of the power vacuum the outbreak had left to start up my business. I just... kept moving."

I gave a humorless chuckle. "Easier said than done."

"Yeah. It hurts. But that's the key, Lax. You've got to let it hurt."

I grimaced. "Does it ever stop?"

"No. But, eventually, if you let it, the pain changes. The bitterness fades. The anger softens. And instead, you feel..." She frowned, searching for words. "Grateful."

I snorted. "For what?"

She shrugged. "The good stuff. The bad stuff. The highs and the lows. All of it. Every moment that you had with them." She gave a heavy sigh. "Nothing's ever going to change the fact that she's gone, Lax. What happened happened. You should have had more time together. But if you let that rob you of what time you *did* have... well, then you really have lost her."

I felt a tear well up in the corner of my eye and wiped angrily at it. I wanted a can. Just a hit. I wanted to make the hurt disappear. But I couldn't. It sat leaden and dull in my chest, weighing me down, crushing me. "I miss her, Sev."

"I know, Lax." She gave a sad, knowing smile. "I know."

"Hah." I made a choking sound somewhere between a chuckle and a sob. "She'd laugh at me if she could see me now. Wandering right back into the crap I was working so hard to get out of." I thought back to the conversation I'd had with Kess right before we boarded the *Panama*. "She mentioned that once, you know. Said she didn't think I had it in me to leave the salvage life behind."

Sev chuckled. "Gotta hand that to her. That was what she was best at, I think. Understanding people. Talking to her always made me feel like she knew something about me that even I didn't." She grinned. "It was infuriating."

I felt a wry smile creep over my lips. "Tell me about it. I never could figure out why she was with me. Like she saw something in me that I just couldn't."

"Well, it wasn't your rugged good looks."

I chuckled. "No. No, it wasn't that."

"You're a good person, Lax," Sev said after a short pause. "That's what she saw. She saw a man who had been dragged through hell and back and still somehow held on to his heart. A man who had seen the worst that humanity had to offer but still had it in him to care about other people. So don't go getting down on yourself like you always do when things go wrong. You're still the same man, Lax. Despite it all."

"Maybe," I said skeptically. "But it was so much easier to be good when she was with me. I've never really been the type to *want* things. She was. She always had ideas. Goals. Dreams. All I ever wanted was to be with her."

"Kess would want you to be happy, Lax," she said. "She'd want you to move forward. Whatever that means for you. Whatever it takes for you to feel whole again. So start with that."

I nodded slowly.

Sev yawned. "*I'm* exhausted. I'm gonna go back to sleep. You figure out how to make it out of this big job of yours. And don't think all this mushiness between us changes any part of this situation we're in, Lax. If my daughter gets hurt, I will tear your eyeballs out and stuff them down your throat."

I grinned. "Would expect nothing less."

"Good." She studied me for a moment longer, her eyes searching my face. "Take care of her. And take care of yourself."

"You got it. And, Sev?"

"What?"

"Thanks. For this."

She smiled. "Any time, Lax. I mean, I charge extra for dead-of-night therapy sessions, but it's your wallet."

"Night, Sev."

"Night, Lax."

Her face vanished, replaced by a message that read *Link Severed at Source*. I sat there watching the message blink until it vanished too. Just thinking. Remembering. It hurt. I let it.

# TWENTY-EIGHT

They didn't blindfold me this time.

Some of the rebels—the ones not on our crew—gave me strange looks as Tekka, Artemis and I made the trip through the secret tunnels to the Khendars' residence. They didn't say anything, though, when they saw how Tekka talked to me.

Artemis was silent. Any vulnerability I'd seen in her was gone, pulled back into the tough, cold persona she used as a shield. I hadn't been able to speak with her since last night's debacle. Hell, she wouldn't even make eye contact with me. Judging by the odd looks he kept giving us, Tekka could tell something was off. He never said anything, though.

When we reached the sitting room we'd met the Khendars in last time, we found it empty. A waiting servant explained that the Khendars would be with us shortly.

"In that case," Tekka said, "I'll be right back. Just a few things to attend to."

That left Artemis and me alone. She sat down. I walked over to the window, looking out over the city below us.

"Gotta admit," I said, "this place is growing on me. It's beautiful."

"You should have seen it *before* the war," Artemis said softly.

I stole a glance at her. She was looking resolutely ahead. "What was it like, growing up here?"

"It was too good to be true," she said after a moment of contemplation. She glanced at me, meeting my eyes, and shrugged. "A perfect childhood. Of course, I didn't realize that until long after everything had fallen apart."

I nodded. "I know that feeling. Well—the not realizing how good things are until they're gone. Not so much the perfect childhood part."

She chuckled. "That's life, I suppose."

Silence fell.

"Last night," I said.

Artemis stiffened. "That was my mistake. It won't happen again."

"No," I said. "It wasn't your mistake. It was mine."

Artemis paused, studying me. I turned towards her, then took a deep breath. "Look, Artemis. I'm all kinds of screwed up. I've been in a dark place for a long, long time, and I'm still working on dragging myself out of it. But if you can give me just a bit of time and patience, I'd like to think I can unmake that mistake."

She searched my eyes for a few moments. "It wouldn't work. Not in the long run."

I shrugged. "Doesn't mean it's not worth trying."

She narrowed her eyes. "And the job still comes first. No matter what."

I nodded, not taking my eyes from hers. "Of course."

She opened her mouth to say something else. Before she could, though, I heard the door open behind me.

"Apologies for our delay," Restell Khendar said as he and Nalis entered. Tekka came right behind them. "Let us begin."

.  .  .

Dinner tonight was some sort of stew, from a source of meat native to Brahma. It took all my restraint to keep myself from simply lifting my bowl and gulping it down in a few swallows. Instead, I gripped the tiny spoon as delicately as I could between my massive fingers and raised it carefully to my lips as Nalis spoke. "Is everything prepared?"

"Yes." Artemis took a sip of wine. "We'll depart in two days, then be waiting when the *Revelation* arrives. After that, it's simply a matter of doing what we set out to do."

"Very good," Restell said. "And how do you feel?"

Artemis glanced at me. "Confident. Hopeful. And..." She hesitated. "Perhaps a bit nervous."

"I would be worried if you weren't," Restell said with a sage nod. The sun shining over him and his wife from the large window behind them made them look regal in their fine Brahmian robes. "Fear, like any emotion, exists for a reason. It protects us—reminds us that we are mortal. So long as it remains under our control instead of the other way around, fear is a valuable companion."

I nodded along with him, taking a sip of broth. I figured he could have said the same thing in about half as many words, but I agreed with the gist of it.

"And on your side?" Artemis asked. "How goes the fight for Brahma?"

"Brahma is but one square on this chess board," Nalis said. "If all goes according to plan with the *Revelation*, the fight will expand significantly beyond our planet."

A nervous knot formed in my gut. I was used to high-stakes jobs, but the idea of sparking a civil war—of *my* actions being directly responsible for ushering humanity into a new era of bloodshed—was on an entirely different level. I was still getting used to it.

*Don't think about that.* I dipped my spoon back into my

bowl. *It's just a regular salvage job. Get in, get what you need, and get out. Alive.*

"Unrest is spreading throughout the stars like weeds," Nalis continued. "The Paragon is stretched to its limits. The only thing holding them intact is their alliance with Divinity. If you're correct about the *Revelation*, that could change."

My mind drifted back to what Tekka had said to me when it had just been the two of us around our campfire. *A whole army of you boys.* I was on board with the idea of taking the monopoly on ultracells away from the Paragon. But the idea of using the Paragon's weapons—the ones that had allowed them to subjugate all of humanity—seemed wrong, somehow. The universe was already worse for having had one army of Vanguards rampaging through it. Would another one make it better?

Nalis's voice pulled my thoughts back to the present. "Mr. VanDunn," she said, "Tekka has spoken highly of you and your friend Nadus. And if there's one thing that we've learned as we've fought this battle, it's that one should never judge a weapon based solely on its peculiarities. Regardless of what happens on the *Revelation*, you've already done us a great service by recovering the *Guardian*."

I glanced over at Tekka, who gave me a subtle wink, then turned back to the Khendars and gave an awkward nod. What was I supposed to do, bow? Were they gonna give me a medal or something? "Thanks," I finally said, the words sounding flat and lame in my own ears. "Glad I could... help."

"And if everything *does* go according to plan," Restell said, addressing Artemis and me simultaneously, "then we'll have many more plans to make. Provided you are willing, we could make great use of you and your crew."

A faint but sharp sound caught my ear. Like something brittle and delicate cracking. I looked up, frowning, but saw nothing out of the ordinary.

Artemis glanced at me, her eyes searching. "The job first," she said. "After that... we'll have to see."

There was another cracking sound, this one much louder, as several small, black cylinders broke through the glass window behind the Khendars.

Restell and Nalis turned around in confusion. Tekka shouted and dove across the table towards them. Artemis's eyes widened as I grabbed her and shoved myself backward, pulling both of us to the floor.

I pressed my hands over Artemis's ears. *"Close your—"*

There was a deafening concussion and a flash of white light.

# TWENTY-NINE

Someone was talking.

No—yelling. My vision was blurred, but I could see the outlines of several dark figures moving around the table.

I blinked and shook my head, trying to bring all of the vague details into focus. One of the figures loomed over me and I felt the unmistakable cold rigidity of a rifle barrel pressed against my temple.

"*LIE FLAT ON THE FLOOR!*" somebody screamed into my ear.

The ringing in my ear subsided, clarity gradually returning as my unnaturally fast healing kicked into action. I blinked upward. It was a Paragon enforcer, clad in tight-fitting black body armor and wearing a jumppack strapped to his back. Several others were standing over Artemis, the Khendars, and Tekka, all of whom were clutching at their ears and groaning. The table and floor were littered with shards of broken glass. The bastards had softened up the window, probably with a laser cutter, tossed a few concussion grenades through, and then used their jumppacks to leap through it.

"*ON THE FLOOR!*" the enforcer screamed. I grunted as he

brought the barrel of his assault rifle down and slammed it into my temple, but complied, spreading out my hands and lying flat on the floor. Peacebreaker was in my shoulder holster, but if I reached for it I'd end up with a magazine's worth of lead in my skull. So I just grimaced and held still.

"Dining room secure," said one of the enforcers, evidently the commander, as he stepped back and surveyed the carnage. Their faces were all concealed behind their helmets and tactical visors, but I could picture the satisfied look on his face. "Five targets incapacitated. Identifying now."

An enforcer standing over the Khendars raised a datapad showing an image of Restell. "Facial scan is good, we got the Khendars."

I tried to worm my head around to get a look at Artemis only to grimace as the enforcer standing over me hit me again. "Stay down," he snapped.

The enforcer with the datapad stepped towards me. "These two the ones the tip told us about?"

"Probably." The commander glanced towards me. "Let's get 'em ID'd, though." He looked up and pointed towards the doors leading out of the room. "Get those hallways clear—"

There was a banging sound like a door being kicked open, followed by the deafening sound of gunfire.

The room immediately erupted into chaos. The rifle that had been trained on my temple raised. I rolled onto my back, sweeping the enforcer's legs with one arm. He fell with a startled grunt, still clutching at his gun. I grabbed the assault rifle and shoved it backward, slamming the butt of the gun into his throat with a sharp crack. He wheezed and let go, hands clutching at his flattened windpipe.

Still lying flat on my back, I raised the rifle and quickly assessed the situation. Several of Tekka's rebels had burst through one of the hidden doors and opened fire on the enforcers, who had returned the favor with a volley of their own.

What the rebels had in courage they lacked in training and firepower. The enforcers' body armor had shielded them from most of the gunfire, while the rebels were unprotected. In the three seconds it had taken me to take down my captor, the enforcers had gunned down three rebels, painting the walls of the richly decorated room with their blood. Two were left standing, screaming as they fired wildly into the room. Two enforcers—besides the one twitching futilely next to me—were groaning on the floor, evidently more stunned than hurt. That left five still standing.

I aimed at the throat of the enforcer commander and squeezed the trigger. The gun bucked in my hands and the enforcer staggered, blood spraying from his neck. The enforcer standing next to him turned, spotted me, and aimed, only to stumble backward as a volley of bullets from the rebels in the doorway struck him.

I sat up and opened fire on the remaining three enforcers. One of them staggered as Tekka fired into the back of his knee with a hidden pistol. The other two activated their jumppacks and vaulted backward, retreating through the window.

More rebels were pouring into the room, finishing off the wounded enforcers. I dropped the assault rifle and crawled to Artemis's side. With a jolt of horror, I realized that her side was coated in blood.

Suddenly, I wasn't on Brahma anymore. I was in a dark corridor, surrounded by death, watching Kessa bleed out.

*I think it got me...*

She blinked up at me, groaning. "That was loud."

*We're not getting out of this...*

"You're hit," I growled.

She frowned down at the blood, then poked at it. "Not my blood."

I let out a sigh of relief. The world snapped back into place around me. "Come on, let's get out of here."

Tekka rose, helping the Khendars to shakily rise to their feet. Another rebel charged into the room, panting.

"They're assaulting the front of the estate too," the man was saying. "Got the whole building surrounded."

"Pull everyone back," Tekka growled. "We retreat into the tunnels, then bring them down behind us. How did they know?"

I glanced towards the fallen enforcers. One of them was still alive, his hands held nervously above his head as a rebel lowered her weapons towards him.

"Wait," I said, holding a hand out to the rebel. She paused. I stooped, picking up the datapad, and held it up in front of the fallen enforcer.

"Your CO said you were looking for us," I growled. "Why?"

The man just shook his head, face invisible behind his visor.

"We don't have time for this," Artemis snapped.

I lifted my foot and slammed it down directly onto his face. There was a cracking sound as his visor fragmented. The enforcer let out a yelp as I reached down, grabbed him by the neck, and flung him into the far wall, sending shards of his shattered visor skittering across the floor.

"*WHY?*" I bellowed, stalking towards him.

He held up his hands defensively. "We got a tip! A tip. An anonymous source. It's all on that datapad." He pointed at the device I was clutching. "It's all there."

"We've gotta go," Artemis hissed, heading for the door.

I nodded towards the rebels. "All yours," I growled, and followed after Artemis. A single gunshot sounded behind me as I rounded the corner into the hallway.

"Someone talked," Artemis growled as we followed Tekka towards the hidden entrance to the tunnel system.

The floor shook beneath me as a deep boom thundered from the front of the house.

"This isn't a sting," I muttered. "This is a damn *warzone.*"

"I've put out an order for all cells throughout the city to mobilize," Tekka said. He was holding up Nalis with one shoulder, while another rebel was helping Restell. "Targeted strikes on important Paragon assets. It should provide some distraction."

My eyes widened. "You're gonna throw the whole city into chaos."

Tekka glared at me over his shoulder. "The city's been in chaos since the invasion. Now the chaos will just become impossible to ignore."

I opened my mouth to respond. But it was right about then that, for the second time that afternoon, the world around me exploded.

This explosion was significantly more violent. I grunted as I was hurled against the wall, my skin stinging from the force of hundreds of tiny pieces of debris burrowing into it. Something heavy struck me in the head and pain lanced through my skull.

I groaned and sat up, coughing through the haze of smoke and dust. From the angle of the damage, it looked as if the enforcers had fired an explosive through the window into the dining room. They *really* wanted us dead.

Hazy shapes moved down the hall. I squinted after them. Tekka was helping the Khendars towards the elevator that led down into the tunnels. Artemis was right behind them. She turned back towards me, beckoning. "Come on!"

I growled and pushed myself to my feet, moving unsteadily towards her. Before I could take more than a few steps another explosion rocked the building. There was a groaning, splintering sound and suddenly I was falling, grunting as I bounced off of broken timbers and shattered stonework only to land heavily on my side.

I moaned, trying to figure out what had happened. My vision was blurry and my ears ringing. I rolled onto my back, blinking groggily up. Through the dust and debris I could see a massive, gaping hole in the ceiling above me.

*Move.* I needed to move. I pushed myself up only to sag back to the floor with a groan. I could hear gunshots and screaming. I was bleeding from multiple wounds. Gunshots? Shrapnel? Had I impaled myself on a broken timber as I fell? Maybe all three.

The world seemed to flicker around me. I gritted my teeth forcing myself to stay conscious. Artemis had been up with Tekka, so at least she'd have made it out. Now I just needed to drag myself out of here. Somehow. Maybe... after a short rest...

"LAX!"

Someone was grabbing me. Shaking me. I snapped back to reality to see Kessa standing over me. No. *Artemis.* She'd come back for me.

"Why didn't..." I groaned. "You should have gone with Tekka."

"Shut up," she growled. "And move. I'll help, but there's no way I can pull you up alone."

She grabbed my hand and pulled. She was surprisingly strong. I gritted my teeth and staggered to my feet, leaning gently against her to keep from falling.

"There you go," she said. "Come on. This way."

I followed groggily as she led us through the ruined house. Something was burning. We walked through a gust of dark smoke. Timbers crashed to the floor behind us.

Suddenly we were in daylight. I blinked around at the Gharseva backstreet she'd led us onto. Corpses littered the pavement—some of them enforcers, others rebels, while others appeared to be civilians caught in the crossfire. Whatever kind of resistance the enforcers had anticipated, they clearly hadn't been ready for a full-on war.

An explosion boomed—this one distant. I craned my head to see smoke rising from several points in the city.

"Come on." Artemis tugged me down the street, over several bodies, and between two buildings. "There's a safehouse nearby with another way into the tunnels. I told Tekka to meet us there."

I lost track of time. Chaos surrounded us in the streets as panicked civilians fled towards their homes. It was all I could do to stay on my feet, letting Artemis pull me along. By some miracle—or, more likely, because of Artemis's knowledge of the city streets—we managed to avoid running into any enforcers.

Eventually we stopped at the back of a modest-looking building. Artemis pounded on the door and shouted something. A code of some sort.

I glanced up and down the alley we were in. It was empty, except for an old man who seemed to be wandering in a daze. He was too far away for me to see his face.

"They're coming," Artemis said, breathing a sigh of relief.

I sagged against the wall, breathing heavily. "What the hell happened?"

"Like that enforcer said," Artemis said grimly, "somebody tipped them off. They were looking for us, specifically."

*The Penitent.* I grimaced. We'd let our guard down. Somewhere, somehow.

"Are you alright?" Artemis asked me.

"Yeah." I glanced down at myself. I was coated in blood and dust. "I mean... I think so. Probably."

She gave a relieved smile. "Good. Can't do this job without my salvage expert."

Movement from the street caught my eye. I turned my head to see the dazed old man had come closer. He didn't look dazed anymore. His face was cold and resolved. He was walking towards us with a purposeful stride.

I recognized him.

"*Eladrius?*" I asked, incredulous.

He drew a pistol and fired in one fluid motion.

There was a cracking sound. Artemis's head snapped back. She crumpled. I let out a shocked cry and ducked into the doorway as best I could. Another bullet zipped through the corner and winged my arm.

The door behind me suddenly flung open. I fell through it, collapsing onto the floor inside the safehouse. I blinked up to see Tames standing above me, holding a submachine gun. She stepped through the doorway and fired wildly down the street.

*Artemis.* I jolted upright. Artemis was lying crumpled in a pool of blood in the street just outside the doorway. Tames was standing over her, obscuring my view of her face.

"*Artemis,*" I croaked.

Tames swore bitterly, grabbed Artemis, and dragged her inside. She fingered her pulse.

"Dead," she said.

I got just a glimpse of Artemis's face. Eyes open and empty. Blood was leaking slowly from the bullet hole in the side of her skull.

My breath caught in my throat.

"Bastard slipped away. We have to go," Tames snapped. "This place is compromised."

*No.* I couldn't believe it. It made no sense. Eladrius, the kindly priest who had taken pity on me aboard the *Jonah*— Nadus's mentor—was here. And he had just... he'd shot...

My mind refused to accept it. "We have to—we can't leave her—"

"Enforcers could be here *any second,*" Tames snapped.

"I don't *care!*" I grabbed Artemis and tried to drag her with me. Her body flopped limply as I tugged on her arm.

"*Lax.*" Tames knelt, bringing her face closed to mine. "She's *dead.* If we don't want to be too, we *have. To. Move.*"

"I..." I gritted my teeth. "I can't. Not again."

She swore and stood up, crossing the room and opening a hidden trap door. "I'm getting the hell out of here. If you decide to follow, shut the door behind you."

She vanished. I stared at Artemis a moment longer.

"I'm sorry," I muttered, then turned and followed Tames, leaving Artemis stretched out on the floor.

I staggered through the darkness for what felt like an eternity, guided only by a dim flashlight Tames held. Artemis was dead. Somehow I couldn't quite wrap my head around the fact. Somehow I believed that when we got back to the *Orpheus* she'd be there waiting. But she wouldn't be. Her corpse was slowly bleeding out on the floor of the safehouse.

*Eladrius.* Was I insane? Had my brain simply conjured a familiar face for the killer? It made no sense.

Voices ahead. Lights. I tensed, mustering what energy I had left to fight, only to relax as I saw Tekka striding towards us, leading several exhausted-looking rebels in tactical gear.

"Hey," I said, my voice haggard. "They got—"

Tekka grabbed me by the shirt and shoved me against the wall.

"*What*," he growled, "*happened?*"

"They killed Artemis," I wheezed. "I... I don't know who. I think—"

"*No.*" He spat the word. "The *attack*. Who tipped them off?"

"I don't know," I said weakly. My thoughts felt slow.

He bared his teeth in a primal growl. His face was covered in dirt and blood. One of his ears had been mangled beyond recognition. His eyes were wild with fury and desperation.

"It's *all gone*," he snarled. "*All of it*. Everything we've fought for. Everything we built up. Destroyed. All because we *trusted you*."

My eyes flitted to the pistol strapped to his waist. His hand was inching closer to it. I could disable him if I needed to. But then his buddies would just mow me down. And even if they didn't... the results didn't seem worth the effort. All I could see was Artemis. Eyes blank. Crumpling into the street.

"Do it, then," I growled.

He narrowed his eyes, letting go of me and letting me sag to the floor so he was looking down at me. "What?"

"Kill me already." I felt a sudden surge of energy as I glared up at him. "You hate me so much. Finish it."

"Oh, no." He shook his head. "I'm not gonna kill you. I need you."

I frowned. "What?"

"That's right." He grinned. A bloody, wild grin. The reckless smile of a man pushed to the brink of madness and desperation who has one trick left to play. "We've still got a job to do, *puppet.*"

THIRTY

I stared through the *Orpheus*'s bridge window down at Brahma. A sullen, uncertain silence hung in the air around me.

"You're *sure* it was Eladrius?" Nadus finally asked, his voice taut. I groaned, massaging my forehead. I'd already spent a few hours in the medbay, but I couldn't handle waiting there anymore. Everything hurt. I was bruised all over, had a bullet hole in my arm, and a dozen other scrapes and cuts from my fall. "Sure as hell *looked* like him."

"Alright, for the sake of argument, let's say that Eladrius *is* some sort of secret assassin," Rose said. "That he's this *Penitent* that's been hunting us. How the hell would he even have known where we were? That we were working with the Khendars?"

Realization hit me like a bullet. I dug through my pocket until I found the routing chip Eladrius had given me. "Last night," I said. "I tried to contact him. Using this."

Bentley leaned forward and narrowed his eyes. "And you just... plugged it in? Didn't test it first or anything? Even with some rudimentary malware on the chip he could have stolen our messages, our location..."

"I—" I felt my shoulders sag. I remembered the odd way the

screen had flickered when I'd first plugged it in. "I wasn't thinking straight."

Nadus sagged into a seat, looking deflated. "He didn't show up until after I'd started working for Artemis. He always seemed so different from everybody else on the ship. So focused on me. I just..." He trailed off, his head drooping.

"He must have known who Artemis was," I said. "Or had at least some idea. Her father was well known for being obsessed with the *Revelation*. Maybe he caught on to her trail that way somehow." I thought about our night on the *Jonah* and groaned. "It's been him from the start. He must have tracked us on Albeni 7 and hired those thugs. Then lost us until I plugged in the routing chip."

I found myself wishing desperately that I hadn't used all of the frigicerin. Damn, could I use a can right now. Every time I closed my eyes, Artemis's face was there, eyes glassy. Or was it Kessa?

"So," Rid said softly, "what happens next?"

"What happens *next*," Tekka's voice announced, "is that we *finish the damn job*."

He emerged from the hatch, then settled into a seat. He'd cleaned himself up, but he still looked battered. His eyes still had that dangerous rage I'd seen in the tunnel. "At the end of the day this changes nothing," he said. "The *Revelation* is still out there. We still know where it's going to be. We have all of our gear. We've trained. You lot will still get your loot. And my lot"—he gave a grisly smile—"have nothing left to lose."

I exchanged a glance with Nadus, who frowned. Tekka was right, though it hurt to think about. Other than Tekka and Tames, the rebels who'd been training with us had never left the *Orpheus*, so we still had a full crew. Only Artemis was missing.

"For all we know there could be more traps for us out there," Nadus said. "Whoever did this isn't likely to stop."

"Neither are we." Tekka gestured at us. "I mean, look at you lot. This *Penitent* has tried to kill you twice now, and you're all still alive. It's all *my* friends that are dead."

I looked up sharply. "The Khendars...?"

His eyes flashed with anger. "Gone."

I felt a chill. We'd led the Paragon straight to them. No—*I* had led the Paragon straight to them. Eladrius—the Penitent, whatever that meant—had used them to get at us.

Nadus crossed his arms. "Look. I'm sorry that this happened. And for any part we had in it. But this *does* change things. Most of us joined this job because Artemis hired us." He gestured around at Bentley, Rid, Shell, Rose, and me. "We need some time to regroup and figure out what we want to do from here."

Tekka stared for a moment, then let out a long burst of air through his nostrils. "Fine. But this job is happening, with or without you. If you won't help, we'll go get the *Guardian* and take that."

He descended the chute.

I sighed and closed my eyes, cupping my forehead in my hands, dimly aware of the sounds of everybody quietly making their exits. Eventually, though, all was silent, only me and my thoughts left on the bridge.

You'd have thought that I'd be used to things like this by now. Sudden upheavals that changed everything. Reversals of fortune that shattered plans and tossed dreams out the airlock. I'd experienced enough of them, after all. And yet, here I was again, caught utterly off guard.

Artemis was dead. It hurt. More than I'd expected it to. I was still struggling to make sense of what had happened. She'd gone. She could have escaped with Tekka. But she'd come back for me. So now I was here, and she was still down there.

"You alright?"

I opened my eyes to see Rid sitting across the room from me, watching me intently. Apparently, I hadn't been alone. He had the same look in his eyes that he'd had way back on the prison station, when I'd been having a nervous breakdown. Concern. Back then I'd been convinced that he was just worried about saving his own skin. Now, though, I realized that wasn't the case at all. He was worried about me.

I gave a dry, humorless chuckle. "Yeah. I'm alright. All things considered."

"You're hurting," Rid said, looking away from me.

"You're damn right I'm hurting." I grimaced. The wound in my back still hurt, my body taking longer than usual to heal the deep, broad wound. "Yet here I am. As always. Like a big damn idiot." I sighed and shook my head. "Why am I doing this, Rid?"

He cocked his head at me. "Doing what?"

"Doing—*this*." I gestured vaguely around me. "Any of this. I should have walked away. Should have stayed in prison. Should have..." I gritted my teeth and closed my eyes, letting my weary head drop into my hands. "Should have died on the *Panama*. Or down in the war. Or down there, instead of Artemis."

There was silence for a long moment.

"I don't know," Rid said, finally.

I looked up, watching him. He shook his head. "I don't know why anything happens. Or doesn't happen. But I do know that they need you." He jerked his head towards the hatch. "*We* need you."

I frowned. "*We* need Artemis. The one calling the shots. The one who knew what she wanted."

"We took her orders. Still would. But we *follow* you." Rid shrugged. "There's a difference."

He got up, gave me a nod, and slid down the hatch, leaving me, once more, alone with my thoughts.

I sat there for a long time, just thinking, and hurting. I thought about my old crew. About Kessa's smile, and Sevani's perpetual stream of sarcastic comments, and Liung's equally perpetual stream of dumb jokes. I smiled as I remembered the night we'd gone out drinking after a good run, and Black, ever serious and down to earth, had drunkenly proposed to the bartender. I sat there and I waited for it to hit me like it always did: the guilt, the bitterness, the anger, washing away all of the good feelings and leaving me feeling empty and alone.

But it never came.

Instead, I just felt... I'm not sure how to describe it. Not happy, not exactly. But not exactly sad, either. Maybe some strange combination of both. It hurt. But under the hurt, like a seedling yearning for the surface, I could feel something else growing. A sort of calmness. Maybe a simple sense of acceptance.

And then I thought about Rid, jumping up and down in the low gravity of the *Orpheus's* cargo bay with that stupid grin on his face. Shell, taking her first stumbling steps in her exo. Rose, with her mother's self-assured smirk, chasing me down in the corridors of Albeni 7. Bentley's perpetual smart-assery, and Nadus's reliable, ever-present practicality. And I thought about Artemis. For all her talk of cynicism and self-preservation, she had given her life in an attempt to save mine. Maybe. Who knew what had been going through her mind in those last moments? But I liked to think that they'd been something along those lines.

I'd had her wrong from the beginning. Figured, like me, all she was looking for in life was a score. A road to a better life for herself. It wasn't an unreasonable thing for a person to want. But that had never been her goal. She'd been trying to change things. To make this dark, bloody universe of ours better.

And now she was dead, left lying in her own blood in an abandoned safehouse, and I was up here, flying off into the sunset. Off to sulk in some deep, forsaken corner of space and lick my wounds. Turning tail and running. Waiting for whatever happened to me next.

My knuckles tightened. *Not this time.*

When I stepped onto the bridge the next morning, Nadus was already there, sitting next to the central hologram and staring blankly at the map of the *Revelation*.

"Morning," I said, settling into a seat across from him.

He grunted in reply, not looking me in the eye. I looked over the schematics, frowning as I worked through the details in my head. We had counted on having Artemis with us on the ship, working the computers while Bentley did what he could from the *Orpheus*. We'd have to work around that. Besides Artemis's absence, though, our plan would still work the same, assuming everybody else bought in. I felt a sudden spike of remorse at the thought of doing it all without Artemis. Funny—not so long ago, I'd felt nothing more than a vague dislike towards her. Now I found that I missed her.

"I don't get it," Nadus said.

I glanced at him. "Get what?"

He shook his head. "Any of it. I thought I was finally figuring life out. For the first time in as long as I can remember, the universe was starting to make sense. It felt like the things that happened were happening for a reason. Little threads, light and dark, in a tapestry we're too tiny to comprehend, but still important. Still meaningful. Each leading on to another. And then something like *this* happens." He gestured vaguely towards the schematics of the *Revelation* flickering in the air between us. "Artemis is dead. Turns out Eladrius was lying out of his ass to me the entire time, just using me to get to her. And I'm left here trying to figure out what it all means, or if any of it ever meant anything to begin with."

I gave a humorless chuckle. "I quit trying to work all that out a long time ago. After I lost Kessa I sort of just... gave up on the idea that there's any sort of order to the universe. Any grand design. Maybe I'm wrong. Hell, I hope I am. But from where I've been all my life, it's sure hard to see."

"It's funny," Nadus said, slowly. "Artemis made no secret of the fact she thought my faith was pointless. But still, you could tell from the way she talked, the way she looked at the universe, that she saw a purpose to it all. Some sort of end goal to everything she did, that made her get up in the morning and keep fighting."

"And now we know what it was," I said. I found a slight, sad smile on my face. "For all her hard-assery, she was a self-sacrificing revolutionary at heart. Who'd have thunk?"

Nadus laughed. "I'd have thunk. Took a while, but I could see it eventually. The things she really cared about." He gave me a sidelong look. "The *people* she cared about."

We fell silent for a moment, Nadus's face becoming serious again.

"We've *got* to finish the job, Lax," Nadus said.

I nodded. "I know. We won't be able to do what she wanted, though. We don't have the connections or the know-how or, hell, the *ambition* to do what she wanted to do. She wanted to make history. To take the Paragon down. I don't think I can do any of that. But..."

"...but we gotta try," Nadus said.

I nodded. "Yeah, I guess we do. Even if it just means finishing the job."

Nadus snorted. "Might be hard with just the two of us."

"It isn't."

I turned to see Shell climbing the hatch. She settled into her usual seat, thumb rubbing the handle of her knife in that peculiar way of hers. "I'm in."

"Me too." I turned again to see Rose climbing up the hatch. She sat down in the pilot's chair, swiveling it around so she was facing us. "Besides," she said, her mother's smirk on her face, "it's my ship, so you'd have a hell of a time getting there without it."

I figured that now wasn't the best time to bring up the fact that I technically owned a bigger majority of the *Orpheus* than Sev did, and instead just nodded.

Rid came up after them. He collapsed into a chair, looking bored, then glanced over at me and raised one eyebrow. "We doing this?"

I glanced over towards Nadus. He smiled, ever so slightly, and gave a nod.

"Wait." There was a crashing sound from down the hatch. A moment later Bentley's head poked up. "Guys, we can't give up. I know things seem bleak, but I've thought about this a lot, and—"

"We're past that, Bent," Rose said.

"Oh." Bentley blinked. "Well. Great."

"And you're going on board with us," I said, giving him a full-toothed grin.

He blinked again. "Uhm. Well. What I meant to say is, have we *really* thought this through? I mean, these are our lives we're putting on the line. Is a handful of credits worth that much risk?"

I ignored him, turning to the hovering schematic. "Alright, then. It's confirmed. We've still got plenty of time to get there. We'll need to make a few tweaks to the plan. But, for the most part, Tekka was right. Not much changes."

Excited murmurings filled the room. I took a deep breath. "I'll go tell Tekka."

Artemis might be gone, but we were still here. And come hell or high water, we would finish what she'd started.

# THIRTY-ONE

TWENTY DAYS

The blueprints of the *Revelation* spun lazily in front of me, suspended above the holoprojector in the middle of the bridge. Looking at it I felt a sudden rush of déjà vu. Like I was back on the *Jonah* again, watching Artemis explain her plan for the first time.

Except I wasn't. And Artemis was dead.

"First step when we get there," Rose was saying, "will be running some scans. I don't want to get ambushed. If somebody else *is* waiting in the area, the *Orpheus*'s stealth systems will let us slip away from them—or *past* them."

"What about the black hole?" Rid asked. "You guys mentioned there was one near where the *Revelation* will be dropping."

Rose shrugged. "It's a little close for comfort, but shouldn't be a problem. We'll be well outside of its grasp."

Tekka nodded. "Do you think this Eladrius could have stolen the co-ordinates?"

Bentley shook his head. "I dug around. I think any breach

was confined to the communications systems. We haven't transmitted that data to anyone, so we should be good."

"What we *should* be asking ourselves," I said, "is if he already knows where it will be."

That got the group's attention. I went on. "He's clearly been tracking Artemis since long before most of us got involved. Starting with Nadus. It's not too far of a stretch to assume that he knows more about what's going on with the *Revelation* than we do."

"Alright." Tekka turned his attention back to the hovering image of the *Revelation*. "Let's say we're alone. Or at least that we can make it undetected to the *Revelation*. What next?"

"Actually getting onto the ship will be tricky," I said. "Warships aren't exactly made to be easy to board. However, we do have an opening. Based on the data from the shuttle black box, we've determined that it ejected from port 93R, here." I pointed out a spot towards the front end of the ship. "Which means that we can board it there."

Nadus frowned. "How does that work? It's not like we'll be able to dock the *Orpheus* to an escape pod port."

"No," I agreed. "But we can put at least a few personnel through it. And whoever does go through it will be relatively close to the bridge." I studied the blueprints for a moment. "Here's what I'm thinking. We split into two teams. The first one goes through the escape pod port. Their goal is to play it stealthy. They'll make their way to the bridge. Once they're on the bridge they should be able to open up one of the docking ports so the *Orpheus* can dock and drop off the second group."

I pointed at the relevant points on the hologram. "Team one will have two jobs after that. First will be looking for that data Artemis wanted. Second will be causing a distraction. The bridge is the most defensible place on the ship. If they can hunker down there and attract the swarm, that'll clear the way for team two to hit the power generators and grab as many ultracells as they can."

"So who do we send where?" Shell asked.

I looked over at Tekka. "Gathering the ultracells should be the easy job," I said. "Less chance of running into rippers. Whoever's on the bridge will be fighting for their lives, guaranteed. Nadus and I can lead team one while you take team two."

Tekka shook his head. "If the bridge is where the data is gonna be, that's where I'm gonna be. Your people"—he pointed at Rid, Bentley, Shell, and Nadus—"plus you, me, Jin, and Rathen can be team one. Tames and the rest of my people will be team two."

I glanced at Tames. "You good with that?"

She nodded.

"Good." I turned back to the plans. "Once we're loaded up on ultracells and we've found the data we're looking for, team two will head back to the *Orpheus* and team one will escape through the bridge escape pod port. Whatever malware took the *Revelation* out will have jammed it, but if we use some explosives we should be able to clear it out and use the port. Rose will swing around and pick us up and we'll be done."

"It seems like a good plan." Rose leaned across the hologram. "Except that it's just a lot of guesswork. How do you know that the rippers will be where you think they are? Or that the bridge will be intact enough for you to run the ship from it?"

"We can't," I said with a shrug. "But that's the nature of the salvage game. The only way of knowing what's on that ship is by setting foot on it. We'll use scanners to try to get a read on where the rippers are lurking, but..."

My voice trailed off. *Green dots, flashing red...*

"Well, even the scanners can give a false negative," I said finally. "The bottom line is that this plan is the best-case scenario. We'll keep on planning, come up with contingencies. But a good salvage run is a marriage between careful planning and quick adaptation. So be prepared to think on your feet." I looked around. "Any questions?"

Several hands shot up. I chose Shell first.

"Do we even know what intel Artemis was looking for?" she asked skeptically.

I turned to Tekka. He shrugged. "Not much point in secrecy now, I suppose."

He explained it. I filled in any details he missed. Artemis's history, and why she'd been convinced that the *Revelation* held Divinity Technology's secret ultracell plans. When he finished, everybody fell silent.

"So this is..." Bentley's eyes widened as he considered all the implications. "Not just money big. I mean, not just big for us. This is... galaxy big."

"Maybe." I shrugged. "We don't even know if we'll find anything. Artemis might just have been plain wrong."

"Then why did she get murdered?" Nadus asked grimly.

I paused. That was an excellent point. One I hadn't given much thought to myself.

The conversation moved on. My thoughts kept getting pulled back to Artemis, though. The closer we got to this job, the more eerie it all felt. No part of it seemed logical. Like a fistful of puzzle pieces that I just couldn't fit together.

Only one way to find out, though.

———

## TWO DAYS

I watched the seconds slip by on the clock hanging in my bunkroom. It was a paradox, I'd found. Each second passing felt like an agonizing eternity, and yet was gone all too quickly. Drifting away, moment by moment, rushing past me and into whatever great, boundless void time runs into.

The first leg of the journey had been the shortest. A quick trip to the Brahma foldgate, back to the Alpha Centauri system, and then through another foldgate to the Ebisu system foldgate.

From there it had been eighteen days straight in nullspace. A far longer journey than anyone normally made. Anything more than a few days by nullspace travel away from a foldgate generally wasn't worth visiting. Maybe that was the point, though. I still couldn't make any damn sense of it all. Why go through all this trouble with sabotaging the *Revelation* just to go here?

I sighed and rose. That was more than enough meaningless musing for one day. I left my room and started down the hallway, thinking through what other preparations I needed to make. We were now less than forty-eight hours away from the *Revelation*'s drop time, so if there was a time for last-minute prep, it was now.

I spotted Rid's door and remembered that I'd been meaning to do a last check with him and make sure his equipment was all good to go. Granted, I'd already checked it a few times, but one last inspection couldn't hurt.

"Rid." I pushed the door open. By the schedule we'd been keeping it was evening, but not so late he'd have gone to bed yet. "I want to—oh."

There was a flash of movement as Rid and Rose peeled their lips apart, suddenly sliding to opposite sides of the small bed. Rid gave me a look like he was a kid caught with his hand in a cookie jar.

"...Yes?" he asked nervously.

"I—" I frowned. "How long has *this* been going on?"

"A while now," Rose said coolly, her eyes defiant like she was daring me to complain. "You have a problem with it?"

I tried to imagine what Sevani might do to me if her daughter returned pregnant. I shook my head slowly and cautiously. "No. Just... don't do anything stupid."

They both stared at me expectantly. "You need something?" Rid asked after a moment.

I cleared my throat. "I... no, I guess I don't. Sorry. As you were."

I turned away. They at least had the decency to wait until the door was part-way closed before they started back at it. The door clicked behind me and I stood there dumbfounded for a moment, then shook my head and walked away.

---

## ONE HOUR, TWO MINUTES, AND FORTY-THREE SECONDS

"You're sure it's best if I go with you guys?" Bentley's hands were shaking slightly as he climbed into his exo. He had painted the pauldrons bright red and decorated them with images of garish-looking flowers, matching the shirts he was always wearing. I'd encouraged the rookies to paint their armor. It was a good little morale booster, and it helped to tell them apart too.

"Yes, Bentley." I stepped up behind him, making sure that he had climbed into the suit correctly, and then hit a button. There was a whirring sound as the armor closed around him, leaving only his face exposed.

"*Absolutely* sure?" he said, his voice quivering slightly.

I sighed. "Bentley. Look at me."

He craned his head, peering up at me.

"You're going to be fine," I said. "We've got each other's backs. We need you. You're an important part of the team. We can't do it without you."

He frowned. "I know *that*."

I sighed. "Alright. Bear with me here. Forget the rippers. Forget the *Revelation*. Close your eyes. Think about yourself, on a beach in a fancy resort on Rethi, or Hawkin, or, hell, even Earth, sipping a cocktail and resting easy because your bank account has more credits in it than you could ever possibly spend. You with me?"

He shut his eyes. A few seconds later, a slight smile broke across his face. "That's nice."

"See? Not so bad." I slapped his armor and moved away. "That'll be you in a week."

Rid had already climbed into his suit and was now pacing back and forth near the door. I stepped up next to him. In the exo he stood a few inches taller than me. He grinned down at me. "Hi down there!"

I chuckled. "How does it feel?"

He nodded, looking down at the armor. He had painted his dark green. "Good. Damn good."

"Excellent. You're gonna be up first, so be ready."

He nodded. "I know. Don't worry about me."

I grinned and turned away, checking on the others one by one. Shell was grimly determined. Nadus calm and focused. Tekka was making the rounds with his own men, making small comments here and there, ensuring that Tames and her team were ready for their part of the job. I frowned as I studied him. Over the course of the long journey our relations with the rebels had gradually shifted from frosty back to camaraderie, even if it was more cautious than it had been before. A long shot from where we'd once been, and from where I'd been hoping we'd be for this job. But, like Rid was always saying, you've gotta play the cards you're dealt.

Rose was sitting at the far end of the cargo bay, watching as the rest of the crew geared up. I sat down on top of a nearby crate of ammo, turning to look at the bustling preparations alongside her.

"Scans still clear?" I asked.

She nodded. "Been scanning nonstop since we dropped out of nullspace. We're the only ones here."

"Good." Somehow I found myself surprised by that. Just

one more thing that didn't make sense. Then again, very little about the *Revelation*'s strange story made sense.

"Is this how my mom always felt?" Rose gritted her teeth, frustration glinting in her eyes. "I mean—I know that my job is important. Maybe the most important. But still. To watch your friends gearing up to go into danger without you, knowing that once they're out of the ship, all you can do to help them is to be there on the other side and hope they make it through in one piece..." She shook her head. "It's torture."

"Your mom did mention it a few times, yeah," I said, chuckling. "Always threatened to come in there after us if we took too long. *Don't*," I said, raising a finger and cutting Rose off as she opened her mouth to speak, "get any ideas. I promised your mom that I'd keep you safe and keep you on the *Orpheus*. Promise me you'll stay here, alright?"

She grimaced. "So my life is more valuable than Shell's, or Rid's, or Bentley's?"

"Not necessarily. But I haven't made promises to a vengeful, motherly crime lord to get them home in one piece. If anything happens to you, I might as well just give myself up to the rippers. So help me out and *don't* do anything stupid, alright?"

She nodded.

"Good." I squeezed her shoulder. "You know what to do. And I'm only a comms call away if you have questions."

"I know."

I glanced up towards the clock hanging near the hatch. Twenty-nine minutes and fourteen seconds until go time.

"Shouldn't you be getting geared up?" Rose's voice held a hint of playful accusation. "Or are you planning on going in your T-shirt?"

I sighed. "I know, I know." I moved over to where my armor was mounted and paused. Generally I left my armor undecorated, but somebody had taken the liberty of painting over the pauldrons on my Jericho. They'd painted a—

"You like it?" Rose's voice held a hint of worry. She stepped up beside me, staring up at the starry night painted across the shoulders of my exosuit. "I know that you have this painted on your ceiling, so I figured that you must like it a lot."

I was silent for a long moment, just standing there, staring at those warm, yellow stars. They were a bit crude, painted with nowhere near Kessa's skill or care, but still... I figure it's the thought that counts.

"It's perfect," I said, and felt a smile spreading across my face.

"Good." Rose took a deep breath. "Alright. I'm heading off to the bridge."

"Wait." She turned towards me, surprise on her face, and I stepped forward and wrapped her in a hug. I held her close for a moment, then let go and stepped back. "That's for your mom," I said. "If... If I... well, you know. Just tell her I'm sorry."

Rose smiled. "I will."

I took a deep breath, then climbed into my exo. I hit the button to close it and felt the familiar pressure of the metal closing around my body, wrapping its protective, empowering layers over me like a cocoon. It felt like coming home. When it was done, I stepped back, away from the mounting frame, then pulled my Jackhammer from the rack and checked it. All good.

I glanced over at the clock. Eighteen minutes and one second.

"Alright," I said. "Team one, let's go. Into the airlock."

Shell, Bentley, Nadus, Rid, Tekka, Jin, and Rathen strode forward, through the airlock doors. Tames and her seven mercenaries held back, watching us go.

I stepped through the airlock doors to join the rest of my waiting team. "We're all here," I said through the radio.

"*Roger.*" Rose's voice crackled through the speakers overhead. "*Closing the airlock. Prepare for depressurization.*"

"Helmets on, everybody." I activated mine via neurointerface and heard the familiar whirring sound as the visor closed over my face. For a moment, the world was darkness, the only sound my own breath. Then there was a jolt of sensation as the Jericho's optical scanners came online.

My eyes flitted down to the countdown timers I had programmed into the bottom left corner of my vision. 00:04:13. I watched the seconds slip by, each both an eternity and yet gone all too soon, as I stared out the airlock window. The *Orpheus* was flying just in front of where the *Revelation* was supposed to drop out of nullspace. As soon as it appeared, we'd decelerate just enough to put us where we needed to be to get through escape pod port 93R.

Nobody said a word.

Not until 00:00:48, at least, at which point Bentley's voice crackled over the comms. "How awkward would it be right now if it just... didn't show up?" He gave a nervous chuckle. "And then we'd just... I don't know... *not* climb into a ship infested by horrifying biologically engineered monsters?"

Nobody laughed.

00:00:21.

"Come on, Artemis," I whispered, too softly for anyone but myself to hear. Myself and, maybe, on some off chance, Artemis. It's a big universe. Who knows?

00:00:03.

00:00:02.

00:00:01.

"Showtime," I said.

And it was there.

## THIRTY-TWO

*"Holy crap,"* Rose's voice said over the comms.

It was all I could do to agree.

I'd seen battlecruisers before. Plenty of times. Inside and out. I'd seen them rain down fire and destruction upon the heads of the innocent. But never before had I been as affected by the sight of one as I was now.

The *Revelation* loomed behind us, a massive black shape blotting out the stars behind it. So far as I could tell, no lights on the ship were blinking. If it hadn't been for the fact that I knew it was there, it would have been easy to miss altogether.

*"Going in,"* Rose's voice came over the comms. *"The doors will be opening in four minutes."*

The massive black shape loomed closer, until I could make out the details in its surface. The orbital cannons, the missile ports, the docking bays. As we drew nearer and the *Orpheus's* lights flashed across the surface, I read the word REVELA-TION painted in huge, broad letters across the side of the ship. A sense of awe—almost reverence—settled over me.

A battlecruiser. The type of ship you sent when you wanted to subjugate a planet. Three thousand meters of steel, firepower, Vanguards, and rippers. And we were about to break into it.

"*That's a lot of ship,*" Rose said. "*One sec. Running scans for ripper life signs. Let's see just how many of those things we're...*" Her voice trailed off. "Huh," she said, sounding confused.

"What is it?" Jin asked.

"*The scan's showing a clean ship,*" Rose said. "*I'm not detecting any ripper signatures.*"

A chill ran down my spine. Same as the *Panama*.

"That's a good thing, right?" Bentley said. "I mean... how is no rippers *not* a good thing?"

"Because it's unexpected," Rid said quietly. "And unexpected is always bad." I couldn't help but feel a quick surge of almost paternal pride. The kid was starting to sound like an old soldier already.

An eerie feeling was settling in my gut, but I shook it off. "There will *definitely* be rippers," I said insistently. "Plan on it. Maybe the hull is too thick for the scanner. Maybe there's a fault. Either way, expect rippers. Better to be overprepared than under."

Silence fell. We drew closer.

"Wish Artemis was here," Nadus muttered.

I nodded solemnly. It felt like *I* had taken a long and bloody road to get here. I could only imagine how Nadus felt, much less how Artemis would have felt. But she was gone. Now there was only the job.

"*We're in boarding range,*" Rose's voice said. I peered through the airlock window and saw the words PORT 93R printed above a round hole in the surface of the *Revelation*. The airlock doors slid silently open, and suddenly there was nothing between us and the *Revelation* but empty space.

"*Bon voyage,*" Rose's voice said. "*See you soon. Be safe. Have fun. Please keep your hands inside the ride at all times.*"

Nobody laughed. I took a deep breath, then pushed against

the floor and shoved myself towards the port. "Leaving the *Orpheus*."

For a long moment I floated through literal nothingness, watching the words PORT 93R grow bigger and bigger. The only sound was my own breathing recycling within my life-support systems. Finally, I collided with the side of the Revelation with a slight jolt, my magboots locking onto the hull.

I turned and looked back towards the *Orpheus*. I felt my eyes go wide. My old ship looked tiny and delicate next to the *Revelation*. My companions, leaping one by one from the airlock and using the thrusters on their exos to guide them towards the *Revelation*, looked smaller still. And, behind it all, painting the scene in sharp silhouettes, Sagittarius A burned with an ominous, otherworldly orange light.

I peered down through the open porthole. It was roughly three meters wide and circular. Inside I could see nothing but darkness, gaping ominously up at me.

"Alright, Rose," I said. "We're good here."

"*Roger.*" I caught a glimpse of her raising a thumb through the cockpit of the *Orpheus* as she steered away, heading towards the docking bay Tames and her team would be using to enter the battlecruiser. "*Keep me posted.*"

I turned back to my team. All of them were watching me.

"Do the honors?" Nadus said, holding an open palm towards the gaping black hole.

"Cowards," I scoffed, but didn't move. Instead, I took a deep breath, staring down into that darkness. My floodlights sheared through the darkness like a blade through flesh. I couldn't see much from out here—just the empty port where the shuttle had once sat.

"We doing this?" Tekka's voice buzzed in my ear. "Or are we going to sit out here admiring the view until we get sucked into that big old black hole over yonder?"

"I'm going, dammit," I growled. Taking a breath as if I was a diver taking a plunge into deep water, I deactivated my magboots from the *Revelation*'s hull, bent over, grabbed onto the edge of the port with one gauntleted hand, and pulled myself into the darkness.

Using the directional control thrusters built into my Jericho, I guided myself through the empty escape shuttle port, past the *Revelation*'s thick armor hull and down into the loading bay that doubled as an airlock. Escape shuttles were designed for immediate use, the idea being that once the survivors had strapped themselves into the shuttle, the room would seal behind them so that the shuttle could launch, using the force of decompression to eject it from the ship while simultaneously protecting the *Revelation* from losing atmosphere.

Here, things had evidently not gone according to plan. Everything I saw told the tale of a desperate struggle for survival. Smears of blood coating the floor where the escapees had dragged their wounded comrades to the shuttle. Several blackened marks on the walls where it appeared they had used explosives to manually launch the shuttle. Finally, and most importantly to my current situation, a jagged hole where the airlock door should have been separating the loading bay from the rest of the ship.

"What happened?" Rid muttered through the comms, coming in behind me.

"They had to launch the shuttle manually," I said, pointing at the blackened patches. "Rippers must have been tearing down the airlock door, trying to get at them."

"Eugh," Rid muttered. I could only agree. Hell of a tight spot: trapped in a loading bay with a shuttle that wouldn't launch, separated only by a few centimeters of steel and glass from ravenous rippers. They'd been lucky they'd gotten out. No, better than lucky—they'd been clever. They'd figured out a way, despite all the odds, when nobody else had been able to.

Only to land on a hostile planet and be executed by rebels a few weeks later.

Life can be a real bastard sometimes.

I pulled my thoughts back to the present, using my thrusters to glide through the airlock and peer around the corner into the hallway beyond, my Jackhammer held at the ready. Here there was at least some illumination: the dull red throb of emergency lights, flaring up one moment to paint the seemingly unending corridors in a macabre red, and then fading out once again to plunge them into utter darkness. Back and forth, on and off, red and black, blood and darkness.

But there was no movement. I let out a long breath and lowered the barrel of my gun. "We're clear," I said. "This way. Try not to touch the walls. The less racket we make the better."

I held up my wrist and tapped the button on my control panel. Immediately, the blue image of my holographic map blurred into view, displaying the schematics of the *Revelation*. A tightly packed cluster of green dots towards the front of the ship marked the position of my little group.

The rest of my crew piled in after me, taking turns expressing their astonishment in their own various ways. I kept my eyes on my map, studying the confusing mass of shafts and corridors. Currently, the mass of green dots was clustered on a corridor labeled 11-M-5. Eleventh deck, maintenance, and the fifth of its kind. It ran lengthwise along the ship, occasionally twisting to work its way around a weapons station or thruster or other system. Escape shuttle 93R had been positioned roughly three fourths of the way towards the front of the ship.

I zoomed in on the corridor while I waited for the rest of the crew, floating in the middle of the corridor, and followed the long line with one armored finger. I knew where it would lead, of course—I'd spent hours tracing it over and over—but I traced it one more time regardless. The bridge was located on the seventh deck, a few hundred meters away in what I'd estimated would take us a half-hour of careful travel to traverse.

I pivoted, spinning around in the zero-G to get a glimpse of my team. They had all made it through the doorway and were now soundlessly gliding down the hallway after me, Tekka and one of his men pulling the supply pod behind them. I held out a thumbs up. Shell, next in line behind me, returned it.

"Alright, then," I said. "Let's get moving." I turned and activated my thrusters, propelling me gently down the corridor. They weren't much, just a little nudge in the right direction, but they provided powerful directional control, and that was important to keep us from bumping into the walls and making too many disturbances.

"The walls," Rid's voice said, low and serious.

I turned my head to see what he was talking about and felt a chill run down my spine. There were patches of crimson splattered across the walls in various locations all down the hallway, scattered randomly. At one point I saw what looked like a bloody handprint. At another I noticed a set of three deep grooves in the wall. The marks of a ripper's claws.

"Stay frosty," I said.

Something clinked against my visor, startling me. It took me a second to realize that it was a bullet casing. I frowned at it, then focused and looked past it, my eyes widening. There were thousands of them glinting in our floodlights, drifting at an almost imperceptibly slow rate, still retaining the smallest bit of momentum from when they had been originally fired. I had to hold back a curse. The crew hadn't gone down without a fight. But from the look of things, they'd gone down regardless. And they'd likely been at least as well armed as us.

I saw more chunks of debris. A twisted and torn piece of Jericho armor here. A discarded APS-7 shotgun there, drifting aimlessly. A helmet with a jagged hole torn through the back of it that reminded me uncomfortably of watching as Black's head was impaled on a ripper's tailspike.

"*We shouldn't be here,*" I heard Bentley whispering, his voice taut with fear. "*This is a bad idea. We shouldn't have come here.*"

"Keep the chatter down," I said, whispering instinctively. The sound would make no difference—no sound would travel beyond our exos, after all—and yet it still felt somehow wrong to speak at anything louder than a murmur. As if that deep, infinite silence was the only thing between us and the rippers. Besides—fear is a highly infectious disease. Best practice is to shut it down before it can spread and multiply. I wasn't sure anything I could say would cure Bentley's fears, but I could at least try to quarantine them and keep them from infecting the rest of the crew.

We reached the corner. I found myself holding my breath as I carefully maneuvered myself around it, peering down. More of the same: long, foreboding darkness, full of little pieces of debris glittering in the light of our flashlights like distant stars, trapped inside this massive ship.

"Where are all of the bodies?" Shell asked.

"They're all rippers now," Nadus said. "That's how they do it. Eat up every last bit of organics they can. Split and repeat."

I looked ahead and spied a terminal built into the side of the wall. I moved closer to it, inspecting it. The screen was a shattered mass of fragmented glass, but a blinking red light below it indicated that it was still online. The words SYSTEM MONITOR 11-M-19 were printed above the terminal. System monitors were positioned along every manned shaft in the ship, allowing technicians and passersby to get a reading on the ship's conditions as necessary.

"Bentley." I pointed at the terminal. "You're up. Get plugged in. I want an update on the ship's condition."

"Yeah." Bentley maneuvered himself next to the terminal,

carefully opened a panel below it, and then fumbled through his gear until he found the hardware he was looking for and plugged it into a port in the terminal. A few seconds later, the display screen he was carrying blinked into life. He studied it in silence for a few moments.

"Well?" Tekka's voice prodded. "What's it say?"

"It's... a lot," Bentley said. The terror in his voice seemed to have been chased away by curiosity, at least for now. "The ship is in bad condition, but not much seems damaged. The port we entered through seems to be the only hull breach. Gravitational generators are offline—"

"No, really?" muttered Shell, staring at an empty bullet casing drifting lazily past her head.

"Decks eleven, ten, nine, and eight are fully depressurized," Bentley continued. "After that the life-support systems are functioning just fine. It looks like none of the emergency airlocks higher than deck seven activated."

"Can you tell what happened from that console?" I asked.

Bentley peered over at me. "What do you mean?"

"We know that somebody sabotaged the ship," I said. "From everything we've seen it looks like somebody issued a computer command that released all of the rippers and shut down the ship's emergency and security features."

"Nothing looks out of the ordinary." Bentley tapped a few buttons. "The ship's wireless network is still functioning. I'll tap into that and keep on looking. Most likely, we won't find anything until we get to the bridge."

"Alright, then." I activated my thrusters and started moving in the direction of the shaft that would take us down to deck seven and the bridge. "Let's keep moving."


The layout of a battlecruiser can be difficult to wrap your head around.

People tend to think about spaceships being built like a waterboat, with one side of the ship facing down, and everything on the ship built along a horizontal axis, one deck stacked on top of another like a sandwich. That's how the *Orpheus* works. A ship as big as a battlecruiser, though, is structured very differently.

If the *Orpheus* is a sandwich, a battlecruiser is a burrito. Or an onion. Or a... well, you get the point. It has layers. The entire ship is built along one long, central gravity-generator core. Rather than stacking on top of it, all of the decks wrap around that core, layered on top of each other like... well, like an onion.

One massive, oblong, dark, deadly, steel onion, carrying enough firepower and rippers to decimate the population of an entire planet.

Even when a ship as big as a battlecruiser is fully functioning, it can be difficult to get around quickly. A myriad of elevators, magnetic rail-guided transport cars, moving walkways, and other devices expedite the process of going from one end of the ship to the other, but it's still an ordeal. From what I could tell, none of those systems were currently functioning, and even if they had been, I'd have been hesitant to activate them for fear of waking up rippers. As the *Revelation* now was—powered down to essentially a poorly lit hunk of metal floating through space—traversing it took even longer. To make things even worse, we were traveling slowly, exercising an overabundance of caution to prevent ourselves from making even the slightest disturbance.

The elevator shaft was long, dark, and empty. I breathed a sigh of relief at that. When we reached the deck seven airlock Rid got the door open and let us inside, where Bentley plugged his device into the terminal and began the pressurization process.

"How close are we?" Shell asked.

"Close." I glanced down at my wrist computer and noted rising oxygen levels. "Just a hundred meters down this corridor and to the right." I switched over to Rose's channel. "Rose, you in position?"

*"Waiting on you, boss,"* she replied. *"The boys here are itching to get their hands on that loot."*

"Good. Just a few minutes, then th—"

Three long, black claws suddenly tore through the airlock door. There was a hissing of gas and a moment later the flimsy emergency barrier exploded inward, ruptured by the force of the rapid pressurization. In the null gravity the force of the blast sent me careening backward.

Screaming filled the comms.

## THIRTY-THREE

"*CONTACT!*" somebody shouted.

I spun, shoving somebody out of the way as I oriented myself towards the breached airlock. Three rippers had leaped through the airlock and were now crawling over Jin's thrashing form. Sparks, chunks of metal, and splashes of blood flecked upward as they tore through the armor.

The screams did not stop.

I brought up the barrel of my gun, but before I could get off a shot, the airlock suddenly flared with angry orange light and the sound of a Jackhammer being fired. The rippers flailed as a storm of exploding rounds smashed into them, detonating in little bursts of light and gore. Within a few seconds the three creatures were little more than floating chunks of flesh and bone, held together by ragged strips of skin.

"Got 'em," Shell gasped, adrenaline lacing her voice.

"We're not done yet." I peered through the cloud of gore. Movement, down the corridor. The scraping sound of claws pushing off against the walls. But no good visual.

I estimated where the rippers would be and used my neurointerface to fire a concussion grenade from my shoulder-mounted launcher. There was a flash of light and an audible *BOOM*.

"Nadus, after me." I pushed off against the wall, sending myself gliding over my companions and into the corridor.

I grimaced as I pushed through the slowly expanding cloud of gore and fired up one of my thrusters to push myself down towards the floor. I counted maybe a dozen rippers in the corridor, all of them pressed up against the wall like squashed bugs from my concussion grenade. As I raised my Jackhammer, they recovered, pushing themselves off towards me, their claws glinting in my floodlights.

I activated my magboots, anchoring myself to the floor, and opened fire. The first few exploded into meaty chunks. One towards the rear drew its tail back for a strike. I ducked as the spike darted forward, leaving a deep groove in the side of my helmet. A moment later I heard another Jackhammer open fire and watched as the next several rippers joined their companions in death, the concussions of the exploding shells scattering them in every which direction. I fired a burst at the last cluster, and it was over.

"Clear," Nadus said, his voice steady.

"For now," I said. "Move forward a few meters, cover the corridor. More will come. Everybody out of the airlock! *Now!*"

"Jin is hurt!" Rathen called over the comms, his voice lined with panic. "He's hurt real bad!"

I turned and looked back into the airlock. Jin's exo was still spasming, blood squirting up through the gashes in his armor from several breaches. Rathen was kneeling over him, frantically searching through his equipment for a quick sealant spray.

"Move around him!" I called to everyone else. I got shocked compliance in return, the rest of the team filing past the fallen mercenary. "Nadus, start leading the way towards the bridge. Rid, start working on getting that door open as soon as you get there."

I deactivated my boots and pushed myself back down towards Rathen and Jin. Rathen had found the sealant and was spraying it over the gashes in Jin's armor, stopping the blood and air loss.

"Jin," I said. "Can you hear me?"

"Yeah," he gasped. "Damn, this hurts. This *really* hurts."

"We're gonna get you out of here. Just hang tight." I carefully grabbed him by the foot and began pulling him through the air after the rest of the group while Rathen finished sealing his wounds. Jin screamed out in pain, but I didn't stop.

"*Lax?*" Rose's voice was urgent and high pitched. "*Lax, are you guys alright?*"

"Yeah." I grabbed Jin's flailing arm and pinned it in place to his side, grimacing. "Mostly. One man hurt."

A short, pregnant silence on the other side of the radio. "*Is it—*"

"It's Jin," I replied.

"*Oh.*" Rose's voice held an odd mix of relief and dread.

"Contact," I heard Nadus say from the front of the line. A split second later the sound of gunfire tore through the corridor. Sounded like two Jackhammers. Nadus and Shell were at the front, so it had to be them.

"Keep moving him," I said to Rathen, letting them move past me so I could take up the rear and keep an eye on the airlock behind us. With the amount of noise we were making we'd have rippers pouring up through the elevator shaft to get at us before long.

"Clear," Nadus's voice called over the radio again. "Reloading."

"Keep moving," I called. "No matter what. If we get bogged down before we reach the bridge, it's over. And Shell, reload as soon as he's done."

"Yeah," Shell said, her voice ragged. "Intersection. Which way?"

"Right," Nadus and I said at the same time.

The team rounded the intersection one by one. I passed the corpses of the rippers Nadus and Shell had killed. It was hard to tell one mangled mass of flesh from the next, but I estimated there had been six of them. I frowned as I noticed a ripper's dismembered limb float past me. The claws looked... different. Shorter, more sharply curved than usual.

A chill ran down my spine. I'd only ever seen variant rippers in one place before.

"Reached the door," Shell said. "Rid, you're—"

"On it." Rid positioned himself in front of the door and began working.

I shook myself out of my stupor. Whatever was going on with the rippers here, I could figure out along the way. For now, I needed to get this job done. I turned from the corridor to briefly assess the team. The corridor we were now in was just wide enough for two exos to stand shoulder to shoulder. Nadus and Shell had reloaded their Jackhammers and were in front of the group, standing next to each other with their barrels pointed down the corridor. Rid was right behind them, kneeling in front of the door and using a laser cutter to peel back a panel covering the door's locking mechanism. Bentley was behind Rid, standing with his boots clamped to the floor and staring at Jin. Even through the exo, I could see the slight quiver in Bentley's hands, still clutching his computer terminal.

"Bentley," I said. "Weapon out."

He looked up at me. I couldn't tell what was on his face, but I imagined it was shock.

"This is it," I said. "From here on out we're fighting for every minute we survive."

He nodded mutely, snapped his terminal into a holster on his leg, and clumsily drew his Jackhammer from its resting place on his back.

Rathen had pressed Jin up against the wall. Jin had stopped

flailing and was now just whimpering while Rathen tried to reassure him. Tekka pushed past them and took up a position next to me, aiming his gun down the corridor.

Movement down the corridor. Rippers.

I let them get closer before I opened fire. We had plenty of ammo in the cargo crate, but it still wasn't an unlimited supply, so making shots count was important. It was hard to count how many rippers there were, the way they crawled over each other, but I figured there were at least two dozen.

"Hold," I said to Tekka. "Wait until they tense to tailstrike. Rathen, I need you ready to swap out if one of us has to reload."

I heard the rebel step up behind Tekka, but didn't take my eyes off of the approaching rippers. I'd been right, earlier. There was something different about them. Nothing extreme. Just subtle distinctions—shorter claws, longer torsos. Was I going crazy?

More appeared behind the first ones I'd seen, too many to count. They rushed closer, closer, a wall of flesh crawling over itself, driven by mindless hunger and bloodlust, and the foremost one stopped, its muscles tensing as it readied its tail for a strike, and I pulled the trigger.

The Jackhammer pressed back against me, my magboots keeping the recoil from driving me backward. A few seconds later Tekka joined in.

They kept coming. Wave after wave, rushing forward only to shatter against a storm of bullets. But each wave died just a bit closer to us than the last.

The digital ammo counter on my Jericho flashed yellow. Half of my fifty rounds fired. I kept shooting until it flashed orange and then red. When the bullets stopped coming, I shuffled backward, ejecting the mag and slamming a new one into place while Rathen stepped up and took my place. A few seconds later, Tekka's gun went dry, and I swapped places with him, bringing my Jackhammer back up and firing into the horde.

They kept coming.

The corridor became crowded with corpses, the onrushing rippers obscured behind them. A stinger shot out of a cloud of gore and I fired at its base. I must have hit the ripper because the stinger jolted, the impact of the bullets jerking it out of line with Rathen's head and embedding it in the wall instead.

They kept coming.

"I'm in!" Rid shouted.

"*Go!*" I bellowed the word, ducking to avoid another tail-strike. Next to me, Rathen ran out of ammo and retreated, pulling Jin along with him and leaving me alone. I deactivated my magboots and kept firing, activating my thrusters to keep me floored as the force of the recoil pushed me backward, towards the bridge door. I reached out and caught the corner of the doorway with one gauntlet, letting my momentum whip me around and into the hallway beyond.

"Close the door!" I shouted.

Rid hit a button and the doorway began closing. A set of claws reached through the doors before they could close, flailing around blindly. There was a thudding sound as Tekka fired an incendiary grenade through the gap and into the hallway beyond. A second later, the corridor flared with white light and the sound of sizzling flesh. I reached forward, grabbing the ripper's limb, and yanked on it. There was a popping sound as the limb was torn from its melting body and the door slammed shut.

"Will it hold?" Shell asked.

"Lock is intact," Rid gasped. "Should hold."

"They didn't seem to have problems tearing through any of the other doors," Bentley muttered.

"Those were emergency airlocks," I said, discarding the mangled ripper arm. Then I ejected my empty mag and loaded up a new one. I had two loaded mags left strapped to my exo. "This door is sturdy, designed to withstand some damage."

Tekka scoffed, reloading as well. "Then how did we get in so easily?"

"Wasn't easy," muttered Rid.

I turned, inspecting the bridge. It was a big room, maybe forty meters long and half as wide, filled with computers. A few overhead emergency lights bathed the room in red. There was an elevated platform towards the far end of the room, which I guessed was the captain's command deck.

"Bentley. You're up. Get that port open so Tames and her team can board."

Bentley made his way towards the elevated platform, trying to run at first, and then remembering that there was no gravity and using his thrusters instead. Meanwhile, I maneuvered myself into the center of the room and looked around, identifying our escape routes. In addition to the main door that we had come through, there were two small elevators designed to transport high-ranking staff members directly from the bridge to the officers' quarters a few decks below, two sealed doors leading out into the main corridors on either side of the room, and, most importantly, a small hatch near the command deck that led to the bridge escape pods. That would be our way out, if everything went according to plan. And that was one hell of a big if.

I pushed myself back down to the ground. Nadus and Shell had opened the cargo pod and were replacing the spent mags on their exos with loaded ones. I followed suit, then approached Jin and Rathen.

"How's he holding up?" I asked, keeping my voice low and calm.

"Not great," Rathen said. "But I already gave him a painkiller and a coagulant, so he should be stabilizing."

"Jin?" I knelt next to him, inspecting the damage. I spied

eleven breaches. With the sealant covering them it was hard to tell how bad the injuries beneath were. "Can you hear me?"

"I can hear you," he said weakly.

"Good. We're gonna get you out of here." I pointed towards the hatch to the escape pods. "Just as soon as we've gotten the other team onto the ship, Rose is gonna fly back over here and we're gonna get you back onto the *Orpheus* through the bridge escape shuttle port. It goes all the way out, back to the surface."

"Why didn't we just come in that way?" snapped Rathen.

"It's closed and it's blocked," Tekka said. I turned over to see that he and Nadus had started assembling the Hades laser turret that had been packed in the cargo crate. "We won't be able to use it until we clear out the shuttles, and we can only do that from in here."

Rathen cursed, his voice trembling. "We've barely even started and everything's falling apart."

"*Nothing* is falling apart," I said firmly. "We knew there would be resistance. We knew there would be a fight. We're exactly where we planned on being. All we need to do now is hold out till we can find those plans. Most importantly—*stay cool*. If we stay calm, we stay focused. If we stay focused, we stay alive. If we stay alive, we get out rich. Got it?"

Rathen gave a reluctant nod. I slapped him on the shoulder. "Keep me posted on Jin's condition." I pushed off the floor and headed towards where Rid and Shell were standing, their guns pointed nervously towards the door we'd come through. "You two holding up alright?"

"I can hear them," Shell whispered.

I frowned. "Hear what?"

She pointed at my helmet. I realized with a start that my helmet's auditory sensor must have been damaged by the spike that had narrowly missed me. I checked my wrist computer to make sure that the room was safe and then opened my visor, taking in a breath of the *Revelation*'s stale air and craning my ear towards the door. I could hear it now: a flurry of metallic scraping sounds.

"They're trying to burrow their way through the door," I said, a chill running down my spine.

"All of the doors," Rid said.

I hesitated and turned towards Nadus. "Nadus. Did you notice anything…"

"They're different," he agreed, not looking towards me. "Claws are shorter and more curved. Bodies are thicker, heads are bigger."

"*I thought all rippers were the same,*" Rose's disembodied voice said. "*They're clones, so they're identical.*"

"That's the idea," I said, glancing at the arm I'd torn off. It was spinning in a macabre circle in the air. I narrowed my eyes. The claws were *shorter*. I tried to push away my memories of the *Panama*, and the aberrant rippers I'd seen there. What would having shorter claws change? They'd be less effective in combat—less reach. But they'd be better at…

"It's getting louder," Shell said, alarm ringing in her voice like a warning bell.

"The shorter claws make them better at burrowing through hard surfaces," I said, turning to face the door. I resealed my visor and the scratching sounds became distorted muffles. "Judging by those sounds, I'd say we have no more than a few minutes before they start breaking through. Bentley, how close are you to—"

The room suddenly went from ominous red to gentle white. The bridge came alive with computers booting up. A large holographic display in the center of the bridge flickered to life, showing a schematic of the ship.

"In," Bentley said. I glanced up towards where he was huddled over a terminal on the command deck. As I watched, he raised a hand to wipe sweat from his brow, only to realize that his exo was in the way and shake his head in frustration. "We now have full control over the ship."

I breathed a sigh of relief. "Good. Get that bay open so Rose can dock." I whirled, taking stock of our situation. Rippers—of a mystery variety that wasn't supposed to exist—banging on the doors, about to break through. Team two about to board. Which meant that by the plan, all we had to do now was survive until team two had hit the major power generators and loaded up on ultracells, then escape out the shuttle bay. Oh—and we had to find the ultracell blueprints. Or whatever it was the Paragon had been hiding here.

No biggie, right?

"*Bay doors are open,*" Rose's voice said. "*Docking now.*"

I held out a thumbs up to Bentley. He gave me one in return.

"*Boarding now,*" Tames's voice said over the comms. "*See you guys soon.*"

Not *that* soon, I thought. We'd see them after the job when we were all reunited on the *Orpheus*. But given how nerve-wracking our situation was, I could forgive her confusion. I turned towards the door.

"Alright, then. I guess it's time for our distraction. If we stay here, they break through all at once and overwhelm us. Bentley, open the main door part way, just enough for one of them to fit through at a time. After that, start looking for those ultracell files."

He gulped. "On it."

"They're getting closer," Shell said, her voice tense. "Sounds like they'll be through any second."

There was a whirring sound as the laser turret powered up, a long cable extending from it to a wide socket in the wall. Nadus gave it a loving pat. "Let 'em come. We're ready for 'em."

I took a deep breath.

I felt strangely good. Calm, when I should have been

panicking. This was the scenario of my nightmares, after all: stuck on a derelict spacecraft, surrounded by rippers hungry for blood. There was a sort of haunting symmetry to it all. But in that symmetry, that familiarity, I found purpose. I'd *been* here before. I knew what I was doing... mostly.

And I'd be damned if I was gonna lose another crew to these bastards.

The door in front of me groaned, shaking as rippers tried to tear it from its frame. I lifted my Jackhammer.

"Let's give 'em hell."

THIRTY-FOUR

"This is... weird," Bentley said.

"What?" I shouted, not taking my eyes off of the carnage in front of me. After nearly half an hour of slaughter, the small gap we'd opened in the door was full of the charred remains of rippers. As I watched, a ripper that had been cut in half but was still somehow alive managed to pull itself free of the carnage and begin crawling towards us, one claw at a time. I put a single round into its skull and turned towards Bentley, letting Shell take my place next to the laser turret.

As much as these rippers *looked* like the ones that had been on the *Panama*, they didn't act like they had. The rippers that had killed my crew had been careful—tactical, even. Waiting to strike until opportune moments. These ones behaved like regular rippers, throwing themselves at us with no regard for their own lives.

I glanced down at the timer on my wrist computer. We'd been on the *Revelation* for two hours. Most of that had been spent traversing the distance from our entry point to the bridge, and since then we'd been holed up here. Tames and her crew had safely boarded and had been giving me occasional updates on their progress. The important thing was that they hadn't run into any rippers yet. I was pretty sure every ripper in the damn ship was outside the bridge, trying to force themselves through that narrow slit in the door. I could hear them through the walls, scrambling over each other in their frenzy. The chokepoint we'd created was the only thing keeping us alive.

"I've been going through the logs and databases," Bentley said, "trying to figure out where we can find those blueprints. Or, at least, trying to figure out what the Paragon had on this ship. What was so special about it. Nothing says anything about Divinity."

"Not so weird," Tekka said. "They were trying to separate themselves from Divinity, weren't they? That was the whole point of this being a secret project."

"Right," Bentley said. "But... the *Revelation*'s mission briefings—the private, high orders that only the commanding officers had access to—don't say anything about ultracells, either."

"What *do* they say?" I asked.

"Their mission was to proceed to Brahma and begin something called 'Project Eden'. Deploy the payload, keep all allied personnel off the planet, and observe."

I frowned. Certainly didn't *sound* like ultracell plans.

Tekka looked away from the door and towards me. There seemed to be a reprieve in the assault. "I thought Artemis said that Project Eden was the codename for the blueprints."

"Yeah." I ignited my thrusters, sending me gliding towards the command deck. "That's what she said."

Bentley pointed down at his screen as I came to a halt next to him. He had lifted the visor of his helmet and was wearing a perplexed expression.

I cursed under my breath. I should've known that finding the blueprints would be more complicated than just running a search on a computer, but what can I say? A man can dream. I studied Bentley's screen. A query program was sifting through what looked to be terabyte upon terabyte of data from various sources, compiling the relevant findings.

I sighed. "Keep looking. Find any files that are locked behind extra layers of security. It might be hidden."

The screen flickered a few times. "That's weird," Bentley said. "Must be some sort of glitch, maybe a short. I—"

The program he had been running suddenly shut down, leaving only the Paragon Navy's symbol on the screen.

"...the hell?" Bentley hit a few buttons, trying to reopen the program. Instead of opening again, a red box saying ACCESS DENIED in bold, authoritative letters appeared.

I frowned. "You accidentally lock us out?"

"No, I couldn't have. We weren't even doing anything when it shut down. And there's no timeout protocol, I checked." He narrowed his brows. "The only other reason would be..."

The lights overhead flickered, then went out. I whipped around, activating my Jericho's floodlights.

"...somebody else is using the system and blocking our access," Bentley finished.

"*Uh, guys?*" Rose's voice called. "*Something's happening...*"

A calm, robotic voice suddenly crackled to life over the ship intercom. "*Defensive batteries operational. Acquiring targets and initiating defensive measures.*"

Cold horror ran down my spine. "Rose, get the hell out of—"

The doors to the bridge all opened at the same time.

Through each of the two doors on either side of me I saw rippers darting past, swarming their way towards the choke-point we'd created, mindless in their eagerness to consume. As the doors opened, I saw a few of them pause, peering in at us with gaping jaws.

Tekka was shouting something, the laser turret's angry orange beam still searing through one ripper after another as the floodgates opened. Shell and Nadus suddenly transitioned from picking off stragglers to firing full auto into the sudden onslaught.

We were dead if we stayed here. Rippers rushing at us from three sides. The doors were still good chokepoints, but our numbers were too thin to hold them back for more than a few minutes.

Rippers had started to dart through the door on my right. I turned and fired a burst, eviscerating the few that had made it through. "Bentley!" I shouted. "Get the escape shuttle ready to evac! It's go time! Everybody else, lay suppressive fire on the entry points and work your way back towards the command deck!"

The room erupted into chaos. Rathen and Rid took up a position blasting away at the rippers pouring through the door on my left. Bentley pushed off towards the hatch leading into the shuttle airlock, frantically trying to get it open. Tekka swore and detached the laser turret from its stand, wielding it by hand and retreating with Shell and Nadus without ceasing fire for more than a few seconds.

"We're not going *anywhere*," Tekka growled, "Not without those blueprints!"

"They won't do us any good if we're dead!" I yelled. "Rose, we're aborting. Get ready to pick us up!"

"*Little...* busy," Rose's strained voice said in my ear. I heard her grunt. "*The damn ship is shooting at—*"

Her voice suddenly cut off, replaced by static.

My skin went cold.

"What happened?" Rid yelled.

"Gimme a sec!" I took a deep breath. *Calm. Breathe. Figure this out.* I pulled up my wrist computer to inspect my connection to the *Orpheus*, only to see a flash of movement in the doorway. I raised my Jackhammer and fired off a burst at the four rippers that were lunging towards me. The first three were sent spinning backward, spraying the walls with their gore. The second was merely knocked off course as a round blasted its tail off. It alighted against the floor, reoriented itself, and then lunged at me head first. I waited until it was close and then fired a single shot into its open maw. That did the trick.

I brushed aside the ruined corpse as its momentum carried it into me and glanced down at my ammo counter. Seven rounds left.

"Rose!" Rid was shouting into the comms, his voice louder and more urgent than I'd ever heard it. "Rose, do you copy?" Nothing but static returned.

I glanced down at my wrist computer. SEARCHING FOR RELAY, it said in blinking red letters where it usually said CONNECTION SECURE. The *Orpheus* was offline.

"What's the call?" Nadus asked, his voice icy cold with focus as he emptied his mag into a group of rippers and then reloaded. "We can't stay here."

He was right. We couldn't stay here. And now I was increasingly convinced we couldn't run, either. Somebody had taken control of the ship, opening the doors on us and activating the *Revelation*'s formidable defensive batteries. Which meant that, as much as it hurt to consider, Rose and the *Orpheus* had most likely been blasted into oblivion. And, beyond that, even if we took the shuttle and hoped that somebody would happen upon us in this massive, empty, unfrequented void of deep space, whoever was controlling the ship could just shoot us down.

"*We need to go!*" Shell's voice screamed in my ear.

"Bentley, bring the C4 here," I said. I turned to the elevator shaft in the middle of the bridge and maneuvered myself over to it. I ripped the door off with a powered gauntlet, then peered down into the darkness. The shaft was empty. It was wide enough for multiple small cars to go up and down which meant that we could navigate around them. "Put it here. Everyone go down the shaft, then we'll blow the C4 behind us."

Bentley pivoted away from the escape pod entrance and flew towards the elevator shaft in the middle of the bridge.

"How do we know there aren't more rippers down there?" Shell demanded, her voice strained as she dodged a tailstrike.

"We don't!" I yelled. "But if we go out the hatch, the *Revelation*'s guns will just pick us off."

"But Rose—"

"Just *do it!*"

They obeyed. I reloaded my Jackhammer and opened fire on several rippers who were creeping through the door, the fire evidently cooled enough for them to pass without immediately melting.

"It's fixed!" Bentley said.

"Everyone go!" I started stepping backward towards the elevator shaft. "Somebody grab Jin, and the cargo crate."

"What is *that?*" Rathen shouted.

I turned and felt my eyes go wide.

A ripper had come through the door Rathen and Shell had been guarding. Except it wasn't a ripper.

It was a nightmare.

Twice as big as a ripper, and at least the size of my Jericho. Bulbous and muscled. A pair of dark, gleaming wings protruding from its back.

*No. It's impossible. You're not real.*

The ripper—nightmare—demon—*thing* stalked into the room, regarding all of us slowly. Its eyeless gaze settled on Rathen, standing just a few meters in front of it.

Jin screamed.

Rathen just stood there, frozen in place. His Jackhammer shook. "What..." His voice was a hoarse, desperate whisper. "What is..."

The creature lunged forward, almost faster than I could follow. One taloned claw sank into Rathen's breastplate, deep into the armor, then yanked the rebel into a tight embrace.

"*Kill it!*" I bellowed, raising my Jackhammer and opening fire on the monstrosity. Rid jumped backward, scrambling to put distance between himself and the beast. The creature's broad, jet-black wings swung around, concealing it and its prey. My barrage of bullets slammed into the wings, exploded, and—did nothing, leaving only small craters in the glinting surface of the wings.

Biosteel. The same material the ripper's claws were made out of. They weren't wings—they were a shield.

Rathen started screaming.

"*Down the shaft!*" I bellowed, pushing towards it myself. Nadus and Bentley had already vanished into the darkness. I grabbed Rid and shoved him in next. Something slammed into my back and I felt a sharp pain lance through my left shoulder. I tried to turn. To fight back. But the tail was holding me in place—

Shell appeared out of nowhere, looming next to me. She bellowed as she swung her knife, severing the tail. The pressure vanished and I found myself lurching forward, towards the elevator shaft.

"*Go! Go!*" I shoved her towards the elevator. "Tekka, leave the turret! Get over here!"

Tekka bounded into view, dragging a panicking Jin behind him. I turned, fired my Jackhammer wildly into the onrushing rippers and let the recoil drive me backward into the elevator shaft. I spun, pushed off, and activated my thrusters to send me launching down the long shaft, towards my companions, spinning back around to watch in horror as rippers poured through the elevator door after me.

"*Blow it!*" I yelled. "*Blow it now! Nad—*"

There was a flash and a boom. The force of the explosion sent me hurling down the shaft, spinning head over heels so quickly I thought I would vomit. I slammed into somebody, bounced off them, struck a wall, went careening back the other way, crashed into something solid, and stopped moving, my head spinning.

For a long moment, the only sound I could hear was heavy breathing in the comms.

I groaned, pushing myself up, trying to orient myself. We were at the bottom of the elevator shaft, piled in an undignified heap. I shoved off the person below me, letting gravity—or the lack thereof—undo the work of the explosion that had smashed us all together.

I pulled up my wrist computer and turned on the map, then growled in frustration. The map itself still functioned, but all of the communication systems that had allowed me to track the members of our team were down. My map just showed eight blinking dots where Tames's team had boarded the *Revelation* and eight more on the bridge, where we had been when we lost contact with the *Orpheus*.

There were groans and curses as the rest of the team untangled themselves. I looked upward and gave a sigh of relief as I noticed that the top of the elevator shaft seemed to have been blocked by debris in the explosion.

"What happened to Tames's team?" Tekka asked. His voice went cold. "Are they..."

"No. Well... I don't know. When we lost our connection to the *Orpheus*, we lost our quantum communication to the other team," I said grimly. "We won't be able to talk to them unless we get within shortwave signal range."

There was a short silence.

"Now what?" Shell asked. "Won't the rippers be coming after us?"

"They'll be looking for us," I said. "But that explosion should buy us some time. They'll all be swarming towards those corridors, and when they don't find us, they'll start eating whatever they can find."

"And we left them one hell of a feast," Nadus said. "At least, whatever didn't get incinerated by the C4."

Silence fell again. I understood why. Most likely everyone was trying to decide which of the hundred questions we all had bouncing around in our brains to verbalize first. The plan had gone to hell in about a dozen ways.

"What," Rid asked, "*was* that thing?"

Nadus shook his head. "I have no idea. These rippers... something's wrong. They're different. They move different. Look different. Act different."

Nightmares. I clenched my eyes shut. Nightmares. Like on the *Panama*. I'd convinced myself that those memories weren't real. That my traumatized brain was making things up. But... Rathen had just been *eaten* by one of those things.

"Look," I said heavily. "It's a lot to process. But right now we've got to keep moving. Let's get to somewhere safer, then we'll figure out what's going on." *If there is anywhere safer.*

Assenting nods.

I sighed and pointed at the door Rid had anchored himself to. "That should lead into the officer's quarters. Let's start by getting through it. And keep quiet. Nothing knows we're here yet. The rippers are probably still looking for us up on the bridge, if they're not busy cannibalizing their fallen buddies. Let's keep it that way."

Rid went through first, his Jackhammer held at the ready. Due to my position at the top of the pile, I ended up waiting for everyone else to file through the doorway before me. Which was fine by me. Gave me some time to think.

And there was a lot to think about.

Rathen was dead. Rose might be too. Jin was groaning in pain again—he'd been moved far more than he should have been in all of the chaos and he was probably bleeding badly. The cargo crate had been left behind in our mad scramble to escape, which meant that so far as supplies went, we were now limited to what we were carrying. And on top of all of that there was the issue of Project Eden, and the fact that Artemis had evidently been wrong about what it was. If that wasn't enough, my mind still hadn't been able to wrap itself around the monstrosity that had eaten Rathen.

I grimaced at the sheer weight of it all. Everyone expected me to have a plan ready as soon as we found someplace to hunker down. A familiar sense of crushing dread started to settle in on me. Rid, Shell, Bentley, Nadus, and even Tekka and his men were all depending on me to somehow get them out of the mess I had led them into. Tames and her squad, too, if they were alive.

*A plan. Focus on that.*

I took a deep breath, forcing my thoughts into order. All that mattered now was getting off this ship. Every other priority was secondary next to that.

"Bentley," I said into a direct channel with him. "What happened?"

"I don't know," he said, his voice shaking. "Somebody blocked us out of the system."

I frowned. "Meaning..."

"Meaning," he reiterated, his voice rising a few octaves, "that *somebody else* is alive on this ship and is controlling it."

I furrowed my brow in thought. "And there's nothing you can do to fight them back? Hacking wise, I mean?"

"No. Only way to be back into the system would be to shut down whoever's screwing with us."

"Any way you could figure out where they're working from?"

"Could be anywhere. At this point, considering everything they've been able to do, I would say nothing's off the table."

I felt a chill run down my spine. "So, you think that whoever this is..."

"I think it's your Penitent." He gave a nervous chuckle. "Bit of a pretentious name. But yes. I think odds are good that we're dealing with the same person—people—whatever—that made all this happen in the first place."

"Well," I said grimly. "That's just fabulous."

I switched to the main channel. Without the *Orpheus*, our quantum communication systems were down, but we could still communicate locally with our radios. "Here's the plan. We head for the docking bay. It's a long trek, but we should be able to make it. Once we get there we commandeer a gunship and hope its shields are enough to get us out in one piece."

"Will we be able to launch it without control of the systems?" Shell asked.

I gritted my teeth. "We're gonna have to figure that out along the way. Those gunships are armed with enough explosives to decimate an entire citystation, though. If we can't get the launch protocol started, we should still be able to blast our way out."

"What about the others?" Jin asked, his voice weak.

"Nothing we can do for them now," I said. "We were using the *Orpheus*'s quantum comms system to stay in touch with them. There're at least five decks between us and them, so unless their paths somehow cross ours, radio will be useless. And there's no reason our paths *would* cross." I glanced down at the map. "If they've got any brains at all, or hell, if they're still alive, they'll be heading to their nearest docking bay as well."

Tekka scoffed. "Not much of a plan."

"No," I said. "It ain't. But right now it's all we've got."

## THIRTY-FIVE

"You ready?" Shell's voice was hesitant.

I grimaced. "Yeah. Hurry up."

I felt a jolt of pain as she pressed one boot against my back and pushed me forward, tugging on the ripper spike that was embedded in the back of my shoulder with two gauntlets. Within a few seconds, the Jericho's built-in self-sealing system had started to close the gap left in the armor. It wouldn't be as strong as it had been before, but it would at least keep my suit pressurized. I felt blood start to well up, soaking through my padded suit, and then slow to a halt as the suit automatically tightened itself, reknitting the severed threads and acting as a bandage.

I moved my shoulder, testing the wound. Uncomfortable, but not too bad. The stinger hadn't pierced more than an inch or so—I'd been lucky that it had struck me at an angle rather than straight on. The Jericho still seemed to be working fine too. Little miracles. I'd take as many of them as I could get.

"How's everyone doing on ammo?" I asked.

One by one, everyone gave their reports. It was not good. Bentley, somehow, had not yet fired his weapon, and was still carrying four full mags in addition to the one in his Jackhammer. Nadus had the least ammo left, with one full mag on his belt and a half-full one in his gun. Everyone else was scattered between the two extremes. I forced Bentley to give two of his mags to Nadus, figuring that they'd be put to better use there.

I studied the map and plotted our route. I didn't like it, but it would have to do. The docking bay was on the opposite side of the ship from us. The most direct way through would be to cut straight across the ship, down into the core of the ship and through. If we were careful to avoid power generators, we might be able to avoid running into any more rippers.

I glanced down at the timer. Roughly three and a half hours until the black hole had us in its dark embrace.

"Everyone had a chance to catch their breath?" I asked.

"No," Jin groaned.

I gritted my teeth. "I don't like it any more than you do, but we've gotta keep moving. It'll take us the better part of an hour to make it all the way through to the research station, and we're running out of time fast."

I transmitted the route I had plotted to their computers, then let Nadus take the lead. I fell into line near the rear, next to Rid. I winced as I noticed him bump absentmindedly into a low doorframe. I switched to a private channel. "Rid, you've gotta watch it. We make too many vibrations and it'll put us right back in the cooker."

"Yeah." He seemed to shake himself. "Sorry."

I hesitated. "How you holding up?"

He said nothing.

Nadus's urgent voice cut into the conversation. "Careful. Movement up ahead."

I fired my thrusters, reversing my momentum to keep from colliding into Rid. The entire line hovered in place. With too many bulky exos blocking my vision I couldn't see what Nadus was referring to. I turned, looking past Tekka and into the long, dark corridor we had come from. I saw no movement.

"Clear," Nadus said after a minute or so. "Let's keep moving."

I turned back to Rid, not sure what to say but determined to say it, only to find that he had moved ahead in the line, switching places and putting Jin between the two of us. I grimaced. The distance wouldn't make talking any harder with the radios, but the unspoken message was unmistakable. I let it go. As long as he stayed focused he could deal with his grief in whatever way suited him.

Sevani's face flashed through my mind. *If anything happens to her...*

I pushed the thought away. That was a problem I'd have to deal with eventually, but I had plenty of other problems trying to kill me today. *Tomorrow*, I thought. *Focus on that. Live to see tomorrow. Survive.*

Sevani's face finally faded, but the sinking feeling in my gut lingered.


"Somebody put up one hell of a fight," Tekka muttered.

We had made it down into the core of the ship and were now in one of the six central maintenance shafts—a long, wide corridor that ran the entire length of the ship. This was where the maintenance crews had come to access some of the ship's most vital systems, such as the massive gravity generators. Evidently, it had also been the location of a brutal, desperate, and ultimately futile last stand. Bullet casings, discarded weapons, and chunks of damaged armor floated through the air like ghosts.

"Keep an eye out for Jackhammer mags," I said, igniting my thrusters and pushing through the debris towards our goal. "But keep moving. And watch out for rippers. There's a primary power generator not too far from here, which means that there could be steady ripper traffic."

"We oughta make a stop by an armory," Nadus said, staring down the shaft in the opposite direction we were heading. "Restock our ammo. Maybe we can hit one of those generators, pick up some ultracells."

I shook my head. "Too far out of the way. All that matters is getting off this ship alive."

Tekka fired his thrusters in reverse, abruptly coming to a halt. I cursed and managed to stop before I collided with him. He pivoted, facing me.

"What *matters*," he growled, "is finding those plans."

"What *plans*?" I snapped. "Bentley didn't find anything. Did you not see that *thing* that killed Rathen? We're *completely* out of our element here."

"If we don't find those plans," he said, moving closer to me, "then *all* of this was pointless."

"If we *die*, then all of it is pointless," I retorted.

Tekka's gauntleted fist shot out, grabbed me by the exo and pulled me close. It made no difference—we were all talking over comms anyways—but I got the idea. "The entire Brahmian resistance movement is *dismantled* because of this fool's errand," he snarled. "Do you understand that? An entire planet's hopes at independence *gone*. Because of *you*." His voice fell from a growl to a cold sneer. "But you don't care about that, do you, Vanguard? You don't care what you're bludgeoning as long as you're bludgeoning *something*."

I swiped his hand away. "I care about getting my crew out of this mess *alive*. Nothing else matters."

"Nothing else matters?" He sounded like he was on the verge of screaming. "*Nothing*? How about the dozens of patriots who died at Gharseva because you couldn't cover your tracks? Or the *millions* of Brahmians who died in your invasion?"

I looked for something to say. I found nothing. Jin reached a weak hand towards Tekka, trying to calm him down, but Tekka shook him off.

"You want to fix it?" Tekka asked, voice hard and venomous. "You want to take back all the lives you destroyed? You can't. But if you do this..." He took a deep breath, his voice steadying. "It's the closest any of us might ever get," he finished weakly.

I clenched my eyes shut. *No.* It made no sense. I didn't even know where we would start looking. And those nightmares were out there, somewhere, hunting for us. *And* somebody, somewhere on this ship, was controlling it, determined to kill us. We should be trying to get out. Doing everything we could to escape.

Bentley suddenly cleared his throat, breaking the tension. All eyes turned to him. "I... I have some news," he said timidly.

"Good or bad?" Shell asked.

"Uhm... some of both." Bentley looked down at his datapad. "The bad news is that the ship seems to be accelerating."

Rid perked up. "Why didn't we feel it?"

"Gravity generators account for it," I said absently as I thought about the implications of what Bentley said. "Moving where?"

"Moving towards..." Bentley's voice trembled. "The black hole."

There was a shocked silence.

"Why the *hell*," Tekka muttered, "would we be..."

"Whoever's driving this thing is going full suicide mode," Shell said. "Don't you see? That's the point of this whole thing. Whatever is on this ship—whether it's the plans, or these weird rippers, or something else—they're trying to take it all down with them."

I thought about it. It made sense... sort of. There were a dozen problems with the conclusion, but it seemed like the most logical one for now.

"How long till we're in the black hole?" I asked.

"I don't know," Bentley said. "I don't have a ton of access. I'm just sort of poking around, seeing what I can influence. Which isn't much. But that *does* lead me to the good news."

Everyone fell silent.

"Well?" Rid snapped.

"Oh. Uh." Bentley took a deep breath, trying to compose himself. "Sorry. Just a... *little* stressed. I think I found out where all these orders are being sent from."

Tekka and I exchanged a glance.

"Obviously it wasn't the bridge," Bentley said, "which made me realize that maybe, if I accessed the—"

"Doesn't matter." I waved his words away. "Where is it?"

"There's a research center farther down the ship, near the docking bay where Rose dropped off the other team," he said. "A closed area. All of the orders that have been giving us these problems seem to be coming from there."

"If we can get there and figure out who's messing with the systems..." I mused.

"...then we find out what the *Revelation* is hiding," Tekka finished.

"And we improve our odds of getting out of here alive a hundredfold," I said.

"We better hurry, then," Shell said. "For all we know, this ship is already in the black hole's grip."

"You got co-ordinates?" I asked Bentley.

"One sec." He manipulated his datapad. A moment later, a path appeared on my minimap tracing the fastest route.

"Alright." I fired my thrusters. "Let's go. Be fast but be quiet. We're wide open in this maintenance shaft. If rippers catch us we're screwed."

We moved as a unit down the maintenance shaft, checking corridors for any sign of rippers as we passed them. I saw no rippers. I saw other things, though. Debris, left behind by the original crew. I scanned it as we passed, keeping an eye out for anything that might come in handy. A Jackhammer—but no mag. I passed it. An SVAG submachine gun. I brushed it aside. A bandolier of thermal grenades. I snagged it out of the air and looped it through my utility belt. A long, bulky weapon that took me an embarrassingly long moment to recognize as an APMP-17. A can opener—that was what we'd called them back in the Vanguard. A heavy anti-armor gun, capable of cutting right through a Jericho. I grabbed it and slung it over my shoulder. It wouldn't be much good against regular rippers, but if we came across another one of those nightmares, it might be enough to pierce those wings.

Thinking about that was enough to drag my thoughts back to the *Panama*. The more I compared the two scenarios, the more eerie the similarities became. In both cases the *Orpheus*'s scans had failed to detect the rippers. The *Revelation* had the same bizarre, overgrown nightmare rippers I'd seen on the *Panama*.

And, I realized with a sinking feeling, both ships had met their fate in the outskirts of the Brahma sector.

I switched to a direct channel. "Bentley," I said. "Do you have a way of seeing how many escape pods launched?"

His voice sounded confused. "Why? Artemis said they only ever found—"

"Just... see if you can find out." I forced myself to breathe. "I've got... a hunch."

"Alright. Except... well, there's no record, because the pods were locked down, so they didn't actually *launch*, per se, so much as they were forcibly ejected. Then again, I could check the status report..."

"Movement ahead," Shell said.

"Everyone hide!" I looked around wildly. There was a corridor entrance a few dozen meters ahead of us. I maxed out my thruster power and jolted towards the corridor, veering into it. Tekka came right behind me. Then Shell. Then Bentley. Then Nadus, dragging Jin.

I peered out from behind the corner. Sure enough, I could see something white and spindly moving down the maintenance shaft towards us, leaping from wall to wall.

"Where's Rid?" Shell hissed.

*Crap.* I whipped my head around. Rid was moving towards us but he was still several dozen meters away.

"I'm almost there," he gasped.

I turned back down the hall. The ripper was almost on top of us. It didn't seem to be looking in our direction, but its head was swiveling back and forth. This ripper was smaller than the other ones, with longer limbs and a bigger head. A scout of some kind?

"Rid," I hissed. "Stop. You won't make it. Hide behind that pillar."

The ripper's head turned towards me. I jerked back behind cover, breath catching in my throat.

Rid darted towards one of the columns extending across the maintenance shaft—just in time. The ripper flitted back into my view and landed on the opposite wall from us. I shied back even further into the shadows of the corridor, praying it couldn't see us.

It froze where it was, claws keeping it in place on the wall. Its head twitched.

Beside me, Tekka raised his Jackhammer.

"*Don't*," I hissed. "Even if you kill it, the noise will attract more."

He cursed softly and lowered the gun.

The ripper suddenly tensed its legs. I braced myself for it to charge us. Instead, though, it pushed itself away down the corridor, going back in the original direction it had been going.

I breathed a sigh of relief. "Alright. Rid, get over here."

"Yeah." Rid spun towards us, firing his thrusters, and—

A loud clanging sound rang out down the corridor as his boot slammed into the column.

The ripper froze.

"*Don't move!*" I snapped, holding a warding hand out towards Rid. He flailed, trying to get himself back behind cover.

The ripper turned and pushed itself back in our direction, angling itself towards the column.

"Now what?" Tekka hissed.

"I..." I tried to think. "Rid. When I say, pivot around to the other side of the column. On your left."

"Will that work?" Bentley asked anxiously.

The ripper was almost here. I shook my head. "It has to. Move... *now.*"

The ripper came to a halt on the column opposite from Rid. Rid pulled himself around to the other side just as it scurried across, claws sinking into the surface of the column where he'd been just seconds before.

"Ok," I said. "Now—*wait!*"

Something launched past me. Shell. She had her knife drawn. She darted like a missile towards the ripper.

It turned its head towards her.

She lunged, striking out with the knife, and the blade sank into the base of the ripper's skull. It spasmed, claws flashing. Shell grabbed it by the neck and twisted the knife, jerking it free and severing through the ripper's spinal cord as she did so. The creature's head twitched, hanging by a loose thread of flesh while its body danced a macabre, weightless jig.

"Holy *crap,*" Bentley breathed. "I can't believe that worked."

"We don't know if it did," I said. "If there are other nearby rippers they might have picked up the signal. This way. *Fast.*"

.   .   .

We tore down the maintenance shaft in the original direction we'd been going. I kept an eye in front of us the whole time, scanning for movement, looking away only to check my minimap.

*Almost there...*

Crap. Movement ahead. Rippers. Lots of them, heading our way.

"Uh, Lax?" Rid's voice was nervous.

"Almost... there..."

The ripper in the lead landed against a wall, turned towards us, and then dove in our direction.

"This way!" I pivoted around a corner towards the corridor the minimap said we should go down. Almost there. Once we were through we'd have to go through just a few levels to reach—

There was a mechanical whirring sound. The door slammed shut in front of me.

*Crap.*

I spun. A ripper was lunging towards me, tail tensing to strike. A gunshot rang out before it could and it went spinning away, spiraling gore.

"Uhh..." I looked around wildly until I spotted another corridor. "There!"

I dove towards it. It snapped shut.

"*Dammit!*" I twisted around, suspended in the middle of the maintenance shaft. More rippers than I could count were scurrying towards us, leaping from wall to wall.

"Look!" Rid suddenly pointed. I followed his finger. What looked like a security camera was watching us from the ceiling.

"Bastard is watching us," Tekka panted as Shell raised her Jackhammer and put a round through the camera.

"Back this way!" I turned and fired my thrusters, heading back the way we came. It'd take longer but we'd have a better chance of evading these rippers. We blasted towards the corridor we'd taken shelter in when Rid had almost been caught, then turned down it. I craned my head back to make sure everybody else followed behind. They did.

So did the rippers.

I grabbed one of the thermal grenades from the bandolier I'd plundered, pulled the pin, eyeballed the distance, and pushed it gently towards the rippers. The grenade drifted calmly past my crewmates one by one.

The lead ripper pushed hungrily past it, focused on its prey. Several more rippers surged behind it.

The grenade vanished in a flash of white light. There was a roaring sound. My Jericho's visor compensated for the flash, keeping it from blinding me as I watched. The first seven rippers died instantly as the thermal grenade stripped the flesh from their bones.

I darted around a corner. Everyone else followed suit. I motioned for them to keep going, then pulled the pin on another thermal grenade and left it floating mid-air in the entryway of the new corridor we'd gone down before following after them. A few seconds later I heard another roar of heat followed by a wet *sizzling* sound.

"Will that throw them off our trail?" Shell panted.

"Maybe," I grunted.

I'm not sure if it actually worked, if we just got lucky, but we didn't see any rippers for a while after that. We scurried through levels of the *Revelation* like rats in a maze, following the co-ordinates Bentley had sent. We went through storage areas and galleys, mess halls and bunkrooms. Past training facilities and washrooms. Every now and then we froze as we heard scraping sounds echoing. Rippers, scurrying down nearby hallways as they searched for us.

Finally, we reached a large, locked door labeled RESEARCH.

"Rid," I said.

He got to work. I stayed next to him, Jackhammer held at the ready.

"Any idea what's gonna be on the opposite side?" Shell asked.

"Research," Bentley said. "Probably. Just a... guess..." His voice trailed off as he realized nobody was laughing.

"Answers," I said.

The door opened suddenly. I swung inside, Jackhammer raised.

I was in a large, open space.

Desks lined the walls. The center of the room was filled with various vats containing dark liquids. A set of cryogenic chambers were set against the far side of the room. One of them was open.

"Dammit," I muttered, lowering my gun. "There's nobody—"

Movement. A gunshot echoed in the confines of the room. There was a metallic whining sound as a bullet ricochet off of my Jericho's armor.

I fired my thrusters, propelling myself towards the source of the gunshot. I caught a glimpse of a figure darting around one of the vats. Another gunshot sounded and another bullet bounced harmlessly off of me.

"Son of a..." I dove towards the figure, cutting him off on the other side of the vat. It was a man who looked to be in his fifties, with graying hair, wearing a white coat with Paragon insignia. His eyes widened as I loomed above him. Without an exo and thrusters, he couldn't move around as well as I could.

"Gotcha," I growled through my exo's speakers. "Put the gun down and—"

He raised the pistol and pressed the barrel against his head.

There was a flash of movement behind him as Shell grabbed the pistol and wrenched it away from him. He gave a cry of pain as the bones in his hand snapped. Tekka approached from the side, pinning his arms. The man's eyes bulged.

"Careful!" I shouted. "Don't crush him."

Tekka loosened his grip. The man wheezed.

I turned to Rid, Bentley, and Jin. "Get that door closed and locked again," I said. Rid nodded and got to work. "Jin, are you alright?"

"Yeah." He still sounded weak. Unsurprising, considering we hadn't had time to treat his wounds. We'd been running since everything went to hell on the bridge. "I just... need..."

"Get him out of his exo and look at his cuts," I said. I turned back to our prisoner. He'd resigned himself to his fate, staring down at the floor.

I raised my visor. My vision flickered for a moment as my exo stopped projecting images to my head. I took a long, deep breath of stale air.

"Let's start with the basics," I growled. "Who the hell are you?"

## THIRTY-SIX

The man looked up at me, face resolute. "My name is Ramar Vent."

There was a long silence. He looked around at each of our faces as if he expected the name to provoke a reaction.

"I..." I shook my head. "Sorry. Not ringing a bell."

Ramar Vent's determined glare faltered into confusion. "I... wait, who are *you*?"

"Vultures," I said.

"Freedom fighters," Tekka said at the same time.

Ramar fixed his gaze on me. "You're not a..."

"I'm a Vanguard, yeah," I said, finding myself vaguely irritated. "*Ex*-Vanguard. I got released after the... oh."

Tekka raised his visor too. From the look on his face, I guessed he'd come to the realization at the same time I had. "You've been in cryo, haven't you?" he said, glancing towards the line of cryochambers. "You don't know."

"The war is over," I said. "Has been for sixteen years."

Ramar tensed. "Did they... is Brahma... or..."

"Oh, they got Brahma," Tekka said grimly. "They got everywhere."

Ramar sagged, eyes hollow. "It was all pointless, then," he muttered. "All of it. A waste."

Tekka and I locked eyes. "I mean..." I shook myself. "Wait. *What* was a waste?"

"*This.*" He gestured with his head around us. "All the deaths, all the subterfuge and treachery." He grimaced. "The Penitent."

I narrowed my eyes at that. He went on, though, before I could ask for an explanation. "How many are left?"

"How many what?" Tekka asked.

"Worlds," he said. "How many worlds have been spared? Any?"

I scratched my head. "None. The Paragon conquered Brahma. They were the last ones. Paragon still rules everything."

Now it was Ramar's turn to look confused. "So... the ultra-rippers..."

"They used regular rippers," I said. "Not whatever freaks you have here."

He stared at me for a moment, eyes wide as he tried to process what I'd said. Finally he gave a heaving sigh of relief.

"Um, guys," Bentley said. "I know this is all interesting and stuff, but should we maybe stop the ship from flying into a black hole?"

"Oh." I had somehow completely forgotten about that. I turned to Ramar. "Stop the ship."

"No," he said.

I narrowed my eyes at him, then looked around. There was a table full of computers at the far end of the room. I pointed. "Bentley, see if that's what he's been running the ship from."

"On it," Bentley said.

"You need to tell us what's going on here," Tekka growled. "You're obviously a Paragon defector of some kind. Which puts us on the same side. We're trying to free Brahma."

Ramar gave a weak smile. "I am a defector. But that doesn't mean we're on the same side."

"Then whose side *are* you on?" Tekka demanded.

"Humanity's," Ramar said simply.

I raised an eyebrow. "If you're the one who set the rippers loose on this ship, you've shed an awful lot of blood to be making claims like that."

"It was a lesser, but still regrettable, evil," Ramar said sadly. "Had there been another way I would have chosen it."

I shook my head, turning away. "Bentley, what've you got?"

"Working on it," Bentley said. "He does have the security footage up, though."

I moved over next to him, setting aside the anti-armor rifle I'd picked up and inspecting the screens. Sure enough, several of them displayed images of various parts of the ship. My eyes widened as I studied them. Rippers. Rippers *everywhere*. Of all shapes and sizes. Some were familiar, like the ones that had attacked us on the bridge and pursued us through the corridors. Others were smaller, like the scout that had been hunting for Rid. I spotted a few of the big ones with the wings stalking dark corridors.

"These rippers," I asked Ramar. "What are they?"

"Ultrarippers," he said softly. "That's what we were calling them, anyways." He shook his head in disgust. "That was a long time ago, though. Before I made this plan. Back when we actually thought this could *help* people."

I frowned. "Project Eden?"

"Yes." Ramar smiled faintly. "So you *do* know something about my work."

Tekka growled and spun Ramar, pinning him against one of the vats. "Tell us," he snarled. "Tell us *everything*. From the beginning."

"I never wanted this," Ramar said. "Any of it. I joined the Department of Research to *improve* lives. Not to—"

"*What did you do?*" Tekka spat.

"We took the gloves off," Ramar snapped, the words gushing out like an angry flood through a failing dam. "Rippers have always had carefully coded limits in their DNA. Parameters that kept them from evolving out of Divinity's control." He slowed down, the hot anger in his voice gradually cooling into remorse. "The Paragon wanted more. They wanted to get out from under Divinity's thumb. And so, they assembled a team to unravel Divinity's secrets. We spent years analyzing, dissecting, experimenting, on Vanguard and ripper alike. We didn't learn much. But enough. Enough to strip away the safeguards and limits that Divinity had set. To let the Divinity gene run free."

"The Divinity gene?" I asked.

Ramar nodded grimly. "The common link between Vanguards and rippers. The foundation upon which Divinity Technologies is built, and their most jealously guarded secret. It's what makes you heal so quickly. What makes rippers able to regrow limbs when they mitose. Even after all of our research, we still don't know how they created it, or how to isolate or reproduce it. All we can do is breed rippers. So that's what we did. We started our own independent ripper breeding program. Rippers that would evolve and adapt to their surroundings as necessary. That were more than just mindless killing machines."

I frowned. "Why?"

"To prove that they *could*." Ramar gritted his teeth. "The Paragon wanted to have something to show at the end of the war. Something more than just conquered planets. They wanted to prove that they *deserved* their place. The idea of the ultrarippers was that they would start out violent, but gradually change. Adapt. Become one with their new environments. The Divinity genes they possessed—that allowed for unparalleled growth and healing—would be distributed into the environment. A new Eden would be created. A garden of endless bounty. But, of course, that's not what would have happened."

I worked through the implications of that. A new type of ripper, able to adapt beyond its original intent, but still at least as deadly and voracious. My eyes widened. "They wanted them to spread. Evolve. Like a disease."

Ramar looked towards me, meeting my eyes and nodding. "I... couldn't do it. I knew what we were unleashing. Up to that point I had somehow persuaded myself that everything we were doing—all the monstrosities we were creating—were simply stepping-stones on the path to doing some actual good."

He moved closer to me, his eyes wide and earnest—almost like he was confessing, *begging* me to believe him. "I realized the magnitude of my sins. The terrible arithmetic of the consequences of my actions. I don't think that there's any way to atone for such evil. But I resolved to try. To do everything I could to undo what I had done."

"You wanted to wipe it all out." I remembered what Artemis had said. After the *Revelation* had disappeared, scientists had disappeared, research stations had been torched. "Make it so the Paragon could never recover your work."

He nodded. "I knew of others who felt the same way. And so, the Penitent was born."

*The Penitent.* My eyes narrowed. "You were behind it all. The attack on Albeni 7. Selling out the Khendars on Brahma." My fingers tightened around the grip of my Jackhammer. "Killing Artemis."

Ramar sighed, raising his hands defensively. "I assure you, *I* have been here for the past twenty years. I don't know anything about any of the events you just listed. However, I left behind some associates with the sacred task of ensuring that nobody would discover what had happened to the *Revelation*. Clearly, they failed. Most of my comrades gave their lives for the cause. Due to my rank, I was the only one in a position to carry out the final task, escorting the *Revelation* to a place it could do no more harm. Gone forever."

"The black hole," Shell said.

"But..." Bentley shrugged, not taking his eyes from the computer screens. "Why not just steer the ship into a nearby sun? Or self-destruct it? Why wait twenty years?"

"Not thorough enough," Ramar said, his voice sounding tired. "The Divinity gene is incredibly resilient. There was a slight chance samples could still have been recovered. Using a black hole was the only way I could be sure I'd done my job. This was the only black hole within range of a single nullspace journey from Brahma. So..." He shrugged. "Here I am. Clearly, however, I went wrong somewhere, or you wouldn't have figured out I'd be here. Someone must have managed to get a message out... or perhaps an escape pod got loose..."

I wanted to be angry. Full of righteous vindication. After all, this man was indirectly responsible for Artemis's murder. As I thought about that escape pod, though, a chill ran suddenly down my spine.

"Bentley," I said slowly, "Did you ever figure out if there was a second escape pod?"

"Really?" He gave me a quizzical look. "That's your priority right now? Not, you know, escaping this black hole?"

Ramar looked over towards Bentley, his face taut. "You can't change course. It's set. The entire ship is being overrun by malware right now. If you shut it down, the ship's security systems will immediately trigger a self-destruct sequence."

Bentley rubbed at his forehead. "Which means..."

"No undocking, no changing course, no using escape pods," Ramar said grimly.

"That's solvable," Shell said. "We just need to time our escape so that we leave before the self-destruct sequence starts."

I glanced towards Tekka. He was studying the vats. I saw

his eyes rest on a smaller vial of goo-like material with a label that read SAMPLE X32.

"So this is it?" he mused. "No ultracells. No Vanguards. Just... more rippers."

"I'm afraid so," Ramar said. "So sorry for any disappointment."

Tekka nodded slowly.

"Alright," Bentley said, holding up his datapad. "I've think I've got a handle on the situation. We've still got a few hours before we're too close to the black hole to escape. As soon as I override the malware, we'll have control of the ship, but an irreversible, thirty-minute self-destruct timer will start."

"So we just need to get to the docking bay, find a ship, and then start it," Shell said.

"You don't understand," Ramar growled. "The ship *has* to be obliterated. Do you *want* these things to get back into the Paragon's hands? Do you want to see them spread across the stars, across one planet after another?"

"We're just trying to *survive*," Nadus said. "We won't take any of it with us."

"Yes," Tekka said quietly. "We will."

All eyes turned to him.

He sneered back at me. "Why so shocked? This was the mission from the beginning. Find what the Paragon was hiding. Turn it against them." His eyes grew excited. "Imagine what we could do with this. How badly we could hurt them. How badly we could make them *pay*."

I frowned. "It wouldn't just be the Paragon you'd be hurting. Even if what he says about the spreading isn't true. Rippers destroy *everything*. They're impossible to control. You'd be dooming millions of innocents."

"Millions of complicit Paragon citizens, maybe," Tekka said coldly. "And saving *every future generation* from Paragon tyranny in the process."

I shook my head unbelievingly. "You *seriously* think that."

He narrowed his eyes at me. "Like I said on Brahma. I wouldn't expect you to understand."

Shell raised her hands. "Guys. We can work this out later. For now we need to get *out of here*."

I glanced at Ramar. Tekka was still pinning him to one of the vats. Ramar was staring at me, eyes pleading.

"You *can't*," he hissed.

"Bentley," I said. "I need to know about those escape pods."

He threw his hands up. "Still with that? I can't see how it's relevant to—"

"*Now.*"

"Fine." Bentley started typing, muttering under his breath. A few moments later, he paused. "Huh. Weird. Looks like there are two missing escape pods."

Two escape pods.

Two ships, dead-in-transit, found years later. Each one inhabited by strange, aberrant rippers.

The *Panama* had been smuggling stolen ultracells to Brahma during the last days of the war. They'd responded to an SOS signal from deep space, then disappeared. And when we'd boarded the ship, Liung had found a Paragon escape shuttle in the bay.

It all lined up. The strange behavior of the rippers. The fact that they hadn't shown up on our scanners—they must somehow have adapted in such a way that defied the usual scanning techniques. The nightmare rippers that I'd been so sure were a product of my tortured imagination.

My throat went dry. My breathing turned ragged. I realized that everyone was staring at me, with expressions ranging from confused to concerned.

"I'm sorry, Tekka," I said, trying to keep my voice calm. "But we're not taking this with us."

He narrowed his eyes. "Oh?"

I shook my head, still reeling from the discovery. "We'll go to the docking bay, find a ship, and leave. But the data, and the samples, stay here."

"What if I disagree?" Tekka said coldly.

I fired my thrusters, maneuvering until there were only two meters between us. I stared him down. "Then we'll have a problem."

Dead silence fell over the room.

I assessed the situation. Our Jackhammers were both slung at our sides. Tekka had one hand still pinning Ramar to the vat, with the other resting on the handle of his weapon. Rid and Nadus were kneeling next to Jin, applying bandages to his wounded chest after having removed his breastplate. Shell was standing a few meters behind Tekka, while Bentley was off to the side at the computers.

"Not good odds," I said. "Don't be stupid."

"My odds are better than you think," he said quietly.

I frowned at that. Then glanced down at my wrist computer. The minimap showed a cluster of green dots gathered in the research station. Seven, to be precise, representing all of us.

Just outside of the research station, however, opposite the side we had entered, were eight more blinking green dots.

# THIRTY-SEVEN

There was a whirring sound behind me. I glanced carefully over my shoulder to see Tames gliding through the doorway, Jackhammer held at her side. The other seven members of her squad filed in behind her and spread out.

Nadus slowly straightened. Shell carefully placed a hand on her own Jackhammer rifle. Rid looked up at the standoff, cursed under his breath, and went back to desperately trying to patch Jin up. Bentley just sat at the computers, staring at us.

I looked back to Tekka. He watched me cautiously. Neither one of us were in a good position, but mine was certainly worse. He had Shell and Nadus at his back, ready to open fire on him if he made a move, but I had Tames and seven other rebels behind mine.

"Tekka," I said carefully, keeping my eye on him. "We don't have to do this."

"You're right," he said. "Just get the hell out of here and let us gather some samples. I don't want to kill any of you. But if you stand in my way..."

Nadus's voice sounded in a private channel. "What's the play here?"

My eyes shifted from Tekka, to Ramar, still pinned against the vat, to Nadus and Shell behind them, then to the vat itself and the reflection of the exo-clad rebels waiting behind me.

"Lower your guns," Tekka said before I could answer. His voice was hard and angry. "This doesn't *have* to turn violent."

"Let Ramar go," I said. "Then we can talk."

"Why do you care?" Tekka growled. "What happened to just wanting your profit?"

"I've seen these rippers in action, Tekka," I said. "And so have you now. I don't care how righteous your cause is. I'm not letting you cut these monsters loose."

Bentley started slowly inching his way along the side of the wall towards Nadus, Shell, Rid, and Jin. Jin had perked up slightly and was watching the scene unfold through his open visor with wide eyes.

"I'll do whatever it *damn well takes* to beat the Paragon," Tekka said quietly. "Including killing all of you if I have to."

In the reflection of the vat, I saw the rebels behind me slowly raise their weapons.

"Nadus," I said in a private channel. "Go back the way we came. Then make your way to the docking bay. I'll meet you there."

"What are you gonna do?" Nadus asked, not moving.

The barrel of Tekka's gun inched up towards me.

Ramar's eyes shifted sharply towards the vat he was pressed against.

Inside the vat's murky depths, something moved.

"I have no idea," I said.

Then I raised my Jackhammer and fired.

The room exploded into chaos. Tekka jerked Ramar aside, sending him spinning backward away from the fight, then aimed his Jackhammer at me and opened fire. A barrage of bullets slammed into my back as the rest of the rebels started shooting, sending me spinning wildly in the zero gravity. I fired my thrusters, trying to orient myself, but the hail of gunfire didn't stop. I thudded against the far wall, shielding my visor with my arms as best I could.

"*Go!*" I yelled at Nadus.

Nadus fired at the rebels with one hand as he grabbed Rid with the other, letting the recoil push them back towards the door. Shell and Bentley followed them. I couldn't see Ramar anywhere.

A bullet slammed into the back of my helmet, smacking it against the wall. I growled and turned to face the rebels, raising my Jackhammer, only to have it torn out of my hands by a volley of gunfire.

"I never did get to kill any of you during the war," Tekka growled. He loomed over me, then activated his magboots to stick to the floor. "Guess there are second chances in life after all."

He pointed his Jackhammer at me and held down the trigger. Warning signs flashed through my vision as a dozen different exosuit systems were compromised. I tried to look past him towards the vat, only to cry out as bullets slammed into the front of my visor, damaging the cameras that fed into my neurointerface and making my vision fuzz.

Tekka's gun ran empty. He growled, ejecting the magazine and reaching for a new one as his companions moved behind him. "All this talk of being a killer—the Paragon's ultimate weapon." Tekka scowled. "I'd have thought you'd put up more of a fight."

"Vanguards aren't the Paragon's ultimate weapon," I groaned.

Tekka slammed a new magazine home. "Oh?"

"Rippers are," I said.

There was a splintering sound from behind them. Everybody whirled to see the large vat—the one Tekka had been holding Ramar up against, the one I'd fired a single shot into at the beginning of the gunfight—splinter, crack, then explode outward as a monstrous shape burst free.

A nightmare.

Screams. It took Tames first, sinking four sets of biosteel claws into her. Tekka swore, turning away from me and firing wildly at the giant ripper.

I pivoted towards the computer desks. My exo was slow and unresponsive, my movements sluggish. Only one thruster was still working. I activated it, sending me scraping along the floor towards my goal. I glanced over my shoulder to see a spray of scarlet as the nightmare tore Tames into three different pieces, then pounced onto its next target, bullets bouncing harmlessly off of its biosteel wings.

I crashed into the computer desk. I reached out blindly. It was here. I'd left it here. *There.* I reached for it with clumsy hands, grabbed at it—

Something grabbed me by the arm and pulled at me, twisting me onto my back. Not the nightmare. Tekka loomed over me, his back turned to the carnage the ripper was wreaking among his men. He pressed one boot against my chest plate, pinning me to the floor.

"All you know," he growled, "is *destruction.*"

He reached down, grabbed the lid of my already damaged visor, and pulled. My vision blurred as my neurointerface stopped projecting to my brain. Cold air rushed over my skin.

"What's that you said about how to kill a ripper? You can't heal what's not there?" Tekka aimed the barrel of his Jackhammer directly between my eyes. "I'm guessing it applies to Vanguards too."

A flash of light. Tekka staggered sideways, releasing the pressure from my chest. I managed to spare a glance sideways to see Jin holding up a smoking Jackhammer. Through his open visor his eyes were clenched in equal parts pain and determination.

"It's wrong," he said weakly. "We... we can't... be like them..."

Tekka stared at the boy for a moment, sighed, raised his gun, and fired a single shot. Jin's body convulsed as the explosive round struck him square in the face.

Tekka turned back to me with a growl. "Now, where were—"

He froze as he stared down the barrel of an APMP-17. The anti-armor rifle I'd found in the maintenance tunnel and had left by the computers. The rifle that Jin's distraction had given me just enough room to reach for.

I wish I'd had something to say. Something clever and biting. But my head was hurting like hell from the beating Tekka had given me. And I've always figured bullets speak louder than words anyways.

I pulled the trigger.

The rifle leaped in my hands. Tekka's head snapped backward as the bullet punctured through front of his helmet and out the back. His body went stiff, pinned in place by his magboots.

I groaned and turned, trying to assess the chaos. The nightmare was hunting down the remaining rebels one by one. They'd given up trying to kill it and were now focusing on fleeing. I tried to move in the direction my crew had gone but my thrusters weren't working. I could barely move my limbs.

Suddenly someone was above me. Ramar.

"This way!" he hissed, pushing off against Tekka's corpse towards a closed door.

I tried to follow, but my exo's movements were sluggish. *Fine.* I used my neurointerface to trigger the self-destruct. A series of tiny explosions blasted away the joints locking me inside the exo suit. The armor fell away, leaving me free. I pushed off against the wall, reaching the door just as Ramar finished inputting a code.

I glanced over my shoulder to see the nightmare turning its gaze towards me. *Crap.* I reached for the open doorway, clawing at the frame, and pulled myself through. Ramar hit a button and the door sealed shut behind me just as the nightmare lunged. There was a heavy thud as its weight slammed against the steel. A few moments later, the screaming resumed as it gave up and went back to hunting down rebels.

So much for teamwork.

## THIRTY-EIGHT

I looked around, gasping for breath. "Where are we now?"

Ramar ignored the question, pivoting to face me.

"The two escape pods," he demanded. "What did you mean by that?"

I groaned, feeling at my side. Everything hurt. "I meant... I've seen your ultrarippers before. On a dead-in-transit cargo ship in the Brahma sector. Wings and everything. Your containment failed. There are already more of these rippers out there on the loose somewhere."

His eyes narrowed.

"So," he said, voice heavy. "It doesn't matter anyways. It's all been in vain."

"I..." I shrugged. "Maybe."

He fell into deep thought, hands steepled. I glanced towards the closed door we'd come through. The sounds of screaming and gunfire had stopped.

I grimaced. "I'm going out."

He frowned at me. "Without an exo?"

"If I have to." I reached down towards my side. Peacebreaker was still sitting in its holster. "But no matter what happens, I'm getting my crew *out of here.*"

"The ultrarippers," he said suddenly. "Why didn't you agree to take them?"

I glanced sharply at him. "What do you mean?"

He shrugged. "Your team would have stayed together if you'd simply agreed. Why?"

I hesitated.

Why hadn't I agreed to it?

"Because I've spent my whole life wandering from one mess to another," I said quietly. "I never wanted to be a Vanguard. Never wanted to be complicit in the Paragon's wars. But I was anyways. Then I got out. Found a crew. A family. Then I lost them to these... ultrarippers of yours." I shook my head slowly. "No way in hell am I letting myself be a part of unleashing more of them onto the world."

He studied me for a few moments.

"What's your plan now?" I asked hesitantly. "Just... go down with the ship?"

"That was the original plan. Needless to say, plans have changed."

He moved with a sudden sense of purpose, walking towards the far end of the room. There was yet another door there. I followed him through it into a smaller room. The walls were lined with tools, weapon racks, and crates of munitions. In the center of the room were four slightly elevated platforms, each one holding an exo that looked unlike any I'd ever seen. Slightly bulkier than the Jericho, with two slim emitters of some kind attached to each of the forearms. A large protrusion behind the exo's shoulders made it look almost hunchbacked.

"The new plan," Ramar said, "is to get the hell out of here so I can go tie up my loose ends. Something tells me my odds of that are better with you by my side than alone."

I inspected the exo. Despite my exhaustion, I found myself gawking. "I've never seen one like this."

"The Paragon knew that the new breed of rippers likely meant even more exposure to our own troops," Ramar said. "So they had a special, anti-ripper exo developed. This is just a prototype, of course—no idea if they ever actually put them into use."

"Prototype?" I stepped up next to it, studying it. "It works, right?"

"Oh yes. Quite well."

I pointed at the emitters on the arms. "What are these?"

"Thermal blades. Each one emits a one-meter-long sheet of sheer thermal energy, reaching 4,000 °C at its highest capacity."

The thought of going toe to toe with rippers, even equipped with such high-tech weaponry, made me hesitate slightly. I'd need to go about this carefully if I was going to get us out of here. "Awful risky letting a ripper get that close to you. One wrong move and you're dead."

"The Icarus provides some extra insurance." He ran a hand along the sleek black outer shell. "The armor is what we call conduction-charged. Simply put, anything that comes into contact with it with any significant amount of force will be repulsed."

That got my other eyebrow to raise. "How do you keep this thing powered?"

In answer, he pressed a button on the Icarus's mounting frame. A compartment on the exo's bulky back opened.

"That'll do it," I admitted, staring at the ultracell nestled within. I hesitated. "And if something makes it through and hits that ultracell..."

"Icarus," Ramar said simply.

.  .  .

"Your friends are moving along one of the outer maintenance corridors now," Ramar said, looking down at his datapad. He had climbed into an exo of his own to keep up with me. "Slowly and carefully. They seem to have realized that the rippers are watching for them."

I nodded in response. We had left behind Ramar's hideout and were now moving as quickly as we could towards the docking bay. The Icarus handled like a dream, its bulkiness not slowing me down in the slightest. I felt strangely energized. Like I'd gotten my second wind. Less than an hour ago I'd been staring down the barrel of Tekka's Jackhammer, certain I was about to die. Now I had a new suit of armor on, the most advanced weaponry I'd ever used at my fingertips, and—most importantly—a shot at saving my crew. Next to that, everything else was secondary.

"*Nadus*," I said into a general broadcast channel. "Nadus, Rid, Bentley, Shell. Anyone. Can you hear me?"

"They're too far away for radio," Ramar said. "Too many floors between us. Plus, the override program turned on the *Revelation*'s signal jammer. No waveform signals will make it more than a dozen or so meters."

"Figured it was worth a shot."

"We *could* patch all of them into the *Revelation*'s communication system," Ramar said thoughtfully. "But we'd still have to be able to reach them first."

"Can you still use the ship intercom?"

"Ah!" He sounded slightly annoyed that he hadn't thought of it first. "Of course." He manipulated a few controls on his datapad. A few moments later, an image in my heads-up display indicated that a new communication channel was available for me to use.

"Perfect." I cleared my throat, then used the Icarus's neurointerface to connect.

"This is Lax," I said as clearly as I could. I bit back a smirk as I tried to imagine the shock on their faces as my voice suddenly crackled to life from the ship's overhead speakers. "Long story, but I'm alive and on my way. Along with Ramar. He's going to give you some instructions to connect to the *Revelation*'s comms systems so we can talk. Listen to what he says very carefully."

Ramar took over. "Yes, um, find the nearest system monitor console and..."

There was a flash of movement from ahead. Ramar's voice faltered as a ripper lunged from around a corner, saw us, then used its tail to redirect itself towards us, maw already open and claws extended.

"Keep going!" I snapped at Ramar, raising the Jackhammer I'd plundered from his little experimental armory. I put two shots into the ripper's chest and one more into its skull as its ruined body drifted closer.

Ramar took a shaky breath and resumed speaking, explaining in careful detail exactly what they needed to do. The Icarus was already hooked up to the *Revelation*'s comms, which left me free to take aim and fire as several more rippers came charging down the hallway.

"That's it," Ramar said after a few moments.

"Good. Let's hope they figure it out. We need to keep moving." I fired my thrusters, leading us past the corpses of the rippers I'd killed. "Hopefully we didn't attract too much attention there."

A flash of activity behind us. I swerved, raised the Jackhammer, and fired, letting the recoil push me down the corridor. Ramar let out a startled yelp as he dove to the side. Several rippers that had emerged from a ventilation shaft shuddered and died in bursts of scarlet viscera. One made it through, leaping from the wall, to the ceiling, straight towards Ramar.

*Ah, hell.*

The scientist cringed backward, holding his datapad up as if the ripper's claws wouldn't tear right through it. Before they could, though, I was there. I used the neurointerface to trigger one of the Icarus's thermal blades. There was a flash of white light as I swung upward, intercepting the ripper's blow. The creature spasmed as the blade sheared straight through flesh and biosteel skeleton alike, cleanly severing its claw from its arm. I brought my arm back down in a diagonal slice that bisected the demon into two steaming chunks of flesh.

"Damn," I said, staring at the glowing white blade. I issued a mental command and it flickered then vanished. "Where has *this* been my whole life?"

Ramar pulled himself to his feet. Even through his exo, I could see his hands trembling slightly as he gave a relieved sigh. I had no doubt that Ramar was plenty brave—you had to be to bet against the Paragon in the way that he had—but he was clearly no fighter.

"You good?" I asked, reloading my Jackhammer.

He nodded, putting one hand on the stock of the Jackhammer strapped to the front of his exo. "Yes, I... well, I've never actually been that close to a ripper in an uncontrolled environment." He forced a dry chuckle. "Somehow, it's even more terrifying than I assumed it would be."

I opened my mouth to reply and then paused as another voice suddenly spoke in my ear. "*Lax. Lax, can you hear me?*"

I blinked. "Nadus? That you?"

Nadus gave an incredulous laugh. "How the *hell* are you still alive?"

"Sheer dumb luck," I said, unable to stop myself from grinning. "How are you guys holding up?"

"So far so good," Nadus replied. "We're closing in on the docking bay."

"Stay where you are," I said. I started moving again, using my thrusters to take me down the hallway. "You guys went straight up and along the outer edge. We're coming from underneath you. There's an elevator shaft nearby that should take us to you."

Nadus suddenly swore viciously.

"What?" I asked.

"We're at the docking bay," Nadus whispered. "And there are... a hell of a lot of rippers here."

I frowned. That made no sense. Why would the rippers congregate in the docking bay?

"They knew you'd try to flee," Ramar said, as if he could hear my unspoken question. I turned sharply towards him as he continued speaking. "In the... well, my little uprising, most personnel aboard the ship tried to flee towards the escape pods and the docking bay. So they've adapted. And now that there are humans aboard the ship again, they assume that's where you'll be headed."

Fantastic. Smart rippers.

"Right now, just stay put and don't attract any rippers," I said. "If that swarm up there gets any ideas, we're screwed. We're gonna have to figure out a way to distract them."

"Roger that," Nadus said.

"Better hurry," Shell interjected. "This ship is still headed straight towards that black hole." She went suddenly silent. After a long, tense moment, she spoke up in a whisper. "And there are rippers everywhere. It's only a matter of time before they find us."

I looked backward to see several rippers at the far end of the corridor. "Just stay hidden and alive. We'll be there as soon as we can." I switched to the private channel between Ramar and me. "Hurry! We're almost to the elevator entrance."

The rippers spotted us and pushed off against the wall. I fired a few rounds as Ramar pressed past me. The first ripper died but the others surged past it. I swore, then turned and followed after Ramar. No point in sticking around for a fight.

For every ripper I killed, a dozen more would arrive. The only thing we could do now was run.

"Here we are," Ramar gasped as he steered through a large doorway. I followed behind him.

This elevator was much larger than any of the other ones we had used so far. It was designed for transporting goods from the docking bay to the various cargo and storage areas distributed across the various decks. As I peered up into the long, dark space, I imagined it as it would have been in the prime of its life: rife with activity, flowing with equipment on its way down to the core, soldiers on their way up to the deployment boats, and crates of rations, medical supplies, and anything else that might be needed by the ship's massive population being moved to the cargo bay. Now, though, it was dark and silent. As still as the grave.

Then the dull throb of the emergency lights flared to life. Only for a moment, but it was enough.

I swore. "Rippers inbound."

Ramar stared up in horror, then suddenly jolted into activity, flying towards the nearest elevator car. "Get in!" he shouted.

I hesitated, then followed. If nothing else, riding the elevator up would provide us some shelter. They'd know where we were, though, and they'd tear through the transport's walls like children unwrapping a present.

A flash of movement from below. I jerked my head just in time to see a ripper's tailspike darting directly towards my face.

My head jolted backward, spinning me in the zero gravity. I blinked. I should be dead. My skull skewered just like Black's had been on the *Panama*. But I wasn't. It took me a moment to remember what Ramar had said about the Icarus's conduction-charged armor.

I grinned, activating my thrusters to stop my spin and orient myself towards the ripper that had attacked me. Seeing its surprise attack had failed, it pushed off against the floor of the elevator shaft and launched itself towards me.

"My turn." I held my Jackhammer in my left hand as I activated the thermal blade attached to my right wrist, then used my thrusters to pivot out of the ripper's path and cleanly decapitate it. Its momentum carried it on up the darkness of the elevator shaft, the two pieces drifting gradually apart the farther they went.

The emergency lights flared again. My eyes widened. The long, wide-open expanse of the elevator shaft above me was speckled with the silhouettes of hundreds of rippers gliding swiftly towards me.

"*Hurry!*" Ramar shouted.

I turned to the car he'd entered, only to hesitate as I saw more rippers rushing from the direction we'd come. A few of them started towards me, but the rest darted for the elevator car.

"Start it moving," I said, firing my thrusters and maneuvering between the rippers and Ramar.

I took out the first wave with the Jackhammer, letting the recoil push me back towards the car. The gunshots boomed in the otherwise silent elevator shaft. A few seconds later, another sound started: a loud mechanical grinding as the transport began to move slowly upward.

I pivoted, flipping head over heel and locking my magboots to the top of the car. The rippers were entirely focused on me now. I didn't like fighting in such an open space—more directions to be attacked from—but it did give me one very distinct advantage: the rippers could only maneuver by pushing off against a surface. In a wide, open area like this, one missed dive meant they couldn't get back in the fight until they hit the far wall. I used this to my advantage as I chose my targets, shooting only at the ones that looked as if they were on an intercept course.

But then there were the rippers attacking from above. I

clenched my teeth as I turned my attention upward. Every few seconds, as the emergency lights turned on, they'd appear, and then vanish, only to reappear closer with each flare of red.

"Are you secured to the top of the lift?" Ramar asked.

"Yeah, for now." I activated one of my thermal blades, hacking at a ripper that had gotten too close.

"Hang on," he muttered, sounding distracted. "This is going to get a little bit bumpy."

Another flare of red light. More rippers on top of me. I ducked and spun and sliced. "What are you doing?"

"Hang on," he muttered again. "I'm trying to..."

Something struck me on the back. There was a flash of dull white light as the blow was repelled. I disengaged my magboots and spun, dispatching two rippers with one swipe of the thermal blade, then grunted as a ripper slammed into me from above, sending me lurching over the edge of the elevator car.

"...turn the gravity generator on," Ramar finished. "Got it!"

I shot one arm out and grabbed at the edge of the transport's roof—and missed. The gap between me and the car widened even farther as the ripper that had knocked me off dove towards me, claws scraping against my chestplate with a flash of sparks and sending me spinning.

"*Wait!*" I cried desperately. For how slow the elevator seemed, we had already traversed a dizzying distance from the bottom floor below. I activated my thrusters, pushing towards the car. The gap grew smaller, the edge growing closer, but I could feel gravity's fingers clutching at me now, dragging me down, down—

I grunted as I slammed into the top of the roof, felt myself start to slide backward, reached and grabbed and pulled desperately, fingers scraping, finding a hold, digging into the metallic surface, pulling me up—

I gasped as I rolled onto my back, safe on top of the car. Relief swept over me, then anger. "What the *hell* were you—"

"Look," Ramar said.

I looked up. The rippers that had been divebombing towards me were suddenly moving much faster now, falling rather than gliding, arcing towards the floor rather than shooting directly at me, flailing uncontrollably in gravity's unfamiliar grasp.

"You crazy son of a bitch," I muttered, an unbelieving smile spreading across my face. Ramar had powered up the ship's gravity generators, and the rippers seemed to have no idea how to react to it.

There was a wet thud as a ripper slammed into the edge of the car next to me, spinning away into the darkness below. Then another. And another. And then it was raining rippers, an unholy downpour of vicious killing machines rendered suddenly helpless against one of nature's most basic tenets. I fought back a laugh as I pressed myself against the wall, trying to avoid the falling bodies as best I could.

"*Lax!*" Nadus's voice shouted in my ear. "What's going on?"

"Ramar turned on the gravity generators," I said, grunting as a ripper glanced off the edge of my shoulder pauldron before striking the roof of the transport and splattering gore across it. I looked up. The downpour of rippers had slowed to a trickle as rippers standing at the top of the elevator shaft tested the limits of gravity, several of them toppling off the edge. "We're in the elevator now. Should be back up to you in just a few minutes."

"That's a whole new issue," Nadus said. "The rippers are going nuts, but they're still all over the place. Trying to get to you, I think, but they don't know how. We need to get them out of the way or there's no way we're making it to a ship."

"What's our play, Lax?" Shell's voice asked.

*A way out.* I felt a bead of cold sweat form on my brow, the temporary relief of having survived my last close call quickly fading. *A way out.* There had to be one. Rid, Black, Kessa, Artemis, Shell, Liung, Rose, Nadus, Bentley, Rawlins... their faces flashed through my mind over and over again in an endless loop of hope and pain and loss and triumph.

*A way out.*

A large shape loomed above me, monstrous in the vivid red light. One of the winged nightmare rippers, peering down at me over the edge of the elevator shaft. I realized abruptly that there was no roof to the top of it: rather, it opened up directly into the docking bay like some sort of massive, square-shaped well. The rippers that had gathered in the docking bay were now watching me, waiting for the lift to bring me to them like a meal served fresh on a silver platter. They seemed to be congregating around the nightmare ripper, keeping an almost respectful distance from it. As if it had first claim on dinner.

"We could just rush them," Shell said. "They don't seem to be used to the gravity. Maybe we can charge through them and make it to the ship."

"Not a chance," Nadus responded grimly. "Too many of 'em. We'd get bogged down."

The lift continued moving up, inch by terrible inch. The lights flared again and glinted off the edges of the giant ripper's biosteel wings, making them look like they were coated in blood.

*A way out.* We were so close, and yet so far.

"We can cause a distraction," Rid was saying. "Sneak around one side."

*A way out.*

"There's nothing that would distract them enough," Nadus said. "Anything we do will just attract them to us."

*A way... out...*

The winged ripper flexed and tensed as I drew still closer to it, ready to pounce, like a wrathful, dreadful angel. The top of the elevator shaft was crowded with rippers, their attention fixed firmly on me. Too many. Far too many for the crew to fight through—at least, not with the amount of time we had left. Every passing second, our odds of survival thinned. We had maybe half a minute before the elevator reached the top and that swarm was on top of us.

There was no way out. I'd lost again. And once again, it was my crew that was going to pay the price for my mistakes. The only comfort I could take was that this time I'd die with them.

*Unless...*

"Ramar," I said into a direct channel. "Start the undocking procedures."

"That means I'll have to shut down the override program," he said. "The self-destruction timer will start."

"I know. Do it."

The winged ripper's maw opened, revealing its jagged, glistening biosteel teeth.

"When I say to," I said over the general comms, "you guys rush to the nearest ship. Ramar will join you. You're not gonna have a lot of time—as soon as the undocking procedure starts, the *Revelation* will start a timer to self-destruction."

"What about the rippers?" Bentley asked, his voice trembling slightly.

"Don't worry about the rippers," I said.

A light in my heads-up display indicated Nadus opening a private channel with me. "Lax," he said, his voice low and worried. "What are you doing?"

I hesitated. "There's no way out, Nadus. Not for all of us. If I draw the rippers away, I can buy you some time."

"Absolutely not. There's..." He faltered. I could picture his face—angry, conflicted—as he tried to work out another solution. "There's gotta be another way."

"There isn't. And you know it."

Nadus fell silent. I reloaded my Jackhammer, staring upward at the ravenous horde of monsters awaiting me.

I felt oddly peaceful. I couldn't say why that was, exactly. Maybe there's a certain peace that comes with letting go of the need to survive. Maybe after so many hours spent staring death in the face, my mind was finally ready to accept that it was unavoidable. Or maybe, for the first time in years, I was finally certain that I was doing the right thing.

"Just promise me one thing, Nadus," I said. "Take care of my crew."

"You got it," he said softly.

I switched to a private channel with Ramar. "On my call, I want you to turn the gravity back off. I'm gonna use it to get a head start on leading them away. Once I've led them far enough, I'll tell you to turn it back on."

"You're not planning on coming back, are you?" Ramar mused.

"No," I said abruptly. "Just make it to the crew as quickly as you can. They'll make sure you get taken care of."

"Penitence," Ramar said.

I hesitated. "Yeah, I guess so. Good luck with tying up your loose ends."

We were close now. Close enough that one of the rippers tried to leap for me, only to miscalculate the distance and tumble into the depths below. The others drew back only slightly.

Nadus's voice sounded in my ear. "One more thing, Lax."

"Yeah?" I bent my legs. The winged ripper was bracing itself to jump. I was close enough now to count its teeth if I'd wanted to. I didn't want to.

"Give 'em hell."

I grinned. "You got it."

The winged ripper leaped, arcing straight towards me.

"*NOW!*" I yelled to Ramar.

And jumped.

# THIRTY-NINE

Gravity clutched at me, pulling me down, past the lift, just out of the winged ripper's reach. My innards pressed against the top of my ribcage. And then the gravity died.

I fired my thrusters, my momentum slowing and then jolting as I reversed directions. The rippers scrambled in confusion, some of them caught off guard and left drifting helplessly in the zero-G. I took advantage of their disarray to fly up and out of the elevator shaft.

The docking bay was swarming with rippers—more than I'd ever seen in one place outside of a battlefield. I grimaced. All I could do was hope that I could make enough noise to drag them all with me.

I spotted a doorway that would lead me away from where the crew was hiding. I pivoted, putting my back to it, then began firing my Jackhammer wildly into the mass of rippers. The recoil pushed me back and down towards the doorway. When I was close, I spun and fired up one of my thermal blades. I made three quick slices, then used the Icarus's considerable power to pick the triangular, makeshift door I'd created through.

"*Warning,*" a calm, robotic voice called overhead. "*Massive security breach detected. The ship will self destruct in thirty minutes. Please evacuate. Please evacuate.*"

Well, at least Ramar had started the launch procedure. Hopefully that meant he was on his way to join the others. I bent over and managed to squeeze through the hole. Once on the other side, I pivoted, Jackhammer at the ready, only to pause and lower it. As good a chokepoint as this might have been, I wasn't here to make my last stand. I was here to draw the rippers away from the docking bay. The farther off I could lead them, the better the crew's chances of making it out were.

"Come on, you bastards," I growled as rippers began wriggling through the hole. I waited until several had made it through and were launching themselves at me before I engaged my thrusters and retreated down the corridor, occasionally firing a warning shot at a ripper that got too close.

"Where are they all going?" Rid asked over the comms. I could picture the confused expression he must have been wearing.

"Away," Nadus replied grimly. "Come on. This is our window." He switched to our direct channel. "It's working. They're all after you. Some of them are taking other exits, though, so they'll likely cut you off ahead."

"Thanks," I grunted as I swerved out of reach of a ripper's tail strike. I wouldn't be able to run forever. Eventually they'd corner me. All that mattered was that I kept them busy enough for the crew to board that ship. After that...

I rounded a corner and saw more rippers pouring down the corridor from the other direction. I engaged my thrusters and flew straight towards them, firing my Jackhammer. I cleared just enough of a path to slip past them and through another doorway.

"*Come on!*" I found I was yelling with no comms channel active. Just me and the rippers. "Keep up!"

I kept going. Corridor after corridor, always making sure

that the rippers were never more than a few meters behind me, occasionally firing back at them. I heard Ramar and Nadus speaking over the general channel as he joined the rest of the crew. Ducked around a corner.

"*Twenty-five minutes until self-destruction,*" the voice overhead said. "*Evacuate. Evacuate.*"

"We're getting a ship ready," Rid's voice reported to me. "Where are you?"

"I'll be there," I lied. A ripper loomed in front of me, claws flashing off my armor. I swung my Jackhammer like a club, sending the ripper spinning away. I looked down at my armor. There was a long, shallow gash in my armor where I'd been struck. Apparently, the conduction-charged armor didn't make me *entirely* ripper-proof. "Just get the ship ready."

I passed through a T-shaped intersection into another corridor and paused. This hallway was much like the one we had first boarded the *Revelation* through—one of the outermost maintenance corridors of the ship. Rippers were already surging towards me from both directions. I pivoted. The hallway behind me was choked full of them.

No way out.

I grinned.

For the past eight years, something had been broken inside of me. Like Artemis had said, some part of me had died with Kessa. With my crew. Since then, I hadn't been much more than a ghostly revenant, a walking corpse. Using cans to dull the pain. Working mindlessly for Venter, and then for Artemis. Following the little threads of fate back to here, where I'd lost it all.

I activated my magboots, locking me to the floor.

*This* was where it had all begun. This was where the rippers that had killed my crew—that had killed Kessa—had come from. For a moment, I wasn't on the *Revelation* anymore. I was on the *Panama*. Watching, helpless, as rippers tore apart my crew. Except this time I wasn't helpless.

The rippers drew closer. My battle-hungry grin turned into an angry snarl. I tossed aside the Jackhammer.

*Green dots, flashing red...*

I activated both of the Icarus's thermal blades. The shadowed corridor burned with dull white light.

*Beauty in the dark. A splash of red against warm blues and yellows.*

The foremost ripper tensed its hind legs, preparing to leap at me.

"TURN IT ON!" I bellowed to Ramar.

The ripper leaped. I sliced with a thermal blade in a swift downward motion, cleaving through flesh and steel. The ripper's severed body parts drifted past me in the zero-G, bounced off the wall behind me, and then suddenly dropped to the floor as the *Revelation*'s gravity generators powered on.

The crowd of rippers halted, confused, falling over each other, and I waded into them, hacking and punching and crushing and kicking. The Icarus's bulk was slightly harder to maneuver under gravity's full weight, but I used that to my advantage, stomping down hard on fallen rippers, feeling their biosteel bones crunch beneath me.

They flailed wildly, trying to get their bearings so that they could attack me. I didn't give them the time. I was vengeance. I was wrath. I was death incarnate, and some long-suppressed, primal part of me laughed with sheer joy as I killed, and killed, and killed.

Eventually they adapted. Though they could no longer use weightlessness to maneuver effortlessly around me, they were still frighteningly agile. They used their claws to cling to the walls, pouncing at me from every angle and all at once, claws flashing, tails darting.

I kept moving, kept killing, not caring for the direction so long as it was forward, blades never slowing down as I cut down ripper after ripper. Claws scraped along the surface of my armor, tail-spikes slammed into it, only to be deflected each time in a flash of light. My maniacal grin only widened with each repelled attack.

"*Self-destruction in ten minutes,*" said the voice overhead. "*Evacuate. Evacuate.*"

"Lax!" Shell's voice this time, urgent. "Where are you?"

I ignored her. More rippers. More death. More scrapes along my armor, more flickers of light as they were repelled. It was becoming difficult to walk, the corridor's floor strewn with smoldering corpses. I kicked several out of the way, wading forward, clearing a path to nowhere.

"The ship is ready to launch," Ramar said, his voice grave.

"Lax!" Rid's voice was heavy with concern. "Lax, where are you? We've gotta go!"

"Go," I growled. A spike slammed into my back—and stuck, the point embedded in my armor, though it didn't seem to have pierced all the way through. I spun, severing the tail, then reached backward, plucking the spike out and using it to stab another ripper through the gut.

"*What?*" Rid's voice turned angry. "No! What are you—"

"Take care, Rid," I said, grunting as a wave of attacks forced me to take a few steps backward. "You too, Shell and—*ugh*—Bentley. Nadus, get the hell out of here."

"Roger that," Nadus said softly. "Goodbye, Lax."

"No!" Rid sounded panicked. "Why? Just find an escape pod! We'll pick you up!"

"Too risky," I said. "When this thing blows it's gonna be one *hell* of an explosion. You guys need to be as far away as possible." If we hadn't lost the *Orpheus*, it might have worked. But the types of ships they'd be able to find in the docking bay—gunships, troop carriers, etc.—would be too slow and clunky.

I kept killing.

Rid's protests became warped, harder to hear. A frenzied shout. Then a garbled protest. A burst of erratic static.

And finally, nothing. It was just me and the rippers.

I breathed a sigh of relief. It was a strange feeling. But a good one. I'd done it. I'd saved my crew.

*"Self-destruction in five minutes. Evacuate. Evacuate."*

The rippers kept coming. I kept killing. I fought until my back was coated with sweat, until my limbs ached. The conduction-charge was becoming increasingly erratic, the rippers' claws finding more purchase now. My left thermal blade had started to flicker, whether from too much sustained use or from being damaged I had no idea. My jumpsuit was sticky with sweat, my breathing ragged. I was running out of fight, and I knew it.

*"Come on,"* I snarled. At the rippers. At myself. At the universe. *"We're not done yet."*

The rippers drew back, forming a ring around me, watching me, tensing and stepping back as I drew closer. I blinked, my mind too drunk with fury to process it.

*"Come on,"* I growled, taking a stride forward. "Come on, you bastards. Finish it."

They cringed backward. It struck me. They were afraid.

My exhausted panting turned into a chuckle. Then a laugh. *They* were afraid of *me*.

*"Self-destruction in four minutes. Evacuate. Evacuate."*

Something heavy slammed into my side. I grunted as the force of the blow threw me from my feet. I staggered back to my feet to see the nightmare ripper I had narrowly avoided in the elevator shaft staring at me, wings held up defensively in front of it. It snarled, teeth glistening in the dull white glow of my thermal blades. As I watched, one of the blades gave a final flicker and vanished.

*"Self-destruction in three minutes. Evacuate. Evacuate."*

The monstrosity moved forward. I held up my remaining

thermal blade, warding it back, and staggered wearily to my feet. The rest of the rippers were inching closer now, regaining their courage in the presence of what seemed to be their leader.

The thermal blade flickered once, plunging the corridor temporarily into complete and utter darkness before flaring weakly back to life.

"We had a good run," I whispered into a general broadcast channel. I'm not sure who I was trying to reach. Certainly nobody living—there was nobody there to listen. Maybe I was talking to myself. Maybe God. Maybe Kessa. Hell, maybe the rippers. Maybe it didn't matter. Because the truth was that I believed it. It had been a good run. But now it was over.

The rippers tensed, ready to charge.

"*Lax?*"

I blinked. That voice. Faint behind a wall of static, and yet familiar.

"Sevani?" I whispered incredulously.

"*Lax!*" The voice was louder now. "*Lax, it's Rose! Do you copy?*"

An unbelieving, electric thrill ran through my body. "Yeah! Yeah, I copy! Dammit, Rose, I've never been so happy to hear somebody's voice. I thought you were dead!"

"*The* Orpheus *took a hit,*" she said, speaking quickly. "*Took out the quantum communication array. Couldn't get any signal through to you guys until just now. Who was on that ship that just left?*"

The winged ripper seemed to have detected a change in my posture, a sudden surge of energy as Rose's voice revitalized me. It backed up a few paces, reassessing the situation.

"Everybody but me," I said. "Rose, you've gotta get out of here."

"*No way. I have your position now. Head for the nearest escape pod and I'll be there to pick you up.*"

"Not gonna work, Rose." I backed up a few paces. The

rippers seemed emboldened by that, creeping closer towards me. "You've gotta get out of here. You're running out of time."

She scoffed. *"We've got a few minutes to go yet. And I don't wanna end up like my mom, moping on and on for the rest of my life about the ones I left behind. So you can get to the port and we can get out of here together, or we can both find out what's inside of that black hole."*

The winged ripper took another step towards me.

*"Self-destruction in one minute,"* proclaimed the broadcast system. *"Evacuate. Evacuate."*

"I'll be there," I growled.

The rippers charged, and I charged too.

The winged ripper swiped at me with a clawed left haymaker, and I knocked the blow away with one fist while I let my full weight slam into the nightmare, catching it off balance and driving it backward to slam against the wall.

The ripper fought back, clawing at me, biting at me, but I was pissed off and in no mood for screwing around. I hacked at it with the thermal blade, but its wings were thick enough to absorb the heat. I grabbed its jaw, pushing it back to keep it from taking a bite out of my helmet, then slammed it against the wall —once, twice, three times. When it had stopped moving, I put one armored foot against its neck.

And pulled.

There was a moment of resistance, and then the head popped off with a spurt of blood. The nightmare's body spasmed, then went rigid.

The rippers surrounding me wilted again, uncertainty written in their postures. For a long moment they just sat there, staring at me and the grotesque chunk of flesh gripped in my hands.

I took a step forward. They turned and scattered.

"Well, I'll be damned," I muttered.

"Hurry!" Rose shouted.

I started sprinting.

I saw a hatch labeled 149D and punched it open, then climbed up through it, groaning as pain lanced through my torn and battered body. "Almost there. The ship's about to blow, so be ready to catch me."

"*The ship's about to* what?"

"*Blow!*" I struggled with the escape pod door.

"*Oh! Okay, I'm ready to—*"

The floor shuddered violently beneath me. I cursed. Out of time. Out of options. Except for one thing.

"Ejecting now!" I shouted, and hit the button that said LAUNCH.

There was a loud pop as the charges blew, followed by a deafening hiss as the evacuating atmosphere tore the escape pod out through the long port and into the vacuum of space. I found myself screaming as I was sucked out along with it.

And then the only sound was my breathing.

WARNING, read a vivid red message in the center of my HUD.

LIFE-SUPPORT SYSTEMS OFFLINE. BACKUP OXYGEN 80% DEPLETED.

"Better hurry," I gasped. "I'm almost out of—"

I slammed into something hard. I spun through the darkness of space. I couldn't see the black hole, but I could feel myself being pulled towards it. Panic gripped me—

Something loomed in front of me, and I grunted as I smashed into it. I groaned, looking around. I was inside of a small, familiar, box-shaped area. The *Orpheus*'s open airlock.

"*Hold on,*" Rose's voice crackled in my ear.

I grabbed onto a nearby strap hanging from the well and clutched it for all I was worth as the *Orpheus* began accelerating away from the *Revelation*. I got one last look at that monstrosity of a ship—long and black and dangerous—before there was a sudden flash of light and it exploded outward, shattering into a thousand jagged black silhouettes against the black hole's hungry orange light. The pieces of debris were pulled inexorably towards the black hole, arcing away from the *Orpheus.*

I sat there, watching the last remnants of the *Revelation* as they grew gradually smaller, trying to wrap my mind around everything that had just happened. I wasn't sure how I felt about any of it just yet. Disappointed we hadn't found the blueprints. Relieved at escaping alive—and, more importantly, at my crew's escape. Mostly, though, I just felt exhausted.

It was hard to call it a triumph—not only had we failed to find the plans Artemis had sought, but we hadn't even walked away with enough loot to turn a profit. That said, it was hard to call it a failure, either. We'd survived. Most of us, at least.

My crew had made it out. All of them. And so far as I was concerned, that was a win. Now we just needed to catch up with them.

I caught one last look at the *Revelation* as the *Orpheus's* cargo doors closed. I could see chunks of it vanishing into the event horizon now, propelled into the black hole's glowing maw by the force of the explosion. The *Revelation*—along with Ramar's secrets—was gone forever.

Good riddance.

The doors sealed shut. I sagged backward. Just needed to close my eyes for a moment...

# FORTY

## ALBENI 7



I've always figured it's the simple things that make life worth living.

A cold drink. A hot meal. A soft bed. Friendly, happy chatter over the sound of music.

"I didn't know what was happening at first," Rose was saying excitedly, slamming her empty cup onto the table as Rid, Shell, and Bentley leaned in to listen. "Warning systems on the *Orpheus* started going off. I tried to warn you guys, and then the whole ship started shaking and I had to pull right into evasive maneuvers. By the time I was out of harm's way I couldn't hear anything. Then I ran a systems check and realized the comms had been blasted, so I had to suit up and go fix..."

She kept on talking, her voice growing more exultant the further into her story she got. I found my thoughts drifting. She should have died. It was pure luck the first volley from the *Revelation*'s defensive batteries had struck the *Orpheus* where they had. My eyes drifted up, past Rose and her friends to where Sevani was watching us with an unreadable expression.

We'd been on Albeni 7 for maybe three days now. Rose and I had managed to make it back there before Nadus and the rest of the team did, which was the first miracle, while the second was that they'd decided to go back to Albeni 7 at all. But they had, and there had been a joyful, unbelieving reunion as the crew regrouped.

Sevani's eyes moved briefly to mine, then away. I frowned back into my drink. We hadn't spoken much since I'd gotten back. Partly because she'd been busy reuniting with Rose and running her smuggling empire, and party because I had essentially been asleep for the past forty-eight hours. And I *still* felt exhausted.

I was about to push myself to my feet and go talk to her when I heard a scraping sound as a chair was pulled up next to me. I turned to see Nadus settling into his seat with a sigh.

"You're feeling it too, huh?" I asked.

He nodded, rubbing at one bleary eye. "I have *no* idea how they're all still going like this."

"Oh, to be young again."

"I guess." He frowned. "If only to do things differently."

"We can't change the past, or what we did in it. All we can do is be better going forward. Like you said, back on Brahma: do what we can to fix what we broke."

"Yeah." He nodded somberly. "I thought that was what we were doing. Making a stand against the Paragon. Power to the people, all that. Hell, I wanted so badly for Artemis to be right. But she's dead now, and it turns out she was wrong about the *Revelation* from the beginning anyways."

"Yeah."

We sat in silence. Bentley made a joke and the other three laughed.

"It has to have been for a reason," Nadus said finally, staring into his drink and setting his jaw. "It's gotta mean something.

Everything we went through. I don't know what yet. But something's gotta come out of it."

A flicker of movement as somebody walked past the open doorway to Sevani's bar. Ramar Vent. He'd been staying on Albeni 7 until he could find transportation to wherever it was he thought he needed to go. Judging by the backpack he was wearing, I figured he might have found it.

"Yeah," I said thoughtfully. "We'll see. Be right back."

I caught up to Ramar in the corridor outside. He paused as I called his name.

"I'm leaving," he said as I drew closer.

"Looks that way. Where you off to?"

He gave me a searching look, like he was deciding how much to tell me. "Just tracking down some... rumors. I did a little bit of digging and was gratified to find that you didn't lie to me. Not about the *Panama*, at least. Whether or not my rippers are on it..."

"They were there. Where they are now is anyone's guess." I hesitated. "But... I wouldn't mind it if you let me know what you find out."

"Of course." He turned to leave, only to pause. "This isn't over, you know."

"Seems pretty damn over to me. The *Revelation* is gone, my employer is dead, and now all that's left is for you to go make sure you don't have any loose ends. Far as I'm concerned, this is all in the past." I studied Ramar's impassive face. I wanted it to be over. Wanted to put all this behind me. But my words rang hollow in my own ears, like I was trying to convince myself instead of Ramar. "Isn't it?"

"Oh, it might be for you. *Might* be. But whether or not you meant to, you've started something. It's been an... *educational* few days, reconnecting with all of my old contacts. Rumors have been spreading. Whispers that the Paragon betrayed Divinity, and that Divinity might finally have found out. That in the aftermath of the disaster on Brahma, more and more systems are eying the prospect of independence. That galactic war is only a few more crises away." He gave a dark smile. "They say that the balance of power is shifting. That all across the Paragon, people with ambition—people with a vision for the future—are biding their time, waiting until there's just enough of a power vacuum for them to make their play. All because of one lost battle-cruiser."

"But that was *you*," I said. "You did all of that."

"True. But you were there. You found the *Revelation*. You went aboard with a team of Brahmian nationals and emerged without them."

A knot of guilt twisted at my innards. Tekka and his team deserved better than to die the way they had, lightyears away from the planet they'd sacrificed so much for. I couldn't really blame Tekka for what he'd done—hell, in his shoes I'd have been tempted to do the same. But justified as he might have thought he was, he was still wrong. The ultrarippers were a threat to *everyone*, no matter who controlled them.

"Folk'll get suspicious if that gets out," Ramar continued. "It doesn't matter how hard you try to distance yourself from it: you and the *Revelation* are inexorably linked. You have been since you set foot aboard the *Panama*. Call it fate, call it bad luck, call it a string of poor choices, the results are still the same: you're a part of this drama now, and the drama is only just beginning."

I felt a chill run down my spine. Maybe Artemis's plan had worked after all. She'd wanted to destabilize the Paragon. To destroy their deal with Divinity. Suddenly, I wasn't so confident that was a good thing. If the Paragon *did* fall, who was to say something worse wouldn't rise up in its place?

"Or maybe you're right," Ramar said. "Maybe the destruction of the *Revelation* was an isolated incident that will be lost to time for everybody except us and your crew. One of history's unsolvable but insignificant mysteries." He shrugged. "Time will tell. Goodbye, Mr. VanDunn."

He hoisted his backpack higher onto his shoulders and walked away. I watched him go. A part of me wanted to follow him. To follow this thread all the way back to where it had started—for me, at least. Back to the *Panama*. But that was the past. And it was time I moved on.

"Time will tell," I muttered, then turned back into the bar.

Sevani was perched on a stool by the bar, watching with a faint smile as Rose, Bentley, Shell, and Rid were leaning together and discussing something excitedly. Upon seeing me, she pushed a drink in my direction.

"Our guest gone?"

I took the drink. "Don't figure we'll be seeing him again. Leastways, I hope not."

She nodded. "Strange guy."

"I guess you have to be, to do the things he's done." I hesitated, then lowered my voice. "Hey. About Rose. I'm sorry. I did what I could to protect her, but in the end, truth is that she got herself out of a mess I never should have dragged her into. I can't apologize enough for that."

Sevani sighed, her eyes not leaving her daughter's face. "I don't think she'd have had it any other way. She'd have cut loose on her own eventually no matter how I tried to keep her. Damn stubborn girl."

"Sounds like someone I know."

Sevani chuckled. "Children are the universe's way of taking revenge on us, I guess." She took a pull from her drink. "So, what's next for you?"

"I..." My voice trailed off. I stared down into my drink, my reflection staring back at me. *Next.* I'd been putting off thinking about it since I got out of prison, and now it was finally here. "I don't know. I never figured I'd make it this far, one way or another. But here I am."

"Well, if you're interested, I can always use some more muscle around here." Sevani looked around the bar with a sigh. "Business is good, but that means competition, which around here means violence. I can pay you well and get you good housing—well, good as there is in this tin can."

I mulled it over. It didn't sound so bad. Nice and stable. Tolerable level of risk, at least by my usual standards. But the thought of spending my days stuck in yet another rusting space station made me feel claustrophobic.

"Or if you want to go somewhere else," Sev continued, "I can buy out your portion of the *Orpheus*. Should be enough to start a new life for yourself somewhere. Maybe even planetside…"

That had its appeal too. I could reinvent myself somewhere quiet and peaceful. Between my half of the value of the *Orpheus*, plus my share of what profits we'd made selling the Paragon gunship that the rest of the crew had used to escape the *Revelation* in, I'd have quite a neat little sum. Not quitting money, and nowhere near enough for the type of life I'd dreamed of finding for Kessa and myself, but I'd be able to buy some land. Maybe start farming, like my parents. It just didn't feel right, though, doing it alone.

"…but I have a feeling fate's got something else in store for you," Sev said.

I looked up from my cup and turned to see Rose approaching me. She strode up between Sev and me, then placed a handcomputer onto the surface of the bar.

"What's that?" I asked.

She hit a button. A fuzzy holographic image of a small but elegant-looking ship appeared.

"That," Rose said, "is the *Spirit of Generosity*. It's a pleasure yacht, formerly owned by…" She paused, scrunched up her face. "Some rich bastards, I don't remember, but it's all in here and it's not important anyways. What *is* important is that they hit some debris and had to abandon ship in the Redhawk system. According to my source, nobody's been back for recovery yet." She raised an eyebrow. "Now, if a crew of experienced vultures was able to make it there in time, who *knows* what kind of valuables they might find?"

I looked from Rose to the rest of the group. Rid, Shell, and Bentley were watching me hopefully. Nadus was sitting back in his seat, an amused grin on his face.

"They rope you into this too?" I asked.

He shrugged. "Better than mercenary work."

I looked to Sev, who had a knowing smile on her face that reminded me of Kess, then back to Rose. Rose settled into her seat, trying to appear cool and relaxed, but I could tell from the eagerness in her eyes and the way she watched my expression how excited she was. "It's not *quitting* money," she said, "but it should be a good payout. Enough to keep the *Orpheus* running for a few more months, you know?"

I stared at the fuzzy holographic image.

*The balance of power is shifting,* Ramar had said. *You're a part of this drama now, and the drama is only just beginning.* I felt as if I should go find a nice rock somewhere and hide under it from whatever madness was on the horizon. Take what little I'd earned on this job and carve out some sort of meager living for myself.

But I couldn't take my eyes off of that hologram. Or off the eager eyes of my crew gathered around it. Their excitement. Their energy.

Maybe I *was* insane. Maybe the fates had cursed me to orbit endlessly around the same life that I'd once been so desperate to break out of. Somehow, though, I didn't feel like it was such a curse anymore. In my mind's eye I could see that knowing, contented smile that Kessa had always had, all the way up to the very end. *Maybe it's not the life we lived that matters. Maybe it's just who we lived it with.*

"Let's do it," I said.

# A LETTER FROM JAROM

Dear reader,

Thank you for taking the time to read *Vanguard Strike*! I hope you enjoyed it. If you want to continue following Lax on his adventures, I'm happy to report that no wait is necessary! Two sequels, *Vanguard Nemesis* and *Vanguard Annihilation* are out now through Second Sky Books.

If you want to stay up to date with my future releases, you can sign up for my newsletter at the following link. I promise not to share your email with anyone else or spam you, and you can unsubscribe at any time.

*www.secondskybooks.com/jarom-strong*

Finally, it would mean the world to me if you would leave a review for *Vanguard Strike*. It's impossible to overstate how important reviews are to the sale of a book in today's market, especially for a debut novel. If you have additional thoughts about the book I'd love to hear personally from you! I can be reached through my social media or you can contact me directly though the contact form on my website.

Thanks again!

Jarom Strong

# KEEP IN TOUCH WITH JAROM

www.jaromstrong.com

facebook.com/jarom.strong.750
x.com/StrongJarom
instagram.com/strongjarom

# ACKNOWLEDGMENTS

As they say, it takes a village to raise a book (pretty sure that's how that saying goes, anyways), and *Vanguard Strike* was no exception. In one way or another it would not exist without the help of the following people, in no particular order:

My writing and critique groups, who have patiently read one misshapen draft of this novel after another.

The many various industry professionals who have taken the time over the years to encourage and support me, especially Brandon Sanderson, whose personalized advice and enthusiasm for *Vanguard Strike* gave me the confidence I needed to finish it and take it into the querying trenches.

The teams at Second Sky and Bookouture, especially my editor Jack Renninson, whose fine eye gave *Vanguard Strike* the professional touch it needed, along with the rest of the editorial team: Ruth Tross, Melissa Tran, Mandy Kullar, and Jen Shannon. Helen Hawkins and Angela Snowden's work on the proofreading and copyediting stages were also essential.

My agent, Helen Lane, who took a chance on a random, hastily constructed Twitter pitch, and never fails to make me feel as if I'm already a bestseller, as well as my agent siblings, whose positivity and good humor have been a constant source of relief.

My family, for a thousand reasons. My parents, for (cautiously) encouraging my dreams of being a writer for as far back as I can recall; My siblings, for being my most enthusiastic fans and for the many, *many* hours of babysitting that gave me the time to write this book;  Cole, for being an unfailingly supportive and encouraging best friend; Ryan and Casey, whose passion for storytelling have been a constant source of inspiration and validation for me.

Finally, and most fundamentally, my wife Marci, to whom this book is dedicated.

PUBLISHING TEAM

**Turning a manuscript into a book requires the efforts of many people. The publishing team at Bookouture would like to acknowledge everyone who contributed to this publication.**

### Audio
Alba Proko
Sinead O'Connor
Melissa Tran

### Commercial
Lauren Morrissette
Hannah Richmond
Imogen Allport

### Cover design
Tom Edwards

### Data and analysis
Mark Alder
Mohamed Bussuri

### Editorial
Jack Renninson
Melissa Tran

## Copyeditor
Helen Hawkins

## Proofreader
Angela Snowden

## Marketing
Alex Crow
Melanie Price
Occy Carr
Cíara Rosney
Martyna Młynarska

## Operations and distribution
Marina Valles
Stephanie Straub
Joe Morris

## Production
Hannah Snetsinger
Mandy Kullar
Ria Clare
Nadia Michael

## Publicity
Kim Nash
Noelle Holten
Jess Readett
Sarah Hardy

## Rights and contracts
Peta Nightingale
Richard King
Saidah Graham